THREE WEEKS IN PARIS

BARBARA TAYLOR BRADFORD

 DOUBLEDAY / NEW YORK LONDON TORONTO SYDNEY AUCKLAND

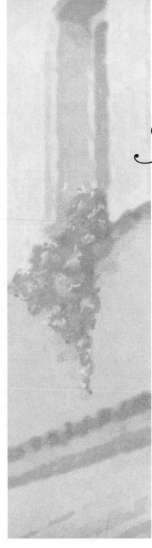

Three Weeks in Paris

PUBLISHED BY DOUBLEDAY
a division of Random House, Inc.
1540 Broadway, New York, New York 10036

DOUBLEDAY and the portrayal of an anchor with a dolphin are trademarks of Doubleday, a division of Random House, Inc.

This book is a work of fiction. Names, characters, businesses, organizations, places, events, and incidents either are the product of the author's imagination or are used fictitiously. Any resemblance to actual persons, living or dead, events, or locales is entirely coincidental.

Book design by Carla Bolte

Library of Congress Cataloging-in-Publication Data applied for

ISBN 0-385-50141-2

PRINTED IN THE UNITED STATES OF AMERICA

February 2002

First Edition

10 9 8 7 6 5 4 3 2 1

For Bob, truly a man for all seasons, with all my love

CONTENTS

PROLOGUE

On the rue Jacob the man shivered and turned up the collar of his overcoat. It was a bitter February day, icy from the wind that swept down from the Russian steppes and across the plains of Europe to hit Paris with a sharp blast.

The sky was a faded blue, the sun watery as it slanted across the rooftops, almost silvery in this cold northern light, and without warmth. But Paris was always beautiful, whatever the weather; even when it rained it had a special quality all its own.

Spotting a cab, he hailed it, and as it slowed to a standstill he got in quickly and asked the driver to take him to the post office. Once he was there, he unwrapped the package of stamped envelopes, seventy-one in all, and dropped them, in small batches, into a mailbox, then returned to the cab.

The man now gave the driver the address of the FedEx office, settled back against the seat, glancing out of the window from time to time. How happy he was to be back in the City of Light, but, nonetheless, he could not help wishing it were a little warmer. There was a chill in his bones.

In the FedEx office the man filled in the appropriate labels and handed them over to the clerk along with the four white envelopes. All were processed for delivery within the next twenty-four hours, their destinations four cities in distant, far-flung corners of the world. Back in the taxi he instructed the driver to take him to the Quai Voltaire. Once there, he headed toward one of his favorite bistros on the Left Bank. And as he walked, lost in his diverse thoughts, he had no way of knowing that he had just set in motion a chain of events that would have far-reaching effects. Because of his actions, lives were about to be changed irrevocably, and so profoundly they would never be the same again.

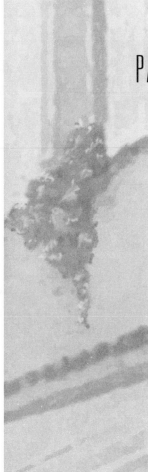

PART ONE

Les Girls

CHAPTER ONE

~⊕~

Alexandra

It was her favorite time of day. *Dusk.* That in-between hour before night descended when everything was softly muted, merging together. The twilight hour.

Her Scottish nanny had called it *the gloaming*. She loved that name; it conjured up so much, and even when she was a little girl she had looked forward to the late afternoon, that period just before supper. As she had walked home from school with her brother Tim, Nanny between them, tightly holding on to their hands, she had always felt a twinge of excitement, an expectancy, as if something special awaited her. This feeling had never changed. It had stayed with her over the years, and wherever she was in the world, dusk never failed to give her a distinct sense of anticipation.

She stepped away from her drawing table and went across to the window of her downtown loft, peered out, looking toward the upper reaches of Manhattan. To Alexandra Gordon the sky was absolutely perfect at this precise moment . . . its color a mixture of plum and violet toned down by a hint of smoky gray bleeding into a faded pink. The colors of antiquity, reminiscent of Byzantium and Florence and ancient Greece. And the towers and spires and skyscrapers of this great modern metropolis were blurred, smudged into a sort of timelessness, seemed of no particular period at this moment, inchoate images cast against that almost-violet sky.

Alexandra smiled to herself. For as far back as she could remember she had believed that this time of day was magical. In the movie business, which she was occasionally a part of these days, dusk was actually *called* the Magic Hour. Wasn't it odd that she herself had named it that when she was only a child?

Staring out across the skyline, fragments of her childhood came rushing back to her. For a moment she fell down into her memories . . . memories of the years spent growing up on the Upper East Side of this city . . . of a childhood filled with love and security and the most wondrous of times. Even though their mother had worked, still worked in fact, she and Tim had never been neglected by her, nor by their father. But it was her mother who was the best part of her, and, in more than one sense, she was the product of her mother.

Lost in remembrances of times past, she eventually roused herself and went back to the drawing board, looking at the panel she had just completed. It was the final one in a series of six, and together they composed a winter landscape in the countryside.

She knew she had captured most effectively the essence of a cold, snowy evening in the woods, and bending forward, she picked up the panel and carried it to the other side of the studio, placing it on a wide viewing shelf where the rest of the panels were aligned. Staring intently at the now-complete set, she envisioned them as a giant-size backdrop on the stage, which is what they would soon become. As far as she was concerned, the panels were arresting, and depicted exactly what the director had requested.

"I want to experience the cold, Alexa," Tony Verity had told her at the first production meeting, after he had taken her through the play. "I want to shiver with cold, crunch down into my overcoat, *feel* the icy night in my bones. Your sets must make me want to rush indoors, to be in front of a roaring fire."

He *will* feel all that, she told herself, and stepped back, eyeing her latest work from a distance, her head on one side, thinking of the way she had created the panels in her imagination first. She had envisioned St. Petersburg in winter, and then focused on an imaginary forest beyond that city.

In her mind's eye, the scenery had come alive, almost like a reel of film playing in her head . . . bare trees glistening with dripping icicles, drifts of new snow sweeping up between the trees like white dunes. White nights. White sky. White moon. White silence.

That was the mood she sought, had striven for, and wished to convey to the audience. And she believed she had accomplished that with these panels, which would be photographed later that week and then blown up for the stage.

She had not used any colors except a hint of gray and black for a few of the skeletal branches. Her final touch, and perhaps her most imaginative, had been a set of lone footprints in the snow. Footprints leading up between the trees, as if heading for a special, perhaps even secret, destination. Enigmatic. Mysterious. Even troubling, in a way . . .

The sharp buzzing of the doorbell brought her head up sharply, and her concentration was instantly broken. She went to the intercom on the wall, lifted the phone. "Hello?"

"It's Jack. I know I'm early. Can I come up?"

"Yes, it's okay." She pressed the button that released the street door, and then ran downstairs to the floor below in order to let him in.

A few seconds later, Jack Wilton, bundled up in a black duffle coat, and carrying a large brown shopping bag, was swinging out of the elevator, walking toward her down the corridor, a grin on his keen, intelligent face.

"Sorry if I'm mucking up your working day, but I was around the corner. At the Cromer Gallery with Billy Tomkins. It seemed sort of daft to go home and then come back here later. I'll sit in a corner down here and watch CNN until you quit."

"I just did," she said, laughing. "I've actually finished the last panel."

"That's great! Congratulations." As he stepped into the small foyer of her apartment, he put down the shopping bag, pulled her into his arms, and pushed the door closed with his booted foot.

He hugged her tightly, brought her closer, and as his lips brushed her cheek, then nuzzled her ear, she felt a tiny frisson, a shivery feeling. There was an electricity between them that had been missing for ages. She was startled.

Seemingly, so was he. Jack pulled away, glanced at her quickly, and then instantly brought his mouth to hers, kissing her deeply, passionately. After a second, he moved his mouth close to her ear and murmured, "Let's go and find a bed."

She leaned back, looking up into his pellucid gray eyes, which were more soulful than ever at that moment. "Don't be silly." As she spoke, a small, tantalizing smile touched her lips and her sparkling eyes were suddenly inviting.

"Silly? There's nothing silly about going to bed. I think it's a rather serious thing." Throwing his coat on the floor next to the shopping bag and putting his arm around her, he led her into the bedroom.

He stopped in the middle of the room, and taking hold of her shoulders, turned her to face him, staring into her eyes, his own questioning. "You went missing for a bit," he said, sounding more English than ever.

She stared back at him, said nothing.

He tilted her chin, leaned down, and kissed her lightly on the mouth. "But I have the distinct feeling you're suddenly back."

"I think so."

"I'm glad, Lexi."

"So am I," she answered.

He smiled at her knowingly and led her toward the bed without another word. They sat down together side by side, and he began to unbutton her shirt; she tugged at his tweed jacket, and within seconds they were both undressed, stretched out on the bed.

Leaning over her, he asked, "And where was it that you went?"

"Not sure. Fell into a deep pit with my work, I suppose."

He nodded, fully understanding, since he was an artist and tended to do the same at times when he was painting. But he had really missed her, and her withdrawal, her remoteness, had worried him. Now he brought his mouth down to her, his kisses tender.

Alexandra felt that frisson once more, and she began to shiver slightly under his touching and kissing, which was becoming provocative. He continued to kiss her as he stroked her thigh, and she experienced a sudden rush of heat, a tingling between her legs.

Unexpectedly, she stiffened. Swiftly, he brought his mouth to her mouth; his tongue sought hers, slid alongside hers, and they shared a moment of complete intimacy.

And all the while he did not stop stroking her inner thigh and the center of her womanhood, his fingers working gently but expertly. To him it soon seemed as though she was opening like a lush flower bursting forth under a warm sun.

When she began to gasp a little, he increased his pressure and speed, wanting her to reach a point of ecstasy. He loved this woman, and he wanted to bind her to him, and he wanted to make love to her now, be joined with her.

With great speed, he entered her immediately, thrusting into her so forcefully, she cried out. Sliding his hands under her buttocks, he lifted her up, drew her closer to him, calling out her name as he did. "Come to me again, come with me, come where I'm going, Lexi!" he exclaimed, his voice harsh, rasping.

And so she did as he demanded, wrapped her legs around his back, let her hands rest lightly on his shoulders. Together they soared, and as he began to shudder against her, he told her over and over again how much he loved making love to her.

———

Afterward, when they finally lay still, relaxed and depleted, he lifted the duvet up and covered them with it, then took her in his arms. He said against her hair, "Isn't this as good as it gets?"

When she remained silent, he added, "You know how good we are together . . ."

"Yes."

"You're not going to go away from me again, are you?"

"No . . . it *was* the work, the pressure."

"I'm relieved it wasn't me. That you weren't having second thoughts about me."

She smiled to herself. "You're the best, Jack, the very best. Special . . . *unique,* actually."

"Ah, flattery will get you everywhere."

"I've just been there, haven't I?"

"Where?"

"Everywhere. With you . . . to some wonderful place."

Pushing himself up on one elbow, he peered down at her in the dim light of the fading day, wondering if she was teasing him. Then he saw the intensity in her light green eyes, and he said softly, "Let's make it permanent."

Those lucid green eyes he loved widened. "Jack . . . I don't know what to say . . ."

"Say yes."

"Okay. Yes."

"I'm talking marriage," he muttered, a sudden edge to his voice. He focused all his attention on her, his eyes probing.

"I *know* that."

"Will you?"

"Will I what?" Now she was teasing him and enjoying doing so, as she usually did.

"Will you marry me?"

"Yes, I will."

A slow, warm smile spread itself across his lean face, and he bent into her, kissed her forehead, her nose, her lips. Resting his head next to hers on the pillow, he continued. "I'm glad. Really so *bloody* glad, Lexi, that you're going to be mine, all mine. Wow, this is great! And we'll have a baby or two, won't we?"

She laughed, happy that he was so obviously delirious with joy. "Of course. You know what, maybe we just made one."

"It's a possibility. But to be really sure, shall we try again?"

"You mean right now?"

"I do."

"Can you?"

"Don't be so ridiculous, of course I can. Feel this." Taking hold of her hand, he put it on him under the duvet. "See what you do to me. And I'll always be ready to make babies with you, darling."

"Then stop boasting and let's do it!" she exclaimed, sliding a leg over him, kissing him on the mouth. "Let's do it all night, in fact. It's one of the things I love to do with you, Jack."

"Don't you want dinner?" He raised a brow.

"Oh, who cares about food when we've something so important and crucial to do."

He started to laugh. "I care. But we don't have to venture out, my sweet. I brought dinner with me. In the shopping bag."

"Oh, so you planned all this, did you? Very devious, you are, Jack Wilton. You wicked, sexy man. I might have known you came here to seduce me. To impregnate me."

"Seduce you! What bloody cheek! You've just displayed the most incredible example of splendid cooperation I've ever come across. As for impregnating you, you can bet your sweet ass I'm going to do that."

They began to roar with laughter, hugging each other and rolling around on the bed, filled with hilarity and pleasure in each other, and the sheer happiness of being young and alive. But after a moment or two of this gentle horseplay, Jack's face turned serious, and he held Alexandra still. "You're not going to change your mind, are you, Lexi?"

" 'Course not, silly." She touched his cheek lightly, smiled seductively. "Shall we get to it then . . . making babies, I mean."

"Try and stop me—" he began, but paused when the intercom buzzed.

The shrilling startled Alexandra, and nonplussed, she stared at Jack. Then she scrambled off the bed, took a woolen robe out of the closet, and struggled into it as she ran to the foyer. Lifting the intercom phone, she said, "Hello?"

"FedEx delivery for Ms. Gordon."

"Thanks. I'll buzz you in. I'm on the fourteenth floor."

———

The carbon copy of the original label on the front of the FedEx envelope was so faint she could barely make out the name and address of the sender. In fact, the only part she could read was *Paris, France*.

She stood holding the envelope, a small furrow crinkling the bridge of her nose. And then her heart missed a beat.

From the doorway of the bedroom Jack said, "Who's it from? You look puzzled."

"I can't make out the name. Best thing to do is open it, I suppose," she replied, forcing a laugh.

"That might be a good idea." Jack's voice was touched with acerbity.

She glanced across at him swiftly, detecting at once a hint of impatience . . . as if it were her fault their lovemaking had been interrupted by the FedEx delivery. But wishing to keep things on an even keel, to placate him, she exclaimed, "Oh, it can wait!" Dropping the envelope on the small table in the foyer, she added, "Let's go back to bed."

"Naw, the mood's gone, ducks. I'm gonna take a quick shower, make a cuppa rosy lee, then start on dinner," he answered her in a bogus Cockney accent.

She stood staring at him, biting her lip.

Observing the crestfallen expression in her eyes, Jack Wilton instantly regretted his attitude. He softened, pulled her toward him, embraced her. "I'm sorry, I *was* a bit snotty, Lexi. *Sorry, sorry, sorry.* Okay?" His eyes held hers, a brow lifted quizzically. "Don't you see, I was put out . . . and you *know* why. I was all ready to make babies." He grinned, kissed the tip of her nose. "So . . ." He shrugged nonchalantly. "Let's go and take a shower together."

"I guess I ought to open—"

He cut her off. "It'll wait." Taking hold of her hand, he led her across to the bathroom and into the shower stall, turned on the taps, adjusted the temperature, held her close again as the water sluiced over their bodies.

Alexandra leaned against him, closed her eyes, thinking of the envelope she had left on the table. She was beginning to worry about it, anxiety ridden and tense inside. She could well imagine who it was from. It could be only one person, and the thought terrified her.

———

But she was wrong.

A short while later, when she finally opened the envelope, it was not a letter inside as she had believed, but an invitation. Her relief was enormous.

She sat on the sofa in her living room, staring at it, and a smile broke through, lighting up her face. Leaping to her feet, she ran across the room to the kitchen, where Jack was cooking, exclaiming, "Jack, it's an invitation. To a party. In Paris."

Jack glanced up from the bowl of fresh tomatoes he was stirring, took a sip of his tea, and asked, "Who's the party for, then?"

"Anya. My wonderful Anya Sedgwick."

"The woman who owns the school you went to . . . what's it called again? Ah, yes, the Anya Sedgwick School of Decorative Arts."

"That's right."

"And what's the occasion?"

"Her birthday." Leaning against the doorjamb, she began to read from the engraved invitation. "The pleasure of your company is requested at a celebration in honor of Anya Sedgwick on the occasion of her eighty-fifth birthday. On Saturday, June the second, 2001. At Ledoyen, Carré Champs-Élysées, Paris. Cocktails at eight o'clock. Supper at nine o'clock. Dancing from ten o'clock on. Hey, isn't that great, Jack, it's a supper dance. Oh, how wonderful."

"Sounds like it's going to be a super bash. Can you take a friend, do you think?"

Alexandra glanced at the invitation again. Her name had been written across the top in the most elegant calligraphy she had ever seen. But it was only *her* name. The words *and guest* were missing. "I don't think I can. It has only my name on it. I'm sure it's just for her family and former pupils. . . ." Alexandra's voice trailed off.

He was silent for a moment, concentrating as he finely chopped an onion. When he at last looked up, he asked, "Are you going to go?"

"I'm not sure. I don't know. It all depends on work, I guess. I've only one small set to finish for *Winter Weekend,* and then that's it. I'll be out of work if something doesn't pop up."

"I'm sure it will, Lexi," he reassured her, glancing at her, smiling. "Now scoot, and let me finish the pasta pomidoro, and before you can say Jack Robinson I'll have dinner for my lady."

She laughed, said "Okay," and went back to the sofa, still holding the invitation in her hand. Sitting down, she stared at it for a moment longer, her mind on Anya Sedgwick, the woman who had been her teacher, mentor, and friend. She had not seen her for a year. It would be lovely to be in her company again, to celebrate this important milestone in her life . . . Paris in the spring. How truly glorious it would be . . .

But Tom Conners was in Paris.

When she thought of him she found it hard to breathe.

CHAPTER TWO

Alexandra awakened with a start, and after a moment she sat up, blinking, adjusting her eyes in the darkness. The room was quiet, bathed in silence, but for a moment she felt a presence, as if someone stood nearby, hovered close to the bed.

She remained still, breathing deeply, pushing the feeling away, knowing this was all it was . . . just a *feeling,* the sensation that he was with her in the room because her dream had been so very real.

But then, it always was whenever she dreamed it. Everything that happened had a validity to it, was vivid, lifelike; even now, as she rested against the pillows, she could smell him, smell his body, his hair, the cologne he used. Jicky by Guerlain. It seemed to her that even the taste of him lingered on her mouth, as if he had kissed her deeply.

Except that he had not been here tonight . . . only in the dream, one so extraordinarily alive in her mind that after awakening she had believed he truly was in the bedroom. But, of course, she was alone.

Suddenly knowing that sleep would be elusive, at least for the moment, Alexa sat up, switched on the bedside lamp, and slid her long legs out of bed. As she glided across the floor, she realized she was bathed in sweat, as she usually was after this oft-recurring dream.

Wrapping herself in her pale blue woolen dressing gown, she hurried through the small front foyer and went into the kitchen, snapping on lights as she did.

What she needed was a cup of tea. Chamomile tea. It would soothe her, encourage sleep. After filling the kettle with water and putting it on the gas ring, she sat down on the stool, contemplating the dream she had with such unusual regularity.

The odd thing was, the dream was always exactly the same. Nothing ever changed. He was suddenly there with her, either coming through the door or standing by the bed looking down at her. And inevitably he slid into bed, made love to her, cradling her in his arms, telling her he missed her, wanted her, needed her. And always he reminded her that she was the love of his life. His one true love.

And the dream was rooted in such uncanny reality, she was invariably shaken; even her body felt as if it had been invaded by a sensual and virile man. It was, she muttered under her breath as she filled the mug with boiling water. At least it was this afternoon. Jack Wilton made love to me when he arrived here today . . . in the gloaming he loved me well.

Yes, a small voice said in her head, but in the dream you just had it was Tom Conners loving you. It's never anybody else but Tom Conners in the dream, and that's your basic problem.

Sighing to herself, Alexa turned on a lamp and sat down in the comfortable overstuffed chair near the fireplace, sipped the chamomile tea, and stared into the dying embers of the log fire.

What was wrong with her? The question hovered over her like a black cloud.

She had made love with Jack and enjoyed every moment of it, and there had been an unexpected and wonderful renewal of passion between them, a passion sadly absent for months. To excuse this, she had blamed tiredness, work, the pressure and stress of designing sets at top speed. But in all truthfulness, something else had been at play. Exactly what that was she wasn't sure. She had pulled away from having sex with Jack, had avoided it. There had been a strange reluctance in her to be intimate with him, and she had mentally recoiled. But why? He was appealing, attractive, good-looking in a quiet way, and had a very endearing personality. He was even funny, made her laugh hilariously.

So many images invaded her, bounced around in her head, and conflicting thoughts jostled for prominence in her mind. She closed her eyes for a moment, endeavoring to sort them out. Suddenly she sat up straighter and thought: My God, I agreed to marry Jack! I'm engaged to him!

This was no joke as far as he was concerned. He was very serious. He had gone on talking over dinner about getting married, constantly touching his glass of red wine to hers, and they had laughed together, and flirted, and been in tune on all levels.

While they hadn't exactly settled on a wedding date, she had sort of acquiesced when he had talked about winter at the end of the year. "In New York. A proper wedding," he had insisted. "With your family and mine, and all the trimmings. That's what I want, Lexi." And she had nodded in agreement.

Once dinner was over, he had helped her stack the dishwasher, and then they had gone to bed. But he had left at five, kissing her cheek and whispering that he wanted to get an early start on a large canvas for his upcoming show.

As for her, she dreamed about another man, and in the most intimate way possible at that. *Was* there something wrong with her? This wasn't normal, was it?

Despite the chamomile tea and its so-called soothing properties, she was suddenly wide awake. Glancing at the small brass carriage clock on the mantel, she saw that it was already ten past six in the morning.

Ten past twelve in Paris.

On an impulse, before she could change her mind and stop herself, she lifted the phone on the side table and dialed Tom's office number, his direct line. Within a split second the number in Paris was ringing.

And then he answered. *"Allo."*

She clutched the phone tighter. She couldn't speak. She could barely breathe. She heard an impatient sound from him, and then he spoke again.

"Tom Conners *ici.*" Then again, this time in English, he said, "Hello? This is Tom Conners. Who is this?"

Very carefully she replaced the receiver. Her hands were damp and shaking, and her heart was thudding unreasonably in her chest. What a fool she was to do this to herself. She took several deep breaths, leaned against the cushions in the chair, staring off into space.

He was there. In his office. He was still in Paris. He was alive and well.

And if she went to Paris, to Anya Sedgwick's birthday party, she would do exactly what she had just done. She wouldn't be able to resist. She would call him, and he would say let's have a drink, because he was like that, and she would say yes, that's great, and she would go and have a drink with him. And after that she would be genuinely lost. Floundering about once more. Yes, a lost soul.

Because to her Tom Conners was devastatingly irresistible, a man so potent, so compelling, he lived with her in her thoughts, and in her heart and mind, if not all the time, for a good part of it.

Even though they had stopped seeing each other three years earlier, and he had been the one to break it off, she knew that if she spoke to him he would want to see her.

You're such an idiot, she chastised herself. Anger flooded her. It was an anger at herself and her lingering emotional involvement with Tom Conners. And she knew it had been foolish to make that call, even though she hadn't spoken to him. Just hearing that arresting, mellifluous voice of his had truly unnerved her.

Alexa now forced herself to focus on Jack Wilton. He loved her, wanted to make her his wife, and she had actually accepted his proposal. All that aside, he was a truly decent human being, a good man, honorable, kind, loving, and generous to a fault sometimes. His success had not spoiled him, and he was very down-to-earth in that humorous English way of his, not taking either himself or life too seriously. "Only my work must be taken seriously," he was forever telling her, and she understood exactly what he meant by that.

She knew he adored her, admired her talent as a scenic designer, applauded her dedication and discipline. He encouraged her, comforted her when she needed comforting, and was always there for her. And the truth was he had stayed in the relationship and had been exceedingly patient with her even when she had been cool toward him physically these last few months.

What's more, her parents liked him. A good sign, since they'd always been very critical when it came to her boyfriends. Not picky about Tom Conners, because he'd charmed them without trying. But then again, they had never really known him, nor had they actually understood the extent of her involvement with him, because their relationship had evolved after she had left Anya's school in Paris.

Jack would make a wonderful husband, she decided. He loved her, and she loved him. In her own way.

Alexandra pushed herself up out of the chair very purposefully, and, turning off the lamp, she went back to bed. Jack Wilton was going to be her husband, and that was that.

Sadly, she would have to forgo Anya's eighty-fifth birthday party. For her own self-protection.

CHAPTER THREE

Seated at the mahogany table in the elegant dining room of her parents' apartment on East Seventy-ninth Street, Alexandra was savoring the tomato omelette her mother had just made, thinking how delicious it was. Hers inevitably turned into a runny mess despite having had her mother, the best chef in the world, to teach her over the years.

"This is great, Mom," she said after a moment, "and thanks for making time for me today. I know you like to have your Saturdays to yourself."

"Don't be silly, I'm glad you're here," Diane Gordon answered, glancing up, smiling warmly. "I was just about to call you this morning, to see what you were doing, when the phone rang and there you were, wanting to have lunch."

Alexa returned her mother's smile and asked, "When's Dad getting back from the Coast?"

"Tuesday, he said. But it could be Friday. *You* know what the network is like. You grew up with networks and their schedules, lived by them when you were a child."

"And how!" Alexa exclaimed. "I suppose Dad's going to see Tim this weekend."

"Yes, they're having dinner tonight. Dad's taking him to Morton's."

"Tim'll love that, it's his favorite place in L.A. I guess he's going to stay out there after all. When I spoke to him last week he sounded very high on Los Angeles, and his new job at NeverLand Productions. He told me he was born to be a moviemaker."

Diane laughed. "Well, I suppose that's true. Remember what he was like when he was a kid, always wanting to go with your father to the television studios, to be on the set. And let's not forget that Grandfather Gordon was a very highly thought of stage director, and for many years. Show business is in Tim's blood, more than likely." Diane took a sip of water, then asked her daughter, "Do you want a glass of wine, darling?" a blond brow lifting questioningly.

"No, thanks, Mom, not during the day. It makes me sleepy. Anyway, it's fattening . . . all that sugar. I prefer to take my calories in bread." As she spoke, she reached for a piece of the baguette that her mother had cut up earlier and placed in a silver bread basket. She spread it generously with butter and took a bite.

"You don't have to worry about your weight, you know, and you look marvelous, really well," Diane remarked, eyeing her daughter. She couldn't help thinking how young she looked for her age. It didn't seem possible that Alexandra was *thirty*. In fact, in the summer she would be thirty-one, and it seemed like only yesterday that she was a toddler running around her feet. My God, when I was her age I had two children, Diane thought, and a husband to look after, and a growing business to run. *Thirty-one,* she mused, and in May *I'll* be *fifty-eight*. How time flies, just disappears. Where have all the years gone? David will be fifty-nine in June. What is even more incredible is our marriage. It's lasted so long, so many years, and it's still going strong. A record of sorts, isn't it?

"Mom, what *are* you pondering? You're looking very strange. Are you okay?" Alexa probed.

"I'm fine. I was just thinking about your father. And our marriage. It's amazing that we've been married for thirty-three years. And what's even more staggering is that the years seem to have passed in a flash. Just like that." She snapped her fingers and shook her head in sudden bemusement.

"You two have been lucky," Alexa murmured, "so lucky to have found each other."

"That's absolutely true."

"You and Dad, you're like two peas in a pod. Did you start out being so alike? Or did you *grow* to resemble each other? I've often wondered that, Mom." Her head on one side, she gazed at her mother, thinking how beautiful she was, probably one of the most beautiful women she had ever seen, with her peaches-and-cream skin, her pale golden hair, and those extraordinary liquid blue eyes.

"You're staring, Alexa. You're going to see all my wrinkles!"

"Oh, Mom, you don't have one single wrinkle. I kid you not, as Dad says."

Diane laughed and murmured, "As for you, my girl, you don't look a day over twenty-five. It's hard for me to believe you'll be thirty-one in August."

"It's my new short haircut. It takes years off me."

"I guess it does. But then, short hair makes most women look younger, perkier. And it's certainly the chic cut this year."

"You once told me short hair was the only chic style, and that no woman could be elegant with hair trailing around her shoulders. And you should know, since you're considered one of the chicest women in New York, if not *the* chicest."

"Oh, I'm not really, but thanks for the compliment. Although I should point out that the whole world suspects you're a bit prejudiced."

"Everyone, the press included, cites *you* as a fashion icon, a legend in your own time. And your boutiques have been number one for years now."

"We've *all* worked hard to make them what they are, not only me, Alexa. Anyway, what about you, darling? Have you finally finished those winter sets?"

Alexa's face lit up. "I completed the last one of the snow forest earlier this week, on Tuesday actually. Yesterday I saw blow-ups of them all at the photographic studio, and they're great, Mom, even if I do say so myself."

"I've told you many times, don't hide your light under a bushel, darling. It doesn't do to brag, of course, but there's nothing wrong in knowing that you're good at what you do. You're very talented, and personally I was bowled over by the panels I saw." Diane's pale blue eyes, always so expressive, rested on her daughter thoughtfully. After a moment she said, "And so . . . what's next for you?"

"I have one small set to do for this play, and after that my contract's fulfilled." Alexa laughed a little hollowly and added, "Then I'll be out of work, I guess."

"I doubt that," Diane shot back, the expression on her face reflecting her pride in her only daughter. "Not you."

"To be honest, I'm not worried. Something'll turn up. It always does."

Diane nodded, and then her eyes narrowed slightly. "You said on the phone that you wanted to talk to me. What—"

"Can we do that later, over coffee?" Alexa cut in swiftly.

"Yes, of course, but is there something wrong? You sounded worried earlier."

"Honestly, there's nothing wrong. I just need . . . a sounding board, a really good one, and you're the very best I know."

"Is this about Jack?"

"No, and now you're sounding like all those other mothers, which most of the time you don't, thank God. And *no*, it's not about Jack."

"Don't be so impatient with me, Alexa, and by the way, Jack Wilton is awfully nice."

"I *know* he is, and he feels the same way about you. And Dad."

"I'm glad to hear it. But how does he feel about *you?* That's much more important."

"He cares."

"Your father and I think he would make a good—a very nice son-in-law."

Alexa did not respond.

————

Half an hour later Alexandra sat opposite her mother in the living room, watching her as she poured coffee into fine bone-china cups. She was studying Diane through objective eyes, endeavoring to see her as clearly as possible. It suddenly struck her what a unique person she was, a woman who was savvy, smart, successful, and highly intelligent as well. And she really did understand human frailties and foibles, because her perception and insight were well honed, and she was compassionate. But would she comprehend *her* dilemma, a dilemma centered on two men?

After all, there had been only one man in her mother's life, as far as she knew, and that man was her father, who Diane Carlson had met at twenty-four and married within the year; they had been utterly devoted to each other ever since. I know she'll understand, Alexandra reassured herself. She's not prudish or narrow-minded, and she never passes judgment on anybody. But how to tell her my story? Where do I begin?

It was as though Diane had read her daughter's mind when she announced, "I'm ready to listen, Alexa, whenever you want to start. And whatever it's about, you'll have all my attention and the best advice I can give."

"I know that, Mom," Alexa answered, adding "Thanks" as she accepted the cup her mother was passing to her. She put it down on the low antique table between them and settled back against the Venetian velvet cushions on the cream sofa. After a second or two, she explained, "Late yesterday afternoon I got an invitation to go to a party in Paris. For Anya. She's going to be eighty-five."

A huge smile spread across Diane's face, and she exclaimed, "Good Lord, I can't believe it! She's a miracle, that woman."

"Oh, I know she is, and aside from looking so much younger than her age, she's full of energy and vitality. Whenever I speak to her on the phone she sounds as busy as ever, running the school, entertaining, and traveling. Only last month she told me she's started writing another book, one on the Art Deco period of design. She's just so amazing."

"I'll say she is, and what a lovely trip for you. When is the party?"

"On June second, at Ledoyen. It's a supper dance, actually."

"That'll be fun, we must find you something pretty to wear. Is it black tie?"

"Yes, it is, but look, Mom, I'm not sure that I'm going to go."

Diane was startled, and she frowned. "Why ever not? You're close to Anya, and you've always been a special favorite of hers. Certainly more than the others—" Diane stopped abruptly and stared at her daughter. "But of course! That's *it*. You don't want to go because you don't want to see the other three. I can't say I blame you, they turned out to be rather treacherous, those women."

With a small jolt, Alexandra realized she hadn't even thought about her former best girlfriends, who had ended up her enemies. She had been focused only on Tom Conners and her feelings for him. But now, all of a sudden, she realized she must throw them into the equation along with Tom. Her mother was quite right, they were indeed an excellent reason she should stay away from Paris. They were bound to be at the party . . . Anya would have invited them as well as her . . . together the four of them had been her greatest pride the year of their graduation . . . her star pupils. Of course they'd be there . . . with bells on.

"You're right, Mom, I have no desire to see them," Alexa said. "But they're not the reason I don't want to go to Paris. It's something else, as a matter of fact."

"And what's that?"

"His name's Tom Conners."

Diane was momentarily perplexed. The name rang a bell, but she couldn't pinpoint the man. She leaned forward slightly, her eyes narrowing. *"Tom Conners.* Do I know him? Oh, yes, now it's coming back to me. Isn't he the Frenchman you introduced to us a few years ago?"

"That's right, but Tom's *half* French, *half* American. If you remember, I did tell you about his family. His father's an American who went to live in Paris in the early fifties, married a French girl, and stayed. Tom was brought up and educated there, and he's always lived in France."

"Yes, so I recall, darling. He's a lawyer if I remember correctly, and very good-looking. But I didn't realize there was anything serious between the two of you. I thought it was a brief encounter, a sort of fling if you like, and that it was over quickly."

"It lasted almost two years, actually."

"I see." Diane sat back, wondering how she had missed this particular relationship. On the other hand, that was the period Alexa had lived in Paris, working with Anya's two nephews in films and the theater. However, she had certainly kept awfully quiet about Tom Conners, had confided nothing. Odd, really, now that Diane thought about it. She said slowly, "Somehow you're still involved with Tom Conners, I think. Is that what you're trying to say?"

"No . . . yes . . . no . . . look, Mom, we don't see each other anymore, and I never hear from him, he's never in touch, but he's sort of there . . . inside me, in my thoughts. . . ." Her voice trailed off lamely, and she gave her mother a helpless look.

"Why did you break off with him, Alexa?" Diane asked curiously.

"I didn't. He did. Three years ago now."

"But *why*?" her mother pressed.

"Because I wanted to get married and he couldn't marry me."

"Is he married already?"

"No. Not now, not then."

"I'm not following this at all. It doesn't make sense to me. I just don't understand what the problem is," Diane murmured, her bafflement only too apparent.

Alexa hesitated, wondering if she could bear to tell her mother Tom's story. It was so painful, so harrowing. But when she glanced at her mother's face and saw the worry settling there, she decided she had no option. She wanted her to understand . . . everything.

Very softly Alexa said, "Tom was married very young to his childhood sweetheart, Juliette. They grew up together, and their parents were friends. They had a little girl, Marie-Laure, and seemingly, from what he told me, they were an idyllic couple . . . the poster couple, I guess. Very beautiful, very happy together. And then something bad happened. . . ."

Alexa paused, drew a deep breath, and continued. "In July 1985 they went to Athens. On vacation. But Tom also had to see a client from Paris, who owned a summer house there. Toward the end of the vacation, Tom arranged a final meeting with his client before he took his family back to Paris. That morning he told Juliette he would meet her and Marie-Laure for lunch at their favorite café, but Tom was delayed and got there a bit late. It was chaotic when he walked into the square where the café was located. Police cars and ambulances were converging in the center, and the human carnage was horrendous. People were dead and dying, there was blood and body parts everywhere, like a massacre had taken place. The police told Tom that a bomb had exploded only minutes before his arrival, more than likely a terrorist's bomb that had been planted on one of those big tour buses, this particular one filled with Americans from the hotel in the square. About sixty people were on the bus, and they all died.

"As the bus was leaving the square, it suddenly blew up, right in front of the café where Juliette and Marie-Laure were waiting for Tom. The impact of the blast was enormous. People sitting at the various cafés around the square were blown right out of their chairs. Many were killed or injured—" Alexa stopped, and it was a moment before she could continue.

After taking several deep breaths, she went on. "Tom couldn't find Juliette and Marie-Laure, and as you can imagine, he was worried and frightened, frantic, as he searched for them. He did find them eventually, under the rubble in the back of the café . . . the ceiling had collapsed on them. They were both dead." Alexandra blinked, and her voice was so low, it was almost inaudible as she finished. "Don't you see, he's never recovered from that . . . that . . . *nightmare*."

Diane was staring at Alexandra in horror, and tears had gathered in her light blue eyes. "How horrendous, what a terrible, terrible tragedy to happen to them, to him," she murmured, and then, looking across at her daughter, she saw that Alexa's face was stark, taut, and drained of all color.

Rising, she went and sat next to her on the sofa, put her arm around her and held her close. "Oh, darling, you're still in love with him. . . ."

"Am I? I'm not sure, Mother, but he does occupy a large part of me, that's true. He's there, inside, and he always will be, I think. But I'm smart enough to know I have no future with Tom. He'll never marry me, or anybody else for that matter. Nor will he have a permanent relationship, because he can't. You see, he just can't forget *them*."

"Or he won't let himself forget," Diane suggested softly.

"Perhaps that's true. Perhaps he thinks that if he forgets them he'd be riddled with guilt for the rest of his life and wouldn't be able to handle it. You brought me up to be sensible, practical, and I believe I am those things. And after we broke up, I knew I had to get on with my life. . . . I knew I couldn't moon around, yearning for Tom. I understood there was no future in that."

Diane nodded. "You were right, and I think you've managed to get on with your professional life extremely well. I'm proud of you, Alexa, you didn't let your personal problems get in the way of your career. All I can say is bravo."

"You once told me years ago that I must never negate my talent by not using it, by wasting it, and I listened to you, Mom. I also knew I had to earn a living, I wasn't going to let you and Dad support me, especially after you'd sent me to such expensive schools, Anya's in particular."

Diane nodded. "Just as a matter of interest, how old is he? Tom, I mean."

"He's forty-two."

Diane nodded, searched her daughter's face intently, and wondered out loud, "Do you love Jack Wilton a little bit at least?"

"Yes, I do love him in a certain way."

"Not the way you love Tom?" Diane ventured to ask.

"No."

"You could make a life with Jack, though?"

Alexandra nodded. "I think so. Jack's got a lot going for himself. He's very attractive and charming, and we get on well. We're compatible, he makes me laugh, and we understand each other, understand where we're both coming from, which is sometimes the same place. We admire each other's talents, and respect each other." She half smiled at her mother. "He loves me, you know. He wants to marry me."

"Would you marry him?" Diane asked quietly, hoping for an answer in the affirmative.

Alexa leaned against her mother, and a deep sigh escaped her. Unexpectedly, tears spilled out of her eyes. Then she swiftly straightened, flicked the tears away with her fingertips. "I thought I could, Mom, I really did. But now I don't know. Ever since that invitation arrived yesterday, I've been in a turmoil."

"You won't be able to resist seeing Tom if you go to Paris, is that what you're telling me?"

"I guess I am."

"But you're stronger than that . . . you've always been strong, even when you were a little girl."

Alexa was silent.

After a short while, Diane said slowly, carefully, "Here's what your loving and very devoted sounding board thinks. You have to forget Tom, as you know you should. You must put him out of your mind once and for all. He's not for you, Alexa, or anybody else, in my opinion. What happened to his wife and child was unbearable, very, very tragic, and so heartrending. But it *was* years ago. Sixteen years ago, to be precise. And if he's not over it by now—"

"He wasn't over it three years ago, but I don't know about now—"

"—then he never will be," Diane continued in a very firm voice. "Your life is here in New York, not in Paris. For the most part, your work is here, and you know you can make a wonderful life with Jack. And that's what you should do—" Diane stopped, tightened her embrace, and said against her daughter's glossy dark hair, "There are all kinds of love, you know. Degrees of love. And sometimes the great love of one's life is not meant to last . . . perhaps that's how it becomes the *great love* . . . by ending." Diane sighed, but after a moment she went on. "I know it's hard to give someone up. But, in fact, Tom Conners gave you up, Alexa. Not vice versa, so why torture yourself? My advice to you is not to go to Paris. That way you won't be tempted to see Tom, and open up all those wounds."

"I guess you're right, Mom. You usually are. But Anya's going to be really upset if I don't go to the party."

"I'm sure she will be." There was a slight pause, and then Diane exclaimed, "There *is* an alternative! You and Jack could go to Paris together. Obviously, you couldn't go looking for Tom if you were there with another man."

Want to bet? Alexandra thought, but said, "The invitation doesn't include a guest. Only my name is written on it. And I'm sure Anya's invited only former pupils and her family."

"But she wouldn't refuse *you* . . . not if you said you were coming to Paris with your . . . fiancé."

"I don't know what she'd do, actually. And I have to think about that, Mom, all of what you've just said . . . and implied."

———

The invitation stood propped up on the mantel next to the carriage clock, and the first thing Alexandra did when she got home was to pick it up and read it again.

Down in the left-hand corner, underneath the letters RSVP, was the date of the deadline to accept or decline: *April the first.* And in the right-hand corner it said Black Tie and underneath this Long Dress. All the information she needed was right there, including what to wear; with the engraved invitation was a small RSVP card and an envelope addressed to Madame Suzette Laugen, 158 Boulevard St. Germain, Paris.

So she had the rest of February and most of March to make up her mind, to think about Anya's birthday and decide what to do, whether to go or not. That was a relief. But she knew she would spend the next few weeks vacillating back and forth.

Deep down she wanted to go, wanted to celebrate this special birthday with Anya, an extraordinary woman who had had such an enormous influence on her life. But there was the problem of Tom Conners, and also of her former friends . . . Jessica, Kay, and Maria. Three women once so close to her, and she to them, they were inseparable, but they were sworn enemies now. She couldn't bear the thought of seeing any of them.

April the first, she mused. An anniversary of sorts, since she had met Tom Conners on April the first. In 1996. She had been twenty-five, he thirty-seven.

April Fool, she thought with a wry smile. But she wasn't sure if she meant herself or him.

Placing the invitation back on the mantel, she knelt down in front of the fireplace, struck a match, and brought it to the paper and small chips of wood stuffed in the grate. Within minutes she had the fire going, the logs catching quickly, the flames leaping up the chimney.

Pushing herself to her feet, Alexandra turned on a lamp. Along with the fire, it helped to bring a warm, roseate glow to the living room, already shadowed as it was by the murky winter light of late afternoon. She felt tired. After leaving her mother, she had walked down Park Avenue from Seventy-ninth Street to Thirty-ninth. Forty blocks of good exercise, but she had finally given in and taken a cab back to the loft.

After glancing out of the window at the lights of Manhattan slowly coming on, Alexa sat down on the sofa in front of the fire, staring into the flames flickering and dancing in the grate. Her mind was awash with so many diverse thoughts, but the most prominent were centered on Tom.

It was Nicky Sedgwick who had introduced them when Tom had come out to the studios in Billancourt to see his client Jacques Durand, who was producing the movie. It was a French-American coproduction, very elaborate and costly. Nicky and his brother Larry were the art directors and were designing the sets, and at Anya's suggestion they had hired Alexa as their assistant. But she had become more like an associate because of all the work and responsibility they had heaped on her.

What a challenge the movie had been, and what a lot she had learned. It was a historical drama about Napoleon and Josephine in the early part of their relationship, and Nicky, who was in charge, was a stickler for historical accuracy and detail. Even now, when she thought of the endless hours she had spent at Malmaison, she cringed. She had taken countless notes, knew that house inside out, and had often wondered why the famous couple had ever lived there. Its parkland and closeness to Paris, she supposed. Nicky had been thrilled with her . . . with her work, her overall input, and most of all with her set designs. In general, it had been a positive experience, and she worked on most of their movies and plays after that, until she left Paris.

The day Tom Conners came out to the studios, shooting was going well, and Jacques Durand had been elated. He and Tom had invited the Sedgwick brothers to dinner when they wrapped for the day, and she had been included in the invitation, since Anya's nephews had by then adopted her, in a sense.

She had been struck dumb by Tom's extraordinary looks, his charm and sophistication. So much so, she had felt like a little schoolgirl with him. But he had treated her as a grown-up, with gallantry and grace, and she had been smitten with him before the dinner was over. Later that night she found herself in his arms in his car after he drove her home; two nights later she was in his bed.

"Spontaneous combustion" he had called it, but not very long after this he had said it was a *coup de foudre,* clap of thunder, love at first sight. Which they both knew it was.

But that easy charm and effortless grace hid a difficult man of many moods, a man who was burdened by the needless deaths of his wife and child, and by an acute sorrow he was so careful to hide in public.

Nicky had teased her about Tom at times, and once he had said, "I suppose women must find his dark Byronic moods sexy, appealing," and had thrown her an odd look. She knew what he was hinting at, but Tom was not acting. He really was in pain on occasion. But it was Larry who had been the one to warn her. "He comes to you dragging a lot of baggage behind him, emotional baggage,"

Larry had pointed out. "So watch out, and protect your flanks. He's lethal, a dangerous man."

Alexa reached for the afghan on the arm of the sofa and stretched out under it. Her thoughts stayed with Tom and their days together in Paris. Despite his moodiness, those awful bouts of sadness, their relationship had always been good, even ecstatic when he shed the burdens of his past. And it had ended only because she had wanted permanence with him. Marriage. Children.

She wondered about him often, wondered who he was with, how his life was going, what he was doing. Still suffering, she supposed. She hadn't been able to convey to her mother the extent of that. She hadn't even tried. It was too hard to explain. You had to live through it with him to understand.

He was forty-two now, and still unmarried, she felt certain of that. What a waste, she thought, and closed her eyes, suddenly craving sleep. And she wanted to forget . . . to forget Tom and her feelings for him, forget those days in Paris . . . she was never going back there. Not even for Anya Sedgwick's eighty-fifth birthday.

CHAPTER FOUR

Kay

I remember dancing with him here, right in the center of this room, under the chandelier, she thought, and moved forward from the doorway where she had been standing.

Her arms outstretched, as if she were holding a man, Kay Lenox turned and whirled to the strains of an old-fashioned waltz that was playing only in her head. Humming to herself, she moved with rhythm and gracefulness, and the expression on her delicately molded face was for a fleeting moment rhapsodic, lost as she was in her thoughts.

Memories flooded her.

Memories of a man who had loved and cherished her, a man who had been an adoring lover and husband, a man she was still married to but who no longer seemed quite the same. He had changed, and even though the change in him was minuscule, she had spotted it from the moment it had happened.

He denied her charge that he was different in his behavior toward her, insisting she was imagining things. But she knew she was not. There had been a cooling off in him; it was as if he no longer loved her quite as much as before.

Always attentive and solicitous, he now appeared to be distracted, was even occasionally careless, forgetting to tell her if he planned to work late or attend a business dinner, or some other such thing. He would phone her at the very last minute, giving no thought to her or any plans she might have, leaving her high and dry for the evening. Although she seethed inside, she said nothing; she was always patient, understanding, and devoted.

Kay had never believed it possible that a man like Ian Andrews would marry her. But he had. Their courtship had been idyllic, and so had the first two and a half years of their marriage, which had been, for her, like a dream come true.

And these were the memories that assailed her now, held her in their thrall as she moved around the room, swaying, floating, circling, as if in another kind of dream. And as she danced with him, he so alive in her head and her heart, she recalled his boyishness, his enthusiasm for life, his gallantry and charm. He had swept her off her feet and into marriage within a month of their first meeting. Startled though she was, she had not objected; she had been as madly in love with him as he was with her. Besides, it also suited her purpose to marry him quickly. She had so much to hide.

A discreet cough intruded, brought her out of her reverie and to a standstill. She glanced at the door, feeling embarrassed to be caught dancing alone, and gave Hazel, the cook at Lochcraigie, a nervous half smile.

"Sorry to intrude, Lady Andrews, but I was wondering about dinner . . ." The cook hesitated, looking at her steadily, and then finished in a low voice, "Will his lordship be here tonight?"

"Yes, Hazel, he will," Kay answered, her tone firm and confident. "Thanks, Hazel. Oh, and by the way, did you see the dinner menu I left?"

"Yes, I did, Lady Andrews." The cook inclined her head and disappeared.

But *will* he be here? Kay asked herself, walking to the window where she stood looking out across the lawns and trees toward the hills that edged the pale blue skyline. After breakfast he had announced he was going into Edinburgh to buy a birthday gift for his twin sister, Fiona; it was their birthday tomorrow and they were having a birthday lunch. But she couldn't help wondering why he hadn't asked her to pick something out earlier in the week, since she went to her studio in the city three days a week. On the other hand, he and Fiona were unusually close, and perhaps he felt the need to do his own selecting.

Turning away from the long expanse of window, Kay walked across the terra-cotta-tiled floor, heading for the huge stone hearth. She stood with her back to the fire, thinking, as always, what a strange room this was, and yet it succeeded despite its strangeness. Or perhaps because of it.

It was a conservatory that had been added on to one end of the house, and it had been built by Ian's great-great-grandmother in Victorian times. It was airy and light because of its many windows, yet it had a coziness due to the stone fireplace, an unusual addition in a conservatory, but necessary because of the cold Scottish winters. Yet in summer it was equally pleasant to be in, with its many windows, French doors, and cool stone floor. Potted plants and wicker furniture painted dark brown helped to give it the mandatory garden mood for a conservatory, yet a few choice antiques added charm and a sense of permanence. A curious but whimsical touch was the Venetian blown-glass chandelier that hung from the beamed ceiling, and yet this, too, somehow worked in the room despite its oddness.

Kay bit her lip, thinking about Ian, worrying about their relationship, as she had for some time now. She knew why there had been this slight shift, this moving away . . . it was because she had not conceived. He was desperate for a child, longed for an heir to his lands and this house, where the Andrews family had lived for nearly five hundred years. And so far she had not been able to give him one.

My fault, she whispered to herself, thinking of her early years in Glasgow and what had happened to her when she was a teenager. A shudder passed through her slender frame, and she turned bodily to the fire, reached out to warm her hands, shivering unexpectedly as she filled with that old familiar coldness.

Lowering herself onto the leather-topped club fender, she sat staring into the flames, her face suddenly drawn, her eyes pensive. Yet despite the sadness, there was no denying her exceptional beauty, and with her ivory complexion, eyes as blue as speedwells and red-gold hair that shimmered in the firelight, she was a true Celt. But at this moment Kay Lenox Andrews was not thinking about her beauty, or her immense talent, which had brought her so far in her young life, but of the ugliness and degradation of her past.

———

When she looked back, growing up in the Gorbals, the slums of Glasgow, had been something of an education in itself. There were times when Kay wondered if she might have been a different person if her early environment had not been quite so difficult and harsh. Inevitably, she always had the same answer for herself . . . she just wasn't really sure.

She knew there were those who said environment helped to create personality and character, while others believed you were born with your character intact, that character was destiny, that it determined the roads you took, the life you ultimately led. She herself tended to accept this particular premise.

The road *she* took was the road to success. At least, that is what she repeatedly told herself when she set out to change her life. And her positive attitude, plus her determination, had helped her to accomplish wonders.

When she was a teenager, the thing that had driven her was the need to get out of the Gorbals, where she had been born. Fortunately, her mother, Alice Smith, felt the same way, and it was Alice who had helped her to move ahead, who had pushed her out into the bigger world. "And a much better world than it is here, Kay," her mother had repeatedly told her, always adding: "And I want you to have a better life than I ever had. You've got it all. Looks, brains, and that amazing talent. There's nothing to stop you . . . but yourself. So I'm hoping to make certain you bloody well succeed, lassie. I promise you that, even if it kills me trying."

Her mother had plotted and planned, scrimped and saved, and there had even been one moment in time when she had actually resorted to blackmail in order to rescue Kay and fulfill her own special plans for her daughter. Alice had enormous ambitions for Kay, ambitions some thought were ludicrous, beyond reach. But not Alice Smith. Nothing and no one was going to stop her grabbing off the best for Kay; eventually, all that shoving and pushing and striving, and sacrifice had paid off. Her cherished daughter was launched with a new identity . . . a young woman of background, breeding, and education, who happened to be stunningly beautiful, unusually talented, and all set to become a fashion designer of taste and flair.

I wouldn't have made it to where I am today without Mam, Kay now thought, still gazing into the flames of the roaring fire, ruminating on her past life in general.

Kay left the conservatory and walked toward the front hall set in the center of the house. It was a vast open space with a high-flung cathedral ceiling and a double staircase, with carved balustrades that ran up to the wide upper hall. The main feature of this hall was a soaring stained-glass window that bathed the front hall below in multicolored light, almost like a perpetual rainbow.

She took the left-hand side of the staircase, running up to the second floor, where her design studio was located in what had once been the day nursery at Lochcraigie.

As she opened the door and went in on this bitter February morning, she was glad to see that Maude, the housekeeper, already had a fire burning brightly in the grate. It was a large, high-ceilinged room with six tall windows, and it was flooded with the cool northern light she loved, and which was so perfect for her work. In this crystalline light all colors were *true,* and that made her designing so much easier.

Stepping toward the old Jacobean refectory table that served as her desk, she reached over and picked up the phone as it began to ring. "Lochcraigie House," she said, walking around to her high-backed chair and sitting down.

"It's me, Kay," her assistant said.

"Hello, Sophie. Is something wrong?"

"No, nothing. Why? Oh, you mean because I'm calling on a Saturday. No, all's well in the world as far as I know. At least it is in mine, anyway."

Kay smiled. Sophie was a darling, full of energy and life, and a joy to work with, and at twenty-three she was bursting with talent, enthusiasm, and ideas. "Then you *are* the lucky one," Kay said at last, wishing that all were well in her little world. She went on. "I just came up to the studio, and as I'm sitting here talking to you I can see that vermilion piece that came from the mill the other day . . . I like it, Sophie, I really do. It's such a change from the colors I've been using this past year."

"I agree. It's really vibrant, but also sort of . . . smoochy."

"What do you mean by smoochy?"

"You know, smoochy, as in kiss-kiss-kiss."

Kay burst out laughing.

Dropping her voice, Sophie now said confidingly, "I called because I finally got that information for you."

"What information?"

"About the man my sister recently heard of . . . you know, we discussed it two weeks ago."

"Oh, yes, of course. Sorry, Sophie, I guess I'm being a little stupid today." She clutched the receiver more tightly, filled with sudden expectancy.

"His name is François Boujon, and he lives in France once again."

"Where, exactly?"

"Just outside Paris. A place with a peculiar name. Barbizon. My sister got me all the information. Do you want to know everything now, or shall I tell you on Monday?"

"Monday's perfectly fine, I'll be at the studio by about ten, and we can talk then. But just tell me one thing now . . . is he difficult to get an appointment with?"

"Yes, a bit, I'm afraid. But Gillian will help."

"Can she?"

"Oh, yes, very much so . . . her girlfriend Mercedes has a strong connection, which is good."

"It certainly is, and listen, I'm very appreciative, Sophie, I really am. Thanks for going to all this trouble."

"It wasn't anything, not really. I was happy to do it. So, I'll see you Monday, then."

"That's right. Have a good weekend."

"I will, and you do the same."

"I'll try," Kay answered, and after saying good-bye she returned the phone to its cradle. Resting her head against the faded red velvet covering the chair's back, she let her eyes roam around the room, her mind whirling with all manner of thoughts. Then quite suddenly she remembered the envelope that had arrived by FedEx yesterday, and she reached for the decorative wooden box on one end of the desk. Lifting the lid, she took out the envelope with its beautiful calligraphy—her name so elegantly written—opened it, and slipped out the invitation.

Once again she read it carefully.

Anya's party was on the second of June, a good four months away. She wondered if she could get an appointment with François Boujon for around that time.

It would be perfect if she could, because Ian hadn't been invited, and so she could travel alone to Paris. Kill two birds with one stone, she thought, and then she sat back in the chair with a jerk, frowning hard. Her vivid blue eyes clouded over, and her expression became unexpectedly grim.

They would be there and she would have to see them. No, not only see them, but socialize with them, spend time with them. Not possible. They were no longer friends.

Alexandra Gordon, the snob from New York. From the elite social set, Junior League, and all that ridiculous kind of thing. Always so toffee-nosed with her, stuck up, snubbing *her.*

Jessica Pierce, Miss Southern Belle Incorporated, with her feminine sighs and languor and the dropping of lace hankies along the way. Poking fun at *her,* teasing her unmercifully, never leaving *her* alone with her taunts.

Maria Franconi, another snob, this one from Italy, with her raven hair and flashing black eyes and fiery Mediterranean temperament. And all those lire from her rich Milanese textile family, flaunting her money and her connections, treating *her* like a servant.

No, it's not possible, Kay told herself again. I cannot go to Anya's party. Because my tormentors will be there . . . how miserable they had always made her life.

She knew what she must do. She must go to Paris sooner rather than later, to meet with this man François Boujon. Hopefully she would get an appointment relatively soon. She would set everything in motion on Monday, ask to see him next month. And it did not matter what it cost.

She put the invitation back in the envelope, placed this in the wooden box, dropped the lid, and turned the key. Then once more she sat back in the chair, her eyes becoming soft and faraway as she thought of Ian. The man she loved. Her husband . . . who must remain her husband at all costs.

CHAPTER FIVE

Even as a child, growing up in the slums of Glasgow, Kay had always managed to escape simply by retreating into herself. When the cramped little flat where she lived with her mother and brother, Sandy, became overly oppressive, she would find a small corner where she could curl up, forget where she really was, and dream.

A great deal of her childhood was spent dreaming, and she found solace in her dreams. She could escape the impoverished, gloomy world she occupied and go to another place, anyplace she wished. It made her young life more bearable.

And she always dreamed of beauty . . . flower-filled gardens, picturesque country cottages with thatched roofs, grassy meadows awash with wildflowers, and grand open spaces with huge, canopied green trees where trilling birdsong came alive. And sometimes her dreams were of pretty clothes, and ribbons for her hair, and sturdy black shoes shining with boot polish for Sandy, and a beautiful silk dress for her mother . . . a pale blue dress to match her eyes.

But as she grew older, Kay's priorities changed, and she began to replace her dreams with a newfound focus and concentration, and it was these two qualities, plus her unique talent, that helped to make her such a great success in the world of fashion.

Now, as she sat at her desk, thoughts of Ian lingered, nagged at the back of her mind. But eventually she let go of her worries about her marriage and became totally engrossed in her work, as she usually did.

In many ways, she loved this old day nursery at Lochcraigie more than her busy high-tech studio in Edinburgh, not the least because of its spaciousness, high ceiling, and clarity of light.

After looking through a few sketches for her fall collection, which she had just finished, she rose and went over to the swatches of fabric hanging on brass hooks attached to the opposite wall. The vermilion wool she had focused on a short while before attracted her attention again, and she unclipped it and carried it over to the window, where she scrutinized it intently.

Suddenly, a smile flickered in her eyes as she remembered Sophie's comment a short while ago. *Smoochy,* she had called the color, as in a kiss, and Kay knew exactly what her assistant meant. It *was* a lovely lipstick shade, one that reminded her of the glamorous stars of those old movies from the 1950s.

As often happened with Kay, inspiration suddenly struck out of the blue. In her mind's eye she saw a series of outfits . . . each one in a different version of vivid vermilion red. She thought of cyclamen first, then deep pink the color of peonies, pale pinks borrowed from a bunch of sweet peas, bright red lifted from a pot of geraniums, and all of those other reds sharpened by a hint of blue. And mixed in with them she could see a selection of blues . . . cerulean, delphinium, and aquamarine, as well as deep violet and pansy hues, a softer lilac, and the lavender shade of hydrangeas.

That's it, she thought, instantly filling with excitement. A winter collection of clothes based on those two colors—red and blue—interspersed with other tones from these color spectrums. What a change from the beiges, browns, greens, taupes, and terra-cottas of her spring season.

Turning away from the window where she still stood, Kay went over to the other fabric samples and searched through them quickly, looking for the colors she now wanted to use. She found a few of them and carried them back to her desk, where she spread them out. Then she began to match the color samples to the sketches she had already done for her winter line, envisioning a coat, a suit, or a dress in one of the reds, purples, or blues.

Very soon she was lost in her work, completely oblivious to everything, bubbling inside with enthusiasm, her creative juices flowing as she began to design, loving every moment of it.

At twenty-nine, Kay Lenox was one of the best-known young fashion designers on both sides of the Atlantic. In London her clothes sold at her boutique on Bond Street, and in New York at Bergdorf Goodman. She had a boutique in Chicago and one in Dallas, and another on Rodeo Drive in Beverly Hills.

Her name was synonymous with quality, stylishness, and wearability. The clothes she designed were elegant, but in a relaxed and casual manner, and they were extremely well cut and beautifully made.

The fabrics Kay favored gave her clothes a great sense of luxury . . . the finest light wools, cashmeres, wool crepes, soft Scottish tweeds, suede, leather, crushed velvet, and a heavy silk she bought in France. Her flair and imagination were visible in the way she mixed these fabrics with each other in one garment—the result a look entirely unique to her.

Kay worked on steadily through the morning, and so concentrated was she, and focused on her designs, she almost jumped out of her skin when the phone next to her elbow jangled.

Picking it up, she said "Lochcraigie" in a somewhat sharpish tone.

"Hello, darling," her husband answered. "*You* sound a bit snotty this morning."

"Ian!" she exclaimed, her face lighting up. "Sorry. I was lost in a dress, figuratively speaking."

He chuckled. "Is your designing going well, then?"

"I'll say, and I had a brainstorm earlier. I'm doing the entire winter collection in shades of red running through to palest pink, and blue going to lilac to violet and deep purple."

"Sounds good to me."

"Did you find a gift for Fiona?"

There was a moment's hesitation before he said, sounding vague, "Oh, yes, I did."

"So you're on your way home now?"

"Not exactly," he replied, clearing his throat. "Er, er, I'm a bit peckish, so I'm going to have a spot of lunch. I should be back about fourish."

The brightness in her vivid blue eyes dimmed slightly, but she said, "All right, then, I'll be here waiting for you."

"We'll have tea together," he murmured. "Bye, darling."

He hung up before she could say another word, and she stood there puzzled, staring at the receiver in her hand, and then she went back to work.

———

Later that afternoon, when she had eaten a smoked salmon sandwich and drunk a mug of lemon tea, Kay put on a cream fisherman's knit sweater from the Orkneys, thick woolen socks, and green Wellington boots. In the coat room near the back door she took down her dark green coat of quilted silk, pushed her red-gold hair under a red knitted cap, added a matching scarf and gloves, and went outside.

She was hit with a blast of freezing air, and it took her breath away, but her clothes were warm, the coat in particular, and she set out toward the loch, in need of fresh air and exercise.

This was one of her favorite walks on the estate, which in its entirety covered over three thousand acres. A wide path led down from the cutting garden just beyond the back door, past broad lawns and thick woods bordering one side of the lawns. In the distance was the narrow body of glassy water that was Loch Craigie.

At one moment Kay stopped and stood staring across at the distant hills, partially obscured this afternoon by a hazy mist on their peaks and lightly covered in snow. Then she swung her head, her eyes settling on the great stone house where she lived, built in 1559 by William Andrews, then new laird of Lochcraigie. From that time onward, the eldest son had inherited everything through the law of primogeniture, and fortuitously there had always been a male heir to carry on the Andrews name. An unbroken line for centuries.

Ian was the laird now, although no one ever used that old Scots name anymore, except for a few old-timers from his grandfather's day who still lived in the village.

Aside from these vast lands, the Andrews family had many other interests, primarily in business, including manufacturing, publishing, and textiles. Everything belonged to Ian, but he was a low-profile millionaire content to lead the quiet country life.

Kay began to walk again, striding out at a steady pace, her eyes thoughtful as she contemplated her own past. She couldn't help wondering what Ian would say if he knew of her mean and poverty-stricken beginnings. He would be horrified, shocked, and perhaps even disbelieving. . . .

She let these thoughts float way up into the air, and took several deep breaths. Her troubles began when she was a teenager, but she had always known they would end, that she would have a different life when she was older.

And now she did. She had everything she had ever wanted, had ever dreamed about . . . a husband who was not only young and handsome but an aristocrat, an ancient historic house she called home, a big career as a fashion designer, fame, success. . . .

But no child.

No heir for Ian.

No boy to be the laird of these vast estates and holdings, one day in the far distant future, when Ian was dead and they proclaimed a new master of Lochcraigie.

She sighed under her breath. It was an old story. After a moment she increased her pace, almost running down to the loch. The body of water was flat and gray, leaden under the wintry sky, and she did not plan to linger long. The air had grown much colder and there was a hint of snow on the wind. But she walked along the edge of the water for fifteen minutes, always enjoying the tranquil view, the sense of peace that was all-pervasive here.

On her way back, she took the paved path that led past the Dower House where Ian's mother lived. For a moment she thought of dropping in to see her mother-in-law but changed her mind. It would soon be four o'clock and Ian would be home; she longed to see him, to assuage her anxiety about him. She had plans for tonight, big plans, and she wanted him to be in the right frame of mind. If she were absent when he arrived, he could be put out.

And so she passed the Dower House and climbed the narrow steps, thinking of Ian's mother. She was a lovely woman, with impeccable manners, manners bred in the bone, and a kind and loving heart. She had always been *her* champion, and for that Kay was grateful.

Margaret Andrews had been born a Hepburn, and her family was somehow distantly related to the ill-fated James Hepburn, Earl of Bothwell, third husband of Mary Queen of Scots, who had died a terrible death in Denmark, imprisoned in the dungeons of a remote castle. Kay hated the story of Bothwell's death. It always upset her; she couldn't bear to think of that virile, vigorous, and handsome man dying in such a ghastly way. And yet the story haunted her . . . she chastised herself now for her morbid thoughts of Bothwell and ran across the lawn to the terrace in front of the conservatory. A second later she let herself into the house.

———

Kay knew at once that Ian was in a good mood as he walked into the conservatory just after four. He was smiling, and when she went to greet him he hugged her close and kissed her cheek. "You look bonny," he said to her as he moved away, went and stood with his back to the fire.

She smiled back at him. "Thank you. Hazel just brought the tea in, Ian. Shall I pour you a cup?"

He nodded. "It was a long drive back, and I thought I was going to hit snow, but so far it's held off."

"Not quite," Kay said, and pointedly looked toward the French doors. "It's just started."

He followed her gaze, saw the snowflakes coming down, and heavily so. But he laughed and said, "It looks as if we might get snowed in, Kay."

"I don't care! Do you?"

"No. Well, let's have tea, then."

They sat down on the wicker furniture grouped in front of the fire, and Kay poured for them both, looking across at him surreptitiously as she did.

Ian appeared to be happier this afternoon than he had in a while, more lighthearted and carefree than was usual. He also looked younger, unusually boyish, but perhaps that was because his fair hair was tousled from the wind and he wore an open-neck shirt under a pale blue sweater with a V neckline. Very collegiate, and vulnerable, she thought, and smiled inwardly, thinking of her plans.

Ian said, "Actually, I hope the snow doesn't stick. It really would be quite awful if we had to cancel tomorrow's birthday lunch."

Kay nodded in agreement. "Let's not worry. I heard a weather report earlier on the radio, and it's supposed to be sunny tomorrow, and also much warmer."

Ian smiled to her and surveyed the tray of finger sandwiches and fancy cakes.

"By the way, Ian, what did you end up getting Fiona?"

"What do you mean?"

Kay gave him a baffled look, her eyes full of questions, and exclaimed, "The gift, for her birthday. What is it?"

"Oh, yes . . . a pair of earrings. Rather nice, I'll show them to you later."

They fell into a companionable silence, sipping their tea and eating the little finger sandwiches and cream cakes in front of the blazing fire. Outside the windows it was snowing heavily now, and the flakes settled on the ground, but neither of them noticed, preoccupied as they were with their own thoughts.

Kay couldn't help feeling taut inside, even though Ian appeared to be so relaxed and at ease with himself and with her.

He was more like his old self, and this was a good omen. She planned to seduce him later, planned a night of lovemaking, and it was important that he was in the right mood. She believed he was . . . at least at the moment. She prayed it would last. And with a little luck she would get pregnant. She must. So much depended on it.

For his part, Ian was thinking about his trip to Edinburgh. It had been interesting, to say the least, and he was glad he made the effort to go. And he was happy with the purchases. He hoped Fiona would like his gift; certainly it had been carefully chosen. He focused on his wife, and he couldn't help thinking how beautiful she looked, and desirable . . . he let *that* thought slide away. . . .

Kay broke the silence when she confided, "The FedEx envelope I received yesterday was an invitation . . . an invitation to go to Anya Sedgwick's eighty-fifth birthday party in Paris."

"I don't have to go too, do I?" Ian asked, suddenly frowning, looking worried. "You know how I hate traveling."

"No, of course not," she answered quickly. She didn't bother to tell him only her name was on the invitation. But she did think to add, "I'm not going to go either."

Ian stared at her, apparently puzzled and surprised. "Why ever not?"

"I don't really want to see people I haven't seen in seven years . . . I lost touch with my friends when I graduated."

"But you've always admired Anya."

"That's true, she's the most fascinating woman I've ever met, a genius too."

"Well, then?" He raised a sandy brow.

"I don't know . . ."

"I think you should go to her party, Kay, just out of respect."

"Perhaps you're right. I'll think about it."

CHAPTER SIX

By the time they finished their tea, the snow had settled on the ground, and it was continuing to fall steadily. Outside, it was growing darker and darker; the dusky twilight of late afternoon had long since been obliterated, and already a few sparse early stars sprinkled the sky.

But in the snug conservatory all was warmth and coziness. The fire roared in the great stone hearth, constantly replenished with logs and peat by Ian; the table lamps cast a lovely lambent glow throughout, and in the background music played softly.

Ian had turned on the radio earlier to listen to the weather report, and after hearing that heavy snow was expected, he had tuned in to a station playing popular music. Now the strains of "Lady in Red," sung by Chris De Burgh, echoed softly around the conservatory.

The two of them had been silent for a while, and at one moment

Ian looked across at Kay intently, his eyes narrowing. "You're very quiet this afternoon, and you look awfully pensive. Sad, even. Is something the matter, darling? What are you brooding about?"

Kay roused herself from her thoughts, and shook her head. "Not brooding, Ian. Just thinking . . . people *do* suffer for love, don't they?"

His brows drew together in a small frown, but his expression was hard to read. After a split second he answered her. "I suppose some do—" He paused and shrugged offhandedly. "But what are you getting at *exactly?*"

"I was thinking of Bothwell earlier, and the way he loved Mary. How he died because of her . . . well, in a sense he did. And that awful death . . . chained like a poor dog to a pole for years . . ." Her voice trailed off and she let out a long sigh. *"He* suffered for love. It's so heartbreaking, that story, when you think about it."

"But it happened hundreds of years ago. And I do believe my mother's been filling your head with stories again—"

"Yes, but they're all part of Scottish history," she interrupted peremptorily. "I can never get enough of it. I guess I didn't pay enough attention at school . . . but your mother's rectified all that. She's been a wonderful teacher."

His searching hazel eyes rested on her, and then he half smiled. "My mother's the best teacher I know. A genius at it, especially when it comes to the history of the clans. She held me enthralled when I was a child."

"She's told me a lot about the noble families, but so much more as well. I've learned a great deal about the Stuarts. How extraordinary they were, so bold and courageous, and very beautiful to look at."

"And very ill fated," he shot back pointedly. "At least some of them were. Foolish Mary, led by her heart and not her head. She was no match for crafty Elizabeth Tudor, I'm afraid. Not in the long run. Her cousin was so much cleverer."

"The problem with Mary and Bothwell is that they were so entangled in the politics of the times. It doomed them."

"*That's* an old familiar story, isn't it?" Ian shook his head, laughed a bit cynically. "She was trying to keep a throne and protect her heir, and he wanted to sit next to her on his own throne, and the lords were in rebellion. God knows, it was a dangerous and hellish time to live."

"Your mother explained everything. She's a bit of a nationalist."

He laughed. "So are you!"

"Something must've rubbed off."

He smiled at her indulgently. She was full of romantic notions, but then, perhaps that was a female prerogative.

There was a small silence.

Eventually Kay murmured, "Your mother once told me that suffering for love is a noble thing. Do you agree with her?"

Ian burst out laughing. "I'm not so sure I do! And let's not forget that my mother is something of a romantic, always has been, always will be, just like you are. But come to think of it, no, I don't want to *suffer* for love. No, not at all. I want to relish it, enjoy it, wallow in it."

"With me?" A red-gold brow lifted provocatively.

"Is that an invitation?" he asked, eyeing her keenly.

She simply smiled, but beguilingly so.

Ian rose and crossed the room, took hold of her hands, and brought her to her feet. And then he led her over to the fireplace, pulled her down onto the rug with him.

He smoothed his hand over her red-gold hair, shimmering in the fire's glow, and held strands of it between his fingers. "Look at this . . . Celtic gold . . . it's beautiful, Kay." She was silent. Her eyes never left his face. He began to unbutton her white silk blouse, leaned forward, kissed her cheek, her neck, and her mouth, then moved her into a prone position. He kissed her with mounting passion.

But after only a moment, Kay pushed him away. "Ian, stop! We can't. Not *here!* Someone might come in."

"No, they won't."

"Maude might, or Malcolm. To clear way the tea things."

He laughed dismissively. But, nonetheless, he got up and walked over to the door set in the wall, to the right of the fireplace. This led to the main house.

Risk, Kay thought. He loves taking risks, taking awful chances. It excites him. And I mustn't fight him now. He wants to make love . . . I must seize this moment.

She heard him locking the door, and his footsteps echoing on the terra-cotta tiles as he came back to her.

Ian knelt on the floor next to Kay. He took her face in both of his hands, brought his lips to hers gently, gave her a light kiss.

"What about the French doors?" she asked, pulling away, glancing worriedly toward the terrace.

"Nobody's going to be out in this weather, for God's sake! There's a snowstorm brewing!"

He doesn't care, she thought. He doesn't care if someone sees us through the windows. Or walks in. But she knew this wouldn't happen. He was right. Everyone was snowbound tonight, safe in their homes. His mother down the hill in the Dower House; his sister, Fiona, ensconced in her cottage by the loch; John Lanark and his family secure in the estate manager's house close by the Home Farm. No one would venture out unless there was an emergency.

Ian had taken off her cardigan and white silk blouse, and was fumbling with the hooks on her bra. She helped him unfasten it, then reached out for him, pulled him into her arms. They fell back on the rug together, and she kissed him hard, deeply. He responded with ardor, and then almost immediately he sat up, pulled off his sweater, struggled out of his shirt, threw them impatiently to one side.

Kay followed suit, and within a few seconds they were both

completely undressed, naked on the rug in front of the fire. Ian sat back on his haunches, looking down at her. She never failed to stir his blood. She was such a beautiful woman, tall, slender, long limbed; and her skin was pale as ivory. But now, in the firelight, it had taken on a golden glow and her red hair was like a burnished halo around her narrow face. How very blue her eyes were, riveted on his.

Staring back at him, Kay saw the intensity in his luminous hazel eyes, twin reflections of her own filled with mounting desire. She lifted her arms up to him.

In answer, he stretched himself on top of her. How perfectly we fit together, he thought.

"I want you," she whispered against his neck, and her long, tapering fingers went up into his hair. "Take me, take me."

He wanted her as much as she wanted him, but he also wanted to prolong their lovemaking. Sometimes it was too quick. He was too quick. Tonight he had the great need to savor her, to pleasure her, before he took his own pleasure with her.

And so he kissed her very slowly, almost languorously, and thrilled when her mouth opened under his. He felt her tongue groping for his, and he was more inflamed than ever.

As he began to caress her breasts, her hands moved down over his broad back, settled on his buttocks. Smoothing his hand up along her leg, he slipped it between her thighs; her soft sighs increased as he finally touched that damp, warm, welcoming place. She arched her body, then fell back, moaning.

Now he could hardly contain himself and he parted her legs and entered her swiftly, no longer able to resist her.

Kay began to move frantically against him, her hands tightly gripping his shoulders, her whole body radiating heat and a desire for him he had not seen in her before. Excited beyond endurance, he felt every fiber of his being exploding as he tumbled into her warmth, and she welcomed him ecstatically.

———

William Andrews, who inherited Lochcraigie on the death of his bachelor uncle, had a growing family, and so it was necessary to provide a larger dwelling to accommodate them all. To this end, he built a new house, which was finished in the late summer of 1559, and for the past four hundred and forty-two years it had stood unflinching on the small hillock above the loch.

Across all these decades the large bedroom, which overlooked the long body of water and the rolling hills beyond, had been called the Laird's Room. From William's day on it had always been the private enclave of the head of the family, from the moment he inherited the title and property until he died.

Like the rest of the rooms in this great stone manse, the bedroom had a grandeur and dignity about it. Of spacious proportions, it had eight windows, one placed on each side of the central fireplace, and three set in each end wall. The fireplace itself was also grand and soaring, with an oversize iron grate to hold big logs and slabs of peat, these kind of massive fires necessary in the dead of the Scottish winter. Its mahogany mantel matched the dark beams that floated across the ceiling and the highly polished, pegged-wood floor.

The elegance of the room was not only to be found in its beautiful proportions but in its furnishings as well. Set against the main wall, and facing the fireplace stood the mahogany four-poster, with its carved posts, rose silk hangings, and coverlet.

The same rose brocade, with a self-pattern of thistles, covered the walls and hung as curtains at the many windows. It was faded now, having been chosen by Ian's great-great-grandmother, the famous Adelaide, renowned in the family for her installation of the Victorian conservatory.

Although she had taste and a great eye for decorating as well as for fashion, Kay had not tampered with anything in the master bedroom. For one thing, Ian loved the room just the way it was, and so did she. So there was no good reason to upset him by making changes to a setting already quite beautiful, and one loaded with tradition and family history.

In particular, she admired the handsome antique chests, dressing table, and other smaller pieces from the Jacobean period, and the Persian rug in the center of the room. This was very old, its rose and blue tones faded, but it looked perfect against the dark pegged wood, and it was priceless, she knew that. A beautiful gilded mirror over one of the chests, antique porcelain lamps and vases, and a charming old grandfather clock standing in one corner were items in the bedroom that Kay cherished as much as Ian did.

Several comfortable chairs were arranged near the fireplace, and Kay curled up in one of them now.

It was late, well past midnight.

Ian was already fast asleep. She could hear the faint rise and fall of his deep breathing; the only other sounds in the room were the crackle of the logs in the grate and the ticking of the clock in the corner.

Kay was thinking of Ian. She had been overwhelmed by his passion tonight, not only in the conservatory after tea, when he had taken her by surprise and made amazing love to her on the floor, but then later in their bed, when desire had overtaken him yet again. He had been unable to get enough of her, or so it seemed.

She had found herself responding in kind, meeting his passionate sexual needs head-on, as wild and demanding as he was.

Hope rose in her that she had conceived.

Kay wanted a child as much as her husband did, not that Ian ever made reference to his longing for a son. But she knew deep within herself how much he yearned for an heir, a boy to follow in his footsteps as the Laird of Lochcraigie.

What would happen if she didn't conceive? Not ever? Would he divorce her and find another woman to bear him a son? Or would he shrug and hope that his sister, Fiona, would marry and provide a male child to inherit the title and vast family holdings? The awful thing was, she had no idea what Ian would do.

Rising, Kay walked over to the window and looked out. It was still snowing; there was a high wind that sent the crystalline flakes whirling about, and on the ground they were still settling. There was a blanket of white below, and under the pale moon this pristine coverlet seemed woven with silver threads. The wind rattled the windows all of a sudden, but the house stood firm and solid, as it always had. William Andrews of Lochcraigie had built a manse that had defied time and the harsh Scottish winters.

If only she had someone to talk to, Kay thought, pressing her face against the cold windowpane. She had never discussed their childlessness with Ian for fear of opening a Pandora's box, or with her mother-in-law for the same reason. If only Mam were still alive, she thought, and unexpectedly a surge of emotion choked her. Her mother had made her what she was, and put her where she was in a sense, but her mam was no longer around to reap the benefits or share the joy. Her brother, Sandy, was long gone, having emigrated to Australia eight years before, and she never heard from him anymore. Sadly.

I have no friends, at least not close friends, she realized, and thought instantly of Alex Gordon. They had been so very close once, until their terrible quarrel. Sometimes, when she wasn't closing her mind to those wonderful days at Anya's school, memories of Alex enveloped her, and she found herself missing the American girl. Not the Italian though; Maria had been a pain in the neck. And Jessica, too, had been difficult. Furthermore, Jessica had been mean to her, teasing her and putting her down. Miss Jessica Pierce was cruel and vindictive.

A long, rippling sigh escaped from her throat, and she felt a sadness settle over her. But there *was* Anya Sedgwick. She had always been good to her, not only as a teacher and mentor but as a true friend, almost like a loving mother. Perhaps she should go to Anya's party after all. If she went a few days prior to the party she could meet with Anya privately, unburden herself perhaps. But why wait until June? she now wondered. And thought instantly of François Boujon. Once she had an appointment with him she could make a date for lunch or tea or dinner with Anya, who would be thrilled to see her, she had no doubts about that.

Suddenly, boldly, Kay made a decision. She would go to the party anyway. Out of respect for Anya, as Ian had suggested earlier.

She couldn't help wondering how her three former friends would behave toward her. She had become a fashion designer of some renown, after all. And although she seldom used her title away from Scotland, she was, nevertheless, the Lady Ian Andrews of Lochcraigie now.

CHAPTER SEVEN

Jessica

Jessica Pierce was in a fury.

She stood in the elegant den of her Bel Air house, looking down at her boyfriend, Gary Stennis. He was almost falling off the cream velvet sofa, sprawled out across the cushions, dead drunk.

Her cool gray eyes, always keen and observing, swept around the room.

Everything looked neat, undisturbed, in the superbly decorated room. Except for the messy jumble of things he had managed to accumulate on the low antique Chinese coffee table in front of the fireplace. A piece that had cost her the earth and was impossible to duplicate, since it was the only one in existence.

The unusual ebony table, beautifully inlaid with mother-of-pearl orange blossom trees, was littered with a number of highball glasses, one of her best Baccarat crystal goblets, a bottle of Roederer Cristal, half full, and an empty bottle of her Château Simard Saint-Émilion 1988. One of my better red wines, she thought as her eyes settled on an antique crystal dish. With a flash of irritation she saw that this valuable signed piece of Lalique, a gift from a client, had been carelessly used as an ashtray. It was full of cigarette butts. And God knows what else.

Sighing under her breath, Jessica picked it up and sniffed. The unmistakable aroma of cannabis was missing. For once he had not been smoking pot with his friends and colleagues. She put it down, relieved.

A sudden frown furrowed her brow, and she leaned closer to the coffee table, staring at the crystal goblet. It bore traces of lipstick on the rim. But it had obviously been a business meeting, of that she felt sure.

Pages of his new script were scattered on the floor, along with a yellow legal pad on which innumerable notes had been scrawled. In his handwriting.

Straightening, now focusing all of her attention on Gary, she studied him for a moment, and through dispassionate eyes. His salt-and-pepper hair was mussed, his face was gaunt and pale with dark smudges under his eyes. In sleep, his mouth had gone slack, was partially open, and in combination with his furrowed neck, it made him look curiously old, worn-out.

Washed up, she thought, and felt a tinge of sadness.

But no, he wasn't that. At least, not yet.

Gary was still a brilliant screenwriter, one of the best, if not *the* best, in the business, and his past was filled with tunes of glory. And Oscars.

He had written many of the greatest screenplays ever put on celluloid and for some of the most talented stars, male stars especially. During his most celebrated career he had made, lost, and made several fortunes, married two famous movie stars, divorced them, and fathered a daughter with one who no longer spoke to him.

And now, at the age of fifty-one, he was courting her and entreating her to marry him.

When he was sober.

Quite frequently these days he was drunk. And because of this addiction, which he refused to admit was an illness, she knew deep down she would never marry him. In her innermost soul she knew she would never be able to cope with an alcoholic on a long-term basis, and that was what he was on his way to becoming, if he wasn't already there.

Constantly Jessica begged him to go to AA, but he merely laughed at her, and somehow managed to charm her into believing he didn't need Alcoholics Anonymous. In her quiet moments, when she was alone, she knew with absolute sureness that he did. Just as she knew she should break up with him.

On two occasions Jessica had thrown him out; he had managed to charm his way back into her life. Well, he was charm personified, everyone knew that, and *the* master when it came to words. He had earned millions and millions from his words, hadn't he?

"Don't forget, he's a writer, he knows exactly what to say to press *your* buttons," her friend Merle was always saying. Her retort to Merle never varied. "And don't *you* forget that Jeremy's an actor. He knows which role to play to punch *yours*. Once an actor always an actor, Merle."

Merle usually laughed, and so did she. They knew their men, that was a certainty. And they're both wrong for us, Jessica thought; she turned swiftly on her high heels, went out of the den, and closed the door quietly behind her.

She was still furious with Gary for being in this inebriated state when she got home, and the best thing was to let him sleep it off.

Jessica had been in Santa Barbara for five days, supervising an installation at a client's new house, and Gary had promised her dinner tête-à-tête at home tonight . . . no matter what time she arrived. A dinner he would cook. He was a great chef when he wanted to be, and a great lover when he was stone-cold sober.

Yes, she loved him, with certain qualifications. Nonetheless, he made her madder than a wet hen at times. Like right then.

When she reached the circular front hall with its glassy black granite floor and elegant curving staircase, Jessica picked up her hanging clothes bag and overnight carryall and headed upstairs to her dressing room next door to the bedroom.

As she went into the octagonal-shaped room she caught sight of herself in one of the four mirrors, and after hanging up the clothes bag and putting the carryall in a corner, she turned and stared at herself in the nearest glass.

Stepping closer, she moved her long blond hair back over her shoulder, then straightened her jacket. What she saw was a tall young woman of thirty-one, not bad-looking, quite elegant in a white gabardine pantsuit and high-heeled mules, with a string of pearls around her neck and pearl studs in her ears. But it's a slightly tired woman tonight, she muttered, then went back downstairs.

Jessica's brown leather handbag was on a Louis XIV bench in the front hall. Picking it up as she walked past the bench, she hurried down the carpeted corridor to her office. Pushing open the door, she turned on the light switch and moved forward to her eighteenth-century French *bureau plat* in front of the window.

The first thing she saw, propped up against the Chinese-yellow porcelain lamp, was a FedEx envelope.

———

Jessica sat staring at the invitation for a long time, lost in her thoughts as she found herself carried back into the past.

A decade fell away.

She was young, just twenty-one, and starting out at the Anya Sedgwick School of Decorative Arts, Design, and Couture, situated on the rue de l'Université in Paris, where she had gone to study interior design.

In her mind's eye she could see herself as she was then . . . tall, very thin, with straight blond hair falling to her shoulder blades and skin without a blemish. A small-town Texas girl on her first visit to Europe. An innocent abroad.

She had been captivated by Paris, the school, Anya of course, and the little family pension on the Left Bank, where she lived. It had all been new, different, and stimulating. So very exciting, and far removed from San Antonio and her parents. She missed them a lot, while managing to enjoy every new experience at the school and in her daily life.

And it was in Paris that she met Lucien Girard and fell in love for the first time. It was at the end of her first year that she and Lucien were introduced by Larry Sedgwick, Anya's nephew. She was just twenty-two; he was four years older, an actor by profession. She smiled inwardly now, thinking of the way she teased Merle unmercifully about living with an actor.

Lucien and she had been the perfect match, completely compatible. They liked the same movies, books, music, and art, and got on so well, it was almost uncanny. They shared the same philosophy of life, wanted similar things, and were ambitious for themselves.

Jessica had believed she knew Paris well—until she met Lucien; he had quickly shown her she knew it hardly at all. He took her to wonderful out-of-the-way places, charming bistros, unique little boutiques, art galleries, and shops, and obscure pretty corners filled with peacefulness. He showed her interesting churches, little-known museums, and he had taken her on trips to Brittany, Provence, and the Côte d'Azur.

Their days together had been golden, filled with blue skies and sunshine, tranquil days and passion-filled nights.

He had taught her so much ... about so many different things ... sex and love ... the best wines and food, and how to savor them ... with him she had eaten mussels in a delicious tangy broth, omelettes so light and fluffy they were like air, soft aromatic cheeses from the countryside, and tiny *fraises du bois,* minuscule wood strawberries fragrant with an indefinable perfume, sumptuous to eat with thick clotted cream.

With him, everything was bliss.

He had called her his long-stemmed American beauty, had utterly loved and adored her, as she had him, and their days together had been sublime, so in tune were they, and happy. They made so many plans. . . .

But one day he was gone.

Lucien disappeared.

Distraught, she tried to find him, teaming up with his best friend, Alain Bonnal. His apartment was undisturbed; nothing had been removed. His agent had no idea where he was and was as baffled and worried as they were. He was an orphan; they knew of no family member to go to, no one to appeal to for information. She and Alain checked hospitals, the morgue, listed him as a missing person. To no avail. He was never found, either living or dead.

That spring of 1994 Lucien Girard had disappeared off the face of the earth. He might never have existed. But she knew very well that he had. . . .

Suddenly jumping up, Jessica hurried across the office to the large French armoire where she kept fabric samples, opened the drawer at the bottom, and pulled out a red leather photograph album. Carrying it back to the desk, she sat down, opened the album, and began turning the pages. It was a full and complete record of her three years in Paris studying interior design. Almost everyone she had met and cared about was in there.

There we are, Lucien and me, she thought, staring down at the photograph of them on the banks of the Seine, just near the Pont des Arts, the only metal bridge in Paris. She peered at the picture, instantly struck by their likeness to each other; Lucien had been tall and slender also, with fair coloring and bluish-gray eyes. The love of my life, she thought, and swiftly turned the page.

Here were she and Alexa, Kay, Maria, and Anya, in the garden of Anya's house. And here was a fun picture of Nicky and Larry clowning it up with Alexa, and Maria Franconi looking mournful at the back.

Jessica experienced an unexpected feeling of great sadness . . . Lucien had disappeared and everything had gone wrong after that. *"Les girls,"* as Nicky Sedgwick called their quartet, had quarreled and disbanded. And it had all been so . . . so . . . silly and juvenile.

Jessica closed the album. If she went to Anya's birthday party she would undoubtedly run into her former friends. She shrugged mentally . . . not knowing how she really felt about them. Seven years. It had all happened seven years ago . . . a long time, a lot of water under the bridge.

And could she actually face being in Paris? She didn't know. Paris was Lucien.

Lucien no longer existed.

That had to be true, because he had never surfaced, never reappeared. She still heard from Alain Bonnal occasionally, and he was as baffled as she continued to be; they had come up with every scenario they could think of, and were never satisfied with any of them, never sure what could have happened.

Accept the invitation. Go to Paris, just for the hell of it, she told herself. Then changed her mind instantly. *No, decline. You're only going to open up old wounds.*

Jessica closed her eyes, leaning back in the chair . . . her memories of Paris and Lucien were golden . . . filled with happiness and a joy she had not experienced since her days with him.

Better to keep the memories intact.

She would send her regrets.

———

Gary said from the doorway of her office, "So, you finally decided to come home."

Startled, Jessica swung around in the chair and stared at him. He was leaning against the doorjamb, wearing crumpled clothes and a belligerent expression.

He's an angry drunk, she thought, but said, "You look as if you've been ridden hard and put away wet."

He frowned, never having liked her southern Texan humor. "Why did you get back so late?" he demanded.

"What difference does it make? You had passed out dead drunk on my sofa."

He let out a long sigh and slid into the room, came to stand by her chair, suddenly smiling down at her. "I guess we got to celebrating. Harry and Phil were crazy about the first draft of the script, and after making our notes, a few changes, we were pretty sure it was almost good enough to be a shooting script. So . . . we decided to celebrate—"

"I guess it just got out of hand."

"No. You just got back very late."

"Nine o'clock isn't all that late."

"Why *were* you late? Did Mark Sylvester detain you . . . in some way?" He cocked a dark brow and glared.

"Don't be ridiculous! And I don't like the innuendo. He wasn't even there. And I was late because there was a lot of traffic on the Santa Barbara Freeway. And how was Gina?"

"Gina?" Gary frowned, then sat down on the sofa.

"Don't tell me Gina wasn't here tonight, because I smelled her perfume in the den. And she's always at your script meetings, drinks my best red wine, and leaves her lipstick on the wineglass. Harry hasn't taken to wearing lipstick, has he?"

"Your sarcasm is wasted on me, Jessica. And I fail to understand why you're always so hard on her. Gina's been my assistant for years."

And partner in bed when you see fit, she thought, then said, "This ain't my first rodeo . . . I know what's what."

Gary leapt to his feet, color flooding his face. He looked apoplectic as he said, "I can see the frame of mind you're in, and I'm not staying around to get in the way of your whip, missy. I'm going to my place. I'll get my stuff tomorrow. See you around, kid."

Jessica did not respond. She merely stared at him coldly, understanding suddenly how truly tired she was of having him use her. And misuse her house.

He strode out and slammed the office door behind him. A moment later she heard the front door bang and the screech of wheels as he drove out of her front yard at breakneck speed.

And at this precise moment Jessica Pierce realized she actually didn't care that he had left in a temper . . . or that she had pushed him at a bad moment, and he had almost snapped.

She opened the red leather album and turned the pages, staring at the photographs of her three years in Paris, and with a flash of unexpected insight she recognized how little Gary Stennis meant in her life. Yes, she had feelings for him, and in the early stages of their relationship she had truly believed they had a chance of making it together on a long-term basis. But now the odds of it working were remote. If she were honest with herself, she knew she shouldn't string him along anymore. It wasn't fair to him, or to herself for that matter. She ought to end the affair.

Well, maybe she just had. He had left in a huff and might never come back.

She thought again of Lucien, gazing at a photograph of him standing between her and Alexa outside Anya's school on the rue de l'Université. How young we all look in the picture, she thought. Young, innocent, with life ahead of us . . . how unconcerned we were about the future . . . about our lives. We thought we were invulnerable, immortal.

"Lucien," she murmured out loud, tracing a finger over his face. "What happened to you?"

She had no answer for herself, just as she never had. His disappearance was a mystery. It was one that would never be solved.

CHAPTER EIGHT

To Jessica the Pacific had never looked more beautiful.

The deepest of blues, glittering brilliantly in the afternoon sunlight, it was dazzling to the eye as it stretched into infinity.

Her gaze remained focused on the ocean as she turned inward, fell down into her thoughts, asking herself what her life was all about, where she was heading, and where she would end up.

In the last twenty-four hours she had felt extremely depressed about her relationship with Gary, which she now believed was doomed to failure. The end was coming, of that she was sure; she could only hope it would not be too messy.

It was Monday afternoon, and Jessica was sitting in the small antique gazebo she had shipped from a stately home in England. It now stood at the tip of Mark Sylvester's property in Santa Monica.

On a bluff facing the sea, the gazebo was a peaceful spot, a place for reflection and tranquillity, as she had known it would be. Mark loved it, just as he loved the new house. She had been quite certain he would approve, but it was a relief, nonetheless, to know he was actually thrilled with it. He was moving in next weekend, and today she had walked him through for the first time since the furnishings had been installed.

Everything's gone right with the house; everything's gone wrong in my personal life, she thought, her mind settling on Gary. She had called him yesterday, wanting to be conciliatory, to make amends, but he had not picked up. Nor had he returned his messages. At least, not hers.

So be it, she suddenly thought. I must get on with my life, move on. I have to in order to save myself. Instinctively, Jessica felt that Gary Stennis would only drag her down with him. She paused in her thoughts, frowning to herself. There it was again, the frightening idea that Gary was on a downward spiral.

"What a strange conclusion to come to," she murmured to herself, then stood up and left the gazebo.

Slowly, she walked up toward the house, through the beautiful gardens that had been planned and executed by one of the world's great landscape designers from England. They were in perfect harmony with the new house, built where the old one, a Spanish hacienda, had once stood.

In its place, shimmering in the sunlight, was a Palladian villa of incomparable symmetry and style. Built of white stone, it had the classic temple façade of arches and columns made famous by Andrea Palladio, the Renaissance architect.

Jessica paused for a moment, stood gazing at the new villa, and realized once again how much it reminded her of one of the great houses on Southern plantations. But, as she well knew, these, too, had been Palladio adaptations, as were so many of those lovely Georgian mansions in Ireland.

Jessica had hired an architect renowned for his expertise in Palladian architecture to design the villa, and she had worked very closely with him to achieve what she knew Mark liked and wanted. Inside, the central hall was the pivotal point, with all the rooms grouped around it for total symmetry, following Palladio's basic rule.

Once the house was completed, Jessica had decorated the interiors in her inimitable and distinctive style, using lots of pastel colors and cream and white for the most part. Her well-known signature was a room based on a monochromatic color scheme, the finest antique furniture and art money could buy, combined with luxurious fabrics, carpets, and stylish objects of art. Since Mark had given her carte blanche and an unlimited budget, she had been able to create a house of extraordinary beauty and style, and one totally lacking in pretension or overstatement.

Walking along the terrace, Jessica opened the French doors leading into the library, and found herself coming face-to-face with Mark.

"Where did you disappear to?" he asked, looking at her curiously.

"You became so involved with your business call, I thought I'd better leave you in peace. I went for a walk."

"I didn't need privacy, you could have stayed," he replied, and sat down on the sofa.

She took a seat on the opposite sofa and said, "I'm glad I put the gazebo down there on the bluff . . . I enjoyed a few minutes of perfect quiet, just whiling away the time, watching the ocean."

"It's a great spot . . ." His voice trailed off, and he eyed her for a moment before saying, "You've looked awfully troubled all morning, Jessica. Want to talk about it?"

"Not sure," she murmured.

"He's been around the block too many times for you, and he's—" Mark cut himself off, stared at her, suddenly looking chagrined.

She stared back at him, her eyes wide with surprise.

"I'm sorry, Jessica, I shouldn't have said that. It's none of my business. I overstepped the boundaries there."

"No, no, it's okay," she said swiftly, offering him a small smile. "I was staring at you only because I'd thought the same thing myself yesterday. I'm afraid Gary and I are at odds at the moment, and I'm not sure the situation will change."

"Leopards and their spots, and all that," Mark volunteered, and shook his head. "I guess he's drinking again."

"No, no, not at all, it's not that," Jessica was quick to say. "We're at odds because of other things. To tell you the truth, it's partially my fault. I've been so involved with my work in the last six months, I'm afraid I've neglected him some. And also, I think we've just grown apart."

"That can happen when there are two careers going strong. Separations, preoccupations." He rose and walked over to the built-in bar at one end of the library. "Would you like something to drink? A Coke? Water?"

"I'll have a cranberry juice, please, Mark." She laughed. "I know there's a bottle there, I put it in the refrigerator on Saturday morning."

He nodded, stood for a moment pouring their drinks, wondering why Jessica had become involved with Gary Stennis in the first place. She deserved so much better. He was a nice guy, and still good-looking in a washed-out, faded sort of way. That was partially due to the booze and hard living over the years. In one sense, Gary was bordering on the edge now, almost but not quite a has-been in the business.

It's one helluva cruel town we live in, he thought, pouring cranberry juice into a highball glass. He knew full well what the industry thought of Stennis, that he had only a couple of scripts left in him, and that was about it. Once he had been the greatest, in Mark's considered opinion. But the booze and the women had taken their toll, got to him, laid him out flat at times. Life could be pretty tough on the fast track of Hollywood fame and fortune, accolades and alcohol.

He smiled to himself. You had to have the strength, willpower, and ruthlessness of a Genghis Khan to survive here.

As he walked across the room, he couldn't help thinking what a good-looking woman Jessica was. She looked especially wonderful today. She wore a pale-lavender-colored suit with a shortish skirt and very high-heeled shoes; he had always admired her long, silky legs. She was a bit too thin for his taste, but striking nevertheless, and her coloring was superb.

"Thanks, Mark," she said as he put the drink in front of her on the glass-topped coffee table.

His thoughts stayed with her as he went back to the bar to get his ginger ale. Jessica Pierce was one of the nicest people he knew. There was a sweetness and kindness in her nature that was most commendable, and which he admired.

He *knew* that she *knew* that Gary was drinking heavily, and that she had avoided agreeing with him, of admitting this, in order to protect Gary in his eyes. Honorable, loyal girl. Too nice for Stennis, as it happened.

When he returned and sat down opposite her, Mark raised his glass. "Cheers, Jessica. And thank you for making this place so beautiful. You're just . . . miraculous."

She smiled at him, her eyes suddenly sparkling with pleasure. "Thanks, Mark, I'm glad you love your new home. Cheers." There was a moment's pause. "And thanks for trusting me, giving me carte blanche to do what I wanted."

"I'm a bit in awe of you, you know. In awe of your knowledge, your taste, your restraint, your flair, your style. You're just the . . . the . . . whole enchilada, Jess."

She laughed at his turn of phrase, took a sip of her drink, and studied him for a moment. She found herself wondering for the umpteenth time why Kelly O'Keefe had left him, had sued for divorce last year. He was such a nice man, at least he was with her, fair, reasonable, and a pleasure to work with, plus he had a good reputation in Hollywood. But she was aware he was a tough businessman, which is why he was a successful producer. Wimps didn't make it in the movie business. At least not to the big time.

Jessica knew Mark Sylvester was forty-five, but he didn't look it. In fact, he seemed much younger, like a man in his mid-thirties; he was lean, tanned, somewhat athletic in appearance, with a pleasant if angular face, and very knowing, alert brown eyes. Kind eyes that could turn as hard as black pebbles if he was displeased. She'd seen that look directed at one of his associates a couple of times, and she was glad it was not she who was on the receiving end.

"You're staring at me, Jessica."

Laughing self-consciously, she admitted, "To be honest, Mark, I was thinking about you and Kelly, and your divorce, wondering why on earth she would leave you."

He gave her a quick, speculative look and replied, "I let that idea penetrate the town. But in actuality, Jessica, I was the one who asked for the divorce."

"Oh, I didn't know."

"Nobody did. Nobody does. They think she wanted it."

"I see."

Mark sat back on the sofa and looked off into the distance for a split second, a reflective expression entering his dark eyes. As if coming to a sudden decision, he sat up straighter and said, "I've never really explained about the divorce. Not to anyone, Jessica. However, I trust you in a way I can't quite explain. So, here goes. I had a problem with Kelly. She drank a lot, and that was hard for me to take. In fact, she was well on the way to becoming an alcoholic."

Jessica was so startled to hear this, she exclaimed, "But I would never have guessed! She was always so . . . *proper.*"

"Leave it to an actress. She was pretty good at hiding it."

"But you were . . . the *perfect* couple."

"Wanna bet?" he asked, shaking his head. "Anyway, I let her

down as lightly as possible. It was all relatively amicable. She got a nice chunk of dough from me, and off she went to New York. I think she's managed to get herself back on track there, and in a sense she's a little more anonymous, although not much."

"Is she still drinking?"

"She's eased off a bit. I think the break-up of our marriage and the divorce really . . . sobered her up. If you'll forgive the pun." He grinned wryly. "She seems to be making a big effort, and I just hope she continues to do so." He leaned back in his seat, crossed his long legs. "In the meantime, I've got to get on with my own life . . . and what are you going to do, Jessica?"

"I've got a couple of houses to remodel in Beverly Hills, and—"

"I meant what are you going to do with your life . . . *and* Gary Stennis?"

Letting out a long sigh, she slumped down on the sofa. "I don't know. Well, that's not true, I know what I *should* do, and that's end the relationship. It's over really, Mark, it's just a case of easing out of it."

"I've known Gary for years; he's written several movies for me in the past. He's a great guy, don't misunderstand me, but he's always been a tad self-destructive."

"Do you really believe that?" She gave him a hard stare.

"I do. And he is. Listen to me, there's no way you can ease out of this situation. You've got to bail out. Just go. Take a deep breath and jump."

"I guess you're right about that. Pussyfooting around doesn't solve a thing, and it can be more painful in the long run."

"You'd better believe it, Jess."

She nodded, and then, changing the subject, she asked, "And what're you going to do now that you've got the new movie in the can?"

"There's a play I want to buy. It's in rehearsal, about to go on in

New York. I think it'll be a big hit on Broadway. It's dramatic, and it would make a good movie, my kind of movie. Unfortunately, the playwright won't let his agent deal with me. He wants to do that himself. So I'll be going to see him in about two weeks. Then I'm going to Paris on movie business. I might be shooting there later this year."

"I just received an invitation to go to a party in Paris."

His eyes lit up, and he exclaimed, "Will we be there at the same time?"

"I don't know. I don't think so. My party is on the second of June. It's for my former teacher, who's going to be eighty-five."

"Sounds great, but what a pity, I'll probably have left by then. I would have taken you out one night. We could've painted the town pink, if not bright red."

She half smiled, then turned her head, looked across at a painting.

Observing her intently, he said, "You've got that sad look on your face again."

"Receiving the invitation sent me spinning backward in time . . . seven years back, actually. And it opened up a lot of old . . . *wounds,* I guess you could call them. I haven't been quite the same since."

"Brought back memories, did it?"

"Yes." Unexpectedly, tears filled her eyes.

Mark leaned forward. "Hey, honey, what's all this? Tears? It has to be a man." A dark brow lifted questioningly.

Jessica could only nod.

"An old love . . . a broken romance . . . yearning for him? Do you want to talk about it? I have a good strong ear for listening."

Sighing, she said slowly, "Yes, an old love, a wonderful love. We made so many plans. Actually, we planned a future together, and then it ended."

"From the sound of your voice, he broke up with you."

"No, he didn't. He disappeared."

"What do you mean?"

"One day he disappeared. It was just as if he'd dropped off the edge of the world without a trace. I never saw him again."

"Tell me the story, Jessica."

And so she did. Speaking slowly and carefully, she told Mark everything there was to tell about Lucien Girard—their first meeting, their relationship, and how she and Alain Bonnal had tried so hard to find him after his disappearance.

When she had finished, Mark said in a thoughtful tone, "We have three choices here. Either he was killed and his body disposed of remarkably well, or he's alive and walking around with amnesia. Or finally, he chose to disappear on purpose."

"But why would he do that?" she exclaimed, her voice rising. She sounded aghast.

"Anyone who disappears has their own reasons for doing so. And usually it's hard to find them, because they've thought everything out very carefully. They're only ever found when they want to be."

"Someone who disappears obviously does so because they want to start a new life," she began, and stopped. Leaning back against the antique Aubusson pillows on the blue linen sofa, she sat thinking for a few seconds. Then, looking across at Mark, she volunteered, "Alain and I wondered if he'd been mugged, or killed, and his body taken out to sea. We both accepted at the time that it would be relatively easy to dispose of a body. Like you, we'd even thought of memory loss."

"People have been known to recover their memories." He rubbed his chin with his hand, went on. "*Random Harvest.* Memory loss always evokes that movie in my head. Greer Garson, Ronald Colman. A good movie, a classic now, and one of my favorites as far as old movies go. *Very* sentimental though."

"I never saw it."

"You're too young."

"No, I'm not. You're not much older than me, Mark."

He grinned. "Fourteen years. Anyway, if ever you see it'll be on late-night television, so tune in."

"I will."

He continued. "I always think in terms of movies, you know. It's just a peculiar little quirk I have. But getting back to your friend Lucien . . . please take me through it again, Jess. I mean the part about him saying he had to go away for a few days."

"We were having dinner; it was the last time I saw him, actually. Over dinner he said he'd be out of town for a few days, that he was going to Monte Carlo to shoot a commercial. I thought that was great and told him so. We made plans for the following week. Oh, and he told me he was leaving for Monte Carlo the next day."

"Did he call you from there?"

Jessica shook her head. "No. I didn't really expect him to, since I knew he'd be extremely busy. But after a week's silence I grew anxious. I phoned his apartment, there was no answer. Then I spoke to his friend Alain Bonnal, who was also perturbed because Lucien hadn't shown up for a lunch date they'd made. We went over to Lucien's apartment building and spoke to the concierge. She told us he was still away. And she mentioned that she had seen him leave, that she spoke to him as he went out with his suitcase."

"And no one else had heard from him?" Mark asked quietly.

"No. As a matter of fact, Alain and I went to see his agent, and he was as baffled as we were."

"It's all very odd. And the police never came up with anything? Never had any information for you?"

"No, they didn't. And neither did the hospitals or the morgue. Alain continued to check with them for a long time, even after I left Paris and came home to America. But there was never anything."

"How upsetting it must've been for you. No wonder you were so distraught." He shook his head, looking perplexed. "I hate that kind of situation, one that doesn't have a satisfactory explanation."

Jessica said nothing, but the look she gave him was full of gratitude.

Mark leaned back against the cushions, and after a split second he asked her in a somewhat cautious tone, "Is there any reason you can think of, *any* reason, why Lucien might want to engineer his own disappearance?"

"None at all, Mark. I've racked my brain about what happened to him for years now, but the thought that he had done a disappearing act never crossed my mind. He wasn't that sort of man; he had a true sense of honor. Lucien had more integrity than anyone I knew. Or know."

"I certainly trust your judgment. Obviously, you knew him well enough to know what he was capable of doing or not doing." There was a brief pause before he asked her, "Have you ever been back to Paris since then?"

Jessica shook her head. "And I'm not even sure I'll be going to the party."

"Oh, but you must!" he exclaimed. "To toast your former teacher, wish her well . . . becoming eighty-five is quite a milestone in somebody's life."

"I know it is, but Paris does not hold happy memories for me, Mark, as you can imagine. To me, Paris is Lucien . . . I don't think I could bear to feel the pain of losing him, experience the hurt all over again. I'm sure I wouldn't enjoy the trip at all."

"I understand what you're saying, but we've all got to live with pain of some kind or other. Life is hard, Jess, and it's always been hard. Nobody ever said this world was an easy place to live in, it's hazardous and full of dangers. People suffer such terrible things. Actually, you'd be surprised what a person can live through. Human beings are tremendously resilient, you know. The secret is to be strong, to keep on fighting."

"I just don't know. About going, I mean."

He said, "I've got an idea. Would you like me to come with you in June? Hold your hand?"

So startled was she by this offer, she gaped at him speechlessly. Finally, she answered, "You'd come to give me courage?"

"If you want to put it that way."

Jessica was truly touched by such generosity of spirit on Mark's part, and she fell silent. They were genuinely good friends; she had designed several of his homes and his offices, and they had become close buddies. That he would want to help make her visit to Paris easier, if she did go, was something that took her breath away. "Thank you for making such a lovely and generous gesture. . . . I'm grateful, Mark, really I am." A sigh trickled out of her. "I do love Anya Sedgwick, and she was an extraordinary influence on my life . . . but . . . oh, I don't know. . . ." She shook her head several times and gave him a helpless look.

"Sometimes having another person with you makes a tough trip much easier. And, as I said, I might well still be in Paris then anyway, since I'm hoping to shoot part of my next movie there."

"So you just said," she answered. "But I haven't made a final decision about attending Anya's party. I found the invitation waiting for me only when I got home on Saturday evening. But whatever I decide, you'll be the first to know."

Mark gave her a warm smile; he was filled with affection for her. But he did ask himself why he had suddenly insinuated himself into her life. He had startled himself as well as her, and he was puzzled by his actions.

As for Jessica, she was wondering the same thing. And asking herself whether or not she had the guts to go to Paris to confront the past. She simply didn't know.

CHAPTER NINE

Maria

Her life had changed. Miraculously. Overnight. She could hardly believe it had happened.

For the last few days she felt as though she were walking on air. Her demeanor was more positive than it had been for a long time; she was excited and filled with anticipation, and in a way she had not been for years. In a certain sense, it was as if she had suddenly been reborn.

The change in her had started last Friday, when she had returned to her office after lunch. On her desk was a FedEx envelope from Paris. Momentarily baffled, unable to properly read the sender's name and address, she had pulled the little tag on the back and taken out the white envelope inside.

The way her name was written in beautiful calligraphy told her at once that this was an invitation. She could not imagine what event it could be for, and when she had removed the card from the white envelope she had been thrilled as she quickly scanned it, reading every word.

Her heart had tightened and she had felt a rush of genuine happiness running through her . . . how wonderful to be invited to this very special occasion for Anya; what an honor to be a guest at the festivities for her.

Anya Sedgwick was a unique person in Maria's life, and also a favorite teacher, and she had done more for her than anyone else. Except for Fabrizio. And Riccardo, of course.

It was Anya who had taken her under her wing when she had started at the school, who had encouraged her creativity, led her into new areas of design, and opened up the worlds of art, music, and culture in general. She had been like a mother to her at times, as well as her champion, and a truly good friend.

When she had first begun to attend the Anya Sedgwick School of Decorative Arts, Design, and Couture, Maria had made a lot of other friends as well—besides the three who had eventually become her closest friends until the quarrel.

In her opinion, it had been about nothing of any great consequence. The parting of the ways should have never happened . . . they had been at loggerheads with one another at one moment in time, and there appeared to be no other alternative but to go their separate ways. She had been upset after this break in the friendships, and at a loss, floundering a little without the other girls in her life.

Surely they would attend Anya's eighty-fifth birthday party? How could they bear to miss it?

She hoped they would be there; she couldn't wait to see them again, whether they wanted to see her or not. She was exceedingly curious about them and their lives. Having not heard from any of them for the last seven years, she couldn't help wondering if they were married, divorced, had children or not. And she was equally interested to know if they had pursued the careers they had chosen, if they had been successful.

Seven years later there could be no animosity left, could there? *Perhaps*. Maria shrugged. One never knew about people; they could be very strange, as she knew only too well, and to her bitter disappointment.

Maria Pia Francesca Teresa Franconi, called simply Maria by her family and friends, fully intended to go to Paris to celebrate with Anya. In fact, she didn't think about it twice.

Her reaction to the invitation had been positive, and she had already mailed the reply card, saying she would attend.

The invitation to the party, and the prospect of the trip, were the reasons her depression had fled; she was so buoyed up and excited, she could hardly contain herself. To her, the invitation was somehow like the spending money she had received every week when she was a child. Her grandmother Franconi gave it to her each Thursday, but she wasn't able to spend it until the weekend, when her mother took her into Milan. And so the money had burned a hole in her pocket.

And she had done this in much the same way she had looked at her lire as a child, counted the money over and over again, then put her little purse in a very safe place. And she had hardly been able to wait until Saturday and her trip to the shops.

Quite aside from wanting to attend Anya's party, Paris was Maria's favorite place. And also, the idea of escape appealed to her enormously . . . escape from her domineering family, a job that bored her, a family business she had not the slightest interest in, and a personal life that was dull and uneventful.

She *was* going to go to Paris, and she fully intended to have a good time when she got there.

It would not be merely a weekend visit just to attend the celebration. She planned to take her vacation in June, and she would
stay in Paris for a week. Perhaps even two. Or maybe even three.

Three weeks in Paris. The mere thought of it took her breath
away. What a wonderful idea.

Now on this Thursday evening, almost a week since she had received the FedEx envelope, Maria was still ecstatic, as if she had
inhaled some kind of high-octane gas. She couldn't wait to tell Fabrizio about the party and the trip she was planning. Her brother
was coming to dinner; he usually did on Thursdays if he was in
Milan.

As it was, Fabrizio had been away for the past two weeks, visiting some of their clients in Vienna, Munich, and London. He was
the head of sales in their company, Franconi and Sons, manufacturers of textiles par excellence since 1870.

With lightness and speed, Maria moved around the high-tech
stainless-steel-and-glass kitchen in her modern apartment, checking the pasta she had just freshly made from her own dough, stirring the Bolognese meat sauce she had put in a glass bowl a few
minutes before. Moving to the refrigerator, she took out the moz-
zarella cheese and tomatoes, began to slice these items. Once she
had done so, she arranged them on two plates and added basil
leaves. Later she would drizzle oil on top.

As she worked, Maria glanced out of the window, thinking what
a pretty sky it was. Ink-black, filled with crystal stars and a perfect
orb of a moon, it was without cloud tonight.

She could see from the delicate lacy pattern of the frost on the
windowpane that it had turned icy outside. But then, it usually was
cold in Milan in February.

Maria was glad Fabrizio was coming to dinner. She had missed
him while he had been away. He was not only her favorite in the
family but her ally in the business. Not that she really needed one
these days, since she was now twenty-nine and able to stand up for

herself. However, he took her side whenever she had a strong opinion, and agreed with most of the major points she made at meetings. Her grandfather usually did not.

Frequently her father supported her, since he, too, saw the necessity for a number of their lines to be updated. This was something Maria continually fought for, but she was not always successful, much to her irritation.

In the years since she had graduated from Anya's school in Paris, she had become one of the top designers at Franconi, and Fabrizio in particular was forever acclaiming her talent, giving her accolades for her textiles.

Deep down, she didn't really enjoy her work anymore, feeling at times that she was in a rut. And her frustration forever got the better of her.

Thinking suddenly of this, she sighed under her breath, then immediately clamped down on these negative feelings, focusing instead on her brother. His arrival was imminent. This instantly cheered her up. Fabrizio enjoyed her cooking, and they usually had a good time together, no matter what they did.

Like her, Fabrizio, who was thirty-one, was single; like her, he was also forever being nagged at by their mother . . . marriage being the reason for the incessant nagging. Their mother and their grandmothers Franconi and Rodolfo couldn't wait to bounce bambinos on their laps, and were therefore vociferous about this. In fact, none of the older females in the family let the two of them forget that they were in dereliction of their duty.

Their elder brother, Sergio, who would be thirty-four the following week, had been married and divorced and was childless. Obviously, he was beyond the pale as far as the grandmothers were concerned; mostly this was because of his marital history, his taste for the fast track and flashy women.

Sergio was the heir apparent. But Maria knew that Fabrizio was the true favorite in the family. And she fully understood why. He was the best-looking. Tall, blue-eyed, and blond, he was a true Franconi in appearance, while she and Sergio were dark and took after the Rodolfos. Furthermore, Fabrizio was the smartest, the brightest, and he worked the hardest. Without even trying, he endeared himself to everyone. Even strangers quickly fell under his spell.

No blots on his page, she thought, smiling inwardly. Fabrizio was the star, and she did not resent this one bit. She loved and admired her brother more than anyone in the world. And she trusted him implicitly. He had two characteristics she put great store in: honor and integrity.

———

Ten minutes later, Fabrizio stood leaning against the doorjamb of her kitchen, watching her as she finished cooking, sipping a glass of red wine, looking nonchalant.

He was filling her in about his trip, and she turned and smiled at him, glowing inside when he told her that it was her revamping and updating of their famous Renaissance Collection that was making such a difference to the company.

"The reorders are tremendous, Maria," he explained. "And so I toast you, little one, for designing a line that has been such an extraordinary success." He raised his glass.

Picking up her own goblet of red wine, she touched it to his. "Thank you, Fab. And won't Grandfather be surprised? He was so against my ideas." She laughed delightedly. "I can't wait to see his face when you tell him."

"Neither can I. Not only that, the customers were really singing your praises. They like what you have done with some of the other older styles as well. I told them I would be showing them a whole new line next season. A line not based on any of the company's standards."

"You did?" She stared at him, her dark eyes holding his.

"Yes. And so I am looking to you, Maria, to produce a collection that bears *only* your signature."

"That's quite a challenge! I'll try." She paused for a moment. "Fabrizio . . . ?"

"Yes?" He stared at her alertly, detecting a new note in her voice. "You sound excited."

"I am. I got an invitation last week to go to Anya's eighty-fifth birthday party in Paris."

Fabrizio stiffened slightly, although he endeavored to disguise this, and his face did not change when he asked as casually as possible, "And when is this party?"

"Early June."

"I see. . . ." He let his voice trail off noncommittally, wanting to hear what else she had to say.

"I'm going, of course. I wouldn't miss it for the world. I've already sent in the reply card, accepting, and I plan to stay for two or three weeks."

Her brother frowned. "Two or three weeks!" he exclaimed, and looked at her askance. "Whatever for?" This announcement *had* surprised him.

"Because I love Paris, and I want to have my summer holiday there."

"But we always go to the house in Capri in the summer."

"Not this year . . . at least I won't be going."

"*They* won't like it."

"I don't care. I'm twenty-nine, almost thirty years old, and I think I can spend a vacation alone for a change. Don't you?"

"But, yes, of course, you're an adult." He smiled at her gently, decided to say no more, and swallowed the rest of his wine without further comment.

Later, after dinner, he would have to tell her she could not go to Paris. He dreaded the thought.

CHAPTER TEN

Maria watched her brother surreptitiously, pleased that he was savoring his food, obviously enjoying the dinner she had so painstakingly prepared for him.

After eating a little of the spaghetti Bolognese, which was one of her specialties, she then put her fork down and reached for her glass of red wine.

She took several swallows, then said, "I am feeling so much better, Fabrizio, much less depressed. I know it is receiving the invitation to go to the party that has cheered me up."

Lifting his head, he looked at her intently, swallowing his dismay. "I'm glad you're feeling better. But perhaps this change is really due to the way Father has been backing you and your ideas lately."

"It's nothing to do with work. Nothing at all!"

"All right, all right, you don't have to get excited."

"I'm not excited. I'm simply telling you the way it is. And I do know what makes me happy. The thought of going to Paris has been . . . very liberating these last few days."

This was the last thing Fabrizio Franconi wished to hear, and he took a few more forkfuls of the pasta before pushing the plate away. "That was delicious, Maria, and thank you, and you're the best cook I know."

"You'd better not let either of our grandmothers hear you say that," she shot back, smiling at him. Then, rising, she took their plates out to the kitchen.

"Can I help you?" her brother called after her.

"No, no, everything is under control." Maria returned a few seconds later, carrying a plate of warm cookies. "I didn't make dessert, because you never eat it. But I did make coffee. Would you like a cup?"

He shook his head. "No thanks. I'll savor my wine."

"How was London?" she asked, sitting down opposite him.

"Cold and wet. But it was good to be back even for a few days. You know, I do have genuinely happy memories about my days at school there. I enjoyed that period of my life, my days at Harrow. Didn't you enjoy your schooldays in England?"

"Yes, I suppose so. But to be honest, I loved the time I spent at Anya's school so much more." Her face changed, became animated as she added, "By the way, her birthday party is black tie. I'll have to get a new evening dress, and I can't wait to go shopping for something special."

For a second her brother was silent, wondering how to begin. After a few moments of reflection, he said in a soft voice, "I wish you hadn't already accepted that invitation, Maria. I think it was a little premature on your part."

"What do you mean?" she asked, her voice rising slightly. She had detected something odd in his voice, detected trouble brewing. "Oh, my God! You think Mother will interfere, that she'll try to stop me going!"

"You know very well she won't do that. You're twenty-nine, as you just pointed out to me."

"Then why do you say I was premature?"

He was silent, staring into his glass of red wine. When he looked up, his expression was unreadable. Very carefully, he began. "You know you can't go to Paris because—" And then his voice faltered.

She stared at him.

He stared back at her.

The face he looked into was one of the most beautiful faces he had ever seen. The face of a Madonna, worthy of being painted by a great artist. She had huge, soulful eyes as black as obsidian, clouds of thick glossy black hair falling to her shoulders, a perfect oval of a face with dimples in her cheeks when she smiled. And each feature was delicately and clearly defined as if carved from ivory by a master sculptor.

Maria's eyes impaled Fabrizio's as she murmured shakily, *"You don't want me to go because I'm so . . . heavy. That's what you mean, isn't it?"*

"I can't stop you going if you want to go so badly. After all, to quote your friend Jessica, whom *you* are always quoting, you're free, white, and twenty-one. But that is just my reason, Maria. *Jessica.* And also Alexandra and Kay. Three very good reasons why you ought not to go to Paris. You are not merely heavy, you are *fat,* and I know you will feel awkward and *humiliated* when you see your friends. Because they are bound to be as svelte and good-looking as they always were."

"You don't know that!" she cried, and then closed her eyes convulsively. *Of course he was right.* They would look gorgeous, she had no doubts about that. And she would feel like a beached whale, a big ball of blubber. Yet she wanted to go to Paris so much, she couldn't bear the idea of declining the invitation, and so she said somewhat defiantly, "I can still go. I don't care what they think."

Fabrizio got up, walked over to the sofa, and said, "Come and sit here with me, let's talk this out, little one." He gave her an encouraging smile, and she smiled back, although the smile instantly wavered as she rose.

Once she had joined him on the sofa, he took her hand in his and looked into her eyes lovingly. "Since you do want to go so badly, there is a way. However, it is going to be tough."

"What do you mean?"

"First of all, let's talk about your love of cooking. It is an enjoyable hobby, I know, but you do it because you are frustrated about many things."

"But I cook for you," she protested.

"That is true, but you also cook for yourself. You comfort yourself with food, Maria."

She did not say a word.

Fabrizio continued: "If you're going to go to Paris, then I suggest you lose some weight. You have a good three months to do that. You will look so much better, and you will feel better."

"Diets don't really work for me," she mumbled.

"They would if you really stuck to them," he shot back swiftly, giving her a penetrating stare. "You have to stop all of this cooking. *Immediately.* Cooking for me, for your friends, and most important, you've got to stop cooking for yourself."

"Do you think I could stick with a diet, Fab?" she asked, sounding suddenly hopeful.

"I certainly do. I will take you to a diet doctor tomorrow, and she will put you on a regime that is suitable for you. Then you can enroll at my gym and start working out every day. Quite aside from your trip to Paris, and getting in shape to meet old friends, your health will benefit."

She almost visibly shrank back against the sofa and gaped at him, her eyes wide, her expression fearful. "I don't think I could cope with everything all at once, Fabrizio. . . ."

He shook his head impatiently. "Oh, Maria, you *can*. I know you can."

Tears gathered in her eyes and she began to weep. "It's too hard for me to diet and work out. And diet and work out. It's so monotonous, and I'm always hungry."

"Then I suggest you cancel your trip to Paris, because you won't enjoy the trip looking the way you do."

———

Later, after Fabrizio had left, Maria stood in front of the full-length mirror, staring at herself through self-appraising eyes.

For the first time in several years she saw herself as she truly was. The blinders were off, and she faced reality. And finally she admitted that her brother was right. She had put on a lot of weight in the last few years.

Yes, I'm fat, she said to herself. No, not just fat. Very fat.

Staring at her body totally naked, she saw that she was huge, her arms thick from the shoulders down, her thighs wide, like the great hams hanging in her grandmother's winter larder.

She blinked several times as tears welled, and turned away from the mirror, filled with self-loathing. Reaching for her silk robe, she drew it on quickly and went and lay on her bed, pushing her face into the pillow.

She let the tears flow, sobbing as though her heart would break, until finally there were no tears left in her. Exhausted, she lay there on the damp pillow, consumed by her longing to go to Anya's party, her weight problem, and her current plight. What to do? What to do? she asked herself repeatedly.

Fabrizio was correct. The ideal thing would be to utilize the next few months to get the weight off, but she was so afraid of failure and of the hardship of exercise and dieting, she was ultimately paralyzed. And she was aware that she would feel exactly the same tomorrow. She always gave up before she even started.

Riccardo, she suddenly thought. It all began when they pushed Riccardo Martinelli out of my life. Closing her eyes, Maria looked back into the past, as if down a long, dark tunnel, seeing him standing at the end of it. How she had loved him, and he her, but her parents had considered him to be unsuitable, and they had broken up the love affair. He had gone away and she had never seen him again. Four years ago it had happened.

That was when she had started to put on weight, after Riccardo had exited her life. One thing was true, she *did* eat for comfort and consolation. She pampered herself with food because she had lost him, because her parents and grandparents were domineering, always trying to control her, and also because she was desperately lonely. She hated her job, was sick and tired of designing textiles, found the whole experience constraining.

Escape.

That was what she really wanted.

Permanent escape from Milan. From her family. From her job.

But you can't escape from yourself, Maria, she reminded herself, sitting up, pushing her hair away from her face. You have a big, terribly fat body that is ugly and ungainly, and no man is going to love you with your elephantine shape. You can't blame the family for your eating, at least only indirectly. You and only you are responsible for what you put into your mouth.

She thought of this over and over again as she sat propped up against the pillows, and then after a while she left her bed and went to sit at her Venetian-mirrored dressing table, staring intently in the looking glass.

She saw herself as she really was; it was a beautiful face staring back at her. If only she did not have this awful body . . . all hideous rolls of fat. Everywhere.

You *can* do it, she insisted in her head. You *can* lose weight. You have great motivation now. Going to Paris . . . to see Anya . . . to make friends again with Jessica, Alexandra, and Kay. And maybe if you get thin enough you can go and see Riccardo. She knew where he was, what he was doing; she knew he was not married.

Perhaps her lover still yearned for her as she yearned for him. She wondered about this for a few minutes, then she got up, threw off her robe and went again to stare at herself in the full-length mirror. She was gross. What man would want you with a body like this? she asked herself.

Turning away in disgust, she wrapped herself in the robe and went through into the kitchen. Snapping on the light, she opened the refrigerator door; her hand reached in for the large slab of cheese. Instantly, she withdrew her hand, closed the door, turned away empty-handed.

Slowly she walked back to her bedroom, vowing to herself that she would *try* to lose weight.

PART TWO

Doyenne

CHAPTER ELEVEN

Anya Sedgwick was so startled, she sat back on the sofa and stared at her visitor seated opposite. There was a questioning look in her eyes, and her surprise was evident.

After adjusting her back against the antique needlepoint pillows, she frowned slightly and asked, "But whatever made you do it so . . . so . . . *impetuously?*" She shook her head. "It's not like you. . . ." Her voice trailed off; her eyes remained fixed on his handsome face.

Nicholas Sedgwick cleared his throat several times. "Please don't be angry with me, Anya."

"Good heavens, Nicky, I'm not angry." She gave him the benefit of a warm smile, wanting to reassure him, to know that he was still in her good graces. He was her favorite in the family, and although he was not her child, not even of her blood, she thought of him as a son. He was very special to her.

"All right," she continued. "You're giving me a birthday party, and you've already sent out lots of invitations, which perhaps precludes canceling it. So you'd better tell me about it. Come along, I'm all ears."

"I wanted to do something really special for your birthday, Anya," he replied, leaning forward with an eagerness that brought a boyish look to his face. "I know how much you enjoy Ledoyen, so that was my restaurant of choice. I went to see them and I've booked the entire restaurant for the evening. There's going to be a cocktail period, then supper, and dancing afterward. And a few surprises as well, along the way."

"I'm sure there are lots of surprises in the works, knowing you," she laughed.

"So far I've invited seventy-five people, but we can have a lot more, double that amount, if you wish."

"Seventy-five already sounds a few too many!" she exclaimed, but immediately smiled at him when she saw his crestfallen expression. "I'm only teasing, Nicky. Continue, darling."

"After I visited the restaurant, did a tour of it, I was filled with all kinds of ideas for the party, and I suppose I got overly enthusiastic, very excited. I went ahead and created an invitation, which I had printed, and I had the calligrapher address the envelopes. Once they were ready, I posted them. But I panicked the day I put them in the mail. It struck me that I had preempted the rest of the family, that I took control, so to speak."

"As you usually do," she asserted in a mild tone.

He nodded; he was relieved she sounded so benign. She was obviously surprised by his actions but definitely not annoyed with him.

"Anyway, Anya, I was going to phone you in Provence that day, but I decided against it. Sometimes speaking on the phone is very unsatisfactory." Nicky lifted his hands in a helpless gesture, and finished: "So, here I am, telling you now, and hoping you won't want me to cancel it."

"I don't know." She gazed across at him, shaking her head. "I really don't know, Nicky."

"You *must* have a celebration for your eighty-fifth birthday. It's such a milestone . . . and you should be surrounded by everyone you care about."

"Do I care about so many . . . *seventy-five* people?" She frowned, screwed up her mouth, looking reflective.

"Let me rephrase that, Anya. I've tried to include those who love you, and the people who have been special in your life in one way or another."

"Well, there are quite a few of those still alive," she conceded, her reflective expression intensifying. "Did you bring the invitation list?"

"Yes, I did." He smiled wryly as he added, "I'm afraid I was sneaky. I had Laure take most of the addresses from your files." Not waiting for a comment from her, he rushed on. "Here's the list." Pulling it out of his jacket pocket, he rose and went to join her on the sofa.

———

After lunch, when Nicky had finally left, Anya went back to her upstairs sitting room. It was a room she had continually gravitated to ever since she had come to live here over half a century ago now, a place to entertain family and friends, relax and read when she was alone, or listen to the music she loved so much.

And, just as important, it was her preferred place to work, surrounded by comfort, her beloved photographs, books, and possessions gathered over a lifetime and so meaningful to her. The large antique desk piled with papers, which stood in one corner, was testimony to her lifetime ethic of disciplined hard work.

Walking briskly across the floor, Anya paused briefly at the window, staring down into the yard below, thinking how bleak her garden looked on this cold February afternoon.

A painting in grisaille, she murmured under her breath, as usual thinking in terms of art. All those grays and silvers mingling . . .

The trees were skeletal, bereft of leaves, were dark etchings against the pale gray but luminous Paris sky. And the wet cobblestones in the yard gleamed with a silvery sheen after the recent downpour.

Mature sycamores and lime trees encircled the house, and there was a lovely old cherry tree in the middle of the courtyard that dominated the scene. Now its spreading bare branches cast an intricate pattern of gray shadows across the yard. But in spring it bloomed softly pink, its branches heavy with cascades of luscious blossoms; in the heat of summer its cool, leafy canopy offered welcome shade.

As bleak as the garden was today, Anya was well aware that in a month or two it would be glowing green with verdant grass and banks of ferns, dotted with the variegated pinks of the cherry blossoms and the little impatiens set in borders around the lawn.

By then, the picket fence enclosing the lawn and garden at one end of the courtyard would be gleaming with fresh white paint, as would the many planters and the ancient wrought-iron garden furniture. A sudden transformation took place every spring, just as it had for as long as she could recall. She had been here in the summer of 1936, when she was twenty years old, witnessing it for the first time.

Now Anya's glance took in the tall ivy-covered wall which, along with the many trees, made the garden and house so secluded and private, shielded as it was from its neighbors. She had always been enchanted by the garden, the quaint courtyard, and the picturesque house with its black-and-white half-timbered façade. It was a house that looked as if it had been picked up lock, stock, and barrel in Normandy and deposited right here in the middle of Paris.

It stood just a stone's throw away from the busy Boulevard des Invalides, and around the corner was the rue de l'Université, where her now-famous school was located.

Anya smiled inwardly, thinking of the surprise most people had when they came in from the street through the great wooden doors and confronted the courtyard. The ancient house, which had stood there for over a hundred years, and the bucolic setting so reminiscent of Calvados country, usually took everyone's breath away.

As it had hers when she had first visited this house the day she was celebrating her twentieth birthday . . . so many years ago now . . . sixty-five years to be exact.

She had come here with Michel Lacoste. To meet his mother. He had been the great love of her youth, her first husband, the father of her two children, Dimitri and Olga.

This house had belonged to his mother, Catherine Lacoste, and to Michel after his mother died. Michel and she had begun to raise a family here . . . and then the house had become hers when Michel died.

Too young to die, she muttered under her breath as she turned away from the window.

Of late, so many memories and recollections of the past were constantly assailing her. It was as if her whole life were being played out for her on a reel of film, one that passed before her eyes at very frequent intervals. Perhaps that was part of growing old, remembering so many things that had happened long ago. And not remembering the events of yesterday.

However, she could not dwell on the past at this moment. Nicholas Sedgwick, her great-nephew through her second husband, Hugo Sedgwick, had forced her to look to the future. To June the second, to be precise, and the fancy party he had planned for her.

In fact, her birthday was actually on June the third, and she had reminded him of that over lunch. Naturally Nicky had known. He should never be underestimated. But, as he had carefully explained to her, he was not able to book the restaurant for the actual night of her birthday, June the third being a Sunday.

Seating herself at the desk near the fireplace, glad to have the warmth of the blazing logs nearby, Anya looked again at the invitation, thinking that it was tastefully done. But then, Nicholas was known for his great taste. She turned her attention to the guest list he had prepared, focusing on the names.

His choices had been correct, and in some instances rather clever, since he had thought of certain old friends she rarely saw these days—but would like to visit with again, she decided suddenly.

There were about ninety people on his original list, although Nicky had mailed only seventy-five invitations so far.

He played it safe, she thought shrewdly, and studied the names once more. She approved of the family and friends he had already invited, along with some of her former pupils from different years. Always the best and the brightest.

In particular, she was pleased to see he had included four brilliant girls from the class of 1994. Jessica Pierce, Kay Lenox, Maria Franconi, and Alexandra Gordon. Most especially Alexandra. Her favorite pupil during the 1990s, perhaps even her most favorite pupil of them all over the many long years she had owned the school. My special girl, she thought.

Anya sat back in the chair, thinking of Alexandra with love and affection, and focusing on her involvement with that poor, bedeviled Tom Conners. All Nicky's fault, since he had introduced them. Well, if she were honest, that wasn't exactly the way it was. Tom had come to the studio to see a client, if she remembered things correctly. So she could not blame the meddling hands of her nephew. Not this time.

And was it ever anybody's fault when lives went awry?

Surely it was fate, destiny, stepping in . . . she considered her own life and the role fate had played in it. She was absolutely certain it was her destiny to end up where she was today, having lived the life she had lived. And so she did not worry about what might have been. She never had.

CHAPTER TWELVE

Although she enjoyed the milder climate of Provence in the winter months, and frequently went there, Anya was, nevertheless, glad to be back in Paris. And back in the house that meant so much to her, filled as it was with her life's history.

This room in particular told the whole story. Encapsulated within its walls were mementos gathered over the years. Some she had bought, others were gifts, yet more were inherited; certain things she had even created herself.

The decoration of her sitting room depicted a woman of discernment, taste, and talent, a woman with an exotic background who had ventured forth courageously when young.

She had followed her heart and her dreams, given free rein to her creativity, believing in her destiny as a woman and an artist. She had lived her life to the fullest, had never regretted anything she had done, only the things she had not found time to do or to accomplish.

After studying the guest list for her birthday party and making notes, adding a few names, she had put it to one side. But she had continued to work at her desk, going over papers that had accumulated during the couple of weeks she had been in Provence. Finally growing a little weary, she put down her pen, sat up straighter in the chair, and glanced around.

Anya smiled, thinking that at this moment the room had a lovely golden haze to it, even though it was gray outside and dusk was rapidly approaching. But then, it had a sunny feeling at all times, as she had fully intended.

Although she had started her professional life as an artist, Anya was talented in many areas, and she had a great flair for interior design. Years ago, wanting to introduce a mood of summer sunshine into this large, high-ceilinged sitting room, she had covered the walls with a yellow-on-yellow striped fabric. This had long since faded from a sharp daffodil to a very pale primrose, but it was nonetheless mellow and warm.

In vivid contrast to these now muted yellow walls were great swathes of scarlet taffeta, which Anya had selected for the full-length draperies at the two windows. They hung on rings from wooden poles, falling straight, but then halfway down they softly billowed out like the skirts of ball gowns.

Anya loved these curtains, the stunning effect they created, and when the bright color faded she simply replaced them with new ones made of identical fabric. She was forever fussing with them, puffing them up with her hands, and sometimes even stuffing tissue paper behind them for the desired bell shape.

These draperies were her pride, gave her immense pleasure. Even though Nicky tended to tease her about them, he secretly admired her nerve, knowing that only Anya Sedgwick would have dared to use them, secure in the knowledge that they were a knockout. She had wanted to surprise, and she had succeeded admirably.

Naturally, Anya paid no attention to his teasing, confident in her own taste and choice of colors. In fact, this whole room was a play on scarlet and yellow, with white accents showing up in the paintwork. Also cooling the strong colors was a pale apple-green silk used on several French *bergères,* these elegant chairs scattered around the room. Anya believed the muted tones balanced a room essentially commanding because of its vibrant colors.

In front of the fireplace there was a large overstuffed Chesterfield sofa covered in scarlet velvet; the same fabric was used for two huge, chunky armchairs, typical Anya Sedgwick touches. She always opted for comfort as well as style. Even the rectangular coffee table was of her own invention. Originally an old wrought-iron garden gate that she had found at a local flea market, she had hired a metalworker to weld on short iron legs, and then she had topped it with a thick slab of glass. She was very proud of her unique coffee table, and glanced at it now, nodding her head in approval.

The fire blazing in the hearth added to the sense of warmth and intimacy on this wintry afternoon, and Anya considered herself blessed to have such a wonderful haven for herself; she had been back from Provence for only two days, and she had felt the cold immediately after she had arrived. She still felt cold at times, even though the house was warm.

Old bones, she mumbled as she pushed herself to her feet. Old bones . . . getting *older.* She moved around the desk and went toward the fireplace but then paused for a second to admire some of her things.

It was as if she had momentarily forgotten, during her absence in the south, how beautiful her possessions were and wanted to reacquaint herself with them, touch them, remember who had given them to her, remember what they meant to her.

That's not in the right spot, she thought as her sharp eyes settled on a silver samovar. This had been put on a circular table skirted in a red-and-yellow toile de Jouy standing between the two windows.

Leaning forward, she pushed the samovar into the center of the table, where it was meant to be, then stood back, gazing at it lovingly; it was very special to her.

This samovar had been resolutely carried out of Russia by her mother when they had left for good, a woman who had been determined that certain precious family objects would not be left behind.

Anya had no recollection of this event, but her mother had told it countless times to her, and to her siblings, and so it had become part of her family history.

As she walked past a console table, she stopped to admire her mother's collection of icons, some of them quite ancient, and all of them very valuable. These had also been in their luggage when they had fled the Bolsheviks, deemed so bloodthirsty by her father.

At the other end of the console, family photographs from Russia were displayed. These were in gold Fabergé frames encrusted with green malachite and blue lapis stones, and had been deeply treasured by her parents. How they had missed their families, whom they had left behind in Russia; they had missed Mother Russia too, despite the country's ills, the turmoil and bloodshed of the revolution.

And these photographs of handsome men, finely dressed, and beautiful women in fashionable gowns and splendid jewels were poignant reminders of the murdered Romanov monarchy, a lost aristocracy, a vanished world of money, power, and privilege, a decimated society that had once been theirs.

Anya turned away from those evocative family photographs that had been her parents' legacy to her along with so many other things they had brought out of Russia.

Briefly, her eyes scanned the bookshelves along a wall at the far end of the room. All were filled with a diverse and eclectic mix of books, some of which she had written, while others had been penned by her friends. Soon, she hoped, another of her works would be on a shelf over there, her book on the Art Deco period, which she was finishing at that moment. It would go to the publisher in a month.

It was an automatic reaction, the way her eyes then swung to a striking painting, one that exuded dominant force and hung on the wall adjoining the bookshelves. It was a landscape, all sharp angles and planes, a modern painting awash with deep greens, rich yellows, and dark reds, these colors balanced by earthy browns and coppery, autumnal hues. It was a most powerful painting, and it was by her father, Valentin Kossikovsky, the great Russian artist. It held her eyes, as it always had and always would. She was full of admiration for the extraordinary talent that had been his.

Finally she looked away, moved on.

There were a couple of her own paintings hanging here. One in particular stood out. She had painted it over sixty years ago, and it was the full-length life-size portrait of a young woman.

Hanging above the fireplace, it was the focus of interest at this end of the room; everyone was drawn toward it, instantly captivated when they caught sight of it.

Anya now approached the fireplace, stood staring up at the canvas, and as usual her eyes were critical. Yet she could never fault this painting, even though it was one of her own works, which she generally had a tendency to overly criticize.

The painting was of her sister Ekaterina, Katti for short, painted when she was just twenty years old. What a beauty she had been.

And there was her own name, Anya Kossikovskaya, and the date, 1941, in the left-hand corner, at the bottom of the painting.

She herself had been twenty-five when she had asked Katti to sit for the portrait, and reluctantly her sister had agreed. For a great beauty she was singularly without vanity, and modest in her opinion of herself.

When the painting was finally finished, her father had been amazed, and momentarily rendered speechless. And when he had found his voice at last, he had marveled at Anya's work, and he had called the painting a treasure. Immediately, he had asked the renowned London art gallery that represented him and handled his own work to show it, and they had obliged him. They had even gone as far as to give Anya an exhibit of her other paintings; this had immediately sold out, much to her surprise and delight.

Many people had tried to buy the painting of her sister, which she had called *Portrait of Ekaterina,* because it was so arresting. But she had wanted to keep it for herself. For a short while, at least.

In the end, even after the show was over, she had still not been able to let it go. The painting was special to her, meaningful and extremely personal. It was important in a way she found hard to explain, except to say that it had become part of her.

And over the long years, many other people had tried to buy it, but her answer was always the same: *Not for sale.*

Anya focused appraising eyes on the painting, studying it, endeavoring to be objective, wanting to analyze its extraordinary appeal to so many different people.

Here was her darling Katti, blond, beautiful, with high, slanting cheekbones, a broad forehead, wide-set eyes, and an impossibly slender, aristocratic nose. Her sister appeared literally to shimmer in the clear light that she had somehow managed to capture on canvas. The painting virtually glowed with incandescent light, usually a hallmark of her work.

Katti's eyes were a lovely blue, like bits of sky, and they reflected the color of the blue taffeta gown she was wearing.

Even now Anya felt, as she had always felt, that if she reached out to the painting, her fingers would touch silk not canvas, so real did the fabric appear to be with its folds and shadows and silvery sheen. She could almost hear it rustle.

Once more, it struck her how English her sister's appearance was; actually, the entire painting had a sense of Englishness to it.

And why would it not? she asked herself. She had painted the portrait on a sunny afternoon at the height of summer in the garden of a manor house in Kent. The background had a hint of Gainsborough about it, even if she did say so herself. Not that she was comparing herself to the master, that great eighteenth-century portraitist, but rather to the way he had painted English landscapes of the time. Somehow he had been able to marry the landscape to the human subjects in his portraits, which was rare. It was this technique she had attempted to emulate, and nothing else. No one had ever been able to compete with that extraordinary artist Thomas Gainsborough except perhaps for Sir Joshua Reynolds, another great master of portraiture in eighteenth-century England.

Were people drawn to this painting because of the girl portrayed in it? she wondered. Or was it for its Englishness? Or perhaps the shimmering pastoral landscape depicted behind the girl? Or the mood of the bygone age it seemed to capture? She had no idea; she had never known what it signified to other people, what powerful emotional response it evoked in them. But it did, that was certain.

Turning away though she did, her thoughts stayed with her sister; Katti had been born in England, but deep down, Anya believed, she had a truly Russian soul. She was so like their mother, Natasha, had been, almost a carbon copy. Their brother, Vladimir, also born in London, was wholly English and did not appear to have a hint of his Russian heritage in him. He was three years younger than Katti, eight years younger than she.

Both her siblings were alive, and for this she was inordinately grateful. She knew they would be thrilled to come to her birthday party; the three of them had remained close and loving over the years, had been there for each other when they were needed. They did not live far away, just across the English Channel, in the beloved country of their birth.

Obviously Nicky had placed them at the top of the guest list, along with the rest of her extended family. Anya laughed out loud when she thought how large it was, and its eclectic mix. She considered it something of a genuine gypsy stew.

Her sister, Katti, and Katti's husband, Sacha Lebedev, another Russian born in England of émigré parents from Moscow via Paris, and their sons, Charles and Anthony, and their daughter, Serena. And Serena's husband, and the wives of the Lebedev boys. Her brother, Vladimir, his wife, Lili, and their three sons, Michael, Paul, and Peter, and their wives.

And then came her closest, her children by her first husband, Michel Lacoste. Her daughter, Olga, and her son, Dimitri; there would be Olga's children, her granddaughters Anna and Natalie, by Olga's former husband Adam Mattison, with whom she was still friendly. Anya had seen his name on the list, and she was glad of that. She had always liked Adam. Dimitri would bring his wife, Celestine, and their daughter, Solange, and son-in-law, Jean-Claude.

Oh, and then there was the Sedgwick tribe, whom she had inherited from Hugo, her second husband, and whom she loved as much as her own. Larry and his wife, Stephanie; Nicky, her special favorite, and his wife, Constance. But no, perhaps Constance would not come, since she and Nicky were apparently at loggerheads, estranged at the moment. She had not noticed Connie's name on the guest list. And of course there was their sister, Rosamund, who had never married, although she had often been engaged. She was expected, along with her current partner, Henry Lester.

It was indeed a complex mixture, but they were all members of her family, and she cared for each and every one of them. The party's going to be fun, she thought, sitting down on the scarlet velvet sofa. She leaned back against the soft cushions, enjoying the warmth of the fire, the floral smell of the scented candles, the comfort of the surroundings in general, the tranquil atmosphere that prevailed.

The painting of her sister, Katti, had triggered innumerable memories . . . memories of the past, of people she had loved who were gone forever . . . others whom she loved and who, fortunately, were still alive. . . .

Eighty-five, she thought, I can't believe I'm going to be eighty-five in just three months. I feel so much younger inside.

Anya smiled to herself and looked up at the painting of Katti. She felt as young as that girl there, who gazed back at her with such innocent eyes. . . .

––––

She had been born in St. Petersburg in 1916, virtually on the eve of the Russian Revolution, although she had no recollections of that city as it was then. Nor did she know of the tumultuous events of 1917 and 1918, which had led her parents to flee their country.

But her father, Prince Valentin Kossikovsky, had recounted everything to her when she was old enough to understand. The politics of these chaotic times was his favorite subject, and besides this he was a mesmerizing raconteur, one who held her fascinated with his tales and reminiscences.

Her parents were from Russia's most elite and privileged society; her father was a man of ancient lineage, great wealth derived from vast family-owned lands in the Crimea, a variety of industrial holdings in Moscow, and financial interests abroad. Her mother, Nathalie, always called Natasha, was the daughter of Count Ilya Devenarskoe, also a landowner and man of wealth.

At the time of her birth, Anya's father was acquiring a name for himself as an artist of formidable talent. His mother and siblings regarded his painting as more of a hobby than anything else; in fact, his mother, Princess Irina, thought it was an avocation rather than a vocation.

But, as it eventually turned out, she was totally wrong. Valentin Kossikovsky *had* found his true *vocation* when he began to paint seriously, and in time he would astound art lovers around the world with his work; he was to become as famous as his talented contemporary, Marc Chagall.

Within fifteen years of his departure from Russia, Valentin would be acclaimed as one of the great Russian painters of the twentieth century, along with Kandinsky, Chagall, Rodchenko, Ender, and Popova.

However, in 1917 Valentin was not thinking of fame but of escape. Anya was now a year old, and he was worried about the safety of his child and young wife. To a certain extent, he was involved in politics, as were other Russians of his ilk, and he was well aware of trouble brewing. Smart, intuitive, and well informed, he was certain that Russia was about to plunge into disaster and turmoil from which it would never recoup. He had long anticipated the revolution, had seen it coming, and accordingly he had made certain financial plans.

At this time, as Anya learned in later years, her father believed that they had been brought to the brink of ruin by the German wife of the tsar, who was born Princess Alix of Hesse. Until the day he died, Valentin Kossikovsky tended to blame Tsarina Alexandra for the revolution, as did so many of his contemporaries and some members of the imperial Romanov family. Within the circle of his small family, he quietly castigated her, characterizing her as deluded, manipulative, controlling, and interfering. As for Tsar Nicholas II, Valentin thought he was weak, vacillating, and somewhat under the thumb of his wife.

And yet Prince Valentin Kossikovsky also knew, as most educated Russians did, that basically Nicholas was a good man and not the tyrant he was purported to be by the Bolsheviks. History would prove Valentin to be correct on this score; in time Tsar Nicholas II was deemed a martyr.

As matters drew to a head within the Duma, the national government, at the beginning of 1917, Valentin literally held his breath, worrying, waiting, weighing the odds, wondering what moves to make.

Then unexpectedly, in March of that year, Tsar Nicholas II abdicated, on behalf of himself and the tsarevitch, in favor of his brother, Grand Duke Michael Aleksandrovich.

For a short time Valentin thought disaster had been averted, that Michael would become a constitutional monarch like his first cousin, King George V of England. This is what the government said they wanted.

Valentin, like most of the aristocracy, admired Grand Duke Michael, who was a celebrated war hero, a forthright man of honor, honesty, and great ability who favored constitutional monarchy, had advocated it in the past to his brother.

Valentin often told Anya when she was growing up that he had met Grand Duke Michael with her uncle Sergei, who was in the army and stationed at Gatchina, where Michael was stationed. "We frequently ran into each other at the riding school of the Blue Cuirassiers. He would have made a good emperor."

Although she knew the story by heart, Anya always pleaded to hear it again. "What happened to Michael, Papa? Tell me the story, please, please."

And her father would explain: "Michael was tsar for only a day. He abdicated immediately, because that was what the Bolsheviks wanted him to do. Since *he* wanted to prevent bloodshed, he signed the papers of abdication. But he didn't prevent the killing or the terrible bloodbath, Anya. Michael was the last Emperor and Autocrat of All the Russias, and the first of the Romanovs to be murdered, just a few weeks before his brother Nicholas and his family were killed in cold blood in that cellar in Ekaterinburg."

Grand Duke Michael was murdered at two A.M. on June 13, 1918. The ghastly murder of Michael and his secretary, Nicholas Johnson, took place in the woods outside Perm, the town where they had been under house arrest in the local hotel. But the murders were not known about then; news of Michael's death did not come out for a long time. At first it was assumed he had managed to escape with Johnson, and that they had fled Russia.

Valentin and Natasha had not believed this story. They were convinced there had been foul play on the part of the Bolsheviks. Five weeks later, when the tsar and his family were so brutally murdered, the news leaked out almost immediately. Valentin made his moves with great speed. He went to see his uncle Sandro, his father's first cousin, who was a very close friend of Admiral Kolchak's, at that time the Supreme Commander of the White Army.

A lot of strings were pulled by a lot of people, and Valentin, Natasha, and their baby daughter, Anya, were finally able to leave Russia six months later, in January 1919, getting out via Finland. From Helsinki they went to Sweden, and from Stockholm they traveled to Oslo. After spending several weeks in Norway, they were finally able to board a British merchant ship and set sale for Scotland.

Waiting for them there was Valentin's older sister, Olga, who in 1910 had married a wealthy English banker, Adrian Hamilton, and moved to London.

Anya's first conscious memories from her childhood were of England, and, in particular, her aunt's beautiful manor house in Kent, where years later she would paint the portrait of Katti on the terrace.

It was in this house, Haverlea Chase, that the Kossikovskys lived until they found a place of their own. Valentin and Natasha spoke several languages, including English, and so they adapted quickly to life in the bucolic English countryside. And for the first time in years they felt safe from harm.

After six months of living in Kent, Valentin knew he must move on. He and Natasha quickly found a small but attractive house in Chelsea; what made it so attractive to them was the conservatory in the garden. Built almost entirely of glass, this was ideal as a studio in which Valentin could paint.

Fortunately, Valentin Kossikovsky had wisely moved money out of Russia in 1912. It ended up in England, where it was well invested by his banker brother-in-law. And so unlike many other White Russian émigrés who had fled to London and Paris, they were not destitute.

It was in this lovely old house in Chelsea that Anya grew up, surrounded by the possessions her mother had managed to bring out of Russia . . . the silver samovar in which she made tea every day . . . the icons arranged on a table in the sitting room alongside the family photographs in their Fabergé frames.

Anya ate Russian food, learned Russian history from her father, and the language from her parents who spoke only Russian when they were alone.

In essence, she was raised as a Russian aristocrat would have been brought up in St. Petersburg. And yet she was also an English girl who grew up in the ways of her adopted country. She went to a private kindergarten as a young child, and then to one of the best boarding schools; later she became a student at the Royal College of Art.

"I'm a funny mixture," she said to Michel Lacoste when she first met him in Paris. "But deep down I know that my soul is Russian." And she continued to believe this for the rest of her life, just as her father, the prince, had intended.

CHAPTER THIRTEEN

The rain did nothing to dampen Nicholas Sedgwick's good mood. As he walked across the Boulevard des Invalides, heading toward the rue de l'Université, he dismissed the sudden downpour as merely an April shower that would stop at any moment. And it did, almost before he had completed this thought.

Closing his umbrella, he hooked it over his arm, and marched on at a brisk pace, humming under his breath. He had just finished the sketches of sets for a new movie to be shot at the studios in Billancourt and in the Loire Valley, and he was thrilled that the producer and director had liked his designs; actually, they had both been bowled over by them.

Nothing like a little success to put a man in a happy frame of mind, he thought as he crossed the boulevard, heading for Anya's school.

And then in a split second his expression changed and a shadow crossed his handsome face, settled in his bluish-green eyes, clouding them over. Professionally, he was at a high point, but in his personal life happiness had eluded him for a long time, and this troubled him greatly.

As far as he was concerned, his marriage to Constance Aykroyd, the English stage actress, was over. He had tried to make it work, but he simply became more and more estranged from her as the months went by, and all he wanted now was to end it. And as peacefully as possible.

But Connie did not want a divorce; she clung to him and to the marriage. He took the line of least resistance, did nothing legally, because he had no real reason to push for the divorce at the moment. There was no other woman in his life; he was so busy with his work he didn't have much time to start seeing lawyers, setting the legal wheels in motion. Although deep within himself he knew that this was an inevitability if he was going to get his freedom. Certainly Connie was not about to set him free of her own accord, even though he had moved out many months before.

Nicky sighed to himself, thinking how difficult and temperamental Connie had become. And anorexic. He was really very upset by her these days. She was so painfully thin she appeared to be starving herself to death, looked like one of those tragic Holocaust victims released from Bergen-Belsen at the end of the war. He shuddered involuntarily; just *thinking* about her ghastly appearance appalled him. She was a walking skeleton.

Suddenly Nicky was thankful there were no children involved in this disastrous marriage. It would be a clean break when it finally happened, and with no additional casualties of the divorce, thank God.

And he was only thirty-eight.

He could start again. He hoped. He smiled to himself. Hope springs eternal . . . that was the favorite line of Hugh Sedgwick, his uncle. Hugo, as he was commonly called, was Anya's second husband; he had been a rather special man, a business genius and the linchpin of the family, the man around whom everyone and every-thing revolved. Charismatic, reliable, and strong, he had been steady as a rock, and the most enduring influence in Nicky's life.

At least my work is going well, Nicky thought as he turned the corner. He and his brother, Larry, were busier than they had ever been, and their theatrical design company, with offices in Paris and London, was thriving.

Not only that, he was particularly enjoying teaching this season. He gave two classes a week, on set designing and decorating, at Anya's school, and this year he had discovered that he had several brilliant students in his class. Consistently, they took his breath away with their work.

Larry, who stood in for him when he was away on a film, agreed with him about their unique talents, was also full of praise.

Nicky had always found it rewarding to encourage and nurture students who showed promise, and he took pleasure in showing them how to develop their work and achieve their goals.

———

Halfway down the rue de l'Université he finally came to the huge wooden double doors that led into the courtyard of the school. He went in through the small side door designed for pedestrians; as he closed it behind him, he hoped Anya would be happy with the de-signs he had created for her birthday party. He was going to show them to her later that day.

Nicky went up in the old-fashioned lift to his office on the fourth floor. This was in the building where the original school had first started and had been housed from the twenties to the forties, which was when adjoining buildings were acquired.

As he stepped out of the lift and walked along the corridor, he couldn't help thinking about the history of this place. The school would be seventy-five years old later this year, and what a success story it was.

If only walls could talk, he thought, going into his office. He put his umbrella in the closet, sat down at his large desk, and began to look at the sketches he had made for Anya's party. But his mind drifted off after a while; his thoughts focused on the school, and what it had become, all because of Anya Sedgwick.

———

Originally, it had been a modest little school of art run by Catherine Lacoste, Anya's mother-in-law.

The young widow of the renowned French sculptor Laurent Lacoste, who had started the school in 1926, she had struggled to keep it going after Laurent's death in the early thirties.

Despite being small, it had a good reputation because of the gifted teachers it employed, mostly artists themselves who needed to earn a steady income to support their art. Even in those days it had a certain prestige because of Laurent Lacoste's name.

Incredibly, and to her credit, Catherine had even managed to keep the school open during the war years and the German occupation of Paris. Somehow it had been able to survive in the terrible and troubled times of the Nazis' domination of Paris, during the many deprivations and hardships of all kinds.

After the end of the Second World War, the school had begun to blossom more fully once again. But in 1948 Catherine realized she could not run it by herself for much longer. She was growing increasingly debilitated by arthritis, and becoming less mobile than ever. Eventually, she had asked her young daughter-in-law to take over the school and run it for her. Anya had agreed, knowing she would have the advice and guidance of her mother-in-law at all times.

Anya and Catherine had always been unusually close. They had initially bonded in 1936, when Michel had taken Anya to meet his mother for the first time. It had been her twentieth birthday, and Anya had once told Nicky that they had sat in the garden drinking champagne and giggling like schoolgirls as they got to know each other. Apparently, they had hit it off in no uncertain terms; Catherine had even predicted, that very afternoon, that Anya and her son would marry one day.

During the war, Michel Lacoste, a journalist by profession, was based in London, where he was a member of the staff of General Charles de Gaulle, leader of the Free French forces, who was headquartered in London.

Anya and Michel, who had fallen in love in Paris before the war, continued to see each other in war-torn England. They were married in 1941 during the Blitz. The wedding took place at the Kossikovsky house in Chelsea, in an austere and badly bombed-out London. Anya was twenty-five, Michel thirty-one.

In 1946, some months after the war was over, Michel had taken Anya and their two young children, Olga, aged three, and Dimitri, aged two, back to Paris.

Life in France in 1946 was full of postwar problems and shortages, just as the rest of Europe was. Because of the shortage of available housing, and their shaky financial situation, Michel and Anya had moved in with his mother. Catherine had been thrilled; she welcomed them warmly, excited and delighted to have her son's young family with her at long last. The war years had been hard and lonely; she welcomed their company, cherished her beautiful grandchildren.

They had all lived compatibly in the lovely old black-and-white half-timbered house where Anya still lived. The house was big enough for them all, and the garden a boon, a place for the children to play and run free, especially in the warm weather.

At Catherine's request, Anya had gone to teach part-time at the school; much to her amazement, she had discovered she had a gift for teaching. And then two years later, when Catherine had asked her to take over, she had agreed to do so, confident in her abilities.

Anya was an astute young woman, and soon, under her guidance, the school began to prosper. Anya had a talent for organization, management, and promotion, plus a keen nose for sniffing out exceptional teachers. Like Catherine before her, she always sought out artists who needed to support themselves in a compatible environment while continuing their own creative careers. It was a policy that had always paid off.

But, perhaps most important, Anya had a vision. In her mind's eye she could see so many marvelous possibilities, exciting ways to expand the little art school by developing its curriculum, adding new courses that taught some of the other important decorative arts.

However, out of respect for Catherine, Anya did not implement too many of her new ideas, nor did she make any really serious changes until after Catherine's death in 1951.

It was at this time that she slowly and cautiously began to upgrade the school, adding the new courses that taught fashion and textile design, as well as costume and theatrical design.

The classes in art and sculpture were still the mainstay of the school, and as always the most important to Anya. But students began to enroll for the other courses, and she and Michel were thrilled.

Her innovations, long in the planning stages, were working, and both of them were surprised how popular the new courses were becoming. So much so, they acquired the adjoining building when it became vacant, and another a year later.

And then in 1955 tragedy struck.

Michel suddenly and unexpectedly died of a massive heart attack; he was forty-five years old. He and Anya had been married for fourteen happy years, and she staggered momentarily because of her terrible shock and devastating loss.

Stunned and grief stricken as she was by Michel's untimely death, Anya continued to run the school. In a way, it held her together, helped to get her through those heartbreaking months. When Nicky once asked her how she had managed to do it, she had replied: "I just kept plodding on. Even though my heart was breaking, I knew I couldn't give in, or collapse. I had so many responsibilities at the school, and many people depended on me for a livelihood, especially the staff, and the teachers. There were my two young children also . . . to raise and educate, and I had a living to earn. I had to keep going, you know. But it was the plodding that did it . . . that was the secret. Anyway, I felt I owed it to Catherine's memory to keep the school open."

Two years after Michel's death, in 1957, Anya met Hugh Sedgwick, an English businessman living and working in Paris. A widower and childless, he had been introduced to Anya by mutual friends who thought these two single people were a good match. Hugo came from a theatrical family; his brother, Martin, and his sister, Clarice, were both actors, and Hugo himself was a bit of an amateur artist, painting in his spare time. They seemed to have a lot in common.

Hugo and Anya had dined together several times when she let the friendship drift away. She was far too involved with her children and the school to be bothered with developing a relationship, and, as she later said, the time was not right for her.

A year later they ran into each other by accident at an art exposition, discovered how much they enjoyed each other that evening, and soon began to see each other once more. Very quickly they became involved, and in 1960 they were married in Paris.

Hugo was an enterprising businessman of unusual acumen and foresight. When Anya asked him to help her with the financial management of the school a year after they were married, Hugo agreed. He happily took over these duties from Anya, who was overburdened. Within a year the school turned yet another corner; it became highly profitable for the first time in its history.

Not only that, its reputation began to grow in the ensuing years. More than ever before, students were flocking to the school, many of them from abroad. It had acquired a certain cachet as well as prestige, not the least because many of its graduates had become famous in their given fields. And Anya's own fame as a teacher and nurturer of young talent had begun to spread. A place at her school had become expensive, and much sought after.

By the mid-sixties it was called the Anya Sedgwick School of Decorative Arts. A few years later the name was changed again, this time to the Anya Sedgwick School of Decorative Arts, Design, and Couture. And it went on growing, and turning out truly exceptional graduates, and Anya's fame was magnified. She had become a legend in her own time

———

The shrilling telephone startled Nicky to such an extent, he literally almost jumped out of his skin. He had been so lost in thought, it took him a moment to recoup and reach for the receiver.

"Nicholas Sedgwick."

"It's Anya, Nicky."

"*Hello!* I was just thinking about you, or, rather, the history of the school."

"And what *exactly* were you thinking?"

"To tell you the truth, I was wondering if you were planning on giving some sort of reception later in the year. After all, the school is celebrating its seventy-fifth anniversary in November."

She began to laugh. "Don't you think my birthday party is enough celebrating?"

Laughing with her, he answered, "One thing has nothing to do with the other. Just a *small* reception, Anya."

"I don't know, Nicky. Let me think about it."

"Yes, do that. And we can talk later. Now, what time shall I come to your office to show you the sketches for the theme of your party?"

"I don't want to see them, Nicky, that's why I'm phoning you. Frankly, I would much prefer the party to be a *total* surprise . . .

every aspect of it. I'll leave it all to you to make the choices and the decisions."

"But, Anya—"

"No, no," she cut in. "I trust you implicitly, darling boy. You have the best taste of anybody I know."

"That's very flattering, I must say, but I do think I'd feel better if you saw them," he protested.

"I want to be surprised. Nothing much surprises me these days, I must admit, so indulge me. I know I'm going to love everything."

"I sincerely hope so," he muttered, then added, "But to be honest, I really was looking forward to seeing you."

"Then you can take me out to tea. That would be *nice,* Nicky, and we can have a little chat, visit for a while. We haven't done that lately."

"What a good idea, and it'll be my pleasure. What time shall I stop by your office to pick you up?"

"I'm not at the school. I'm . . . out. So why don't we meet at the Hotel Meurice, it's very beautiful after its redecoration. Have you seen it lately?"

"No, I haven't."

"Then we'll meet there. At four o'clock, oh, and, Nicky, the main entrance is now on the rue de Rivoli."

"I'll be there. Four sharp."

CHAPTER FOURTEEN

They sat together in the Jardin d'Hiver—the winter garden—just beyond the lobby of the newly refurbished Hotel Meurice on the rue de Rivoli opposite the Tuileries.

Palm trees in tubs and many other exotic plants helped to create the garden feeling so prevalent in this charming and comfortable spot where lunch and tea were served. Floating above, set in the center of the large curved ceiling, was a glass roof in the shape of a dome, interlaced with metalwork. The milky opaqueness of the glass filtered the natural daylight and gave this garden-inspired room a softness that was unique.

"They discovered that glass roof when they started to tear the hotel apart," Anya suddenly announced, looking up at the ceiling and then glancing across at Nicky. "It had been covered up, plastered over, and painted for many years. No one had any idea that the central dome was actually made of glass, until the restoration and refurbishment began several years ago."

"How amazing! And what's even more amazing is the condition of the glass," Nicky exclaimed, following her gaze of a moment ago. "It *can't* be the original, can it?"

"No, actually it is not. It's new glass, and, of course, a totally new dome, Nicky, made in the Art Nouveau style, as you can see," Anya informed him, sounding extremely knowledgeable. "The architects and designers had the original copied. You see, when they found the glass roof up there, it was cracked and broken, ruined in general. It had been damaged by the plaster and paint that had been slathered on for God knows how many years. But it's beautiful now, isn't it? I've always been a trifle partial to Art Nouveau, haven't you?"

Nicky nodded and gave her a curious look. "How do you know all this, about the roof I mean."

Anya smiled a bit smugly. "One of the directors is a friend of mine, and he told me about that glass roof when he showed me around the hotel recently, then took me to dinner here."

Laughing, Nicky shook his head. "Why do I ever ask you a single question when it comes to such things? I might have known you got your information from the horse's mouth."

She made no comment, merely gave a slight nod, and then sat back in the chair, glancing around her. "Catherine Lacoste always loved this hotel," she confided after a moment. "She used to bring me here for tea. Or champagne. It became a favorite of mine too. Of course, when the war came, she never set foot inside the place. How could she? During the Occupation, the hotel was the headquarters of the German High Command, you see. How Catherine hated *les boches.*"

"As did the rest of France."

"Well, thank God for one thing . . . the Nazis didn't destroy Paris, although they could have."

"I shudder at the mere *thought* of that. It would have been ghastly, a true desecration."

"Hitler ordered historic buildings destroyed in 1944, when Allied troops were approaching. But General Dietrich von Choltitz, the occupying governor, was not able to perpetrate such sacrilege. He surrendered the city intact to General Leclerc, liberator of Paris," she explained.

"Hugo once told me something about that," Nicholas said, and picked up his cup, took a sip of tea, eyed Anya over the rim, thinking how well she looked this afternoon. She was wearing a crisply tailored pale blue wool suit, and her much-loved string of large South Sea pearls and matching earrings, which were a must with her, and had become her trademark, in a sense.

Her softly waved, short dark-blond hair was as elegantly coiffed as it usually was, and she looked positively radiant, just wonderful to Nicky. She forever sang the praises of her sister, Katti, considered her to be the more beautiful, but in his opinion this was not the case. They were very similar in appearance, the two Kossikovskaya sisters, but Anya's looks were decidedly the more striking, Nicky believed. Her eyes were larger, and a lovely blue, her nose better shaped, and her high cheekbones, even at her age, were quite sensational. She looked twenty years younger than she really was, and in a variety of ways. One thing on her side was her marvelous health, which she attributed to her Russian genes.

Breaking into his thoughts, Anya asked, "Have you had many acceptances for my party so far, Nicky?"

"A lot, yes indeed, and I'm expecting more this week. The first of April was the deadline I gave, but some people will be late, that's normal."

"Have you heard from Alexa? Has she accepted?"

"No, she hasn't, not yet. But I'm sure I'll be hearing from her any day now."

"She might not come. She's not been back to Paris since she

broke up with Tom Conners, and if you remember, that was three years ago, just about the time she stopped working with you and Larry. I saw her in New York when I was there last year to receive that award—" She paused, gave him a very pointed look, and finished, "I rather got the impression Alexa was avoiding France . . . Paris in particular. Because of him."

"You're implying she's carrying a torch."

"I believe she is."

Nicky sighed. "I always warned her about him, and so did Larry. Repeatedly. Tom's hauling far too much emotional baggage. No woman needs that, Anya."

"Perhaps he's discarded some of it? By now?" A blond brow lifted, and she gave him another penetrating look.

"You'd think so, wouldn't you . . . but I just don't know . . ." His voice trailed off lamely, and then he threw her a helpless look. "Tom was always an odd chap."

"In what way?"

"A loner. Kept his thoughts to himself. Standoffish. Yes, I suppose that's what I mean. He was very independent and self-contained. Not at all confiding."

"Don't you ever see him these days?" Anya leaned forward, her light-green eyes focused on him more intently. "I was under the impression he represented quite a few people in show business."

"That's absolutely true, he did. Probably still does. But I haven't run into him for the longest time, for at least a year. Maybe longer even." His eyes narrowed slightly. "Why? What are you getting at?"

"I do so want Alexa to be at the party. I was just wondering if there was any way we could make it easier for her?"

"By inviting him too?"

"No, no, don't be so silly, Nicholas! That wouldn't make her feel more comfortable, quite the contrary. What I meant was that perhaps he's left Paris."

"I doubt it." Nicky sat up, an alert expression on his face.

"But if he no longer lives here, we could tell her that, don't you see?" Anya pressed.

"Yes, I do. But I'm pretty sure he's still a resident of this fair city. He was born here, it's where he belongs."

"Some people retire, move location, go south to Provence, somewhere like that."

"Not Tom, take my word for it. Incidentally, I did hear from that nice Italian girl, the one who was in Alexa's class. Maria Franconi. She was practically the first to accept."

A wide smile spread itself across Anya's face. "I'm so glad she's coming! She's such a lovely person. And she has such enormous talent, wasted probably these days."

"What do you mean?" Nicky asked, frowning.

"She could be doing a lot more than designing textiles for that antiquated family business she's stuck in, I can tell you that, darling boy. The girl's an extraordinary artist—at genius level." Not giving him a chance to make any kind of comment, she continued. "Kay Lenox will come, that I am certain of, but not Jessica. I don't think she'll be able to face Paris, in view of what happened to her."

"You mean Lucien's disappearance?"

"I do. That was a mystery, one that's never been solved, and I don't suppose it ever will be. *C'est dommage.*"

"I agree with you. And so you think Jessica will forgo your party because Paris holds bad memories, too much pain for her?"

Anya nodded and sat back in the chair. "I really do, Nicky, I've never seen anyone so distraught. I remember it so very clearly, it might have happened only yesterday. One minute she was full of life, happy, madly in love, looking to a future with him, and the next she was plunged into the most horrendous anguish and despair." She shook her head. "I honestly thought she would never recover. It's different when the person you love dies. There's an awful finality to death. But it is final. The end. And there's the funeral, family gatherings, grieving, all of those necessary rituals, and they help, believe me they do. Somehow you go on living, by rote perhaps, and for a long time it's by rote. Eventually, though, you begin to feel a little better. Life *is* for the living, you know. I've come to be a firm believer in that cliché. But when the object of your love just . . . *disappears,* as if into thin air, then everything becomes impossible, and in a peculiar way there's actually no way to deal with the grief and the pain."

"Because there's no closure," Nicky suggested.

"Correct. No body. No burial. No grieving as such. Therefore no closure. No end to the pain, because you don't know what happened to him. It's as simple as that. For Jessica it was a nightmare. I was really concerned for her, worried to death. To be very frank, I thought she was in danger of becoming . . . well, mentally ill. For a while, she *was* demented, couldn't come to grips with the loss, and since Lucien Girard had no family, there really was no one for her to grieve with, or be consoled by in the way she needed. Alain Bonnal was wonderful, but like her he was nonplussed, confused, and, not unnaturally, very baffled. Still, they were supportive of each other, helped each other for a while."

"And nothing has ever turned up? No body has been washed ashore? Or found anywhere else? No information was ever forthcoming from the police?"

"None. I would have told you. Look, Nicky, it was as if Lucien never existed."

For a moment Nicky did not respond. He had known Lucien, and Larry had introduced the young actor to Jessica. What a strange story it was. Finally, he said, "I remember her parents came to Paris to be with her, and then they took her back to Texas. But what actually happened to Jessica, Anya? Did she ever marry? Do you hear from her?"

"Oh, yes, I do, I get notes and cards from her from time to time, or a clipping from *Architectural Digest* when one of the homes she has designed appears in its pages. She's enormously talented, one of the great interior designers of today, and that's partly because of her classical background. And no, she hasn't married. She lives in Bel Air, does a lot of designing for the rich and famous. But she never misses sending me a Christmas card with a lovely message. In fact, I get Christmas cards from Kay and Maria as well."

"And Alex?"

"Oh, she's constantly in touch. I get letters, cards, photographs, and phone calls. Alexa has always been very devoted to me, warm, loving."

"You saw her in New York last year. How was she? How's her personal life shaped up?"

"Very well, but you know that, Nicky. You know what a success she's had in theatrical design. I thought she'd been in touch with you."

"That's true, she has. But she never discussed her personal life. Never."

"And you never mentioned Tom Conners?"

"Sure I did. Once. She bit my head off, was really rather snotty. Therefore, I learned my lesson. Hell hath no fury like a woman in love with a man she can't have because he's a jerk."

"Is that what you really think about Tom?" She gave him a hard stare, her brows puckering.

"Yep." Then he shook his head, looking slightly chagrined. "No, no, not really. In many ways he's a good man. But Tom had a great tragedy in his life and he's let it ruin his life, ruin any chance of happiness with a woman. And that's certainly being a jerk, isn't it?"

"Yes, I tend to agree. And what's more, I can't imagine any man letting a gorgeous young woman slip through his fingers the way he did Alexa." Anya lifted her cup, sipped her tea, then continued. "It's funny, isn't it, how one girl in particular becomes very important in one's life. I've had some truly wonderful students, male and female, over many years of teaching, but there's never been anyone quite like her. At least, not for me. She was . . . the *perfect girl*. No, not perfect, I don't really mean that exactly, because she was flawed then, as she is now, I've no doubt. But she was the embodiment of everything I thought a young woman should be. Do you understand what I mean, Nick?"

"Yes, I do, only too well. I think I was always a bit in love with Alexa when she worked with Larry and me." He smiled ruefully, took hold of her hand. "Maybe I still am. Do you know the reason why?"

"No, I don't."

"It's because Alexandra Gordon is so like you, Anya, and in many ways. That's why you love her yourself, you know. She might have been cast from the same mold as you, and she's a lot more like you than Olga is, and I mean that in the nicest way, I'm not being critical of your daughter. What I'm trying to say is that Alexa is a reflection of you, and quite by accident. Or maybe she modeled herself on you. In any event, she has a lot of your special talents."

"She does, yes, I think you're right."

He laughed. "I'm positive. She's creative but also very competent, that was most obvious when she worked for us. You know, she can do so many other things as well as design sets. You could give her this school to run, and she'd do it very well. She could design costumes, or fashionable clothes, even decorate a house. She's that kind of person, and her work will always be excellent. Yes, she's like you in that sense."

"I think you might be a bit biased, Nicky," she answered with a small smile. "And listen to me, on reflection I don't think we should meddle in her life. I shouldn't have suggested it." She patted his hand still holding hers, and gave him a stern look. "Meddling can be dangerous, we mustn't play God, Nicky."

"Like I sometimes do?"

"Exactly. Hugo used to say to me, what will be will be. And he was right. You know, life does have a way of taking care of itself. So let us leave everything to life, let things take their course. If we don't hear from Alexa in a week or so, I'll phone her, ask her to come to the birthday party. For me." Her eyes were warm and loving as she went on. "I'm glad we're having this visit, Nicky, I've been worried about you, worried about the way you've looked, so strained lately. I know there are problems with Constance. Can you not work them out?"

"I doubt it. The marriage is over, only she won't accept that. But she'll have to eventually. I moved out a long time ago. Now I've got to move on, get on with my life."

"Is there anyone else?" Anya asked softly, a brow lifting speculatively. He was very handsome, dark, striking, as Hugo had been, and she knew most women found Nicky irresistible.

"No, there's no one. I'd tell you if there was." He let out a long sigh, "Look, she and I have grown apart, and quite aside from anything else, I've really been put off by her dieting. Actually, it's gone beyond that. She's anorexic. Connie looks really ill, like a skeleton, as if she's stepped out of one of those wartime concentration camps."

"Let's give those horrendous places their correct name, Nick. *They were death camps.*"

"I know."

"It's an illness, anorexia. You know that, just as bulimia is too. She needs help. Can't you get Connie to see a doctor, one who treats eating disorders?"

"I've tried, so has her sister. She's very resistant to the idea, it's like she has blinders on."

"That's part of the illness, I'm told." Anya leaned back against the chair. "If there's anything I can do, you have only to ask."

"Thanks, Anya."

A compatible silence fell between them. But eventually, Anya murmured in a reflective voice, "Life is strange, unpredictable, so is this world we live in. Here we are, Nicky, sitting in the Meurice so relaxed, having afternoon tea. But just think, sixty years ago the

Nazis were installed in this very hotel, running the German Occupation of France. Why, they had the very destiny of France in their hands. How they were feared and hated. And then, suddenly, they are finished. The conquerors are defeated. French Resistance forces march into Paris and liberate the city. And everything changes yet again."

"Uncle Hugo used to say that the only thing that's permanent *is* change."

PART THREE

Quest ⌒

CHAPTER FIFTEEN

Anya had convinced her to change her mind.

And so, here she was, in Paris in the spring. In May, to be exact. Three weeks before the birthday party on June the second. Far too early. On the other hand, Alexandra Gordon knew she had plenty to occupy herself with during this period.

She planned to spend some special time with Anya; she was going to do quite a lot of serious shopping, wanting to treat herself to new clothes, which she needed, and felt she deserved after the many long months of hard work on the Broadway play. Also, since she had just agreed to work with Nicky on a new movie, which would start shooting in October, it was imperative that she have a number of meetings with him immediately.

And then there was her hidden agenda.

Tom Conners.

She fully intended to seek him out. She needed to understand where he was at this stage in his life. And where she stood with him. And there was something else . . . she had to know how she actually felt about him. After all, she had not seen him for three years; perhaps when they did finally come face-to-face her feelings would be quite different.

In her own mind—most of the time—it was over.

He *had* ended it, telling her there was no future for her with him, that he could not marry her, would not. Nor anyone else. Seemingly, his past had claimed his future.

And yet in a certain way it *wasn't* over for her. Part of her still secretly yearned for him. He occupied a large part of her, continually crept into her thoughts when she least expected. But lately she had come to recognize that none of this was very healthy, and that she could not live with the situation any longer.

Alexa accepted that she had to be emotionally free in order to move forward, that she could not marry Jack Wilton until she had confronted the demons that haunted her. It wouldn't be fair to Jack, who was such a decent human being, or to herself, for that matter.

If she was going to marry Jack, it must be with a free heart, with love in her heart only for him. Anything else would be shoddy.

And so she had come to slay the dragon in his lair.

After that, perhaps she could turn the page, so to speak, and get on with her life. After all, she was almost thirty-one, and it seemed to her that time sped by faster than ever these days.

Alexa had admitted to herself that she had felt much more relaxed once she had made the decision to see Tom. Not only comfortable about coming to Paris for Anya's landmark celebration, but more at ease within herself. It was as if just making the decision to deal with Tom had lifted a burden from her.

———

She had arrived in Paris on Thursday morning, having taken a night flight from New York, and after unpacking and resting for most of Thursday she was now ready for action.

It was eleven o'clock on Friday morning, May the eleventh, and the temptation to call Tom Conners was strong. But Alexa resisted picking up the receiver. She was not quite ready to face him just yet.

And so she glanced around the bedroom, making a last-minute check, and picked up her bag. On the desk, where she had put them, were her dark glasses, her address book, a notepad, and her cell phone, plus the door key. Scooping everything up, dropping them into her bag, she left the room and headed for the elevator.

A few seconds later she was walking across the elegant marble-floored lobby of the Hotel Meurice, which Anya had recommended several weeks before. She was glad she had taken Anya's advice; her room was comfortable and pleasant, and the hotel's location was ideal for her.

Alexa went through the revolving door and down the steps, stood outside in front of the hotel for a moment, undecided what to do. She was invited to Anya's house for lunch at one o'clock, so she had two hours to fill. And lots of options.

She was in her most favorite city in the world, and she knew it well, and since she had not been there for three years, she was filled with excitement, enormous nostalgia, and the desire to visit much-loved parts of the city.

If she turned left, she could walk down to the Louvre, where one of her favorite paintings hung, and it would certainly give her a great deal of pleasure to see it again.

Or she could turn right, walk along the rue de Rivoli, looking in shopwindows until she came to the Place de la Concorde, the Champs-Élysées beyond, with the Arc de Triomphe at the top. Always a heartstopping sight to her.

Then again, the Place Vendôme was just behind the hotel, as was the rue du Faubourg St. Honoré, where some of her favorite clothing boutiques were located. But she was not really in the mood for shopping, trying on clothes. She would do that another day. All day. Making a snap decision, she set off walking toward the Louvre.

What a glorious day it was.

Paris shimmered under a shimmering sky. It was brilliant, awash with sunlight, and there was not a cloud visible. The sky appeared to be high flung, a great arc that looked like an upturned bowl with its inside glazed a soft powder blue. There was no breeze; it was not sultry either. It was, very simply, the most perfect weather.

How magnificent Paris looks today, she thought as she glanced around her, walking along the rue de Rivoli at a steady pace. Then she made a mental note to visit Le Louvre des Antiquaires in the Place du Palais-Royal nearby. She hoped that in this unique gallery of antique shops she would find something really special and original for Anya's birthday. There might be something Russian or English, some small memento that would evoke all the right kinds of memories in Anya.

A flood of her own memories engulfed Alexa; they made her heart clench with their bittersweetness. Memories of Tom and the two years they spent together . . . their sensual lovemaking, their joy in each other. Memories of working on different movies with Nicky and Larry. Such exciting days with them, from whom she had learned so much . . . such exciting nights with Tom, from whom she had also learned so much . . . including heartbreak, heartache. . . .

She was assaulted all of a sudden by the fragrant, mouthwatering smell of fresh coffee. Tantalizingly, it hung on the air, floated to her. Abruptly she came to a stop outside a sidewalk café; immediately she sat down at one of the tables, unable to resist.

"*Café au lait, s'il vous plaît,*" she said to the smiling waiter who instantly appeared in front of her.

"*Mais oui,*" he said, hurrying off.

Alexa sat back in the metal chair, thinking how wonderful it was to be here, how foolish she had been to stay away for so long.

A few seconds elapsed, and then the waiter was back, placing a pot of coffee and a jug of steaming hot milk in front of her. "*Voilà, mademoiselle!*" he exclaimed with a nod, and brought more items to her table swiftly.

"*Merci,*" she said, smiling back at him as he put down a basket of breads, and then she picked up the pot, poured coffee into the large cup, added the frothy milk.

The first sip was delicious; then she eyed the basket of different breads. She could smell the fresh croissants, which had also miraculously appeared on the table, along with small slabs of creamy-looking butter on a plate, plus a dish of dark raspberry jam.

Oh, what the hell, why not? she thought, and took a croissant, broke a piece off, added a touch of butter and a generous blob of the jam. It seemed to melt in her mouth, and she thought of all those breakfasts she had had, just like this one, when she had been a student here.

Nine years ago. She had been just twenty-one when she had started at Anya's school. And from the first day to the last she had enjoyed every moment, never once been disappointed.

There was an extraordinary atmosphere in the school. The series of adjoining buildings along the rue de l'Université were filled with a special kind of . . . *happiness.* That was the only word she could think of to describe the mood in the many different classrooms and art studios. This feeling of genuine euphoria and excitement enveloped everyone who came there. Of course it emanated from Anya, who else? And yet the other teachers were just as inspired, and as inspiring, as she was.

They all inculcated a love of learning in her and the other pupils, and they were the best, always the greatest experts in their given fields, and specially chosen by Anya Sedgwick for a variety of qualities as well as their talents.

How wonderful those years were, she thought now, leaning back in the chair, reminiscing, letting her mind fill with memories of those days. They had been filled with wonder, anticipation, expectation, and a sense of adventure. Everything was ahead of her, her whole life, and the future glowed before her eyes. It held so much promise, glittering prizes.

Yes, all of her hopes and ambitions had been encouraged here by Anya and her other teachers. And what dreams of glory she'd had. Thanks to Anya, so many of them had come true . . . at least as far as her work was concerned. But so much else had gone wrong . . . in her personal life. But that wasn't Anya's fault. And now she aimed to put it right. She had come to deal with unfinished business.

CHAPTER SIXTEEN

The woman was so striking and dramatic-looking, heads turned as she passed.

She was tall, about five feet ten inches in height, well built but not overly heavy, and there was a certain regality to her posture, fluidity in the way she moved with a measured grace.

But it was her face that made people look at her again. The woman was startlingly beautiful, with a thick mane of jet-black hair falling halfway down her back, perfectly curved black eyebrows above dark eyes that were huge, set wide apart, and a most voluptuous mouth.

Her clothes were simple yet elegant in their cut. She wore a black, light gabardine pantsuit, a man-tailored shirt of white silk, and high-heeled black sandals. A black leather bag was slung over her shoulder, and she carried a pair of dark glasses in one hand.

This simple elegance was carried through to her jewelry. There was nothing ostentatious about the watch she wore on her left wrist, the gold bracelet on the other, or the small diamond studs in her ears.

This morning she moved at a slow, leisurely pace through the quiet halls of the Louvre, stopping now and then to gaze at a painting that caught her eye, in no great hurry to get to the picture she had actually come to see. She had plenty of time before she had to leave to keep her luncheon date at the Ritz Hotel in the Place Vendôme, which was not too far away from the museum.

The woman became aware of the stir she caused as she meandered along, self-contained and slightly aloof. She marveled to herself about this. Three months ago she would not have believed it possible that she, of all people, could create such an astonishing reaction in others.

But Maria Franconi had undergone an enormous transformation, and one so extraordinary, so radical, her brother Fabrizio could describe it only as unbelievable and miraculous. And indeed it was both. The miracle was not accidental. It had occurred because of tremendous hard work, rigid discipline, many deprivations of various kinds, and total dedication to a cause: *Immense weight loss in the shortest possible time.*

It had taken Maria not quite three months to lose forty-eight pounds, two pounds short of her goal. She had accomplished this with the help of a doctor, a nutritionist, a personal trainer, and her brother—and a focus so intense it took over her life.

During this time she had thrown herself wholeheartedly into a brutal regimen comprised of punishing workouts, a diet totally free of fat, sugar, and carbohydrates; wine and alcohol of any kind were forbidden, as were chocolates, candy, and most desserts.

If she was hungry, more often than not the very visible results of the dieting were worth it and kept her going, and were actually inspiring to her. Through most of February, March, and April she thought of nothing else but going to Paris to Anya's party, and it was this incentive and her extraordinary willpower that enabled her to continue. She even surprised herself at times.

One day, halfway through her program, there was a sudden and remarkable change in her face. She had always been good-looking, she was well aware of that, but now her face had become dramatically beautiful. There was not an ounce of excess fat on it, and the high cheekbones were more apparent than ever. Her neck was thinner, and therefore looked longer and more elegant, added to the shapeliness of her head.

It soon became apparent to Maria that she was mostly losing weight in her upper torso first. Her shoulders, arms, and back were growing more slender by the day, and her breasts were not so large anymore. What disappointed her was the slowness of the weight loss on her hips. But her trainer had assured her that the weight would eventually drop off, most probably when she least expected it. All she had to do was keep strictly to her regime. And this she did. Vanity was the goad, and it kept her going.

Very simply, Maria Franconi was beginning to like herself, and she could hardly believe her incredible transformation. She also discovered that being beautiful was really quite addictive.

Through her nutritionist, Maria learned all about behavior modification, as well as gained an understanding of the right foods to eat, ones that would keep her healthy. And thin.

And so there was no more cooking for her brother, no more dinner parties for her friends. She virtually locked the doors of her fancy modern kitchen, took her friends to lunch or dinner in restaurants, where she herself ate frugally and stayed away from wine.

Several weeks before she left Milan for Paris, Maria visited a well-known dressmaker recommended by her brother Sergio, who had innumerable women friends who went there. The dressmaker instantly understood the problems and created several well-tailored pantsuits, skirt suits, and a few elegant, simply cut dresses, all in beautiful fabrics.

The clothes were designed to specifically play up her good points, and also conceal certain parts of her body. The secrets were the longer jackets that stopped just below the thigh, cut edge-to-edge without buttons; the narrower trouser legs; and the pencil-thin skirts on the dresses and suits.

These styles helped to slim her lower body, by illusion gave her a leaner and more elongated look. The dark colors she chose, mostly black and various tones of gray, played into this camouflage, and also suited her dark coloring and olive-tinted complexion. In a very short time she had acquired a certain kind of chic, and this, along with her glowing health and lovely looks, made heads turn. She felt gratified. All of her hard work and focus had paid off admirably.

———

Even though she was now in Paris, Maria did not let up on her regime. She knew she would have to follow it for the rest of her life if she was to remain thin. At the moment it was less arduous, but nonetheless she was very disciplined and dedicated. She visited the spa in the hotel every day, swam, did exercises, and worked on the treadmill. All this gave her extra strength and muscle tone, which pleased her.

She also remained on her strict diet despite the tempting French food she had always enjoyed ever since her days here as a student.

Although Fabrizio had been supportive, and had helped her to achieve her goal, he had been against her spending the better part of June in Paris, which she had originally planned to do.

The entire Franconi family went to their spectacular villa in Capri at the beginning of June, where they spent most of the summer. Fabrizio was insistent that she accompany the family, and after a great deal of discussion, sometimes heated, she had finally agreed.

But she was determined to spend three weeks in Paris, which she had promised herself, having that much-needed vacation on her own, doing exactly as she pleased.

And so she had arrived on the third of May, and she planned to stay until the fifth of June, when she would join the family in Capri, traveling via Milan.

Maria had been busy since she had arrived. She had been to visit her beloved Anya several times, had lunched at the house with her and taken her out to dinner at Chez Benoît. She had gone shopping, spent time in art galleries, and been to Versailles, a favorite place of hers.

And she had enjoyed every minute of her freedom, far away from her job and her domineering family.

I escaped, she thought now as she slowly began to approach the painting she had come to see. If only I didn't have to go back . . . if only I could stay in Paris. *Always.* She instantly pushed these longings to one side, not wishing to fall down into unhappy thoughts.

———

The painting was sublime. Incomparable.

Maria stood in front of it for a very long time, gazing at it as if in a trance. It usually had this effect on her . . . held her spellbound.

The *Mona Lisa*.

Painted hundreds of years ago by Leonardo da Vinci, the greatest artist there had ever been on this planet, with the exception of Michelangelo, in her opinion anyway.

To be able to paint like that was the greatest gift in the world, she marveled, mesmerized by the woman's face captured so beautifully on canvas . . . how eloquently it spoke to her.

And how truly gifted Leonardo da Vinci had been, one of the world's greatest geniuses, and in so many different fields. She had known a lot about him before she had attended Anya's school. Coming as she did from Milan, she was familiar with the Church of Santa Maria delle Grazie, where in its refectory Leonardo had painted the *Last Supper*. It was more than likely the most famous *Last Supper* in the world.

It was Anya Sedgwick who had taught Maria much, much more about da Vinci in her classical art classes—her master class. And Maria had never ceased to marvel at his extraordinary achievements in so many other fields. He had been an architect as well as a painter and sculptor, an expert in the art of weaponry, hydraulics, optics, anatomy, and mechanics.

What an amazing man he was, Maria thought. A man of the Renaissance who was perhaps *the* Renaissance man of all time.

To be able to paint like that, she thought, a small sigh escaping her. It was a sigh of absolute yearning . . . she stepped closer in order to look more intently at the *Mona Lisa*.

As she did so, out of the corner of her eye she caught a glimpse of a woman heading her way. Her heart dropped. But she swung her head to make sure she was not mistaken, then swiftly turned back to face the painting.

After one last look at the da Vinci, Maria hurried off in the opposite direction.

———

His table in L'Espadon faced the door, and he saw her the minute she arrived. He pushed back his chair and rose long before she reached the table, a broad smile of welcome on his face.

When she came to a standstill, he took hold of her arm almost possessively, kissed her cheek, and then stared at her intently for a moment.

Maria smiled at him and said as she slid into the chair, "I'm sorry I'm late."

He sat down opposite her and shook his head. "But you're not late, and even if you were, you're certainly worth waiting for. You look very beautiful, Maria."

"Thank you," she murmured, dipping her head slightly.

"I ordered grapefruit juice for you," he went on, "I hope that's all right."

"It's perfect, thanks."

Lifting his wineglass, he said, *"Santé."*

"Santé," she responded, lifting her glass, touching it to his.

"So what did you do this morning?"

"I went to the Louvre. To see the *Mona Lisa* in particular. I'm always mesmerized by that painting."

As I am mesmerized by you, he thought, but said, "What a genius Leonardo was. He was lucky enough to be born with a brain fully equipped to explore and comprehend all human knowledge."

The maître d' arrived with the luncheon menus, and they studied them for a few moments. He knew what he was going to order; he assumed Maria did also. Since he was usually on a strict diet, as she was, they seemed to choose the same dishes. The other evening she had told him all about her strenuous dieting, and her exercise program, had confided a great deal about herself over their second dinner. He had listened attentively, been impressed with her honesty, and sympathetic.

He had seen quite a lot of her since her arrival in Paris, and he wanted to continue seeing her. He was smitten with her, and in a way he had not been taken with a woman for years. But he was aware that at this moment in time caution was in order.

"You are staring at me."

"I'm sorry," he apologized. "I just can't help it. Your face is quite . . . *sublime.* That's the only word to describe it."

Maria laughed lightly and shook her head. "I don't know about that . . . I use that word only when I think of the *Mona Lisa* . . . now, that truly *is* a beautiful face."

"Yes, it is, and actually *you* should be painted by a great artist, a modern-day da Vinci."

The waiter arrived at the table before she could respond. She ordered oysters on the half shell and steamed turbot, and so did he. That they had decided on the same food amused him.

When they were alone, Maria volunteered, "I saw Alexandra Gordon at the Louvre this morning."

His eyes narrowed; he glanced at her alertly. "How was she? She must have been pleased to see you."

Maria sighed. "I didn't speak to her. I suddenly felt shy, a little nervous, and I slipped away before she spotted me. At least, I don't think she did." Maria shook her head, added, "It was foolish perhaps. After seven years, I would like to spend time with her and the others."

"Was it such a bad rift between the four of you?" he asked, riddled with curiosity.

"It seemed like it then. But now it all seems somewhat childish, even silly. . . ." Her voice trailed off lamely.

Understanding that she did not wish to pursue the subject, he moved on. "You're enjoying Paris enormously, aren't you, Maria?"

"Yes, I am. Thanks to you. You've been so wonderful to me. I was so thrilled to come to Paris, to be on my own, away from the family. But, you know, I do think I might have been lonely if you hadn't been around and taken pity on me."

"Anya would have taken you under her wing."

"I like being under your wing, you—" She stopped abruptly, cut her sentence off, looked abashed.

He saw the faint pink blush rising on her neck to flood her face, and he exclaimed quietly, "Don't be embarrassed." Reaching out, he took hold of her hand on the table, squeezed it. After clearing his throat several times, he said in a low voice, "I'm very smitten with you, Maria. And I was hoping you felt the same way."

After a moment's silence, she said, "I do. Oh, Nicky, I *do*."

He tightened his fingers on hers. "I'm so very glad this is not a one-way street."

She merely laughed and looked at him, her dark eyes holding his.

They sat holding hands across the table, staring at each other in silence and with great intensity until the oysters were served.

Finally releasing her hand, he picked up his oyster fork and wondered to himself what was happening to him. Here he was, thirty-eight years old, an experienced man of the world, and feeling like a schoolboy. Daft, he thought, I'm daft. But he knew exactly what was happening to him, and he discovered he was glad.

After eating several oysters, Maria put her fork down and leaned across the table, leveling her gaze at him again. "When I came to Paris over a week ago, I thought I'd take the train to London for a day. To see Riccardo. As I told you, he's working there. But I don't want to do that, not now, Nicky."

"Because of me?" he ventured carefully.

"Yes." She lifted her eyes to his, stared back at him.

Nicky saw desire reflected there, a yearning for him, and his chest tightened. Slowly, he warned himself. Take this very, very slowly. Don't frighten her off. He wanted to possess her, he could not wait to take her to bed, but he knew he must pick the right time.

CHAPTER SEVENTEEN

Coming back to Paris *has* been a mistake, Jessica thought as she walked up the narrow street that ran alongside the Plaza-Athénée hotel, where she was staying. Just as she had always known, there *were* too many memories here, and obviously most of them were associated with Lucien Girard.

They evoked in her an immense sadness for what might have been . . . a marriage that had never happened, children that were never born, a life not lived with the man she had truly loved.

Now she wished she had not phoned Alain Bonnal from Los Angeles last week to make this date for lunch today. She had done so because she had become nervous about being in Paris alone after an absence of seven years. Afraid of memories, she supposed, and recurring sorrow, and the pain of old wounds opening up.

Alain Bonnal and she were friends because of Lucien, but he was not someone she was close to anymore. She had seen him only twice in the last few years, when he had been in California on business. On the other hand, in the past he had been kind, considerate, and helpful, and she had never forgotten his compassion for her when she was full of sorrow, and perturbed.

He was a connection to the past, a past she had not been able to let go of apparently, if she were honest with herself. Lucien, and their intense love affair, had haunted her ever since he had disappeared. And haunted any other relationship she had attempted to have. She truly understood that now. Gary Stennis had been a casualty of her past in certain ways, even though his behavior had been deplorable. Ultimately, he had given her plenty of reasons to end it. Not one regret, she thought, I don't have one regret about saying good-bye to Gary.

Of all the men she had known, Lucien had had the most impact on her. It's not a question of unrequited love, she said to herself as she hurried on, but of an unrequited life. Lucien and I made so many plans, sketched out a future for ourselves together, we even chose names for the children we planned to have. All of those nights we dreamed our dreams and built our future . . .

But it wasn't meant to happen, she thought, heading in the direction of Chez André, where she was meeting Alain. Even his choice of restaurant was a nod to nostalgia, to their shared past with Lucien, since the three of them had frequently gone there together when she was a student at Anya's school.

She had not had a chance to visit Anya yet, but they had spoken on the phone several times. Perhaps tomorrow she would be able to run over to the house to have tea or drinks, as Anya had suggested. Jessica realized how much she wanted to see her old teacher and mentor; despite her misgivings about making the trip, she *had* come to Paris, after all, in order to honor Anya.

Jessica had arrived in Paris three days earlier, but her work had taken up all her time. She had accepted an assignment some weeks earlier, a redecorating job for a valued client who wanted her Bel

Air house to be redone. Jessica had suggested a theme built around French Provincial antiques and fabrics, and the client had agreed.

For the last couple of days she had been seeing the best of the antique dealers, seeking out fabrics in keeping with French country style, scouring the leading rug dealers for Aubusson and Savonnerie carpets. That very morning she had accidentally fallen on a collection of antique toile de Jouy fabrics and had purchased them immediately, along with an extraordinary tapestry she knew would make an elegant wall hanging in the entrance foyer of the house.

Well pleased with her success, she had returned to the hotel to drop off her briefcase, retouch her makeup, and brush her hair. After changing into a lighter weight navy blue gabardine pantsuit, she had raced out, realizing she was running late.

But within a few minutes she was pushing open the door of Chez André and hurrying into the noisy, bustling bistro, which had a typical old-fashioned Parisian charm with its marble-topped bar, polished brass, and air of bygone days. It was full of patrons at this hour, but as she glanced around swiftly, she spotted Alain at once.

He waved when he saw her, pushed himself to his feet, and came around the table to greet her. He made a big fuss over her, and after they had embraced and kissed affectionately, they sat down together on the banquette.

Alain exclaimed, "You are more beautiful than ever, Jessica!" He shook his head wonderingly. "You *never* age. Unlike me."

"Thank you, Alain, for those kind words, but you've always been prejudiced. Anyway, you look pretty good to me."

"A few gray hairs these days, *chérie.*"

"But a young face nevertheless," she shot back, smiling at him, thinking he was just as attractive as ever.

"An aperitif, perhaps?"

"Thanks, that would be nice. I'll have the same as you," she answered, eyeing his kir royale.

After he had beckoned the waiter and ordered her drink, Alain turned to face her and went on. "I know you've come to celebrate your former teacher's birthday, but you said something about buying antiques, carpets, and art for a client's house. How can I be of help?" A dark brow lifted questioningly as he fastened his pale gray eyes on her. Alain Bonnal had always admired Jessica; he was genuinely interested in her life. He had also shared her great sense of loss after Lucien Girard had disappeared, and had been as baffled as she by that strange and mysterious tragedy.

"It's a house in Bel Air, actually," Jessica replied. "A beautiful house, Alain, and one I believe should have been decorated with French country antiques originally. Now the owner has finally decided to go that route." She laughed lightly. "Sometimes when clients ask me to redecorate, they want exactly the same thing they've been living with for years, except *newer*."

"I know what you mean. People do seem to hate change."

Jessica lifted her glass, which had materialized in front of her while they had been talking. "Cheers, Alain, it's nice to see you after all this time."

"Two years. And *à votre santé*, Jessica. Welcome to Paris."

"So you're still not married," she remarked after taking a sip of champagne mixed with kir liqueur.

He chuckled. "I'm afraid I'm a confirmed bachelor. Never found the right woman, I suppose."

She smiled at him, shook her head. "I have a lot of beautiful women I could introduce you to when you come to Los Angeles again," she teased.

He merely smiled, sipped his drink. After a moment, he continued. "You asked me if I had any really interesting paintings, and fortuitously we just received a collection from an estate that is being sold because of the death of the owner. His son wants to sell some of the truly good art, and I think you ought to see the collection. It is most unusual, and I believe you would make some good purchases."

"I'd love to do that . . . come to see them."

"Would you like to visit the gallery after lunch today?"

Jessica thought for a moment. "No, I don't think so, Alain, but only because I'm running out of steam. Jet lag, I guess."

"Then I must feed you immediately." He motioned to the waiter hovering nearby, who brought them the menus, recited the day's specials, then left them to make their choices.

"Oh, my goodness, my favorite!" Jessica exclaimed as she stared at the menu. *"Cervelle au beurre.* That's what I'm going to have."

"I recall how you and Lucien used to love brains. But not for me, I shall have a steak. And what would you like to start with? I see they already have white asparagus."

"That's for me, Alain. Thank you."

Once the food had been ordered, Alain asked for two more kir royales and the wine card.

"Oh, no wine for me, thanks. I'm afraid I can't drink too much during the day," Jessica explained.

"I will order a dry white wine, a Pouilly-Fumé, and if you wish you can have a glass later."

"I'll see how I feel. Are you available tomorrow, Alain? Or perhaps the gallery is closed on Saturday?"

"No, we are open. I will be happy to see you then, and I do think you will be impressed by some of the paintings."

————

As they sipped their aperitifs, waiting for the first course, Jessica talked to Alain about art and her own preferences, which he enjoyed, since she was so knowledgeable. Madame Sedgwick's art classes had been worthwhile, he decided as he listened to her hold forth with confidence.

Alain Bonnal worked with his father and brother in their family-owned gallery, which had been founded by Alain's grandfather, Pierre Bonnal, before the Second World War. It was one of the best in Paris, and was particularly well known and highly thought of,

since it specialized in Impressionist and Postimpressionist paintings, holding a good inventory.

As she talked, Alain studied her, thinking how well she looked.
It seemed to him that she had hardly aged at all. At least, as far as
her appearance was concerned. Of course she was much more mature and sophisticated in her mannerisms and attitudes these days,
but it would have been odd if she had not changed over the years.
Her face was unlined, and she wore her pale blond hair in the same
style, long and straight, falling to her shoulders. And she was slender, had kept her lovely figure.

For a moment, he felt as though time had stood still. But it was
only a fleeting thought, and then it was gone.

Their orders of white asparagus arrived, and Alain murmured,
"Aren't we lucky it's in season right now?"

Jessica nodded, and began to eat, saying between mouthfuls, "I
hadn't realized how hungry I was."

When the waiter arrived with the wine, Jessica agreed to have a
glass, and later, once their empty plates were removed, she sat back
against the banquette. A reflective look settled on her face.

After a moment or two of growing silence between them, Alain
said, "You're looking pensive, Jessica."

"Am I? Well, to tell you the truth, there's something I want to
talk to you about. To do with Lucien."

He nodded, looked at her attentively, his eyes alert, questioning.

She went on. "Recently, I was telling a friend about Lucien's disappearance, and he presented a whole new scenario to me. I'd like
to pass it by you."

"What do you mean by a whole new scenario?" he asked, frowning, obviously puzzled.

"You and I came up with every possibility all those years ago. But
we never considered one thing . . . that Lucien might have disappeared of his own accord. You know, *on purpose.*"

Alain gaped at her, a look of astonishment crossing his pale face.

"Mais non, non, c'est pas possible!" he cried, reverting to French. He shook his head vehemently, and his eyes widened as the astonishment intensified. "He was not that kind of man, Jessica. He would not disappear on purpose. What possible reason had he to do that?"

"He might have wanted to start a new life."

"Ah, non, non! That is *ridiculous!* You and he had so many wonderful plans. And you knew him so well, he had such . . . *integrity.* He was an honorable man. No, no, he wouldn't have done anything like that."

Jessica sat very still, staring at Alain.

It was quite obvious to her that he was startled and dismayed by her suggestion, just as she herself had been when Mark Sylvester had presented this theory to her months earlier.

Ever since then, from time to time, she had wondered about Alain Bonnal, wondered if he had known more about the disappearance of Lucien Girard than he had admitted. Yet he had just proved to her, by his stunned reaction, that he knew only what she knew. Alain had never been very good when it came to dissembling. Only Lucien had been a good actor.

She frowned. A vague half-memory stirred at the back of her mind . . . she couldn't quite put her finger on it. It was something that had lain dormant for years. She struggled, but she could not make it come to life. She gave up, let it go.

Alain, his eyes on her, said in a somewhat concerned tone, "What is it, Jessica? What is wrong? You have the most peculiar expression . . ." He did not finish his sentence.

Slowly, she answered, "You know, Alain, I've always had this weird feeling, deep down inside me . . . a gut feeling . . . that Lucien is still alive. Somewhere out there. And I just can't shake it."

Alain Bonnal had turned white, and he sat staring at her speechlessly, completely dumbfounded.

———

A little later, when she was back at her hotel, sorting through the samples of the fabrics she had found earlier, Jessica thought about Alain Bonnal's stunned disbelief, his total negation of the theory she had put forward.

Was it an act? *Did* Alain know more than he was saying? He had turned so white, looked so . . . *afraid*. Yes, that was it, he had suddenly looked terrified. Had she hit the nail on the head? Did he know for a fact that Lucien *had* staged his own disappearing act? Would a person need help in order to vanish without a trace? Maybe. But then again, maybe not.

"Oh, for God's sake, he's dead!" she cried out loud to the empty room. Something really terrible happened to Lucien when he was in Monte Carlo, she added silently to herself. She was determined to stop dwelling on this most tragic event in her life. It was stalling her, suddenly.

Move on, she instructed herself, you've got to move on. You've got to get a life. You can't live in the past, or—

The shrill ringing of the telephone cut off her thoughts, startled her. Reaching for it, she exclaimed, "Hello?"

"Hi, Jess, it's me. Mark Sylvester."

"Mark, *hello!* How are you?"

"I'm great. How're you doing?"

"A bit jet-lagged, but okay. Hey, it's wonderful to hear your voice. Are you in L.A.? Or London?"

He laughed. "I'm in Paris."

He had taken her by surprise, and there was a brief silence on her part. Then she said, "Where are you staying?"

"Next door. Well, I'm not *exactly* next door, but down the corridor. I'm at the Plaza-Athénée," he answered, suddenly chuckling.

She laughed with him but said nothing.

Mark asked, after a split second, "How about dinner tonight? Are you free?"

"Well, yes, I am, as a matter of fact."

"Then we've got a date. Would you like to go to Tour d'Argent?"

"I'd love it."

"Then I'll knock on your door at eight. Is that okay with you, Jess?"

"Yes, it is. I can't wait to see you."

CHAPTER EIGHTEEN

They sat together in the garden, under the ancient cherry tree, the old woman and her younger companion. The renowned teacher and her favorite former student.

Anya and Alexandra.

Two peas in a pod, Nicky Sedgwick called them because he thought they were so alike. Two women of such disparate backgrounds and upbringing, and yet, if he hadn't known otherwise, he would have said they were of the same blood, the same family. But then, most people thought *he* was a blood relative of Anya's, not her great-nephew by marriage.

In a way, this was understandable, as she had worked her magic on him since the day he was born. He was her creature just as Alexandra was.

Nicky was standing inside Anya's house, staring through the window at the two women. They were drinking their after-lunch coffee at the wrought-iron table, and chatting as animatedly as they always did. They look so comfortable with each other, he thought. Alexa was just like a young woman confiding in her grandmother.

His former assistant was as lovely looking as ever, he noticed, although her dark hair was cut shorter. It was chic, and she was certainly smartly turned out in her man-tailored gray pinstripe jacket and matching short skirt. All the better to see those gorgeous legs, he thought, his eyes sweeping over her. He liked the sleek hair style; it showed off her long neck and pretty ears. She wore gold earrings and a gold chain around her neck. As always, she was understated during the day. Alexa had always had perfect style in his book.

Next to Alexandra Gordon, Anya was the grande dame personified, so regal in her bearing, and as good-looking as ever with her stylish blond hair and perfect makeup. Anya was dressed in what she called her working uniform: gray flannel slacks, a white silk shirt, and a navy blue blazer. It makes her look so English, Nicky decided, but then, she is very English in so many things, even though she has lived in France since her mid-twenties. When she spoke English she sounded like an upper-class Englishwoman; once she launched into her perfect French she could easily be mistaken for a Parisienne; and, naturally, when she spoke her native language, learned at her father's knee, she was as Russian-sounding as the prince had been. That was a special talent, being able to speak foreign languages well. His uncle Hugo had been equally as adept at them as Anya.

Glancing at his watch, realizing that the time was ticking away, Nicky now stepped out into the garden, exclaiming, "Good afternoon, ladies!"

They both stopped talking and looked across at him. Then Alexa leapt to her feet, ran to greet him, threw her arms around his neck. After their long, smoochy embrace, he held her away. "Well, ain't you looking great, laidy," he said in his best Cockney accent.

She laughed. He had sounded just like Jack did when he spoke Cockney.

Nicky said, "I'm sorry I arrived a bit earlier than expected, and interrupted your time with Anya." He now glanced across at his aunt. "Sorry, old thing."

"That's perfectly all right, Nicky dear, we'd more or less finished our lovely, long discussion anyway, hadn't we, Alexa?"

"I suppose so, although you know I can go on listening to you forever," Alexa responded, going back to her chair under the cherry tree.

Anya smiled. "Let's listen to Nicky instead. And, Nicholas darling, please do sit down. I can't stand you hovering there like an anxious waiter in a half-empty bistro nervously waiting to take an order."

Nicky began to laugh as he strode over to one of the wrought-iron chairs arranged around the table and sat down.

Turning to face Alexandra, touching her arm with a loving hand, Anya felt it was necessary to give the young woman an explanation.

She said, "I asked Nicky to do something for me last week, and it has to do with you, Alexa. But I do take full responsibility, I just want you to know that, to understand it was not Nicky's idea, but mine. Now I think he's here to report to me."

Looking puzzled, Alexa frowned, then glanced from Anya to Nicky, but she made no comment.

"A few weeks ago, Anya had the feeling you probably wouldn't come to her birthday party because of Tom Conners," Nicky began. "She felt you might be uncomfortable in Paris because of your past with him, and how you parted. She suggested I make a few inquiries about Tom to ascertain what he was doing, what his status was in general."

"I see," Alexa murmured, sounding noncommittal, but she felt herself tensing in the chair. She crossed her legs, then sat very still.

"Then almost in the same breath I told Nicky not to do it," Anya interjected, looking at Alexa carefully. "Because I felt that for him to poke around in Tom's life was like playing God, and in effect it was being a megalomaniac."

"So I didn't do anything," Nicky remarked. "Until this past week, when Anya used her woman's prerogative and changed her mind."

"He's still in Paris, that I do know," Alexa announced.

She surprised them both, and they exchanged quick, knowing glances.

Alexa noticed this, and went on. "When I received your invitation to the party, I called him at his office, on his private line, actually. Then I hung up when he answered. I guess I lost my nerve."

"So he has been on your mind," Anya muttered. "I thought as much." She felt justified for enlisting Nicky's help.

"Yes, Anya, he has. You see, I want to get rid of this unfinished business of mine. Then perhaps I can move on with my life."

"Good girl!" Anya exclaimed, beaming at her in approval. "Well, I suppose we've done your legwork for you. Or Nicky has, at any rate. He's probably saved you some time, actually."

Alexa nodded. She was now eager to hear what he had to say.

"I made a few calls, spoke to several people I know who know him," Nicky began, leaning forward slightly, giving Alexa a very direct look. "Basically, nothing's changed in Tom's life, Alex. He's not married, nor is he seeing anyone special as far as I've been able to ascertain. Although I do hear there are a few women circling him, so to speak. But that's normal, under the circumstances. He's very good-looking, charming, successful, and a bachelor. It's to be expected. He's still with the same law firm, but then, you already know that. I guess I have to say that everything seems to be status quo." Nicky sat back in the chair, and then turned his head, glanced at Anya.

"And that's all you found out?" Anya asked with a frown. "Nothing more, Nick?"

He shook his head. "Not very much, really. Tom even lives in the same apartment. But one of the chaps I know at Clee Donovan's photo news agency is an old buddy of Tom's and—"

"That's got to be Charles Dugdale," Alexa swiftly cut in, "they're good friends."

"Correct." Nicky gave her a faint smile, and added, "Charlie told me that Tom inherited money from a relative recently, and that he's bought a property in Provence. A farm or an estate, I'm not sure."

Anya's face lit up. "Oh, really, how very interesting! I wonder if he's anywhere near me?"

Nicky burst out laughing. "Anya, you're incorrigible! Always looking for dinner and luncheon guests, eh, old thing? Always wanting interesting company."

"And why ever not? Interesting company's much better than the bores, wouldn't you agree?"

Nicky smiled at her lovingly. "You'll be happy to know then that Tom's place *is* near your house. He's just outside Aix-en-Provence."

"Lovely," Anya replied, her eyes sparkling with pleasure.

"Does this mean Tom is leaving Paris? Leaving the law firm?" Alexa ventured, her eyes questioning.

"I don't know," Nicky answered her. "Charlie wasn't sure about that. I'm afraid you have the sum total of everything I found out, Alex, except that he's fit and well and, according to my friend Angelique, the famous casting director, he's still as good-looking as ever." He grinned at her. "A taller version of the other Tom."

Anya frowned and repeated, "The other Tom? Of whom are you speaking, Nicky?"

"Cruise. Tom Cruise."

"Oh, Nicky, you are such a pest with all of these eternal film references of yours!" Anya mildly chastised him. "Half the time I never know who you're talking about." Reaching out, she now took hold of Alexa's hand and went on softly. "Well, darling, you now know which way the land lies. Why don't you call Tom this week-end? But this time, if a machine answers, please leave a message, for heaven's sake, otherwise we'll get nowhere very fast."

Alexa laughed, suddenly feeling lighter than she had in ages, as if a weight had been lifted off her chest. "Thanks for doing the leg-work, Nicky. I owe you one. And in the meantime, when are we go-ing to get together to discuss the movie? Later today?"

"I'm afraid not," Nicky exclaimed, and glanced at his watch. "I'm sorry, Alexa, but I have to leave. My apologies, Anya, for this . . . hit-and-run visit, but I have to go home to change. I have a special dinner date tonight." Rising, he went over to Anya, bent over his aunt, and kissed her cheek. "I'm taking Maria to dinner, you'll be glad to hear."

"I am indeed very pleased, she's a lovely young woman," Anya re-sponded, and patted his hand resting on her shoulder.

Moving around the table, he went to Alexa and kissed her. "We can lunch tomorrow if you're free," he said.

"I am, Nicky, that'll be great. Where shall we meet?"

"I'll take you to the Relais at the Plaza-Athénée. I know you like it there. Let's meet at one. Okay?"

"That's perfect," Alexa answered.

Anya got up, tucked her arm through his, and walked back to the house with him. "Thank you so much, Nicky, for finding out about Tom. I do appreciate it."

"I think Alexa does too," he murmured in a low, confiding voice. "Don't you think she looks tremendously relieved? Probably to know he's still single."

"Perhaps," Anya replied, not quite sure if this was the case or not. In her long years as a teacher she had learned one thing: Young women could be very tricky.

CHAPTER NINETEEN

"I'm so glad you don't think I'm a meddlesome old woman," Anya said to Alexa after she had ushered Nicky out and returned to the table under the cherry tree. She sat down, sighing lightly as she did. "Some people might, darling girl, and it would truly upset me if *you* did."

"First, I never think of you as *old,* and second, you were not meddling. I suspect you wanted to find out what was happening with Tom in order to protect me," Alexandra asserted. "Forewarned is forearmed. I can just hear you thinking that. Am I correct?"

"Absolutely."

"I'm very surprised I didn't get a lecture from Nicky," Alexa suddenly blurted out, and added, "He was also protective of me years ago, and he and Larry kept cautioning me about Tom. They both said he would only cause me grief."

"I know Nicky can be a pain in the neck at times, but he's a good person, and very devoted to *you*. Anyway, let's face it, Alex, in this instance he wasn't far off the mark, was he? And neither was Larry."

"You're right, as usual." Alexa gave Anya a concentrated stare and asked pointedly, "A few minutes ago, was Nicky referring to Maria *Franconi?* Is that who he meant?"

"I do believe he did." Anya sat back, eyed Alexa, averted her face for a moment, endeavoring to stifle the laughter bubbling in her throat. Alexa had obviously been taken aback by Nicky's announcement about his dinner date. Her expression was one of such horror, it was actually comical. She knew that Alexa and Maria had locked horns at one point, just before their graduation, and there was no love lost there. She's appalled at the idea of Nicky, her favorite, being with Maria, Anya decided.

"I can't believe it! And certainly I don't get it. He's married. To Connie Aykroyd." Alexa shook her head; her expression one of puzzlement mixed with annoyance.

"Not anymore, at least not for much longer. Seemingly, that marriage is over, except for the shouting. And the legalities, of course. Nicky moved out a long, long time ago, and I suppose he feels he can date other women if he wishes. And if the woman is willing."

"And obviously Maria Franconi is . . . oh, my God, Anya, what a weird *mix!*"

"Oh, I don't know about that. I rather think you're wrong, darling. Actually, Nicky's quite taken with her."

"*Really?* How amazing. How is she, anyway?"

"Maria appears to be very well. And pleased that she managed to lose forty-eight pounds."

"Maria got *fat?*" Alexa exclaimed, and then she laughed. Her eyes narrowed. "Oh, dear, oh, dear, all that pasta, I guess."

Anya bit back a smile. She was amused that for once in her life Alexa was being a little bitchy. She said, "People get fat for all kinds of reasons. But at least Maria did something about her weight. She went on a very strenuous fitness regime, and obviously it worked. Because she's so tall, she carries the remaining bit of extra weight very well. And she does have a remarkable face, you know."

"Yes, she *is* beautiful, I'll concede that."

Anya frowned. "From your tone, I can tell you're still troubled by Maria, and her *treachery*. Isn't that what you called it once?"

"She *was* treacherous," Alexa responded in a hard voice, one that brooked no argument.

"Are you still reluctant to talk to me about it after all these years?"

"Yes, I am, Anya. It was awful, very unpleasant, and she was a bitch. She was extremely unfair to me."

After sixty years of experience as a teacher, Anya knew better than to press the point at this moment. Instead, she said, "Jessica is here also, and I heard from Kay Lenox the other day. She'll be arriving imminently, if she's not already here. I do sincerely hope the four of you are going to be able to bury your differences. . . ." She let the sentence slide away.

Alexa looked at her quickly, at once noticing the slightly plaintive tone in Anya's voice. Reaching out, she patted her hand. "Of course we are." She began to laugh, and exclaimed, "I'll beat them *all* into submission . . . they'll behave well at your party, take it from me they will!"

Anya chuckled. "Oh, Alex, you can always make me laugh when you want to, especially when you try to be tough."

"I am tough."

"Not you, darling girl."

"I hope I am. I don't want to be a cream puff. Where is that going to get me in this world? I hope I am *really tough,* because that means I'm strong and resilient. That's what tough means to me."

"Yes, you're right, actually. Let's not mix up the words *tough* and *hard;* they have very different meanings indeed. I cannot bear hard women because they're so hard-bitten, so emotionless, without feelings. What was it Hemingway once said? 'I love tough dames but I can't stand hard broads.' Well, anyway, it was something like that."

Anya looked off into the distance for a few seconds, and there was a small silence. And then suddenly, unexpectedly, she said: "I once knew a man like your Tom Conners, and it became very difficult for me in the end."

"When was that?" Alexa asked gently. She was startled by Anya's angry voice, the odd twist to her mouth. A bitter twist, she thought.

"Oh, long ago. A few years after my darling Hugo died. I met another man, as one does if one is out in the world, living life, doing things, and not becoming a dullard, a bore, by staying at home doing nothing. He was a widower. His wife had died of cancer when she was very young. It *was* a tragedy, she was only in her twenties apparently. But, you see, he used her death constantly to prevent our relationship from going where it should have gone. His dedication to her memory, survivor guilt—all of those things got in the way."

"What happened in the end?"

"One day I left him. It wasn't worth it to me. I couldn't understand why *I* had to be made to suffer because another woman had died too young, too soon. And I was getting awfully tired of being compared to a dead woman who had become a plaster saint in his eyes."

"Did he . . . ever remarry, Anya?"

"Not to my knowledge."

"And where is he now?"

"Oh, goodness, how do I know! Dead probably. Or still marching around with that cross on his shoulders, feeling sorry for himself, being selfish in his continuing grief." Anya shivered slightly and pushed herself to her feet. "It's growing cooler, Alexa, let's go inside. Look, the sun is already hidden by the clouds."

Together they walked toward the lovely old house with its black-

and-white façade so reminiscent of Normandy architecture. Anya led the way, and Alexandra followed her into the small library that opened off the garden.

Anya went around the room, turning on lamps, saying to Alexa as she did, "Darling, do me a favor and light the fire. There's a sudden chill in the air. You'll find the Swan Vestas in that copper bucket filled with logs."

"Right away," Alexa responded, and knelt down in front of the fireplace. There were rolled pieces of newspaper and chips of wood in the grate, and she immediately spotted the matches in the copper bucket, struck a match, brought the flame to the paper. It caught with a *whoosh,* and she knelt there until the chips also ignited, when she put on several small logs. Then she got up.

Dusting her hands together, Alexa walked over to a small upholstered chair and sat down. Anya was already propped up against a pile of pillows on the love seat opposite. "Thank you, Alex."

Then, picking up the conversation where she had left off, Anya continued. "Those sort of men are not worthy of a woman like me, or you either. So do me a favor, and yourself. Deal with Tom Conners. Don't drag it out. And if you find it necessary to walk away, then walk away. Get on with your life without him if there's no alternative. You'll meet another man one day." She gave Alexa a hard stare. "In fact, I'm surprised you haven't done so already."

"Oh, but I have, Anya. Jack . . . that's his name . . . Jack Wilton . . . he's an artist, very talented and successful. He wants to marry me."

"And you, Alex? How do you feel?"

"I like Jack a lot, I love him actually, but . . ." She shook her head. "It's not the same as it was with Tom. As I just said, Jack wants us to get married, and we're sort of engaged, well, unofficially."

She bit her lip and looked away. When she finally brought her eyes back to Anya, they were troubled. "I have too much integrity to marry one man while still yearning for another," Alexa finished quietly.

"Yes, you always have been a very honorable young woman. But what is honor worth if it is honor without courage? Don't be afraid, Alexa . . . don't be afraid to confront Tom, *and* Jack, if you have to . . . take your courage in both hands and be honest in your confrontations."

"I know, you're right, Anya. Honesty is the only thing that works in the end."

"Be brave . . . it's not as hard as you think." Anya smiled at her encouragingly, then glanced at the small desk in one corner of the room. "There's the telephone." She brought her gaze back to Alexa. "Go on, call Tom now. See how he reacts to hearing from you."

For a moment, Alexandra was thrown off balance, and she found herself shrinking back in the chair. And then she stood up very determinedly and walked across the room. She said to Anya as she stood at the desk with her hand on the phone, "What have I got to lose?"

"Nothing. Nothing at all. But you do have everything to gain, one way or another."

Alexa picked up the receiver. She noticed her hand was shaking, but she ignored this and dialed his private line at the office.

"Tom Conners," he answered, on the second ring.

She found it impossible to breathe. Just the sound of his voice had paralyzed her. She was shaking inside. She leaned against the desk, swallowing; her mouth was dry.

"Tom Conners *ici*," he said again in a level tone of voice.

"Hello, Tom, it's—"

He cut her off. "Alexa—where are you calling from?"

Momentarily startled by his instant recognition of her voice, she couldn't speak. And then she said swiftly in a rush of words, "I'm in Paris, and I'm fine, Tom. How're you?"

"Okay, doing okay. Are you in Paris on business?"

"Sort of," she answered, glad that she sounded normal. "But I really came for Anya's eighty-fifth birthday." She glanced at Anya and saw that she was mouthing something. Leaning forward over the desk, frowning, Alexa tried to figure out what Anya was silently saying.

"Invite him if he doesn't invite you," Anya finally said aloud in a stage whisper.

"It's hard to believe Anya's going to be eighty-five," Tom was saying, laughing. "Can we get together, Alexa? Will you have time?"

She felt herself going weak with relief on hearing these words. "Yes. I'd like to see you. When?"

"Are you available this weekend? What about lunch tomorrow?"

"I can't, I'm afraid. I'm meeting Nicky Sedgwick for lunch. I'm going to be working on a film with him later in the year, and we have quite a lot to go over. So I can't really change it."

"That's okay. What about tomorrow night? Are you free?"

"Yes."

"Shall we have dinner?"

"That'll be nice, Tom."

"Where are you staying?"

"The Meurice."

"I'll come for you around six-thirty, is that all right with you?"

"It's fine. See you then."

"Great," he said, and hung up.

Alexa stood clutching the phone, staring at Anya, a stunned expression on her face.

Anya began to laugh. "You look shell-shocked, Alexa. As if you can't believe it."

"I can't," she replied, and dropped the receiver into the cradle.

Anya said, "It wasn't so hard after all, was it?"

"Not really, but I *was* shaking. Inside and out."

"I know. There are men who have that effect on women, and of course they are lethal."

"I guess I *am* still in love with him," Alexa began, but her voice faltered.

"Perhaps you are. But you won't know how you truly feel until you see him tomorrow night."

Leaning back in the chair, Alexa merely nodded, once more finding it difficult to breathe. And then she thought: Tom is lethal. He's always been lethal for me.

CHAPTER TWENTY

Kay wondered, as she walked up the Champs-Élysées, how she could have stayed away from Paris all this time. Even though it was only an hour by plane from London, and not much longer from Edinburgh, she never "hopped over" as many people did, because Ian did not like to travel, and she wanted to be with him on the weekends.

Still, Paris was a city of fashion on all levels, and she was in the fashion business, and she realized now that she should have come more often than she had. There was so much to see here, and to learn, as she had rediscovered in the last few days. Silently, Kay chastised herself.

A moment later she thought of the happy years she had spent at Anya's school; Anya was another reason she should have come over, because the famed teacher had been her great mentor and her truest friend.

Everyday life intrudes, she muttered under her breath, but that's really no excuse. How often she had wanted to confide in Anya, to ask her advice, and yet she had diligently stayed away. This, too, perplexed her. But now was not the time to analyze her behavior, she knew that, and she pushed all such thoughts to one side. There were other situations to deal with, other problems to solve.

Taking a deep breath, Kay glanced about her. Paris *was* the most beautiful city, and she noticed that it was particularly lovely this morning. The sky was a light cerulean blue filled with sweeping white clouds, and bright sunlight washed over the ancient buildings. She remembered now that many of them had been cleaned for the millennium celebrations, and the stone façades gleamed whitely in the clear light, looked as if they had just been newly built.

Staring ahead, Kay's eyes now fastened on the Arc de Triomphe at the top of the long avenue. Underneath that soaring arch the tricolor, the red, white, and blue French flag, fluttered in the light breeze. The sight made her catch her breath . . . there was something so poetic and moving about that simple flag flaring in the wind.

Because it symbolizes a country's courage and triumph, she reminded herself, thinking of the many history classes she had attended at Anya's school.

Anya taught them, although they were not actually part of her master class. She was an expert in the history of the Second World War, having lived through that war, and she loved to teach about it, and what had happened on both sides of the Channel at that terrible time. How horrible it would have been if these magnificent buildings had been blown to smithereens by the Nazi Occupation forces, as Hitler had wanted. In 1944 the Allied armies were rapidly approaching Paris, and Hitler had commanded General von Choltitz to blast the historic monuments so that the Allied forces would be greeted by smoke and debris. Dynamite had already been laid under the Arc de Triomphe, Les Invalides, the Eiffel Tower, and the Cathedral of Nôtre-Dame, among others. But at the last minute, General von Choltitz had not had the heart to blow up such extraordinary edifices.

Close call that was, she thought as she finally came to the Place Charles de Gaulle, where the Arc de Triomphe stood. How dwarfed she felt by this massive structure, built on the instructions of Napoleon to celebrate his greatest victory at Austerlitz. At the time, he had promised his men they would go home through triumphal arches. And ever since this arch had been completed, long after Napoleon had lost his power, it was the starting point for national victory parades and celebrations.

She had once gone up to the top, where she had stood with Anya, Alexa, Jessica, and Maria, looking out across Paris. It was then, and only then, that she had truly understood why the arch was also called the Étoile—the star. It was at the very center of twelve avenues that radiated out to form a star. Many were named after famous generals, and had been part of the modernization of Paris by Baron Haussmann, which had begun in 1852.

As she moved through and around the arch, Kay had a sudden unexpected thought . . . of a woman who, like her, had been unable to give the man she loved an heir . . . the empress Josephine. And eventually Napoleon had had to divorce her in order to father a son by another woman. He had not been particularly happy with Marie-Louise, daughter of the Austrian emperor, even though she had eventually given birth to a boy. It had been a diplomatic marriage, and Napoleon had forever yearned for Josephine. At least so Anya had told them in one of her other history lessons. "His luck changed the day he left Josephine. Unhappiness and disasters followed him to the grave," Anya had explained dourly.

Sighing to herself, Kay wandered away from the great arch, crossed over to the Champs-Élysées, began to walk down this most imposing boulevard, thinking of Dr. François Boujon. She had gone to see him yesterday at his office on Avenue Montaigne to discuss her own inability to conceive. She had an examination and tests, and depending on the results of the tests he had taken, she might have to spend a few days at his clinic in Barbizon, near Fontainebleau. His reputation as an expert on fertility preceded him, and after some years in California he had finally returned to practice in his native France.

Kay had made the appointment with him weeks ago, and yesterday she had been very nervous when she had sat waiting in the reception area of his offices. But within moments of meeting him she had found herself relaxing. He was the kind of doctor who immediately put a patient at ease, at least *she* felt that way.

Dr. Boujon had asked her a lot of questions before the examination, most of which she had answered truthfully. But in some instances she had felt it necessary to lie. And now these lies troubled her, which was one of the reasons she had set out early for her appointment with Anya.

Kay knew herself, and she was well aware that if she sat in the hotel worrying she would drive herself to distraction. Better to be out and about than confined within four walls, contemplating disasters that might never happen.

After a while, she came to Avenue George V, and she walked slowly along the street, heading toward the Place de l'Alma. In the distance, dominating the skyline, she could see the Eiffel Tower, and she remembered something Nicholas Sedgwick had once told her. That wherever she looked in Paris she would see either the Eiffel Tower or the great white domes of the Sacré-Coeur, and that was true.

She wondered how Nicky was, and the others . . . the girls who had been her companions for three years. Once they had been close friends, and it struck her now that their quarrels had been rather harsh at the end. Would they be able to enjoy Anya's party if they didn't make up? She was doubtful. For a long time she had thought of them as being bitchy and unfeeling, but perhaps she was being judgmental after all. Life was too short, wasn't it, and there were so many other things infinitely more important than female quarrels. And quarrels that had happened seven years ago, at that.

Anya had said this to her last night when they had spoken on the phone, pointing out that they should all try to act in a mature manner. And Anya was right.

————

Kay found a table at a small café on a side street just off the Place de l'Alma. She felt quite ravenous all of a sudden and needed to eat; then she remembered she had not really had breakfast, only a cup of tea, and now it was almost one.

When the waiter came, she ordered a tomato omelette, a green salad, and a bottle of sparkling water. Once her order had been taken, she sat back, watching the passersby for a moment or two, but mostly she was thinking about her life, and in particular her husband, Ian, whom she loved so much.

He, who was not at all enamored of traveling, had been forced to fly to New York the other day in order to deal with an unexpected business matter to do with the woolens they produced at the Scottish mills. He had gone instead of his partner, Vincent Douglas, who had broken an arm and a leg in a car accident. And how he had grumbled about going and right up to the last minute.

Poor Ian, she thought, stuck in a hotel in Manhattan. He was such a countryman at heart and in spirit, one who truly felt uncomfortable in most cities, and especially a great metropolis like New York.

He would be gone for ten days, and in that time Kay hoped to finish her tests with Dr. Boujon; she also planned to find the perfect premises for a boutique. Her assistant, Sophie McPherson, was arriving next week, and together they would work with the real estate agent who had been highly recommended.

Although Paris was one of the greatest fashion centers of the world, with haute couture houses, and top-, middle-, and lower-scale manufacturers and designers, Sophie had somehow convinced her there was a need for her clothes.

But the idea of opening a boutique in this fashion-conscious and most stylish of cities had not appealed to her in the beginning; it was Sophie—young, enthusiastic, and highly committed to the running of the boutiques—who had persuaded her otherwise.

Sophie had pointed out that her clothes were selling tremendously well in Britain and the United States, and that they would find a huge market in Paris.

So be it, Kay thought, letting out a sigh. She could try, and hopefully she would succeed. She generally tended to take Sophie's advice, trusting her judgment, knowing that her assistant seemed to have her finger on the pulse of fashion for the young woman of today.

As she sipped the sparkling water, Kay's thoughts drifted in various directions. Soon she found herself focusing on those years she had lived in Paris. Home had been a small, cozy hotel on the Left Bank, and she had loved her tiny room in it, and the quarter where it was located, just off the Place Saint-Michel.

Maybe she would take a walk down the rue de la Huchette later in the day, and pop into the Hôtel Mont Blanc, where she had lived for three years. She wondered if Henri, the lovely old concierge, still worked there. He had always been so kind and considerate, and concerned about her.

Kay's time in Paris had been the happiest years for her, and for various reasons. She was far away from the slums of Glasgow; she was safe, *that* most of all; she was attending the famous school she had dreamed about for years, never believing she would actually become a pupil there at the age of nineteen.

At the Anya Sedgwick School of Decorative Arts, Design, and Couture, Kay had studied fashion design with the renowned teachers Eliane Duvalier and Jean-Louis Pascal. But she had also taken Anya's master class in classical art, as well as her three history classes that dealt with eighteenth-century France, imperial Russia, and the Second World War on both sides of the English Channel.

Kay had enjoyed every one of her classes on various subjects, and her dreams and hopes and ambitions for the future had been fueled and strengthened here. For the first time in her life she had felt special and worthwhile, thanks to Anya's loving encouragement and belief in her. This sense of inner worth had been totally reinforced by the other teachers who had shown their genuine belief in her and her abilities.

When her mother had first sent her away from Scotland, Alice had actually taken her to Yorkshire, to Harrogate at the edge of the Dales, where she had enrolled Kay in an old and respected school, Harrogate College. There were other girls attending the college who were boarders, as she was, and they all became good friends, and once she had settled in, she found great pleasure in learning.

Being away from the bad environment in Scotland had given her a sense of enormous relief; she felt secure, not so vulnerable and exposed anymore. The courses at the college were liberating, and her inbred talent soon found release. It flowered. Her potential was so apparent, so highly visible to the teachers working there, they were frequently startled by it.

She missed her mother very much, and Sandy as well, but her mother never permitted her to come back home. Whenever Alice could, she came south to Yorkshire in order to see Kay, and those times had been very special and meaningful to them both. "Remember this, lassie," Alice Smith would say. "There is no such person as Jean Smith. She does not exist. You are Kay Lenox now. New name. New identity. New life. New future. There's no going back, not in any way."

Her mother's voice seemed to echo in the inner recesses of her mind, always encouraging, always speaking about her new life and her future. In a way, her mother had sacrificed herself in order to give *her* a better life.

She made everything possible, Kay thought. And I do have so much. But I'm always afraid of losing it. I can't enjoy what I have. That is the problem.

Things are going to be all right, she now told herself firmly. They had to be.

CHAPTER TWENTY-ONE

How truly beautiful she has become, Anya thought, staring across at Kay Lenox, who had arrived at her house a few moments ago.

Because it was such a warm and sunny day, Honorine, the housekeeper, had shown her to the table in the garden, which had been set for tea. But Kay had obviously immediately risen from her chair and strolled across the cobbled courtyard.

Now she waited under the cherry tree, gazing off into the distance, one hand resting on the trunk, surrounded by the double cherry blossoms of palest pink that dropped down around her. She was unaware she was being observed, and her face held a dreamy, faraway expression.

Kay is so tall, long-legged, and slender, she looks almost ethereal, Anya commented to herself, wishing she had a camera, so lovely was the image of Kay under the ancient flowering tree.

Sunlight slanted through the branches laden with blossoms, and it was turning her hair into a halo of shimmering red-gold fire. She still wore it long, as she had when she had come to the school at nineteen, and from this distance Anya thought Kay did not look as if she had aged a day since then. She wore a tailored outfit of delphinium blue, composed of very narrow trousers worn with high-heeled blue pumps and a three-quarter-length jacket styled in the manner of a maharajah's tunic. It had buttons down the front and a small stand-up mandarin collar, and it was flattering on her.

The outfit was simplicity itself, but so beautifully made it was elegance personified. Well, she always was enormously talented, a little couturier even when she first came to me, Anya thought to herself.

Stepping into the courtyard, Anya exclaimed, "Kay darling, here I am! So sorry to keep you waiting." She hurried forward, her face radiant with smiles, her joy at seeing Kay after so long reflected in her sparkling eyes.

Kay immediately swung around, then rushed forward at the sight of Anya, almost tottering on those very high heels. She embraced Anya, holding her tightly. After a moment, Kay looked into her teacher's face, and her own happiness was transparent. "It's just wonderful to see you!"

"I might well say the same thing, Kay. But come, my dear, let's go and sit at the table and have a cup of tea, like old times. I want to hear all of your news."

Together the two women walked over to the wrought-iron table Honorine had covered with a linen cloth. All the accoutrements for afternoon tea were set out: Aside from the big silver teapot, matching milk jug and sugar basin, there was a plate of lemon slices. On a tiered silver stand Honorine had arranged an assortment of the small nursery-tea sandwiches, as Anya called them, and plain biscuits. There was also a sponge cake filled with jam and whipped cream. Plus an English fruit cake, dark and rich-looking, its top decorated with blanched almonds.

Picking up the silver pot, Anya poured tea into the china cups, then sat back, staring at Kay.

The young woman was simply spectacular to look at, with her tumbling red hair, cool, polished ivory skin, and blue eyes. "Kay, you are stunning!" Anya finally exclaimed admiringly. "And so grown-up. Very elegant." Her eyes twinkled and she beamed at her. "What a pleasure it is to see you looking so . . . *fantastic.*"

Kay shared her smile. "I guess I *was* a bit awkward and gangly even when I graduated, wasn't I?"

"Never quite that," Anya protested, dropped a slice of lemon into her tea. "And congratulations on your extraordinary success. You've done the school proud. But then, we all knew you would."

"It's thanks to you, Madame Eliane, and Monsieur Jean-Louis, that I am where I am today. And of course my mother. Without her I would have been . . . *nothing.*"

Anya noticed the shadow that suddenly blighted Kay's eyes, fading their color as she spoke of Alice, dead for some time now. Mother and daughter had been very close, symbiotic, unusually devoted to each other. She was well aware that Alice had sacrificed much for Kay.

"We could only guide you, show you the way," Anya finally remarked. "You alone are responsible for your success, Kay."

"I remember you used to tell us that, as individuals, we were the authors of our own lives, and that only we ourselves could accept the accolades, or take the blame if our lives went wrong."

"But that did happen to be *your* philosophy when you enrolled at the school, Kay. I really only gave you the right words to properly express and explain what you appeared to already feel."

Kay nodded, sipped her tea, became silent, her face instantly serious, reflecting her myriad thoughts. She fell down into the past for a few seconds, remembering so many things.

It struck Anya that there was a certain . . . *regality* to Kay, that was the *only* word for it. And an inbred elegance. She was the true lady now in every sense—in bearing and manner as well as title. How amazing life could be for some people. Here she was, shy little Kay, who came to the school looking so undernourished, and quiet as a mouse, now a world-famous fashion designer, immensely successful, and the wife of a genuine aristocrat of breeding and wealth. Lady Andrews, wife of Ian, the Laird of Lochcraigie. Also Kay Lenox, couturier par excellence. There was a duality here, but it did spell triumph, and on a grand scale.

Well, she's simply . . . wondrous, Anya now thought, marveling at her former pupil. She had not known much about Kay when she had first arrived in Paris ten years before. Kay's personal history and background were somewhat shrouded in mystery, but her academic records from Harrogate College had told Anya a great deal. The girl was brilliant, no question about it.

Anya had instinctively known that Kay's early life had been poverty stricken. There had been a sort of tenacious grimness about her mother. Alice had been pretty but a little pinched, and she was tired-looking around the eyes. Thin as a rail, she looked as if she had never had a good meal in her life. In fact, there had been an aura of genuine deprivation about Alice, Anya now recalled, and a sadness that had stabbed at her most forcibly. Alice's sorrow had been a palpable thing, and like a knife in Anya, who had empathized with her.

What Kay has made of herself, the life she has created, is quite remarkable, she thought. She was truly proud of this young woman, who was a genuine success story.

Breaking the silence, Anya said, "I'm glad you came to Paris well before the party. It gives us a chance to visit, to catch up." Anya chuckled and her eyes were merry again. "The others were of the same mind as you, Kay. Alexa, Jessica, and Maria are also here."

"Oh" was all Kay could think of to say, and she wondered how they would all feel when they finally met again after all these years.

Anya was thinking of Alexa and Jessica, who both had unfinished business to deal with. Studying Kay, she asked herself if Kay also had a secret agenda tucked away.

Leaning forward slightly, she focused on the younger woman. "Did you come early for any special reason, Kay dear?"

"Yes, actually, I did." Kay turned to face Anya as she spoke, and continued. "I am thinking of opening a boutique here. My other shops have been very successful, and everyone believes my clothes will sell well in Paris."

"I'm quite certain that's true. And the idea is a marvelous one. Eliane and Jean-Louis will be most impressed and proud of you, as indeed I am."

"Thank you. Also, I have to go to Lyon to see the textile manufacturer who produces my silks and brocades. I have some special colors I want created for my next collection."

"You were always so clever with color. I love this delphinium suit. It makes your eyes look bluer," Anya murmured, then asked, "And how is your husband?"

At the mention of Ian, Kay sat up straighter. "He's well." She shook her head. "Well, I hope he is. He's in New York on business, and Ian's not very fond of cities. He's probably very depressed, and itching to get home to Scotland."

"Ah, yes, the countryman, you once told me."

"Yes." There was a slight pause. "So, the others are here? Have you seen them yet?"

"Maria, yes. Several times, in fact, and Alexa came to lunch yesterday."

"Are they both married now?"

"Oh, no."

"And what about Jessica?"

"I haven't seen her so far. But she's not married either. It appears that you are the only member of the quartet who has found the man of her dreams."

Kay sat back in the metal chair, gaping at Anya, a look of dismay flickering on her face. Unexpectedly, alarmingly, tears gathered in her eyes, were in danger of spilling over onto her cheeks.

"Whatever's the matter?" Anya asked, her surprise and concern apparent.

Kay did not speak. The tears began to fall.

"Darling, what *is* it?" Anya leaned closer across the table, touched Kay's arm to comfort.

Flicking the tears away with her fingertips, Kay said in a hesitating voice, "I'm so worried, Anya . . . about my marriage."

"Do you want to talk about it?"

Kay nodded. She took a deep breath, explained in a low, almost-inaudible voice, "I haven't become pregnant, and that's what's at the root of it all."

"Oh, yes, I understand, darling. Ian wants a son and heir. The title . . . the lands . . . *of course*. Yes, I do see."

Kay swallowed, cleared her throat. "Ian is a kind person, and he doesn't talk about it. He never has. But I just know it's always there, lurking at the back of his mind. And it's a kind of . . . *pressure* for me. It's always hanging over me."

"I know what you mean."

"I came to Paris for another reason," Kay confided. "To see Dr. François Boujon. I'm sure you've heard of him."

Anya nodded. "Yes, he is very famous, and brilliant. And very well respected, I might add. As the world's foremost fertility expert, I am sure he will be able to help you."

"Oh, Anya, I *hope* so."

"Have you seen him yet?"

"Yesterday. I had an examination, and tests—" Kay cut herself off, averted her head, bit her lip.

Anya watched her intently.

Kay brushed her eyes with her fingertips once more; she had begun to weep again.

"Are you all right?"

"I lied to Dr. Boujon," Kay blurted out, turning to Anya. Her eyes were agitated.

Startled by this announcement, Anya stared at Kay. "I'm not sure I'm following you. . . ."

"He asked me certain questions, and I didn't answer truthfully. I lied."

"But *why?*" Anya frowned, looked more perplexed than ever. "Whatever made you do that? It's not like you. You've always been so honest and forthright."

Biting her lip again, Kay did not respond for a moment. Then slowly, she explained. "I didn't want to tell him my *secrets*. I think it's better if people don't know . . . *things* . . . certain things about me."

"Secrets? What kind of secrets?"

"Once, a long time ago, you made a comment to Alexa and me. You said you had always lived by one rule—"

"I remember that day very well," Anya cut in. "I said that I never show weakness, never show face, and that this had worked for me, especially in business, but also in my private life sometimes."

"Yes, you did, and it's been *my* rule ever since. That's why I lied."

"I see." Anya leaned back in the chair, looking at her steadily. "And what *exactly* are you hiding from Dr. Boujon?"

"When he asked me if I'd ever been pregnant, I said no, I hadn't. But that's not true. I was pregnant once. Do you think he realized that when he examined me?"

"I'm not sure—" Anya paused, troubled. She studied Kay for a split second, then asked, "You lost the baby?"

Kay took a deep breath. "I had an abortion."

"Oh, *Kay.*"

"Don't look like that, Anya. *Please*, Anya, *please*. I was abused when I was very young. When I got pregnant I was only . . . *twelve.*"

Anya closed her eyes convulsively and sat very still for a long while. When she finally opened her eyes she thought the garden seemed just a little less sunny, as if the light had somehow dimmed. What a world we live in, what monsters some men are, she thought. Her face was no longer happy and laughing as it had been earlier, had become unusually somber, etched with dismay. And then her eyes filled with compassion and sympathy as she quietly regarded one of her favorite pupils.

Kay exclaimed, "It wasn't my fault, it wasn't!" and her voice was now high-pitched, almost shrill, and she grew agitated once more.

"Darling Kay, I know it wasn't your fault. I know *that* without your having to tell me." Anya reached out, put her hand on Kay's, her touch gentle and reassuring, she hoped.

Looking at her steadily, she saw that Kay's face was drained, whiter than usual, and she said after a moment's reflection, "Will it help to talk about it, do you think?"

"I've never told anybody . . . only Mam knew," Kay whispered.

Anya squeezed her hand, then sat back, poured more tea for them both. She was silent, waiting. Waiting for Kay to feel comfortable enough to speak to her about this most painful and heartbreaking matter.

CHAPTER TWENTY-TWO

It took Kay a short while to compose herself.

She sat back in the chair, took several sips of the fresh tea Anya had just poured, and forced herself to relax. Slowly her agitation and anxiety receded.

Her gaze was level, her voice steady as she looked across at Anya and said, "I think it's best if I start right at the beginning. My mother worked for a fashion designer in Glasgow named Allison Rawley. I was about seven when she first started as a saleswoman. But after a couple of years, Mam was running the shop. You see, Anya, she was a good organizer and manager. Anyway, Allison had a close friend, a titled woman who was English. They'd been at boarding school together, and she sometimes came to stay with Allison, and, of course, she bought things at the shop. This woman, who was a lovely person, offered my mother a job running her

house, with Allison's approval, of course. She thought Mam was ef-
ficient and capable. I was ten at the time."

"And your mother accepted the job?"

"Yes. How could she refuse? It sounded fantastic. The house
was on the Firth of Forth, near a place called Gullane, about thirty
minutes by car from Edinburgh. Her ladyship told Mam there was
no problem about us—Sandy and me—that we could go with her
and that we'd have our own quarters in the house. My mother saw
it as an opportunity to better her position in life, earn more money,
get us out of the city and into the countryside. There was a local
church school in the village, and everything sounded wonderful. So
she took the job."

Kay paused. "I don't think I'll ever forget that house, Anya . . . it
was so beautiful, inside and out. The grounds were magnificent,
and there were views of the Lammermuir Hills and that vast
stretch of water . . . the Firth of Forth. It was magical. But there
was a problem in that house, at least for me . . . his lordship."

"Was he the one who molested you?" Anya asked softly.

Kay nodded. "Not at first. And later, when he did, if his wife was
at the house, he was very careful. But her ladyship traveled a lot.
They had a flat in London and a country house in Gloucestershire,
so she was often away. It all started when we'd been living there for
about a year. I was ten and a half by then. At first it seemed almost
accidental, you know, he would brush against me, squeeze my
shoulder, stroke the top of my head in a fatherly sort of way. But
then he began to waylay me in the grounds, in the woods. He . . .
he touched me . . . you know . . . in the intimate places."

Not wanting to break the flow of her words, Anya simply nodded.

"After a few really bad incidents, I began to struggle all the time
with him, and I protested vehemently. He vowed to sack my
mother, send us all away if I didn't do what he wanted. He said he
would send us into penury, and I didn't know what that meant and

I was scared to death. I also knew what the job meant to Mam, to us as a family. Where would we live if we had to leave? And where was Penury? For the longest time I thought it was some awful place."

"And you never told your mother? Or anyone else?" Anya ventured.

"I was too afraid to say anything . . . afraid of him . . . of what he might do to us. And *could* do to us if he wanted. He was a powerful man, and we were poor, vulnerable, alone. Dad had been dead for years and we had only Grandma in Glasgow and she was poor."

"Oh, Kay dear," Anya murmured. "How terrible it must have been for you." Her face was bleak as she spoke, her eyes pained.

"It was horrendous, and very frightening. Then, as time went on, he became bolder, more aggressive, and he went further with me. I tried to hold him off, and I never stopped protesting and shouting and being voluble. But he shut me up. He was strong, and persistent, and he threatened me with dire trouble if I didn't do exactly what he wished. My only respite was when his wife returned from London occasionally."

"Did you feel you couldn't tell her about this?"

"How could I? Anyway, who would believe me? The daughter of the housekeeper accusing the master? Certainly she wouldn't have believed a word. I would have been branded a liar. I might have even been accused of coming on to him, Anya. Think about *that*. My mother would have been dismissed. So I steeled myself to his attacks, and stuck it out, hoping and praying he would never come back whenever he went to London. He always did. When I was almost twelve, he finally went, well, he went the whole way, Anya. He raped me one Saturday afternoon when my mother was in Edinburgh with Sandy."

Kay stopped again, took a sip of tea. After a few moments, she murmured, "That happened several times and I was in panic, very upset. Traumatized, I think, looking back. Then one day I missed my period, and I knew that what I'd feared had finally happened. I was certain I was pregnant. I was out of my mind with worry, and really terrified."

"And so you finally told your mother?"

"I did. I had no alternative. She was wonderful with me, and appalled about what had been going on. But she didn't blame me at all. She was in a fury, and flew into a blind rage when she went to see him. Straightaway, she threatened him with the law. She accused him of molesting a minor, said she was going to the police and that she would hire a solicitor in Edinburgh. She vowed to sue him. At first he denied coming anywhere near me, but there were no other men on the estate and we were in an isolated spot. Well, there were the two gardeners, but they were old, and the rest of the staff were women."

"So your mother went to the police."

Kay shook her head. "No, she didn't. She was about to do so, when his lordship offered her . . . a deal of sorts. He said he would send us to a doctor he knew in Edinburgh, one who would perform an operation on me, and that he would pay for it. He offered my mother three months' severance, and told her that we must all leave. Immediately."

"What happened? Did your mother accept, Kay?"

"No. She told him she'd think about it, and then in the end she turned it down. I suppose my mother was really quite a clever woman, even though she hadn't had a lot of education. Suddenly she understood she was holding all the cards. His lordship sat in the House of Lords, in London, he was a businessman, and very well known socially. He moved in all of the top social circles, and so did her ladyship. When she realized this, she made a counteroffer."

"And what was it?" Anya asked, leaning closer, her eyes fastened on Kay.

"She made sure she had all the information about the doctor in

Edinburgh, and had *him* make the appointment. Then she told him that what he offered wasn't enough for what he'd done to me . . . years of abuse, molestation as she called it, and rape. And rape over and over again, that had resulted in my pregnancy. She told him she wanted—" Kay broke off, took a deep breath. *"A million pounds."*

Anya gaped at her. For a moment she was speechless. At last she managed to say, "Did Alice get it? Don't tell me she actually got that much money?"

"No. She had asked for a lot because she knew she would have to bargain with him and she wanted room to maneuver. In the end he settled for four hundred thousand pounds."

"Good God!"

Kay nodded, then smiled faintly. "It *was* a lot of money, Anya. I think even my mother was surprised. She was expecting to settle for much less . . . about a hundred thousand."

"He must have been frightened out of his wits to pay that."

"I believe he truly was. He was a successful man, but he didn't have the kind of money his wife did. She was heiress to a vast industrial fortune. The last thing he wanted was to be exposed, at the center of a big scandal. Nor did he want to lose her money. Her ladyship was nice, I told you that, and if my mother had sought the help of a solicitor, gone to the police, she would have ultimately believed *us*. Not him. And she would have divorced him. I'm sure he realized that. Finally."

"And so he paid up?"

"Oh, yes. My mother wouldn't leave until his checks had cleared. Then we packed and went to Edinburgh, where Mam found a small flat for us all." Kay sat back, shaking her head, then she sighed, stared at Anya. Without flinching, she said, "It was blackmail. I recognized that when I was older. My mother saw an opportunity to help me, not only then, but in the future. And so she blackmailed him."

There was a silence.

Everything was very still in the garden. Not a leaf stirred, nor a blade of grass. Nothing moved at all. Even the birds were quiet.

But Anya's head buzzed with all that she had heard, and mostly she thought of Alice Smith, resorting to such a terrible thing as blackmail. And then she dismissed such a silly thought. What that depraved and sickening man had done to Kay was infinitely worse, and who could blame Alice Smith for demanding recompense? For that was what it really was. An eye for an eye, a tooth for a tooth, she thought. Such violence and depravity against a mere child would have caused some people to commit murder. Who could blame Alice for what she had done? The man had been monstrous, obscene.

"The money was used for your education, that's what Alice did with it. Didn't she?"

"Yes, and Sandy's. Some of it paid the rent of our little flat. And the fees for Harrogate College and your school here in Paris. Mam used it only for me, never for herself, except for the rent in the beginning. She always worked hard, and she saved. And the remainder of the money, which she'd put in a savings account at the bank, went to start my fashion business later."

"Alice was wise, Kay, very wise, and in so many different ways. But the abortion? What happened? You haven't really spoken about it. Was it botched?"

"I'm not sure. But that's what worries me, Anya, that the doctor accidentally did something to me all those years ago. Looking back, I think he was a bit inept, he certainly looked seedy, and he smelled of alcohol. Afterward, I bled a lot and I was in terrible pain for days. My mother almost had to take me to Emergency. At the hospital. But then I started to feel better—"

Kay stopped abruptly, looked away, and when she finally turned back to Anya, her eyes were dark with worry. "What if the doctor *did* damage me somehow?"

"I suppose he could have, but I think you would have known. Has everything . . . been all right over the years?"

"Oh, yes, but I'm not sure that means anything. Do you think, I mean, would Dr. Boujon know I'd had an abortion?"

"I told you earlier, I'm not certain, Kay dear. I think he would probably soon spot internal damage if there was any."

Kay looked at her for a moment, her face suddenly stark, her skin stretched across the bones tautly. Tears welled; she pressed her hands to her mouth and began to cry.

Anya rose and went to her, put her arms around her, endeavoring to comfort her as best she could. Kay clung to Anya, pushed her face against her body, sobbing. Anya soothed her, stroked her head, and eventually she became quieter.

After a few moments, Anya murmured, "He doesn't know, does he? You've never told Ian anything of this."

"How could I?" Kay whispered. "He knows nothing of my past. My mother created a whole new identity for me, and she had the money to back everything up. He'd die if he knew where I come from—" She paused, laughed hollowly. "The slums of Glasgow. And of course he'd divorce me. I know *that.*"

"You can't be sure, Kay, people can be very understanding."

"I'm not going to take such a chance, rest assured of that, Anya."

"Words are cold comfort in so many instances," Anya began gently, stroking Kay's hair again. "To say I'm sorry this happened to you is just not enough. It doesn't express the pain and hurt I feel for you, darling Kay. It was horrific, and I can well understand how traumatized and scared you must have been. You were so very young, just a little girl." Anya's voice shook slightly with sudden emotion, and she found she was unable to continue.

After a while, Kay pulled away, released her grip on Anya, and looked up at her. "I lived with fear once he'd started on me. But I was a dreamer, you know . . . I learned to dream in my very early childhood, and it kept me alive. I could escape to a better place."

"You've managed very well . . . I can't imagine what it was like for you. . . ."

"I learned one other thing, Anya."

"What is that?"

"I learned to arm myself against the world."

———

Honorine had come outside to tell Anya she had a phone call, and Anya had gone inside to take it. Kay was alone in the garden.

Her tears had ceased and she sat calmly in the chair, looking at her face in a small silver compact. There were a few mascara smudges around her eyes, and she removed these with a tissue, powdered the area lightly, and refreshed her lipstick. Then she put the compact and other items back in her handbag, and relaxed.

When Anya returned, she glanced at her and exclaimed, "As good as new, my dear. Are you feeling better?"

Kay smiled. "Yes, and thank you for listening, for being so patient and understanding, Anya. It's helped me." She paused, shook her head. "You see, I've never spoken about that part of my childhood to anyone except my mother. I think I buried it all so deep, it was hard to dredge up. Also, I didn't want to tell anyone my secret."

"There's just one thing I'd like to say. When you see Dr. Boujon again, he might ask you if you had an abortion, so be prepared for that. And frankly, Kay, I do believe you should tell him the truth."

Kay recoiled slightly, and stared at her. "That would be a bit hard for me—"

"You don't have to give him any of the intimate details," Anya interrupted. "I mean about the childhood abuse. Just the bare facts. If you *do* have some internal problem, he must be told your medical history in order to make a judgment."

"I suppose so," Kay reluctantly agreed.

"Of course, it's more than likely he'll have good news for you, tell you there's nothing wrong with you, no reason why you can't conceive." Anya peered at her. "Then you'll have to try to relax about getting pregnant. I suppose it goes without saying that adoption is out of the question?"

Kay nodded.

Anya went on. "So often, when a couple adopt a child, the wife immediately gets pregnant. The pressure is off, and I think that's what does it, helps a woman to conceive."

"Ian would want only a biological child to inherit the title."

Anya sat back, thinking Kay was probably right about this, but on the other hand, you never really knew about people. Also, it might not be Kay at all. There was the distinct possibility that Ian might be to blame; he could be sterile, or deficient in some way. She wondered if she dare suggest that he, too, should be tested, and then decided she had better not.

Instead, she reached across the table and took hold of Kay's hand. "You've been very brave and strong all of your life, Kay, and I'm so proud of you. And I want you to know I am always here for you, whatever you might need."

Kay was touched, and she responded, "Thank you for those words, Anya, and for being my friend, my one *true* friend."

This remark made Anya frown, and she exclaimed, "I hope I'm not your only friend, my dear."

"Well, sort of . . . I'm close to my assistant, Sophie, and also Fiona, Ian's sister, but, well, yes, you are my only really intimate friend."

How sad that is, Anya thought. She said, "It's such a pity your little quartet fell apart. You were all *so close* for three years, and then *puff!* Suddenly everything went up in smoke. I've never witnessed anything like it. And I do sincerely hope the four of you are going to come to terms with the situation, make an effort to set aside your differences and be friends again." Anya gave Kay a long and pointed look, and finished, "Take it from an old lady, life is too short to bear grudges, to carry animosity inside, so that it gnaws away like a canker."

"I agree," Kay answered, thinking that of the four of them, she was the least to blame. It was the others who had created the problems, not her.

CHAPTER TWENTY-THREE

Alexa looked at her watch as the phone began to ring.

It was exactly six-thirty. Snatching up the receiver, she said "Hello?" in a tight voice that didn't sound like her own, clutching the phone so hard, her knuckles shone whitely in the lamplight.

"It's Tom. I'm in the lobby."

"I'll be right down," she managed to answer, dropped the phone into the cradle, picked up her bag and shawl from a chair, and left the room.

As she waited for the elevator, she glanced at herself in a nearby mirror. Her hair was sleek, her makeup perfect; she wore a tailored black linen dress that would go anywhere, her only jewelry her watch and pearl earrings.

She took a deep breath as she stepped into the elevator. She was taut, so eager to see him she could hardly wait as the elevator slid downward. She saw him immediately, the moment she stepped out. He stood off to one side, near the entrance to the Jardin d'Hiver, but something had obviously distracted him and he was looking toward the main lobby and the concierge's desk.

Stupidly, ridiculously, she found she was unable to move. She stood, rooted to the spot, staring at him, shaking inside.

His face was in profile, but she saw at once that he was as handsome as ever, and immaculately dressed. He wore a dark blue blazer, gray trousers, and a blue shirt. His tie was silk, a blue-and-silver-gray stripe; his brown loafers gleamed.

She swallowed, trying to get a grip on herself, and then started in surprise as he suddenly turned his head abruptly and saw her at once.

His face was serious, unsmiling, as he walked toward her, his step and his demeanor full of confidence. But then he smiled suddenly, showing his perfect white teeth. His eyes were very blue. She saw, too, that his hair was now gray at the sides.

"Alexa," he said, taking hold of her arm, leaning toward her, kissing her cheek.

She pulled away almost at once, afraid he would hear the pounding of her heart. Swallowing, her mouth dry, she said, "Hello, Tom."

His vivid blue eyes searched her face for a split second, and he frowned. Taking hold of her arm, he said, "Let's have a drink, shall we?" He didn't wait for her answer, and in command, as he always was, he led her forward. They went into the Bar Fontainebleau that faced out through bay windows onto the Rivoli arches, positioned in front of the hotel's main entrance.

He guided her to a small table near a window in a corner, where they both sat down. A waiter was with them in an instant.

Tom looked across at her and raised a dark brow. "The usual?"

She nodded.

"Deux coupes, s'il vous plaît."

As the waiter disappeared in the direction of the long mahogany bar on the other side of the room, Tom looked at her intently, nodding his head, obviously in approval. "You haven't changed. You look exactly the same, except for your hair."

"I cut it."

"I can see that. It suits you. *Très chic.*"

She said nothing.

After a slight pause, Tom went on. "I've read a lot about you, Alexa. In the show business trades. You've been having a great success with your theatrical sets."

"Yes, but I've been lucky in many ways."

"I would say it has much more to do with talent."

She smiled at him weakly, wishing her heart would stop clattering in the way it was. She also wished she didn't have the overwhelming urge to clutch his hand resting on the small table between them. It took all of her self-control not to touch him.

The waiter was back at the table, depositing the two flutes of champagne in front of them.

Once they were alone, Tom picked up his glass and clinked it to hers. "*Santé.*"

"*Santé,*" she said, and gave him a wide smile.

He put down his drink. "At last," he murmured. "I thought that grim look was never going to disappear."

"I didn't know I was looking grim."

"Take it from me, you were." He leaned across the table, focused on her, the expression in his eyes more intense than ever. "I'm glad you called . . . I'm glad to see you, Alexa." When she remained silent, he asked, "Aren't you glad to see me?"

"Yes."

He laughed. "Such a poor little *yes.* So timid."

"Not at all. I *am* happy to see you, Tom. I wanted to see you, otherwise I wouldn't have called."

He reached out, took hold of her hand, held it tightly in his, scrutinizing her carefully. Then he glanced down at her hands. "Not married or engaged or otherwise taken?"

Alexa shook her head, not trusting herself to speak.

"There must be someone," he probed. "Or is every man blind where you live?"

She began to laugh—he had always managed to make her do that—and she shared his sense of humor. She was about to tell him there was no one special, but changed her mind. Instead, she said, "I have one friend. An artist. He's very nice. English." The words came out in a staccato delivery.

"Is it serious?"

"I—I—don't know," she began, and hesitated. "Well, perhaps he is serious."

"And what about you?"

"I'm . . . uncertain."

"I know what you mean."

"Is there someone special in your life?"

"No," he answered laconically.

"I can't imagine you haven't had, don't have, a girlfriend around."

"Of course. But make that plural. And none of them mean much to me."

She experienced such a surge of relief, her whole body went slack. She hoped he hadn't noticed this, said quickly, "I saw Nicky Sedgwick at Anya's the other day. He mentioned in passing that you'd bought a place in Provence. At least, that's what he'd heard."

"It is true. My French grandmother died. She left me a little money. I bought a small farm outside Aix-en-Provence, an olive farm."

"How great! Is it actually operating?"

"Limping." He grinned at her. "But I'm going to put a bit of money into it, hire extra help for the manager who runs it for me. But it will be a hobby, nothing more serious, *naturellement.*"

"So you're not giving up your law practice? Or leaving the city permanently?"

"Now, who could leave Paris? Certainly not I. And surely you know I'm not cut out to be a country boy."

"I do."

He took a sip of his champagne, and continued, "I booked a table at L'Ambroisie. In the Place des Vosges. But first I thought we could take a drive around Paris. It's such a beautiful evening, and you haven't been here for a long time. Three years."

———

A short while later he was leading her down the front steps of the hotel, his hand under her elbow, guiding her. As they moved along the sidewalk, he raised a hand, signaling to a driver a little farther along who was standing next to a car.

A moment later, Tom was helping her into the backseat of a maroon Mercedes and climbing in after her. Alexa slid along the seat, positioned herself in the corner; Tom took the other corner, and she placed her shawl and bag in between them, as if building a barrier.

She noticed him glance down at them, saw his mouth twitch as he attempted to swallow a smile. She suddenly felt slightly foolish, and racked her brain for some kind of suitable small talk, but without success. Once more she was shaking inside and felt as though she couldn't breathe. But this was not unusual. He had always had an extraordinary effect on her, and right from the beginning.

He was talking to the driver in rapid French, explaining where he should drive them . . . around the Place de la Concorde, up the Champs-Élysées, back down to the Seine, over to the Left Bank. She knew the latter was one of Tom's favorite parts of the city, an area where he had often driven her himself in the old days.

Once he had finished giving the driver these detailed instructions, he settled back in the corner, looked at her, and began to talk in an easy and effortless manner. "So, how is Nicky? I haven't run into him for a long time."

"He looks great, and he and Larry are more successful than ever."

"So I hear. And you're going to be working with them? Or is it just with Nick?"

"Nicky only. We had our first meeting today over lunch. And, of course, he always loves to rope me in when it's a costume picture . . . he knows I don't mind the historical research involved."

"And what's the movie?"

"It's about Mary Queen of Scots."

"To be made in France?"

"Well, yes, and in England and Ireland." Alexa broke off, exclaimed, "Oh, Tom, how beautiful the Place de la Concorde looks tonight . . . under this perfect sky."

He glanced out of the window and murmured, "Yes, it *is* a perfect sky, and there is such a marvelous clarity of light this evening. The city looks magnificent at this hour."

"A little bit later than the Magic Hour, but nothing to complain about," she said.

"You and your Magic Hour! Dreamed up when you were a child," Tom laughed.

"You remember?"

"I remember everything."

He reached for her hand, but she quickly put it on her lap, glanced out of the window again, pretending she had not realized he wanted to hold hers in his. She knew if he touched her, she would fall apart or leap on him. She didn't want to do either, and certainly nothing foolish.

"So, tell me more about your movie," he suddenly said, turning toward her.

"Well, as you know, Mary grew up here at the French court, under the patronage of her Guise uncles—"

"Ah, yes, those somewhat ambitious princes of the blood," he cut in.

"Then she married the Dauphin, became Queen of France when his father died, and then was widowed rather soon when very young."

"And then she was sent back to Scotland to be their rightful queen. How much of her life does the movie cover, Alexa?"

"From what Nicky said, the early years . . . her time at the French court, marriage, becoming the French queen, and then her move to Scotland, marriage to Lord Darnley, and her love affair and marriage with the Earl of Bothwell. I believe the script ends when they have to part."

"A romantic story in many ways."

"Yes." Stay away from the subject of romance, a small voice cautioned. She went on swiftly. "I always complain to Nicky when he offers me a costume picture, but actually I do quite enjoy doing historicals. They're very challenging, and I admit it, I like digging into the research, coming up with some authentic houses as well as my own sets."

"You'll certainly find quite a few of those in the Loire Valley. As you know, it's full of châteaux. And have you actually read the script yet?"

"No, but Nicky hopes to have the first draft in a few days. I have a feeling it will be quite good. Nicky says the treatment was wonderful, very well written."

"You suddenly sound excited about the film."

"I am, Tom. I like designing sets for plays, but there's so much more scope, so many more opportunities to be truly creative when it comes to movies."

"Do you know when the film starts shooting?"

"Not exactly. At the end of the summer, early September, I think. Why?"

"I like the idea of having you here in Paris."

"Oh" was all she could say. She was at a loss for words.

———

Not long after this conversation, the car came to a standstill on the Place Saint-Michel. "Come on," Tom said, and opened the door, reached in to help her out. To the driver he said, *"Cinq minutes, Hubert,"* slammed the car door shut, and took hold of her hand.

Striding out, he led her down the rue de la Huchette and up into the rue de la Bûcherie at a rapid pace, without saying a word. As they crossed this small square with its little cafés, going toward the Seine, Tom suddenly exclaimed, "Look, Alexa! You always said this was your favorite view in Paris."

He brought her to a standstill, and together they stood staring across at the Île de la Cité, one of the small islands in the Seine, on which stood the Cathedral of Nôtre-Dame. Alexa turned to glance up at Tom, just as he looked down at her. Their eyes met and held; she nodded, then turned to face the Nôtre-Dame. Its imposing Gothic towers looked magnificent in the early evening light, silhouetted as they were against the deep blue sky, and the taller spire shone in the last rays of the fading sun.

She did not say anything for a few minutes, and then she glanced up at him and said, "Yes, it does have a very special meaning for me, this view."

"And for me too. Do you think I don't remember that we came and stood here the first night we had a date?"

She opened her mouth to speak, but no words came out. He had bent toward her and was kissing her softly. Then he pulled her into his arms, held her very tightly against him, his kisses growing more passionate.

Her arms went around him, and she clung to him.

Finally, when they drew apart, he looked deeply into her eyes, and gently stroked one side of her face with his hand. "I said it before, but I feel I must say it again, I am very happy you phoned me."

"Why did you bring me here, Tom?"

"So that you would know I haven't forgotten anything. . . ."

"Neither have I," she whispered, and her heart clenched as she thought of all the pain he had caused her, as well as the happiness they had shared.

At last she said, "I don't think I could ever come to Paris without calling you."

"And I couldn't bear it if you were here and I didn't know you were." Placing his arm around her shoulder, he walked her back to the car, and at one moment, he said quietly, "I've missed you . . . a lot."

Alexa gave him a look through the corner of her eye. "So have I . . . you."

Tom took a deep breath, blew out air, glanced around him, and then after a moment, he ventured, "Your friend. The Englishman. Does he want to make the relationship permanent?"

She was silent at first, and then she answered in a low voice: "He's talked about it, yes."

"That's what *you* want, isn't it? Marriage, children, a family life?"

"I did want that, with you, yes."

"And not with him?"

Alexandra shrugged, looked up at the sky, squinted into the light, shook her head. Finally, her eyes met Tom's, and she said, "I just don't know. Actually, I don't want to talk about it."

"So sorry, I *am* prying. . . ." His voice trailed off, and then he dropped his arm from her shoulder, took hold of her hand, and led her toward the Mercedes parked just ahead.

They hardly spoke on the way to the restaurant, sat quietly in their respective corners, although the silence between them was not angry but as amicable as it usually was. They were compatible, and comfortable with each other, even when they did not want to talk.

Alexa was in a quandary inside. She couldn't for the world figure out why he was asking questions about her love life. After all, it had been Tom who had broken if off three years ago. Then again, he wasn't acting as if it were over. He had pulled her into his arms and kissed her with growing passion a few minutes ago. She was glad it was he who had made the first move and not her. He had acted suddenly, unexpectedly, and she was so taken by surprise, she had fallen into the trap . . . and into his arms. And willingly so. She had clung to him and kissed him back, and her heart had been clattering as erratically as his. So it wasn't over for him either, was it? She tried to pull her swimming senses together; she knew, only too well, that it wasn't over for her, it had never been over. She doubted that it ever would be.

For his part, Tom Conners was silently chastising himself for falling prey to his emotions in the way he had. From the moment he had seen her standing in the hotel lobby, he had wanted to grab her, pull her to him, kiss her long and hard. Slake the desire he had felt for her for years, fill his need. And he had spoken the truth when he said he was glad she had phoned, that he had missed her, and that he remembered everything about their time together. The problem was, he hadn't meant to say any of those words to her, nor had he meant to start a relationship with her once more. It wasn't that he didn't want to make love to her, of course he did. But he was well aware that he had nothing to offer her . . . not in the long run. And he did not want to hurt her again.

"I'd forgotten how charming the Place des Vosges was," Alexa was saying, breaking into his thoughts, and he roused himself quickly, pushed a smile onto his face.

"It really is the most beautiful old square in Paris, and as you know, it's seventeenth century," he said. "And I think I told you once, my mother grew up in an apartment in one of the old houses at the other side of the gardens over there."

"How is she? And your father?"

"They're both well, thanks, and yours?"

"The same, they're great."

Hubert, the driver, was suddenly opening the door of the Mer-

cedes, and after Tom alighted, he helped her out. They went into
L'Ambroisie together, blinking slightly as they entered the dim interior. Within a split second Tom was being greeted warmly, and
then they were shown to a table for two in a quiet corner of a
medium-size room.

Alexa glanced around once they were seated, taking note of the
mellow old paneling on the walls, the high ceiling, the ancient tapestries, the silver candlesticks with white candles, the big stone
urns brimming to overflowing with fresh flowers.

"It has the feeling of an old house, a private home," she murmured, leaning across the table toward Tom.

"And that's what it was, of course. There are several rooms for
dining, and it's very hard to get a table unless you're famous or a
politician. Or a noted lawyer." He winked at her. "And its undeni-
able charm is matched only by its delicious food. The chocolate
dessert is sublime, and they have one of the best *caves* in Paris."

"You know I'm not a big drinker."

"But you'll have a glass of champagne, won't you?"

"That'll be nice. Thanks, Tom."

After he had ordered their drinks, Alexa said, "You know what
I've been doing lately, because of my name being in the trade pa-
pers occasionally. But you haven't told me anything about yourself.
How have *you* spent these last few years?"

He leaned back in the chair, eyeing her thoughtfully, pondering.

She thought his eyes had never looked more blue; he was very
handsome, debonair in his demeanor, and irresistible. No, lethal.
At least to her. She corrected herself. He would be lethal to any
woman.

He said, "I still represent a number of people in the film industry. In fact, I'm now the head of the show business division of the
law firm. The firm's become rather prestigious in the last two years
because we've had several big, non-show-business cases, which
we've won. The clients are coming in a steady stream these days.

And my own work has been going well." He gave her a lopsided smile. "But nothing special has been happening; in fact, I do lead a rather humdrum sort of life, Alexa."

"I wouldn't call it that, Tom."

The waiter arrived with two extra-tall crystal flutes of champagne, pale blond in color and sparkling, and he was saved the trouble of answering her. He wondered why they were here; he wanted her at home in his bed.

Suddenly the maître d' was standing next to the table, talking to Tom about the menu. It was obvious Tom was a favored client.

Alexa sat back, half listening, her eyes riveted on Tom, mesmerized by him. Humdrum life, she thought at one moment, wished she could live it with him. And then she thought of Jack and was sad.

The only man she wanted was Tom Conners.

CHAPTER TWENTY-FOUR

"I hope you don't mind, but I've ordered for both of us," Tom said, smiling at her. He took a swallow of his champagne before adding, "White asparagus, a taste of the langoustine in pastry leaves, which is their specialty, to be followed by—"

"Lamb," Alexa interrupted peremptorily. "I think you must have forgotten I speak French."

"No, I haven't." He sat back in his chair, his gaze level and steady as he studied her. If only she knew what he remembered. Images of her and their time together were indelibly printed on his brain, and she existed inside him, in his heart.

Alexa said, "And you've ordered your favorite wine, a Petrus, which you once told me should be drunk only on special occasions. Is tonight special, Tom?" She gazed at him, the expression in her light-green eyes as serious as her face.

"Absolutely. We are celebrating your return to Paris."

"I'm just visiting. And not for long."

He threw her an odd look, frowning, and murmured, "Don't talk about leaving, Alex, you've only just arrived. And you're coming back for the film." His blue eyes quickened. "How long will you be here on the movie?"

"I don't know. Nicky hasn't said. But quite a few months, I'm fairly certain of that. There's a lot of preproduction on a film like this, because of the sets and locations, and the costumes as well. Once I get the script I'll know how many scenes are to be shot in Paris. Nicky and I hope to make a schedule next week." She lifted her glass, took a sip of champagne, and asked curiously, "You've never been to New York in the past three years?"

"No. I was in Los Angeles two years ago to meet with a client." He shook his head. "I should have phoned you."

"Why didn't you?"

He reached out, put his hand over hers. "I didn't feel I had the right, I was the one who brought our relationship to an end. I was positive you had met someone else by then, fallen in love, made a new life. Moved on."

Alexa gaped at him, her eyes opening wider, and she thought: Fallen in love, moved on. How can he possibly think that? Doesn't he know how much I loved him, with all my heart and soul, with every fiber of my being? She held herself very still in the chair. Her eyes welled with tears all of a sudden, and she wanted to look away but discovered that she couldn't. She blinked back her tears.

"I've upset you. What is it? What's wrong?" His fingers tightened on hers and he leaned closer over the table, his eyes troubled.

"I guess I'm surprised, that's all . . . that you think I could move on . . . so quickly . . ."

"It's been a long time . . . three years."

"You haven't moved on. Or have you?"

He did not answer at first, and then he admitted, "No, Alex, I haven't." He hesitated slightly, and then asked, "But what about your friend? The Englishman? You must have a relationship with him, since you said he wants to make it permanent."

"Yes, I do, but I have always been . . . uncertain, nervous about the situation. Before I came to Paris, I had a long talk with my mother about him, you, and—" Alexa broke off, gave a strange little laugh. "Some people would think I'm crazy for telling you this . . . feeding your ego, in a way, I guess." She paused, took a deep breath, and finished softly. "I love you, Tom. I always have, from the first moment we met, and I suppose I always will."

He nodded, continuing to hold her hand very tightly in his. His gaze fastened on hers. "I've spent the last few years having meaningless sex with women who meant nothing at all to me. They're a blur. You see, Alex, I didn't want anyone else but you."

She stared hard at him, her eyes narrowing. "Why didn't you call me? Weren't you ever *tempted?*"

"Of course I was! I must have picked up the phone a hundred times. But I felt I did not have the right, as I just told you. I had ended it, and it was not for me to attempt to start a relationship with you again. I also knew I had so many problems to work out in my own head."

"You said at the time that you had nothing to offer, and therefore you were setting me free. But you didn't do that . . . I've been forever bound to you, Tom."

There was a moment of silence.

He sat looking at her, his eyes searching her face, that face he loved. Finally, he said slowly in a low voice, "I've waited a long time for the call you made last night. I could hardly believe it was you. And ever since, I've been anxious, anxiety ridden, really on tenterhooks until I saw you standing there in the lobby."

"Yes, I know exactly what you mean."

He smiled; his eyes sparkled. "Suddenly, there you were, looking so chic and beautiful and not a day older than when I last saw you."

"I'll soon be thirty-one. And you'll soon be forty-three."

"At the end of the month. And don't remind me!"

"It was Anya, you know. She made me call you."

"Oh." He sat back and gave her a long, contemplative look. "Weren't you planning to phone me?"

"I knew I would ultimately. It was all a question of getting up my nerve."

The waiter arrived with the white asparagus; he took a few moments serving it and drizzling the vinaigrette dressing before finally stepping away from the table.

Alexa ate several spears and then sat back in the chair; she drank some of her water.

Tom looked up from his plate, and frowned. "Is something wrong? You're not eating."

"I'm not really hungry."

"I know . . . neither am I."

They stared at each other, exchanging an intimate look full of yearning, fully aware of what they really wanted.

Tom said, "We cannot leave now . . . not until the entire meal has been served. If we do go, I won't ever be able to come here again." He sighed, reached for her hand. "I'll be persona non grata."

"I understand. And after all this time, what's another hour? I'll try and eat a little of each course, and you should, if you can."

"You are right. . . ." He picked up a spear of asparagus. "And this is delicious, you know."

Following suit, Alexa also ate a few more spears, and by the time the langoustine was served, they had both adopted a more relaxed demeanor, were less tense with each other, at least on the surface.

At one moment, picking up his goblet of red wine, Tom toasted her. "Here's to you, Alexa. Welcome back."

"I'm glad to be back," she said, touching her glass to his. She wondered if he was welcoming her back to Paris or back into his life, and she was not sure. She took a sip of wine, said, "Smooth as silk, this Petrus of yours."

He laughed, looked pleased.

Alexa toyed with the lamb on her plate, took a forkful, ate a bite, then put the fork down. Looking across at him, she said, "You mentioned your problems just now. Do you think . . . I mean, well, have you worked them out finally?"

"I believe I have, Alexa, yes," he replied, took a long swallow of the wine, and leaned back in the chair. His face had changed slightly in that brief moment, and the laughter of a second ago had vanished. "It's taken me a long time to settle things in my mind," he said in a sober tone, "to come to terms with everything, but I now have."

"I'm glad. It must make you feel better."

"It does. I do have my moments, when I'm . . . sad, but for the most part I'm much better than I ever was. I slayed the demons."

"How did you manage to do that?" she asked, and then cringed inside when she saw his face. "I'm sorry," she added quickly. "I don't want to pry. I'm just glad you feel better."

"If I can't talk to you about it, then I don't know who I can. I did it on my own, no psychiatrists, no tranquilizers to get me through. I just faced up to what had happened, and most important, I managed to stop feeling guilty."

"That must have been very difficult, Tom."

"It was, but I had enormous incentive. I wanted to be the Tom Conners I was before Juliette and Marie-Laure died. When I told you there was no future for you with me, and you left Paris, I sort of fell apart. I began drinking. A lot." He glanced at the glass of wine on the table. "And not that mother's milk either. Hard liquor. Vodka mostly, because it tastes of nothing. That's all I did in my free time, I sat at home and drank. For six months. But suddenly one day I hated what I had become and I stopped. I also did something else."

"What was that?"

"I decided to do some research."

"*Research?* About what?"

"Terrorism. My wife and child were murdered by terrorists on a warm, sunny day in Athens. Like everyone else in that square that day, they were innocent. I wanted to know *who* and *why*, and so I spent a whole year reading, talking to experts, learning about Muslim fundamentalism, the meaning of Islamic *jihad*, Hezbollah and how it worked, Abu Nidal, Carlos the Jackal, and other terrorists. I was very conscientious, Alexa. Actually, I filled seven notebooks with information. And about four months ago I suddenly realized I was finally free of guilt . . . it had simply fled. *I* hadn't killed my wife and child by being late that day. They had been blown to smithereens by those brutal cowards who fight a guerrilla war in the name of Islam."

Alexa was very quiet for a moment or two, and then she reached out, touched his hand. "Did you ever find out which group blew up the bus of Americans that day?"

"I have a good idea, and so do various governments. But what good does that do?" He sighed. "The main thing is, I managed to rid myself of guilt, and I've felt so much more like a normal person ever since."

"I really am so happy for you, Tom, happy that you have been able to ease your pain. There were times when I didn't know how to help you, when you were in such . . . anguish—" Alexa broke off as the waiter came to the table and began to clear away their plates.

Once they were alone, Tom leaned forward and said quietly, "I'm afraid their chocolate dessert will arrive at any moment. Can you handle more food?"

She laughed. "I'll cut it up and push it around my plate. That should do the trick."

"You may find yourself eating it."

"I doubt that."

"There you go again, doubting what I say. Just like the bees."

"The bees?" She wrinkled her nose, looking perplexed and then she began to laugh. "Oh, my God, yes. The *bees.*"

He chuckled with her.

"Listen to me, Tom Conners! No one else would have believed you either! What person in their right mind would believe that bees were kept on the roof of the Paris Opera House, and that their honey was put in jars and sold. No one, that's who!"

"True."

"But you were so dear when you bought me the jars of honey just to prove it."

He looked into her eyes, squeezed her hand, and asked, "Do you want coffee? Or anything else, Alex?"

"No, thanks, Tom."

"Will you come home with me?"

"You know I will. Where else could I possibly want to go?"

CHAPTER TWENTY-FIVE

They stood in the foyer of Tom's apartment, alone at last as they had longed to be for the last few hours, but curiously silent now as they stared at each other intently.

Although they had laughed in the restaurant, been more at ease with each other, the tension between them had returned once they were sitting on the backseat of the Mercedes in their separate corners.

Acutely conscious of each other, they had hardly spoken a word as Hubert had driven the car through the evening traffic, heading in the direction of the Faubourg Saint-Germain, where Tom lived.

Now the electricity between them was a palpable thing once more, and they both moved forward at precisely the same moment, coming together in the middle of the floor, almost stumbling into each other's arms.

Tom gathered Alexa close, and she held on to him tightly, her body instantly welded to his. He bent down, began to kiss her fervently, and she matched his ardor, responded with equal intensity and passion.

Alexa was shaking internally, her long-pent-up desire for Tom flooding her entire body, and her heart clattered in unison with his. Tom slid his hand down her back and onto her buttocks, pressed her even closer, molded her body to his, and she felt the hardness of his growing passion through her thin linen dress. Suddenly she was suffused with warmth. Her bag and her shawl fell from her hands, but she ignored them as he led her away from the foyer and into the bedroom, his arms still wrapped around her.

It was obvious he did not want to let go of her, and he pulled her down onto the bed with him, began to kiss her once more. His hand went to her breast and he stroked it, played with her nipple, which began to harden under the fabric. A small groan escaped her throat; her hands went up into his thick, dark hair and she felt his scalp with her fingertips. They were lost in their raging desire for each other, wanting only to possess and be possessed.

Tom's kisses stopped abruptly, and he pushed himself up on one elbow, looked down into her face, his own congested with raw emotion. He started to say something, and then stopped, not wanting to break the spell or cool the heat of their rampant feelings.

Gazing back at him, Alexa recognized the longing and desire in his eyes, was swamped by that vivid blue gaze, and she was as overwhelmed by him, and her feelings for him, as she had been from the first moment they met. Her throat tightened. Nothing had changed, she knew that now. She felt undone, helpless, and so in love with him, nothing else, no one else, mattered. Very simply, there was no other man for her. Only he made her feel like this.

Tom touched her mouth with one finger, leaned into her, said softly, "Take your clothes off, darling."

She slid off the bed, did as he asked, quickly shedding everything, and then moved back onto the bed again.

Tom did the same, undressed with swiftness, and she watched him in the dim light of the bedroom, shivering slightly as he came back to her. He was so tall, long-legged, broad-shouldered, the most handsome and masculine man she had ever known, and his desire for her was now very apparent. She longed for Tom to take her to him.

Tom lay down next to her, covered her body with his own, held her in his arms. Against her hair, he said, "I've never stopped wanting you, and only *you*, Alex."

"Oh, Tom darling, Tom," she whispered, and touched his cheek with one hand. "And it's only *you* I want—"

He stopped her words with his kisses, his mouth firm yet gentle on hers. He parted her lips, let his tongue graze hers, and then rest still. As one of his hands moved down to smooth and fondle her round breast, he brought his mouth to it, smothered it with kisses.

Wanting to touch and kiss every inch of her, his mouth moved on, fluttered across her stomach, her inner thigh, and all of those erotic, secret parts of her. Slowly his kisses became more languorous until finally his lips settled on the feminine core of her, and lingered there.

Alexa stiffened and gasped, and went on gasping as he made love to her in this most sensual and intimate way, as he had done from the outset of their relationship. Loving her like this gave him as much pleasure as it did her; he was pleased and gratified when he brought her to climax and she spasmed, called his name, and told him how much she loved him.

Her excitement fed his own arousal. Tom knew only too well that he had never felt like this with any other woman, not before her, or during her recent absence from his life. Suddenly, he thought he was going to explode, and unable to hold back any longer, he moved on top of her. He needed to be inside her, to possess her totally, to make her his own.

Tom pushed himself up, braced his arms on each side of her, and looked down into Alexa's light-green eyes. Her emotions were explicit on her face, and as his gaze lingered for a moment longer, his heart clenched. He knew all of a sudden what she truly meant to him. He also knew what a fool he had been to ever let her go.

As he entered her, she cried his name again, and he told her finally, and with absolute certainty, that he loved her, that she was the love of his life.

————

They lay amid rumpled pillows and tangled sheets, resting quietly in the soft, dim light of his bedroom.

The impact of seeing each other again had been devastating to them both, and they had fallen into their own thoughts.

For Alexa, their passionate lovemaking on this bed for the past hour and a half was merely a confirmation of what she already knew, had known deep down inside herself for the last few years. She loved Tom, always had, always would, and nothing could ever change that fact.

Endeavoring to move on, because he had been unable to make a commitment to her, she had strived for a successful career, a good life, and eventually she had even enjoyed a relationship with another man . . . Jack Wilton. The thought of Jack made her heart sink. She was going to have to tell him she couldn't marry him; she hated the thought of hurting him. But even though there might not be a future with Tom, she could not marry Jack or anyone else. Her heart belonged to this man cradling her in his arms, one leg thrown over her body, his hands clasping hers, as if he were afraid she was going to escape his tenacious grip.

He loved her; she had always known he did. And he desired her sexually. They were intense in bed and out of it; they were compatible. Yet he couldn't take that final step. At least, not in the past. Now he might. He had told her he no longer felt guilt about the tragic deaths of his wife and child. And yet she wondered . . . had he really conquered it?

As far as she was concerned, marriage didn't matter anymore, she just wanted to be with him. "Living in sin" it was called. But she didn't see it that way. If you loved each other, it wasn't a sin. Marrying a man you didn't love, and spending the rest of your life with him, well, that was surely living in sin, wasn't it?

Alexa closed her eyes, imagining the child she had wanted. Correction. *His child.* But if that were not possible, it didn't really matter. Tom was all that mattered to her, and being with him for the rest of her life.

As he lay next to her, Tom was contemplating the dichotomy in his nature. How he loved her, this woman in his arms, with all his heart; sexually he craved her constantly, wanted to be joined to her. They were hot together, and perfectly matched; her passion, ardor, and sensuality in bed had echoed his since their first night together years ago. She truly satisfied him and he knew he satisfied her.

Yet despite all this, he was afraid to make the relationship permanent, afraid he might somehow hurt her in the long run. . . .

But if he lost her again, where would he be? He groaned inwardly. When he thought of all the mindless, meaningless sex he'd had in her absence, he was appalled at himself.

He had told her the truth when he said he had vanquished the survivor guilt. Sixteen years he had lived with that, and he thanked God every day that he was free of it at long last.

When Tom considered the research he had done into global terrorism, and what he had found out, he inevitably shriveled inside at the enormity of it all. The knowledge of terrorism in the future that he now possessed was a burden. He knew too much. It weighed him down, and what he had learned filled him with despair. Apprehension about the years ahead never waned. But there was nothing he could do but go about his daily life, hoping for the best, praying that goodness would outweigh evil ultimately.

Alexa moved in his arms, and he tightened his embrace, but she wriggled around so that he had to loosen his grip, and finally she was facing him.

Her cool green eyes looked deeply into his. "I want to tell you something, Tom." Her face was serious.

"Then tell me." He held his breath, wondering what was coming.

"I want to be with you . . . and being married doesn't really matter to me any longer. Just so long as we're together, that's all that counts."

He searched her face; his eyes, fastened on hers, were filled with love. "And I want to be with you, I feel the same, Alex. But mostly we're so far away from each other. You're in New York, I'm here."

"I know, but I'm coming back soon, to do the movie."

"And after that?"

"I think we can work it out . . . if we want to."

"I know we can, darling." He kissed her, and they clung to each other for a few moments. And they both knew a bargain had been sealed.

After a while, he said against the hollow of her neck, "You're my one true love, Alex."

She moved again, so that she could see him, and stared hard at him, frowning. Then she said slowly, "When we were making love, you said I was the love of your life . . . but . . ." She left her sentence unfinished.

He returned her gaze with one equally as steady. "I know, you're thinking about Juliette, and my feelings for her. Of course I loved her deeply, but we were children together. Childhood sweethearts, Alex darling, and in many ways we were very young. I came to you as a grown man, scarred by life, and you were a mature woman.

You'd lived life a little. And it's a different kind of love I feel for you . . . and so yes, you are the love of my life. Now."

Reaching out, she touched his cheek very gently, and leaned into him, kissed him lightly on the lips. "Everything will be all right. *We're* going to be all right, Tom."

He smiled at her, and she settled down in his arms. He rested his face against her head, ruminating again on the evening they had spent together. It had been marvelous to see her again, to look at her across a dinner table, to make love with her, to hold her here in his arms like this . . . he was lucky.

Tom relaxed, closing his eyes, and he realized then that the pain had finally ceased. That awful pain he had lived with all these long years had miraculously ceased to exist . . . and he was at peace.

———

"Why do you have this photograph in your album?" Tom asked, looking up at Alexa as she came out of the bathroom in her hotel room. It was Sunday morning. They had gone to the Meurice half an hour ago so that she could shed her clothes of the night before, put on something more suitable for lunch. As he waited, Tom had seen the album and picked it up, curious as always.

She glanced at the small red leather photograph album in his hands, and shook her head. "Which one are you referring to?"

"This one," he said, holding the album out to her.

Alexa took it from him and stared down at the photograph he was indicating. It was of Jessica and Lucien. The two of them stood on the Pont des Arts, and she had taken it just a few weeks before graduation.

"It's Jessica Pierce," Alexa explained as she looked up at Tom. "She was at Anya's school with me."

"No, no, it's the man I'm talking about. I was curious why he was in your album. I didn't know you knew him. He's a neighbor of my parents."

Alexa was gaping at Tom. She exclaimed, "That can't be. Lucien disapp—"

"Why do you call him that?" Tom interrupted.

"That was his name . . . Lucien Girard."

"No, no, Alex," Tom argued, shaking his head. "The man with Jessica is Jean Beauvais-Cresse, and he lives in the Loire Valley."

CHAPTER TWENTY-SIX

⁂

Alexa was speechless for a split second, and she sat down heavily on the chair opposite Tom. She had been startled and shocked by his words, and it showed on her face. After looking down at the album and the photograph of Jessica and Lucien once more, she finally managed to say, "Tom, are you sure about what you're saying?"

He leaned back on the sofa, a reflective expression crossing his face fleetingly. "Well, they say everybody has a twin somewhere, but I'm pretty certain this *is* Jean Beauvais-Cresse. Obviously, I could be wrong, but I don't think I am." He leaned forward, held out his hand. "Let me look at the picture again, please, Alexa."

Rising, she bent toward him, handed him the album, and then sat down, crossing her legs, waiting for him to continue their conversation. She was still taken aback, her mind racing as she considered a variety of scenarios and possibilities.

Once he had carefully studied the photograph of Jessica and Lu-

236

cien on the bridge, he flipped through the album again, glancing at some of the other pictures, many of them himself and Alexa.

Finally placing it on the coffee table, Tom said, "Listen to me, Alex, people don't change that much between their twenties and thirties, their looks remain pretty much the same for the most part. The man in the picture appears to be in his mid-twenties at the time. Did you take it?"

"Yes, I did."

"When? About seven or eight years ago?"

"Yes. Not long before our graduation actually, Tom."

"The man I know, well, I shouldn't say I know him, I'm acquainted with him, that's all. Anyway, he's in his mid-thirties now." Tom focused his eyes on her; leaning forward slightly, his hands on his knees, he finished, "I know it's Jean when he was much younger."

Alexa bit her lip and shook her head, her eyes suddenly clouded over. "Then at a certain time he led a double life. Or he led a different life as someone called Lucien Girard."

"Tell me about him and Jessica, Alex."

"There's not a lot to tell. Jessica and Lucien met, fell for each other, and started to date. Soon they were inseparable as they became more and more involved, and in love. She told me they planned a future together, that they wanted to marry. And then one day Lucien disappeared into thin air. Without a trace. She never saw him again."

It was Tom's turn to be startled, and he exclaimed, "Nobody disappears just like that! Like a puff of smoke floating away! Surely he was in touch with her eventually, gave her a full explanation."

"He wasn't. And Jessica was heartbroken. It was all something of a mystery at the time. She and a friend of Lucien's did everything they could to find him, but without success. In the end she just gave up and went back to the States."

"And she never heard from him later?"

"I . . . we . . . well, we weren't in touch by then. We weren't speaking. But if Lucien Girard had turned up, Anya would have known, because Jessica would have told her. And Anya or Nicky would have told me. Remember, I lived in Paris for almost three years after graduation, before I went back home."

Tom nodded, settled back against the cushions on the sofa, enormously puzzled by this odd coincidence . . . that two men could look so much alike. "What a strange and troubling story." He frowned, then asked, "And what was this Lucien Girard doing at the time? Was he a student also? Or was he working? Or what?"

"He wasn't a student, Tom. He was an actor. Not well known, he had only small parts, but he was quite good, from what I heard."

"What else do you know about him?" Tom probed, the lawyer in him coming to the surface. "I'm very intrigued, I must admit."

"I don't really know anything else. Jessica spent a lot of time with Lucien, usually alone, except for the few occasions when we were all together." She shrugged, suddenly at a loss for words.

Tom also was silent. He brought a hand up to his chin, rubbed it a few times as he sat pondering on the sofa. "Well, it's none of my business," he murmured eventually. "Although it's quite peculiar when you think about it . . . uncanny that two men look the same. Maybe identical twins."

"That could be it!" Alexa exclaimed. "Perhaps this Jean fellow who lives near your parents actually has a brother. *Even a twin,* as you've just suggested."

"Yes, that's a possibility. I don't know much about the family. But look, Alex, as I just said, it's nothing to do with us."

Alexa nodded, rose, went to the window, stood looking out for a moment or two at the Tuileries across the street. After a short while she turned around, came back to her chair, sat down, and looked across at Tom. "But what if Lucien and Jean *are* the same person? Don't you think Jessica Pierce has a right to know . . . that he's all right, that he's alive. That way she would have *closure* finally."

"That's true, to a certain extent. Look, Alex, think about this . . . what would be the purpose of telling her, really? Wouldn't it be opening up a lot of old wounds? Anyway, it may not matter to Jessica now. She's probably married to someone else."

"No, she isn't. Anya told me we were all still single, except for Kay Lenox, who's now married to some lord. I ought to give Jessica this information, even though we parted on bad terms. Anya wants us to be friends. Perhaps I owe it to Jessica."

"Honestly, you must think about this carefully," Tom cautioned. "Might it not be rather cruel, hurtful, to tell Jessica that I think her old boyfriend is alive and well and living in the Loire?"

"I suppose so, especially since we don't really know whether Jean *is* Lucien. But what if they are the same man? He was a bastard, wasn't he?"

Tom inclined his head, seeing the truth in what she said. He ventured, "Could it be that Lucien wanted to break up with Jessica, and not knowing how to do it gracefully, he simply . . . *slipped away* . . . never to be seen again?"

"That's possible. Rather cowardly though. Here's another thing, Tom. If Lucien is actually Jean Beauvais-Cresse, why did he become Lucien Girard for a period of time?"

"I don't know . . . I can't even imagine why. . . ."

"A mystery," she muttered, and jumped up. "I'd better finish getting dressed. I'll be only a few minutes, then we can leave for Anya's. We mustn't be late for Sunday lunch. It's a sort of ritual with her."

––––––

Alexa was quiet in the taxi on the way to Anya's house, and several times Tom glanced at her out of the corner of his eye. She seemed preoccupied, and so he knew it was wisest to keep silent.

Settling back against the seat, he thought about their morning together. They had awakened early, and prepared breakfast in the kitchen; later Alexa had wandered around, exclaiming about the changes he had made in the apartment since she had last been there, showing her approval. Then she had called her hotel for messages; the only one was from Anya, inviting her to Sunday lunch. He had heard her on the phone, asking if she could bring him, and then the whoop of jubilation as she had hung up the phone. "She can't wait to see you, Tom! You're invited too."

On their way to lunch they had stopped off at the hotel, so Alexa could put on makeup and change. He glanced at her now, thinking that her clothes stamped her nationality on her. She could be only an American in her blue jeans, white silk shirt, and brown penny loafers worn with white wool socks. A dark-blue cashmere sweater was tied around her neck, and she carried the brown Kelly bag he'd given her years ago.

He loved her looks. Well, he loved her, didn't he, and he knew she loved him. There had never been any doubt in his mind about that; he had been the one at fault in the past. A jerk, if he thought about it.

Instinctively, Tom knew that Alexa was going to tell Anya about the resemblance between Lucien Girard and Jean Beauvais-Cresse. He had seen Alexa put the small red leather album into her bag before they had left the hotel, and he wondered what Anya would have to say. Instantly, his thoughts settled on Jessica, who looked so young, beautiful, and sweet in the photograph. She must have been utterly devastated when her boyfriend had disappeared, and he asked himself again whether it was appropriate, wise, to say anything to her about Jean.

Before he could stop himself, Tom suddenly asked, "Why did you and Jessica part on bad terms, as you put it?"

Alexa turned away from the taxi window and looked at him. "It wasn't just Jessica and me. You see, Tom, there were four of us, and we *all* quarreled. It was a big bust-up."

"What about?"

"It's too complicated to tell you now. I'll fill you in later. But I do think we'll have to meet and make up before Anya's party."

"That might be a good idea." Tom took hold of her hand. "I've been thinking about Jean Beauvais-Cresse, and as I told you, I've barely met him. But I could phone my father and ask him what he knows."

Alexa's face quickened. "Would you mind?"

"No, I'll call him after lunch. And by the way, is anyone else going to be at lunch?"

"Anya didn't say. But Nicky could be there. He's very close to her."

"I'd like to see him again."

"I've just remembered something, Tom. If I remember correctly, I think it was Larry Sedgwick who introduced Lucien to Jessica, not that this means anything really." She bit her lip, staring hard at him. "The idea that Lucien might have been playing games really bugs me. I just don't know what to do about it."

"Nothing right now," Tom answered swiftly in a firm voice. "You can't go around accusing people of once being someone else; you'll find yourself in the middle of a lawsuit."

"I wasn't going to do that," she said a trifle huffily, and glanced out of the window. Immediately, she turned her head and said in a lighter tone, "But you'd always defend me, wouldn't you?"

"With my life," he answered, and put his arms around her.

CHAPTER TWENTY-SEVEN

Anya Sedgwick glanced around her upstairs sitting room through appraising eyes, decided that it looked particularly warm and welcoming this morning.

Red and yellow tulips made stunning pools of vivid color in various parts of the room, and a fire burned brightly in the hearth. Although it was another sunny May day there was a nip in the air, and earlier she had asked Honorine to make a fire. She had always liked to see one burning in this room, even in spring and summer.

Moving around, her bearing as elegant as always, her eagle eyes sought anything that might be out of place; she found little amiss except for a crooked photograph frame on the skirted table. After straightening this, she went and sat down behind her large desk in the corner near the fireplace.

As she waited for her luncheon guests to arrive, she once again looked at the list of acceptances for her birthday party. It had grown somewhat in the last few weeks, since almost everyone had accepted, and new people had been added as well. Nicky had told her only the other day that the number had reached one hundred and fifty. She couldn't wait to greet them all.

She put the list down and sat back in the chair, staring into space for a moment, her blue eyes as clear and bright as they had always been. She truly was looking forward to her eighty-fifth birthday party, and had carefully planned what she would wear.

Anya knew she didn't look her age, and she certainly didn't feel it; nevertheless, she was an old woman. At least numerically.

I've been on this earth eighty-five years and I've lived every one of those years to the fullest, with energy, zest, and enthusiasm. I've been involved, curious, caring, loving, interested in everything and everyone. I've never been bored or jaded, and my mind has always been active, alert, and filled with optimism. She smiled inwardly as she added to herself: *And I've no intention of dying just yet. No plans for that in the works. I've a lot more damage to do. Yes, I aim to be around for a long time.*

The telephone rang, and she picked it up. "Hello?"

"It's Nicky, Anya, good morning. I'm sorry, but—"

"Don't tell me you're not coming to lunch."

"There's a problem."

"What is it?"

"Maria. She's very nervous about coming face-to-face with Alexa."

"Well, she'd better get over it, because she's going to have to do exactly that, and very soon, even if she doesn't do it today. I want this mess cleaned up before the party, and the only way to do it is through confrontation. I'm determined to get to the bottom of their quarreling, Nicky!" she exclaimed in a tough voice.

"I agree," he answered quickly, picking up on her militant tone, which he knew brooked no argument. "You're absolutely right."

"I'm glad you agree. She has to come to lunch today. Actually, I was planning on having a lunch for those four later in the week, so this makes a good beginning."

"Oh, are the other women coming today?" he asked quickly.

"No, no, just Alexa and Tom, as I told you."

"Are they back together?"

"I don't know . . . I understand they had dinner last night."

Nicky sighed. "Well, I hope I can persuade her."

"Don't sound so weak-kneed, Nicky. Be firm. Wait . . . put her on the phone, I'll speak to her myself."

"Oh, I'm not—"

"Don't stonewall me, Nick, and don't lie. I know she's with you, either at your flat or her hotel. You can't pull the wool over my eyes . . . I know you're having an affair with Maria, and more power to the two of you. Please, put Maria on the phone. *Now.*"

"Yes, okay, and calm down, Anya."

A moment later, Maria said meekly, "Good morning, Anya."

"Good morning, my dear. I expect you for lunch at one o'clock. Please be here, Maria. It is extremely important to me that you are present today."

"Yes, Anya. We will come. We might be a bit late."

"Start hurrying, Maria. And please don't be *too* late."

"No, no, we'll hurry," Maria promised, and hung up the phone.

Anya rose, walked around the desk to the fireplace, stood with her back to it for a few moments, thinking about Nicky and Maria. She had seen them on quite a few occasions since Maria's arrival in Paris, and it was very apparent to her that they were completely absorbed in each other. Infatuated, she thought, and then amended that. No, they're in love, she corrected herself, and she just hoped Nicky would be able to sort out his problems with Constance, and as quickly as possible. It had struck her several times that Maria and Nicky were ideally suited, that they should be together on a permanent basis.

As for Alexandra and Tom Conners, there was no question that these two had connected again last night. When Alexa had returned her phone call earlier this morning, she had asked her if this were so. Alexa had answered in the affirmative, adding, *"big time."* Anya loved this expression, and she smiled to herself. She definitely wanted Alexa and Tom to be together "big time," because she had always known that her favorite pupil was still in love with him, that he was undoubtedly the love of her life.

With a sudden flash of intuition, Anya knew that these two *were* going to be together for the rest of their lives, even if they didn't know that yet. She felt it in her very old bones.

———

Ten minutes later Alexa was rushing into the room, her face filled with smiles, followed closely by Tom, who was also smiling broadly.

"Good morning, Anya!" Alexa cried, hurrying over to the fireplace, hugging Anya tightly. In her ear, she whispered, "I'm so glad you made me call him. He's been wonderful."

"I'm happy you're here, Alexa, and you too, Tom," Anya said as Alexa stepped away from her. She stretched out her hand to Tom, who took it, and shook it with a firm grip.

"Thanks for including me today, Anya, and I must say, it's wonderful to see you again after so long."

"You're looking well, Tom," Anya responded, still smiling. "Now, what would you both like to drink?" As she spoke, she glanced over at a chest in the far corner, where bottles of liquor and glasses were lined up on a tray. There were also two silver buckets filled with ice, one containing a bottle of white wine, the other champagne.

"I know Alexa will have champagne, Anya, and so will I. Why don't I pour it, and what about you? What will you drink?"

"The Veuve Clicquot also, thank you, Tom, and certainly you can be bartender."

He nodded and moved across the room. She watched him as he strode away, thinking that she had not seen such a magnificent specimen of manhood for years. It wasn't just that he had a handsome face, beautiful, in fact, if she was honest, but his physique was also extraordinary. She had forgotten how tall and long-legged Tom was, and his barrel chest and broad shoulders gave him a truly masculine appearance.

Anya's eyes remained on him as he poured champagne into the tall flutes that Honorine had put out earlier. He had always been well dressed, she now remembered, and today was no exception. He wore a pale blue checked shirt, navy tie, navy blazer, and blue jeans, impeccably tailored. Custom-made, Anya thought, and then accepted the glass of champagne from him.

The three of them stood in front of the fireplace, and clinking their glasses, they said "Cheers" in unison. Looking up at him, Anya found his eyes blinding for a split second. They were the bluest eyes she had ever seen. If only I were fifty years younger, she thought, and then smiled inwardly, amused at herself. Imagine fancying a man at my age, she thought, and focused on Alexa.

"Is Nicky coming to lunch by any chance?" Alexa asked.

"He is, as a matter of fact, and he's bringing Maria Franconi."

"Oh, no!" Alexa exclaimed before she could stop herself.

"Oh, yes," Anya shot back. "And I think you'd better get used to it, Alexa, since you'll be working with Nicky. Those two have become . . . well, 'an item' is the best way to put it for the moment. That aside, I am hoping you, Maria, Kay, and Jessica are going to make an effort to be civil with each other. I'm planning a lunch for later in the week, so that you can all have it out with each other, if necessary. None of you have ever told me what caused you to blow your friendships apart." Staring at Alexa, she raised an eyebrow questioningly.

"It just so happens that it all started with Maria," Alexa finally volunteered after a moment or two. "But since she's coming for lunch, we'd better not get into it now." Moving toward the sofa, Alexa sat down, and Anya joined her.

Tom lowered himself into the armchair next to them and put his glass on the coffee table. Turning to Anya, he said, "I think Alexa wants to talk to you about something important. Don't you, Alex?"

Taken aback for a moment, knowing he was referring to Jessica and Lucien, she could only nod. Finding her voice at last, she said, "I think Tom ought to tell you what happened this morning, and then I'll take it up from there." She put her glass down, reached for her Kelly bag on the floor, and opened it.

Tom said, "I was waiting for Alexa to change at the hotel, and I happened to pick up a small photo album that was on a table. As I went through it, I saw a picture of a man who's a neighbor of my parents in the Loire. He was photographed with this beautiful blonde. Oh, and I must add, Anya, that in the photo he looked about eight years younger than he does today. I was surprised, because I didn't understand why Alex would have a picture of him in her album."

Anya had listened attentively, and now she glanced at Alexa and said, "Who was the blonde? Jessica, I'm assuming."

"Correct." Alexa handed her the album open at the photograph of Jessica with Lucien Girard.

Anya took the album, gazed at the picture for a second, then looking at Tom, she said, "It's Lucien, as I remember him. But who do *you* think he is?"

"Jean Beauvais-Cresse, a man in his mid-thirties who lives near my parents. He's not a friend, just a neighbor, an acquaintance, and I don't know much about him. But Lucien Girard's resemblance to him is uncanny. He looks like a younger version."

"He could be a relative," Anya pointed out, nodding to herself.

"Indeed he could," Tom agreed. "A twin, a brother, a cousin." As he was speaking, Tom, the lawyer who relied on facts, reasoning, analysis, common sense, and evidence, realized how true his words were . . . a family resemblance between two different men was the answer. It had to be. Taking a deep breath, Tom finished, "Alex feels she ought to talk to Jessica. What do you think, Anya?"

"Not at the moment!" Anya exclaimed. Reaching for Alexa's hand, holding it in hers, she continued. "Jessica shouldn't be told anything about this. It would only upset her terribly."

"Well, actually, I wasn't planning to say anything to her until we'd done a bit of investigating, Anya, and Tom suggested it might be a good idea to talk to his father, ask a few questions," Alexa explained.

Nodding, Anya said, "That is probably a good idea, Tom."

Alexa said, "Anya, you might think I'm being fanciful, but I just have a really weird feeling about this photo. . . . I think it *is* Jean Beauvais-Cresse when he was a young man, and that he and Lucien are the same person. I can't explain why I feel this, but I just do."

Anya said, "Look, I've always been a great believer in gut instinct, and you might well be right, Alexa. But we mustn't say a word to Jessica. We really do have to keep quiet."

"That's correct," Tom exclaimed. "It's very flimsy, there's no hard evidence, nothing concrete to go on. However, I do think I can ask Dad a few pertinent questions, and maybe he can supply the answers we need regarding Jean and Lucien Girard—" Tom stopped as Nicky walked into the room with Maria Franconi.

"I hope we're not *very* late," Nicky said. After kissing Anya and squeezing Alexa's shoulder, he shook Tom's hand enthusiastically. "Tom, it's great to see you! And this is Maria Franconi, I don't think you've ever met."

Maria smiled, shook Tom's hand, and murmured quietly, "I am pleased to meet you."

"It's a pleasure," Tom replied, smiling at her.

After kissing Anya on the cheek, Maria looked toward Alexa seated on the sofa and forced a smile. "Hello, Alexa."

"Hi, Maria," Alexa responded coolly, without smiling.

"Do be a darling, Nicky, and pour Maria a glass of champagne," Anya said.

"Oh, no, Anya, thank you, but I'd prefer water," Maria announced.

Nicky said, "Coming right up, sweetie, but I think *I'll* have a drop of the old bubbly myself." He sauntered across the room as he said this and busied himself at the drinks tray.

"Sit down, Maria dear." Anya indicated the chair next to her, and went on. "I haven't had a chance to tell you this before, but I've studied the photographs Nicky gave me the other day. Maria, your paintings are quite extraordinary. But then, you were an enormously talented artist when you were at the school."

Maria looked extremely pleased when she spoke. "Thank you, Anya. Hearing those words from you about my paintings is very important to me."

Nicky carried the water to Maria, and then stood in front of the fire, regarding all of them. After a moment he took a sip of his champagne, and said, "Cheers, everybody."

"Cheers," Tom answered.

"*Santé,* Nicky darling," Anya murmured.

Alex simply raised her glass to him, and smiled, and then eyed Maria out of the corner of her eye, thinking that Anya had not exaggerated the other day. Maria Franconi was a different person than she had been at the school seven years ago. And she was indeed a beautiful woman now.

Glancing across at Tom, Nicky said, "Did I hear you mention Lucien Girard just now? Or am I dreaming?"

The room went quiet.

Tom glanced at Alexa and they exchanged pointed looks.

Anya said swiftly, "Oh, it was nothing important, Nicky, just a casual remark on Tom's part. Now, I don't want to rush you, but we mustn't linger up here too long. Honorine's daughter, Yvonne, came in to cook for me today, and I know she's making something very special for the first course. So drink up, Nicky."

———

A short while after this, Honorine's curly gray head appeared around the sitting room door, and beaming at everyone, she announced, *"Le déjeuner est prêt, madame,"* and disappeared as swiftly as she had materialized.

Within the next few seconds they finished their drinks, rose, and trooped down the stairs, Nicky and Maria leading the way. Alexa hung back in the sitting room, touching Anya's arm as she did, whispering, "How much did Nicky hear, do you think?"

Anya shrugged, shook her head, and murmured in an equally quiet tone, "I don't really know . . . but not very much, I'm sure." There was a slight hesitation on her part before she added, "But don't forget, he and Larry knew Lucien first. It was actually Larry who introduced him to Jessica. It might be worth asking him a few questions, you know."

"Nicky's okay, but I can't say anything to him because I don't trust Maria. She might tell Jessica, and that would be disastrous."

"She doesn't even know where Jessica is staying," Anya murmured.

"Where is she staying?"

"The Plaza Athénée."

Tom looked back up the stairs, frowned, and called to them, "Come on, Alexa, Anya—Nicky and Maria are waiting for us in the dining room."

The two women descended the staircase, and when they were finally in the entrance foyer, Anya hurried forward, exclaiming, "Sorry, my dears, I'm afraid I'm a little stiff today, Alexa was helping me down the stairs. Sorry I kept you waiting."

"That's all right," Nicky said, came forward, and took hold of Anya's arm, led her into the dining room, which overlooked the cobbled courtyard and the garden. To reflect the outside, which was so visible through the windows and the French doors, Anya had used a color scheme of light and dark greens, accented with touches of white. With its billowing white organdy curtains at the windows, dark parquet wood floor, and masses of white flowering plants, the room looked fresh, airy, and cool.

Pausing at the circular table, made of highly polished yew wood and surrounded by five Louis XV chairs upholstered in a green-and-white-check fabric, Anya rested one hand on a chair and said, "Maria, come and sit at my left, and Tom, please take the chair at my right. Alexa dear, sit down next to Tom, and Nicky, you can sit between Alexa and Maria."

Smiling broadly, she lowered herself into her chair. "I think that works very well," she continued, and looking across at Nicky, she said, "Would you pour the white wine for those who want it, and there's a very nice red to have with the main course."

Nicky did as he was asked, and he had just finished filling their glasses with white wine when Honorine came into the room carrying a large tray. She was followed by her daughter, Yvonne, who held a smaller tray in her hands. Yvonne nodded, murmured a quiet greeting, and followed her mother to the serving table.

Within minutes they had all been served with an individual cheese soufflé and were soon exclaiming about it, pronouncing it delicious. And at one moment Nicky announced, "It's as light as a baby's breath." Everyone laughed at this expression, and the ice was broken a little, but Anya noticed as this first course was being eaten that Alexa and Maria carefully avoided speaking to each other. However, Tom and Nicky had lost no time in getting properly reacquainted, and they were now chatting enthusiastically about the movie industry in general.

She herself turned to Maria and began to talk more fully about her paintings, while Alexa was soon drawn into Nicky's conversation with Tom. He was holding forth on the new film about Mary Queen of Scots, and Tom was obviously fascinated, listening attentively as Nicky explained about the preproduction plans that were slowly coming together.

After the empty soufflé dishes had been cleared away, Nicky served the Mouton Rothschild to everyone except Maria, and Tom poured the mineral water. Not long after this, Honorine came back with a platter of roast leg of lamb, followed by Yvonne with a dish of steamed vegetables and roasted potatoes. When they had been served, the two women left the dining room, but a second later Honorine returned with the gravy, which she placed on the table.

Anya asked her to bring the other sauce, and then explained to them, "I'm very English when it comes to my roast lamb . . . it's my upbringing, I suppose. I like it thinly sliced and covered in mint sauce." She laughed. "The French usually shudder when they see me eating it this way."

"It's because they can't imagine why anyone would want to put a sauce made with vinegar on their meat," Nicky pointed out, and grinned at her. "And as you know, I eat mine exactly the same way."

The conversation at the table was rather mundane as the main course was eaten and enjoyed, the red wine savored, the water drunk. Looking at each of them from time to time, Anya was pleased that they were all here with her today, and that there was an air of civility at the table. She realized quite suddenly that Maria appeared slightly more ill at ease than Alexa. And it struck her that Alexa had undoubtedly spoken the truth when she had blamed Maria for the trouble in the friendships, but it had been so long ago, she wished they could forget about it. As for Maria, she was such a brilliant artist, it was almost criminal to let her rot in a textile company in Milan. But then, Anya knew it was none of her business . . . she could only hope Nicky was going to be the girl's knight in shining armor, that he would rescue her from a terrible kind of servitude.

––––––

Once lunch was over, Anya asked everyone upstairs for coffee, and once again they moved en masse to the floor above.

Anya was pouring the coffee when Tom, hovering over her, asked, "Could I use your phone, please, Anya?"

"But of course," she said, and glancing at Alexa, she went on: "Show Tom into that little den down the corridor, Alexa, please. He can use the phone in there."

Alexa nodded, took hold of Tom's hand, and accompanied him out of the room. Once they were in the corridor leading off the main landing, he pulled her into his arms and kissed her deeply. As he released her, he said, "Let's forget about the movie we talked about seeing later. Why don't we go back to my place instead?"

Alexa smiled up at him adoringly. "You've got a deal, Tom Conners."

"The best one I've ever made," he shot back.

Still smiling, Alexa pushed open the door of the den and said, "Don't be too long."

As she walked back to the upstairs sitting room, Alexa wondered whether to say anything to Nicky about Lucien Girard. Normally she would have done so, but Maria's presence was acting as a deterrent. Very simply, she still didn't trust her. More often than not in those days, Maria's mouth was open and her foot was usually in it.

How she had changed in her appearance though. With a tendency to overeat, she had looked slightly plump all the time she had attended Anya's school. Her face had been lovely but her body too fleshy for a young woman.

Now, if she wasn't yet svelte, she was well on the way to becoming so, and her startling face and her mane of hair gave her a kind of movie-star glamour. Penélope Cruz sprang to mind, and that image was instantly reinforced when Alexa walked back into the sitting room.

Maria was standing near the window, looking casually elegant in burgundy slacks, silk shirt, and matching woolen jacket, the black hair streaming down her back; her face, in profile, was stunningly beautiful.

No wonder Nicky fell for her, Alexa thought, sitting down next to him on the sofa. It was obvious to Alexa that he had fallen completely under Maria's spell.

Hook, line, and sinker, she thought as she picked up her coffee cup and took a sip, then glanced at Nicky. "I can't wait to see the script, and once I've read it, Tom will drive me down to the Loire. He feels sure there are any number of houses that would be a perfect setting for the film."

"He's right. Maybe we'll all go down for a weekend," Nicky suggested.

Alexa gaped at him. "You've got to be kidding!"

Nicky exclaimed, "Oh, I know you're angry with Maria. She's told me all about it. And frankly, I think it's about time you both grew up and behaved like the mature young women you are. It's nonsense, carrying a grudge like that!"

"Hear! Hear!" Anya exclaimed. "It's time to move on."

Maria walked slowly toward the fireplace, looking nervous, hesitant; then she sat down on the edge of a chair and said in a low voice, "I'm sorry, Alexa, for causing you so much trouble. Truly regretful. But I was young, I didn't mean—"

"You betrayed me!" Alexa snapped, determined not to give an inch as she remembered how hurt she had been all those years ago.

"I didn't mean to! It was an accident. An error on my part. I've always been . . . so very sorry, Alexa."

Alexa glared at her. "I was never interested in Riccardo. That was all your imagination. And you blew it into a huge . . . atomic cloud! Into something so enormous, you incited Jessica to action, and she told me off in the most awful way. She took your side, believed you, and she stopped being my friend. Actually, Maria, *you* destroyed my friendship with Jessica."

"I'm so very, very sorry, Alexa," Maria apologized again. Her face had turned a ghastly white, and she appeared contrite, worried.

"You were jealous of our friendship, if the truth be known," Alexa shot back. "Jealous to death."

"I wasn't. That's not true." Maria now looked as if she was on the verge of tears.

"That's enough, girls," Anya said in a strong, firm voice. "I want you both to come over here for coffee tomorrow morning. And I'll have Jessica and Kay here as well, and we'll straighten this out once and for all. I don't want my party spoiled because you four are quarreling. So let us shelve the matter. This is not an appropriate time."

At this moment Tom walked back into the room, and from the look on his face Alexa realized his father had told him something he found interesting. She was certain he wanted to share it with her.

She said, "It's all right, Tom, you can talk in front of Nicky and Maria."

Surprised, he stared at her, his expression puzzled. He raised a brow questioningly.

Alexa nodded, then focused her attention on Maria. "We're going to talk about something that has to do with Lucien Girard. But you cannot breathe a word of it to Jessica. Do you understand that, Maria?"

"Yes. I wouldn't say anything to Jessica . . . or anyone."

Nicky, intrigued, asked, "What's all this about, then, Tom?"

Tom looked at Alexa once more. She inclined her head, and he explained, first telling them how it all started, with the photo in Alexa's album.

"Oh," Maria gasped, staring at Tom. "So Lucien's still alive?"

"We don't know," Tom said hastily, and continued. "The whole idea is a bit flimsy, I must admit, although a couple of things my father said intrigued me. The two men *could* be one and the same."

Nicky sat up straighter on the sofa, frowning. "I didn't know Lucien all that well, Tom, but I don't think he was the kind of man to . . . how should I put it? Lead a double life, play games. Anyway, who is it that so resembles him?"

"A man called Jean Beauvais-Cresse, who's in his early thirties. Earlier, I'd more or less decided that he might be related to Lucien. Perhaps Lucien was a brother using a stage name. Lucien could have been a cousin. However, my father told me that Jean's only brother died about seven years ago."

Maria and Alexa exchanged glances, but neither of them uttered a word.

"What else did your father say?" Anya asked.

"He told me that the brother was the eldest son, and that he was killed in a terrible accident. My parents didn't live in the Loire then, so this is sort of . . . local gossip, and Dad didn't have all the details. The brother's tragic, untimely death caused the father to have a stroke. Apparently he was very attached to the son who died. He was the heir to the title, the lands, the château. Jean, the younger son, was a bit of a black sheep, so my father once heard. He'd been living in Paris for a number of years, and came back only when his father was stricken, to look after him. He inherited everything when the old man died. That's all Dad could tell me."

"But don't you think it sort of fits in with Lucien's disappearance?" Alexa asked. She was convinced it did, and she held Tom's eyes, endeavoring to convey this to him.

He nodded. "The time frame is certainly right," he said cautiously.

Nicky said, "Let's just go over it. Seven years ago, Lucien Girard disappears never to be seen again. Seven years ago Jean's elder brother dies unexpectedly, so that Jean becomes the heir. But what if Lucien, working in Paris as an actor and using a pseudonym, were the eldest son and met a terrible fate? As everyone has always believed Lucien did."

"I thought of that," Tom answered. "But my father said the el- dest son was much older than Jean. By about fifteen years, a son by another wife, the first wife."

"So Lucien and Jean *could* be one and the same person," Anya stated.

"Bearing in mind the extraordinary resemblance and the simi- larities in age, yes. *Possibly.*" Tom now sat down in a chair and con- tinued. "But it's an awkward situation at best, Anya. My father said he'd make a few discreet inquiries, and I'll talk to him tomorrow. In the meantime, no one should say a word to Jessica. It wouldn't be fair. Either to her or Jean Beauvais-Cresse."

"What we need is someone who can verify that Jean was an ac- tor in Paris at one point in his life, and that he used a stage name," Alexa said. "Then we'd have something more concrete to go on." She let her eyes settle on Nicky.

"Oh, no, not me!" he exclaimed. "I hardly knew Lucien. And ac- tually, Larry didn't know him well either."

Anya settled back against the sofa, closing her eyes for a mo- ment. Something had stirred at the back of her mind, but she couldn't quite put her finger on it. And so she let it go. For the mo- ment.

CHAPTER TWENTY-EIGHT

"Let's go for a walk," Tom said as they left Anya's house and came out onto the street.

"Great idea," Alexa agreed, falling into step with him. "Like you, I love the Seventh. It's my favorite part of town."

Tom smiled and took hold of her hand, tucked her arm through his, and together they headed in the direction of the rue de Solferino and the quays running parallel with the river Seine.

It was warmer now and sunny, and the sky above was a clear blue arc, unblemished, without cloud, and benign on this May Sunday afternoon.

The Seventh Arrondissement where they were walking was an elegant area of the city, and Tom's apartment in the Faubourg Saint-Germain was located nearby. Also in the vicinity were such landmarks as the French Academy, the École Militaire, and the Hôtel des Invalides, wherein was housed the tomb of Napoleon.

But Tom and Alexa bypassed most of these historic buildings as they headed onto the Quai Anatole France.

For a short while they walked along the quai, enjoying each other, the weather, and the charming views of the Seine. Its rippling waters glittered in the sunlight, and suddenly a faint breeze blew up, rustled through the trees that grew alongside the Seine, made the leaves flutter and dance in the silvery light.

They paused for a moment, looking down, and Alexa smiled at the sight of the colorful *bateaux-mouches* smoothly moving down the river, leaving frothy trails in their wake.

She had always enjoyed the trips she had taken on them, especially those in the evenings with Tom years ago. Paris at night was romantic and magical when seen from the river on a slow-moving boat, the glittering lights of the city illuminating the inky sky. There was nowhere like it in the world.

Almost as though he had read her thoughts, Tom said, "We must take a *bateau-mouche* one night. I must admit I always enjoyed our evenings sailing along the Seine."

"How funny, Tom, that you would say that. I was just thinking the same thing."

Hand in hand, they walked on, heading toward the Quai Voltaire. Ahead, reaching into the sky, were the great towers of Nôtre-Dame, hazy now in the soft afternoon light of Paris, a light loved by artists over the centuries and so frequently captured on canvas.

To Alexa, Paris had never looked more beautiful than it did today. It was a city that forever took her by surprise. She remembered once getting caught in a thunderstorm, and hurrying through the streets drenched, looking for a taxi. And then unexpectedly she had abandoned the idea of finding a cab, suddenly enjoying walking in the pouring rain . . . and she had been filled with happiness that night, glad to be in this city, the city of her dreams. . . .

As they reached the Quai Malaquais, Tom said, "Let's head

down into Saint-Germain-des-Prés and have something to drink before going home. A coffee, whatever."

Alexa nodded in agreement, and still holding hands they strolled down the Rue Bonaparte, and into a huddle of quaint old cobbled streets. Here there were chic boutiques, antique shops, art galleries, and picturesque cafés that gave charm and character to this arrondissement. Several times they stopped to look in the windows of the boutiques, and paid a quick visit to one of Tom's favorite art galleries, but for the most part they did not linger, moved on at a steady pace.

By the time they reached the Place de l'Odéon, Alexa knew Tom was taking her to the Café Voltaire, once the favorite spot of the eighteenth-century French writer and philosopher of the same name.

They found a table outside and she was glad to sit down, settling into a chair under the awning, relaxing after their long walk. After ordering coffee for them both, Tom loosened his tie and opened the neck of his shirt. "It has become quite warm," he said, glancing at her. "Do you want to take your sweater off?"

"Yes, I will." She loosened the cashmere sweater tied around her neck and laid it across her knees. Turning to Tom, she added, "If Anya invites you to her party, will you come?"

"Only if I can be your date." He hesitated, then raised a brow, asked, "Or is your English friend going to be your escort that night?"

"Of course not!" she exclaimed, looking askance, her voice rising slightly. "Only I was invited, and I'm sure it's the same with the other women. Nicky told me the guests are mostly favored students from past years, her rather extended Russian, English, and French family, and some of her old friends." Alexa gave him a hard stare. "Anyway, I told you last night that I wanted to be with you, and on a permanent basis, married or not. So how could you possibly think I would want to take Jack, even if I'd invited him? I would have to ask him not to come, if that was the case."

She sounded so angry, he reached out, took her hand in his, brought it to his lips, and kissed it. "Such a dear little hand, I love it so," he murmured. "Don't be angry with me, Alexa."

"I'm not, not really." She cleared her throat, changed the subject. "Did your father tell you anything else? Were you holding anything back when we were at Anya's?"

"Not exactly. Dad didn't have much more information. But he did say that Jean Beauvais-Cresse was known to be something of a recluse, not often seen around the village or at the local church. By the way, Dad did tell me he was married, and that there was a child. But that's about it. As I said at Anya's, my parents have not lived in the Loire all that long, and much of what he knows is local gossip anyway."

"I understand." Alexa paused, looked off into the distance.

After a moment or two of watching her, Tom said quietly, "Is there something wrong, Alex? You're looking somewhat pensive."

A little sigh escaped her. "I was just thinking about Lucien Girard. If he *is* Jean Beauvais-Cresse and he just decided to go back to his old life one day, he must be a truly cruel man. Imagine doing something like that to Jessica, or any woman. I know Jessica suffered terribly, and Anya told me she's never married. She's probably been carrying a torch for Lucien all these years."

He frowned. "Do you really think so?"

"Yep, I do." She half laughed, and looked at him pointedly. "Women tend to be like that, you know." Me included, she thought, but refrained from saying so. "And there's something else, Tom. Just think of her *grief,* believing that something really bad happened to him." She sighed. "It makes me so mad."

"I can understand why. Obviously Nicky didn't know Lucien well, and if my father has no additional information, I think we just have to forget I ever mentioned Jean."

"Not so easy." Again Alexa stared ahead, her eyes narrowing slightly, and after a moment or two of thoughtful reflection, she turned to Tom, put her hand on his arm. "I think I have the solution . . . a way to find the truth."

"You do?" Tom sounded surprised, and just a little alarmed by the determined look that had flashed onto her face.

The waiter arrived with their cups of coffee, and once he was out of earshot, Alexa said carefully, "Here's my plan. I think we should go to the Loire and confront this man who so resembles Lucien Girard."

Tom sat back, obviously flabbergasted by her suggestion. For a moment he did not speak, and then taking a deep breath, he replied, "And I think that's asking for trouble . . . perhaps even legal trouble."

"No, no, I didn't put it quite right," Alexa exclaimed. "Let me start all over again. You and I, with Jessica, should drive down to the Loire Valley one day next week, if you can spare the time. Otherwise we have to go on the weekend. Once we arrive at Jean's house, Jessica and I will remain in the car while you go to the door. If Jean answers the door, you can simply tell him you have a client who wants to shoot a historical movie in the Loire, and is looking for appropriate châteaux in which to film the interior scenes. Once you get him engaged in conversation, Jessica and I will get out of the car and walk over to join you. If he *is* Lucien, you'll know, Tom, and so will we. He'll be in shock."

Tom nodded. "I'm following you. And if he's not Lucien, he won't recognize either of you, is that what you're trying to say?"

"Correct."

"But, Alex, Lucien was an actor. He *could* fake it, couldn't he?"

"I don't think he was that good an actor, Tom. He wasn't in the running for an Academy Award."

Tom burst out laughing, shaking his head. "There's just one thing though. You will have to tell Jessica, obviously, and that could open up her old wounds."

"It will. But look, if we solve a seven-year-old mystery and she gets closure *finally,* then that's a good thing, isn't it?"

Immediately, Tom saw the sense in what she was saying, and told her so, adding, "But I'd like to think it through, sleep on it, Alex, before making a final decision. Also, it would be wise to leave Jessica in the dark, for the moment anyway."

"I agree with you," she said.

————

"Where is your parents' house in the Loire?" Alexa asked. She and Tom had left the Café Voltaire and were walking back toward the Faubourg Saint-Germain and Tom's apartment.

"They're in that beautiful two-hundred-mile stretch of the Loire that is known as the Valley of the Kings," Tom answered. "It's between Orléans and Tours, and the reason it's called the Valley of Kings is because there are so many magnificent châteaux there."

"Yes, I learned all about the Valley of Kings in Anya's French history class," Alexa informed him. "Almost three hundred châteaux stand there, including some of the greatest . . . Chambord, Cheverny, Chinon, Chaumont, Amboise, Azay-le-Rideau, Close-Lucé, and Chenonceau, and I know it's a very beautiful area."

"Sublime," Tom said, glanced down at her, added, "But my parents don't have a grand château, Alex. Just a charming manor house in rather lovely grounds sitting on a bend in the River Cher, a tributary of the Loire. Basically it's quite a small estate, and that's one of the reasons they love it. Also, it's only about an hour and a half from Paris, so they can easily move back and forth between their apartment here and the Loire."

"So we could go there and back in one day, couldn't we?"

"Yes. *If* we decide to go and see Jean," he answered quietly. "But as I said, I must think about that idea, and I must also mention it to my father. I don't want to cause any problems for my parents."

"I understand, of course. By the way, did you tell your father the whole story? About Jessica and Lucien, I mean? Or did you just ask him about his neighbor?"

"I told him the whole story. You've met Dad, you know what he's like. He wasn't CEO of a giant American company in Paris for twenty-five years for nothing. He knew what questions to ask, how to get to the root of it all, and I must say he was very understanding, wanted to help in any way he could."

"I knew he would. I always liked your father, he reminds me of you. Or, rather, you remind me of him in so many ways."

Tom laughed. "I'm a chip off the old block, is that what you're saying?"

"Yep. And where is Jean's house? I suppose it must be nearby?"

"Not too far away, and it's not a house, Alex. It's one of those grand châteaux we were just talking about. Very old. Been in the Beauvais-Cresse family for centuries. I think it was built in the 1600s, or thereabouts. It's quite magnificent, and basically it's an agricultural estate, a lot of farming goes on there."

"At Anya's you mentioned something about a title."

"That's right. Jean is the Marquis de Beauvais-Cresse, to give him his accurate name."

"I see." She sighed. "It's such a peculiar story, isn't it? The way Lucien just disappeared overnight . . ."

"There are thousands of cases of missing persons," Tom told her. *"Hundreds of thousands,* if we consider all the countries in the world. People do disappear, and just like that." As he spoke, he snapped his thumb and finger together, then continued. "Some are the victims of foul play and their bodies are never found. Others do suffer an injury that results in amnesia. And then there are those who disappear because they want to."

"I know, that's the problem."

Noticing the disconsolate expression on her face, the sudden weariness in her tone, Tom changed the subject, said, "Have you ever been to Chenonceau?"

"No, I haven't."

"I want to take you there. But that won't be possible if and when we go with Jessica to the Loire. So perhaps you'd come another weekend. We could stay with my parents and I'd drive you over there, it's not very far. You see, this is the thing . . . Chenonceau has a connection to Mary Stuart . . . the *petite Reinette d'Écosse,* as she was called in France in those days."

"What connection?"

"The legendary château was once the home of Henri II, who gifted it to his mistress, Diane de Poitiers, but Henri and his son Francis II, and *his* wife Mary Queen of Scots, all spent a lot of time there."

"How interesting. I'd like to see it, and some of the other châteaux as well. There might be one or two people, owners of châteaux, who would let us film there for a fee."

"I've no doubt."

They walked on in silence for a while. At one moment Tom stopped, took hold of Alexa's arm, and turned her to face him. Looking deeply into her eyes, he said, "Quarrel or no quarrel, you really are being a good friend to Jessica. I admire you for that."

"When Lucien disappeared, her life changed radically," Alex replied. "Never to be the same again, that I surely know. Because his body was never found, there has been no closure. I'm sure that's why Jessica hasn't been able to settle down with another man. In my opinion, that is. And if I have a chance to help her, as I now think I do, why wouldn't I?"

Tom searched her face, then brought her into the circle of his arms. Against her dark head he said softly, "I see into your heart, my sweet Alex . . . and you are truly a good person." She did not answer, and he held her tightly for a moment longer. And then he thought: She fills the empty places in my heart, she makes me whole.

CHAPTER TWENTY-NINE

"I'm so glad you could come early, darling," Anya said, smiling across at Alexa. "I just want to go over a couple of things before the others arrive."

"And I have something to tell you," Alexa responded, settling in the chair opposite Anya. The two women were sitting in the small library that opened onto the gardens. It was another beautiful day, and the French doors were wide open to reveal a view of the cobbled courtyard and the cherry tree.

"What is it you wish to tell me?" Anya probed.

Alexa shook her head. "Tell me first why you wanted me to come earlier than the others, and then I'll explain something to you, an idea I've had."

"All right." Anya sat up a little straighter in the chair and continued. "I want everything ironed out between the four of you today, Alexa. This feud is beginning to be ridiculous, and I'm looking to *you* to create harmony among you."

"I'll do my best, and I agree with you actually. After yesterday's confrontation with Maria, I don't like the thought of any more of them. They're too upsetting. Let's face it, we're all around thirty and we should know better by now."

Anya nodded. "I'm glad you feel like being conciliatory. That's the way to go, and once you've talked it through, I'm going to take you all out to lunch."

"Oh, that'll be nice!" Alexa exclaimed. "But you should let *us* take *you*. To somewhere chic and expensive. We can all afford it now."

Laughing, Anya said, "There's something else I want to mention. I would like Nicky to invite Tom to my party. Would he come, do you think?"

"I'm sure he would." Alexa flashed her a wide smile.

"That's what I thought. I'll tell Nicky to send him an invitation. I'm also going to tell Kay to invite her husband, and naturally Maria will be accompanying Nicky. But I don't know what to do about Jessica. I've no idea if she's in Paris alone or with someone. In any case, I think she ought to have an escort."

"You still haven't seen her yet?"

"No, darling girl, I haven't. I asked her several times to come and have a drink, or lunch, but she's hiding behind her work. I say *hiding* because I think she's staying away on purpose."

"But why?"

Anya made a moue with her mouth, and then explained. "Jessica identifies me with the past, in particular the last few months she was here in Paris, when Lucien went missing. I think deep down she's a little afraid to see me because of the memories it will evoke. Memories of Lucien, the pain she suffered, her anxiety and fear . . . those sort of things. Remember, Jessica hasn't seen me since you all graduated. It's been *seven years*. And she links that time to him."

"I know. But I'm sure she'll open up today, and we can find out if she's here alone or not. I'll do everything I can to make her feel at ease, and Kay too."

"And Maria. Don't forget Maria, Alexa. She was awfully nervous yesterday. Afraid of you, I do believe."

"I suppose I was a bit fierce," Alexa admitted, looking shame-faced. "I'll be nice, I promise."

"Now, what is the idea you said you had? An idea for what exactly?"

"Finding the truth. Remember what you would tell us . . . *the truth sets you free,* you used to say." Alexa took a deep breath and shifted her body in the chair. "I think Jessica and I, along with Tom, should go down to the Loire, seek out this Jean fellow, and confront him."

"You could be on dangerous ground here, Alexa," Anya warned. "As I'm sure Tom has told you."

"Yes, he has. But I wasn't suggesting a real confrontation during which we ask him if he was once using another name and working as an actor in Paris. I just want him to *see* us, Jessica in particular. If he is shocked, we'll know immediately his alias was Lucien."

When Anya was silent, Alexa stared at her and asked, "Well, what do you think?"

Anya ruminated for a few seconds, then posed her own question. "What does Tom think?"

"He's cautious."

"So am I."

"Why, Anya?"

"Alexa darling, you can't go rushing around the countryside accusing people of leading a double life."

"I didn't say we'd be doing that . . . I said we'd go over to his house on a pretext, just to see him, let him see us. Get his reaction or nonreaction."

"I think I'd like to hear what Tom has to say."

———

A moment later Anya was standing up, walking across to the door, a huge smile illuminating her face.

"Hello, Jessica," she exclaimed. "It's wonderful to see you."

"And you, Anya, after so long."

The two women embraced and then Anya stepped back and stared at Jessica, an appraising look in her light blue eyes.

What a lovely woman Jessica had become, elegant in her well-tailored black pantsuit and white silk shirt, her long, pale blond hair falling around her tan face. She was still the all-American girl, tall, long-legged, slender, and as pretty as she was seven years ago. But there was a sadness in her eyes, a wistfulness in her smile, and Anya was sure she knew the reason why. *Lucien Girard.*

Anya also knew she had been right all along about Jessica's reluctance to come and see her. In Jessica's mind she was part of the past, part of another life, one Jessica had buried so deep within her psyche, she did not want to resurrect it. Could not, perhaps. At the same time, Anya was certain Jessica had not really moved on, that deep within her soul she still yearned for Lucien. She was thirty-one and still not married. Anya had immediately noticed there were no rings on her fingers. It seemed to her that Jessica needed closure. Maybe Alexa was right about going to the Loire to discover the truth. Might it not set Jessica free?

"Come in, come in, don't let's stand here in the doorway!" Anya exclaimed, taking Jessica's arm, leading her into the room. "Here's Alexa. And the others should be here any moment."

Alexa had risen and she stepped forward, her hand outstretched. "Hello, Jessica, it's been a long time," she said, striving for genuine cordiality.

Jessica inclined her head, rather curtly Alexa thought, and took her hand, shook it. "Hello, Alexa."

Alexa recoiled slightly; there was such coldness in Jessica's voice, and her demeanor was equally as icy. Fasten your seat belt, kid, she told herself. We're in for a rocky ride.

Anya had noticed Jessica's extreme coldness and she instantly filled with dismay and just a little trepidation. She had been foolish to think everything would go smoothly; there was obviously enormous animosity between the women. She had been somewhat aware of that at lunch yesterday when Maria and Alexa had flown at each other so fiercely, both of them sounding bitter, angry, and ready to continue the estrangement.

Anya said, "Jessica, do sit down," and taking her own advice, she lowered herself onto the sofa.

Jessica did as she asked, glanced around, and then said in a softer tone, "I'd forgotten how lovely the library is, Anya. It's just charming, the way you've redecorated it."

"And I must tell you how proud I am of *you*, Jessica, and your work. The houses and apartments you've designed are simply superb. I've loved seeing them in the magazines over the years. Congratulations, my dear."

"Thanks, Anya. And everything I know I learned at your school."

"The school can't teach anyone taste and style, you know, and you have an inbred sense of style, enormous taste, Jessica. I always told you that."

"Yes, you did, and you helped to make my dreams come true professionally. You and the other teachers were just extraordinary. I'm so lucky, I had the best training in the world, and what's stood me in great stead is my knowledge of history; English, French, and European furniture through the centuries; antique fabrics; and classical architecture. You taught me so much, Anya."

"Thank you again for those kind words." Anya settled back

against the cushions and asked, "Are you by any chance in Paris alone, Jessica?"

"I'm alone, yes."

"I see. The reason I ask is that I thought you may wish to bring someone with you to my party, be escorted by a friend that evening. And if that *is* the case, I will have Nicky send him an invitation."

Jessica blinked, and her brows furrowed together, then she nodded in a positive manner, her face softening. "I think I *would* like to bring a friend, have an escort that night. One of my clients happens to be in Paris. His name is Mark Sylvester, and he's a movie producer from Hollywood. But he's working on a picture, shooting here and in London. He told me the other day that he'll be back and forth between the two cities for the next month or so. I'm sure Mark would love to come."

"I'm delighted. May I ask where he's staying, my dear?"

"The Plaza Athénée, and I'll tell him to expect the invitation. Thanks so much for being so considerate, Anya."

Suddenly, Maria was gliding into the room looking stunning, beautifully put together in an ankle-length black skirt and a matching jacket, long and sleekily tailored. It slimmed her down even more, and underneath the jacket she wore a low-cut black silk blouse. Her long neck was enhanced by a gold necklace composed of ancient medallions, and she wore matching earrings. Her black pumps had very high heels, and she actually looked willowy this morning, Anya thought.

But when Maria spotted Jessica seated on a chair near the fireplace, she came to a sudden halt, looked hesitant. Maria appeared uncertain whether to enter the room or not.

Anya, detecting this at once, pushed herself to her feet and hurried to her, embraced her. "You're looking wonderful," she said, wanting to imbue confidence in her. "Here's Jessica and Alexa, and we're just waiting for Kay."

The words had hardly left Anya's mouth when Kay came walking in from the front portico, exclaiming, "Oh, dear, Anya, am I late? So sorry."

Swinging around, Anya smiled at Kay and shook her head. "No, you're not late at all. But now that you are here, my dear, I would like to get down to business." Escorting Maria and Kay into the room, Anya continued. "The business being solving your problems with each other."

––––––

Anya threw Alexa a pointed look as she returned to her seat on the sofa.

Understanding exactly what was expected of her, Alexa rose, walked over to the fireplace, and stood in front of it. She glanced at Maria and Kay, whom she had not yet greeted, and said, "Hi, Maria, hi, Kay."

Both women acknowledged her, although neither sounded very friendly.

Alexa said, "Anya asked me to speak to you about our falling out with each other seven years ago, just before our graduation. Her birthday party's on June the second, and, understandably, she doesn't want any bad feelings between us on that very special occasion. She thinks we should sort out our differences. In order to do that, I think we must all speak about our feelings, get things off our chests, so to speak."

"I want the air cleared," Anya murmured, and settled back against the cushions, hoping they would be friends by the time she took them to lunch.

Alexa unbuttoned the jacket of her black pantsuit, pushed her hands into her pockets, and went on. "Yesterday Maria and I did begin to sort out our differences, so I'm going to let Maria explain how she and I fell out. Then perhaps Jessica could respond."

Maria was totally taken aback, and she appeared to be startled as she sat up straighter in the chair and looked around at everyone.

After a moment, she cleared her throat, and said haltingly, "Alexa blamed *me* yesterday. She said I told Jessica lies about her. But that's not correct—"

"Yes, it is!" Alexa cut in peremptorily, and then took a step back. "I'm sorry for interrupting, Maria. Please continue."

Looking at Jessica, Maria said, "I didn't tell you any lies. Truly I did not. I told you what I believed to be the truth . . . that Alexa had been flirting with Riccardo Martinelli, my boyfriend at the time, and that she was trying to steal him from me."

Alexa had to bite off another exclamation, this time of denial. She was infuriated with Maria once again. She forced herself to remain calm, clenching her hands in her trouser pockets.

Jessica was nodding. "Yes, I remember that. You explained that you were worried Riccardo was going to become involved with Alexa. Because of *her* behavior. That you thought she was after him. You cried a lot. And, yes, I *did* believe you." Jessica glanced at Alexa. "And I did take Maria's side, there's no question about that."

"But it wasn't true!" Alexa protested. "And don't you think you owed me the benefit of the doubt, plus a chance to defend myself? You condemned me without a trial, so to speak."

Jessica bit her lip. "I guess that's true." She narrowed her eyes, and a thoughtful expression crossed her face. "But I did see you flirting with Riccardo at the party Angelique's mother gave. You were draped all over him when you were dancing, clinging to him, pressing into him. That's what cinched it for me."

Alexa felt bright color flame in her face, and she cried, "I *was* dancing with him, and quite intimately, I suppose. I admit that. But we were *only* dancing. And *I* wasn't flirting with him. *He* was flirting with me. He had a tendency to do that, as you well know, Jessica. And *you* also know it, Maria." Alexa gave Kay a very direct look and added, "I saw Riccardo Martinelli flirting with *you*, Kay, the Sunday night we all went to the Deux Magots for coffee. After your birthday dinner."

Kay sighed. "Yes, that's perfectly correct, Alexa." Kay turned to Maria. "He did flirt with me. And with everyone, if you want the absolute truth. Riccardo couldn't help himself. He was after all of us. I wasn't interested in him though, and in all honesty I don't think Alexa was either. I have to take her side in that."

"Listen to me, Maria," Alexa cried. "You were getting fat, and you knew it and you were a very troubled young woman. Not at all happy with yourself or your relationship with Riccardo. So you dreamed up this idea of me trying to steal him, when all along *he* was at fault, not I. You just couldn't help yourself, I suppose. But you behaved very badly. You took it out on me, and that was not fair play."

"I didn't—"

"Yes, you did! You went running off to Jessica, because you were jealous of our friendship, and you turned her against me, broke up *our* friendship."

Maria was stunned and she gaped at Alexa. But she said nothing.

Alexa went on. "*Why?* Why didn't you come to me? Have it out with me, for heaven's sake. You were really sneaky, and you genuinely hurt me. I was heartbroken about losing Jessica's friendship."

Maria seemed about to burst into tears, and did not respond. She threw Jessica a helpless look, said in a plaintive voice, "I know I accused Alexa, Jess, but I did *believe* she was trying to steal Riccardo from me, and I was so in love with him. Now I realize accusing her was an error, and I apologized to Alexa yesterday. I said I was sorry, and I do say that to you too."

"Maria *was* jealous of our friendship," Alexa announced to Jessica, staring hard at her.

Jessica exclaimed, "Oh, I don't know about that—"

Maria interrupted when she admitted, "I think I was jealous— no, perhaps that is the wrong word. I believe I was envious of your relationship. You seemed to have so much in common. You laughed a lot. At the same things. Sometimes I felt shut out. . . ."

"But we're both Americans!" Jessica cried. "Of course we had a lot in common . . . like growing up with the same values in the same country, for one thing. And liking the same movies, music, and books . . . and hamburgers and hot dogs and Dr Pepper and banana splits . . . And the same clothes and makeup . . . well, the list is endless, Maria. But I truly never thought we were excluding you. Or Kay."

"But you were!" Kay shot back, her voice suddenly and unexpectedly shrill. "And you did it a lot."

"Let's finish with Maria and Jessica," Alexa instructed firmly, giving Kay a warning look.

Jessica shook her head, blew out air. "Gee whiz, to coin an American phrase! I guess I did the wrong thing seven years ago, Alexa. I listened to Maria, a very tearful Maria, I might add, and I made a judgment. A flawed judgment, as it turns out. I guess I should have talked it out with you."

"Yes, you should have, but you didn't want to," Alexa snapped. "You were caught up with Lucien's disappearance. I realized that then, and I acknowledge it now. However, you weren't fair to me. Just because you had serious personal problems should not have precluded you from being straight and open with me. You just stopped speaking to me. . . ."

"I did, yes, and that was wrong. My only excuse is that I *was* extremely upset about Lucien, heartbroken. And I would like to point out that you weren't very helpful or sympathetic at the time." She gave Alexa a hard stare. "I expected more from you, of all people, under the circumstances."

"You expected sympathy, and I gave it to you! But you weren't receptive. And you didn't make it easy. You were far too busy *condemning* me for being a man snatcher, as you put it, and so you never even heard my sympathetic tone of voice. Or my offers to help you in any way I could. You didn't want my help, only Alain Bonnal's."

Jessica sat back; her face had turned pale under her tan. She looked suddenly haggard, and her eyes filled with tears. "I think you might have a point," she admitted finally.

Alexa nodded, and then looked at Maria and said, "And thank you, Maria, for being honest yesterday, and again today."

Anya said, "Yes, it certainly does help to clear the air. And what about you, Kay? Do you have anything to add to this?"

"I . . . well, I don't know. I don't think so."

"Why not?" Jessica suddenly demanded a little harshly, sitting up in the chair, determinedly brushing away her tears. She glared at Kay, who sat opposite her. "You certainly had enough to say about *us* when we were at school here, and usually it was behind our backs! You gossiped about us."

"I certainly did not!" Kay cried, her voice once more rising an octave or two. Endeavoring to get a grip on her anger, reminding herself she was now Lady Andrews, she took several deep breaths, striving for dignity. Then she said, "I never talked about any of you behind your backs."

"You're a *liar,* Kay. You did bad-mouth us—Alexa, Maria, and me," Jessica accused in an icy voice.

"How dare you call me a liar!" Kay looked at Alexa. "*She* is lying. Not I."

Jessica half rose, and then sat back down in the chair. "You did talk about us. I was informed of everything you said, and by a very good source. You said Alexa was superior and a snob, that she was always snubbing you. That Maria was a *rich* snob and treated you like a servant, and that I was a la-di-da Southern belle, forever taunting you, teasing you, putting you down. You called us the three bitches. Not very nice, *Lady* Andrews."

A bright scarlet flush rose from Kay's pale neck to suffuse her face; she blinked back the tears that suddenly filled her eyes. Her hand went up to her throat, and then a moment later she fumbled in her bag for a handkerchief.

Wanting to give Kay a moment or two to compose herself, Alexa turned to Jessica and said, "If you want the truth about how *I* felt, I was heartbroken, Jessica. Your friendship was very important to me. We were two American girls alone in Paris, and we had clicked right from the beginning, and then one day you simply dumped me without a proper explanation. And all along I thought we had such a meaningful relationship."

Jessica stared at her, said nothing, simply twisted her gold bracelet on her wrist. Her eyes were suddenly anguished. She knew deep within herself that she had wronged Alexa, and she was upset. She had listened to Maria, and acted stupidly, without thinking it through. What a fool she had been.

"I felt truly betrayed," Alexa murmured, sighing. "I hope you understand that now."

"I do. I'm—" Jessica cut herself off, took a deep breath. "I'm so very sorry. I have no excuse. Except to say that I was crazy at the time, off the wall with worry because of Lucien Girard's disappearance."

"I know. And I *did* try to help. You just didn't want to hear me, I suppose, because of Maria's story, and perhaps because you were just a little jealous of me."

"Me? Jealous of you? Come on, Alexa. I'm not the jealous type," Jessica responded heatedly, shifting in the chair, glaring.

"That's true, to a certain extent. But you were jealous of my success at the school, and my relationship with Anya," Alexa pointed out very softly, her anger now suddenly dissipated.

Anya sat up alertly, cringing inside, her eyes roaming over the four women, studying them. She remained absolutely silent, and she felt suddenly regretful that she might have played favorites at different times in the past.

"I don't believe this," Jessica exclaimed. "Alexa, how can you say such a stupid thing?"

"It's not stupid. It's true. You and I were in many of the same classes, and I knew then you were jealous and envious because I received such a lot of accolades and won most of the prizes. But you were silly to be jealous. I was a set designer, not an interior designer . . . it's not the same. And you were the most brilliant interior designer in the class, so far above any other student. I knew you were going to be a huge success."

Suddenly Jessica's face underwent change, her anger now replaced by a chagrined expression. After a moment or two of thought, she admitted in a low, deflated voice, "Maybe I *was* jealous . . . yes, that's *true*. I'm . . . sorry, Alexa. I owe you an apology."

"I accept your apology." Alexa glanced at Maria. "And I accept yours too. Now, Kay, let's hear from you."

Kay's white face looked stark against her black dress and jacket, and she shook her head, momentarily unable to say a word.

There were a few seconds of quiet in the library. None of the women spoke. Anya glanced from one to the other, suddenly worried about Kay. She looked as though she were about to faint.

And then Kay finally spoke, breaking the silence. "It's true that I did harbor a few grudges against all of you. We had been so close and happy together for three years, and then a few months before graduation you all changed toward me. I really didn't understand. I thought you didn't like me anymore because I didn't have your upbringing, your family backgrounds. You all slighted me."

Alexa stared hard at her, frowning, totally nonplussed. "But we didn't slight you, and certainly we didn't think you were any different than we were. Did we, Jessica?"

"No."

"Did we, Maria?"

"No, Alexa, not at all."

"But I felt the change in you," Kay protested.

Alexa said quietly, "I think we changed for the reasons we've just discussed. The problems were about me, Maria, and Jessica." She let out a small sigh. "Sadly, you just imagined we had changed toward you, but we hadn't. *Honestly.*"

"We never knew much about you or your background, Kay," Maria volunteered. She smiled at Kay, having now recovered her equilibrium. "You never confided. But you had beautiful clothes, plenty of money, an air of breeding. We did not think of you as being different."

Kay was silent.

Jessica said, "Look, if I ever slighted you in any way, then I'm sorry. I do sincerely apologize, Kay. But I don't believe I did."

"I agree with Jessica, and with Maria." Alexa shook her head. "We never thought you were different, not as good as us. We were simply caught up in our own troubles, as I just said." She gave Kay a huge smile and finished. "We always thought of you as one of us."

"But I wasn't," Kay said slowly. *"I was different."* She stopped, looked across at Anya.

Anya nodded, encouraging her to continue.

"I was a poor girl from the Glasgow slums," Kay confided in a fading voice. "But my mother worked hard to give me an education at a good boarding school in England. And then she sent me here to Anya's school."

"We didn't know," Jessica said. "And we really wouldn't have cared. We loved you for being *you,* Kay, and for your talent and caring ways."

Kay nodded. "I'm sorry," she said in a regretful tone. "But I was so hurt at one moment. I felt you'd cut me out, that's why I said the things I did." She groped again for the handkerchief and wiped her eyes.

The four women sat quietly, saying nothing to each other, every one of them lost in their own thoughts for a few minutes.

Anya had listened to their words very attentively, and she understood that Alexa had told the truth. It *had* all started with Maria, but Jessica had not helped the situation. In a sense, Alexa had been a victim of Maria's jealousy and muddled thinking, and Jessica's readiness to condemn her. As for Kay, she had allowed her insecurity and sense of inferiority to get the better of her. What a loss of true friendship, she thought, filled with an aching sorrow. Such a waste of those years when they could have given each other moral support, helped in other ways. What a shame they hadn't been able to communicate better, more explicitly, when they were here at the school.

Alexa broke into her thoughts when she said, "Let's bury this . . . *garbage!* Seven years have passed. We've all grown up. We're healthy, successful, and, yes, we're truly lucky women. Let's be . . . friends again."

Alexa offered her hand to Maria, who took hold of it and joined her near the fireplace. Jessica then stood up and came over to them. The three women put their arms around each other and looked across at Kay.

"Come on!" Jessica exclaimed, smiling at her. "Make the quartet complete again."

Kay pushed herself to her feet and rushed into their arms. The four of them stood in a huddle, half laughing, half crying. Then, breaking the circle they made, Jessica said, "We're missing one . . . come on, Anya. You belong here with us. For what would we be without you?"

――――

Anya took them to Le Grand Véfour for lunch.

The ancient restaurant, dating back to before the French Revolution, was situated beneath the arches of the Palais-Royal, and it was a historic landmark.

Now the five of them sat at one of the best tables, sipping champagne, surrounded by the distinctive decor of the eighteenth and nineteenth centuries.

Red velvet banquettes were balanced by simple, clean-lined Directoire chairs in black and gold and a richly patterned black-and-gold carpet, also in the Directoire style. Scarred antique mirrors in old gold frames were affixed to the ceiling and to some of the walls; on other walls were Neoclassical paintings of nymphs entwined with flowers and vines, set under glass.

"What a fabulous place this is," Jessica said, her keen eyes taking in every detail of the decor. "I just love the paintings, they look as if they come from ancient Rome."

"I noticed a brass plaque on one of the banquettes bearing the name of Victor Hugo," Alexa said. "And another one with Colette's name. She must have been a regular client too."

Anya nodded. "A lot of writers came here, and also politicians. Why, even Napoleon used to bring Josephine here to dine."

"*Really,*" Kay exclaimed, her ears pricking up. "I hadn't realized the place was that old."

"Oh, yes, it dates back to 1784, but at that time it was called the Café de Chartres. Anyway, I must admit, I never tire of its charm and refined elegance," Anya said. "It's had a sort of rebirth lately," she went on. "For many, many years it was owned by the famous chef Raymond Oliver. But he decided to sell it in 1984 because he was getting very old. It went through a transitional period, but under Guy Martin, the new chef, it's gone back to being one of the top restaurants in Paris. I know you're going to enjoy your food as much as you're enjoying the ambiance."

Glancing at Maria, Anya added, "They make a very nice sole, my dear, so you don't have to worry about your diet."

"You're always so considerate, Anya," she answered, and took a sip of her mineral water.

Anya now engaged Maria in a conversation about her paintings, and the two became very quickly engrossed.

Kay spoke to Jessica and Alexa about the premises she had found for her boutique, and then she tentatively asked Jessica if she would come and look at them later in the week. "Maybe you'll be interested in designing the boutique for me," she explained.

Soon the maître d' was hovering next to the table, telling them about the specialties of the house, and handing around the menus. After studying them for a while, they all settled for sole except Anya, who had decided to indulge herself. "I'm going to have the pigeon stuffed with foie gras," she announced with a wide smile. "And no one is going to make me feel guilty."

It was a warm and happy lunch. All of the women were at ease with each other once again; as Anya studied them from time to time, she realized the quarrel might never have happened. They were as sweet and loving with each other as they had been in their early years at the school. And this pleased her . . . it was the best birthday gift she could ever have.

Before they knew it, the lunch was over and they were trooping out into the street. Alexa began to chastise Anya, complaining that she should not have signed the bill, that they had wanted to take her to lunch. "It should have been our treat," she insisted.

"Don't be silly, darling. It was my pleasure to have you all together again, and so *tranquil* too. I'm very happy the quarrel is behind us."

As they waited for Anya's car and driver, Alexa drew Jessica under the arches at one moment, and said to her quietly, "I need to talk to you about something really important, Jessica. Can you spare me half an hour?"

Jessica looked at her swiftly, then nodded, glanced at her watch. "Let's find a cab. We can talk on the way to the Bonnal Gallery. I have an appointment there with Alain, about a painting for a client."

Alexa was staring at her intently.

Jessica frowned. "You remember him, don't you? He was a friend of Lucien's."

"Oh, yes, I remember him," Alexa answered.

CHAPTER THIRTY

A week later, very early on a warm Saturday morning, they drove to the Loire Valley.

Tom was at the wheel of his large burgundy-colored Mercedes sedan, with Mark Sylvester sitting next to him in the front. On the backseat were Alexa, Jessica, and Alain Bonnal.

Tom peered ahead as they finally exited the environs of Paris and headed out toward the main motorway that would take them to Orléans.

Although it was balmy weather, the sun was hidden by dark clouds that floated across the horizon; they seemed threatening, hinted of an imminent downpour. Tom hoped it would not rain, wanting a fast run down to his parents' house near Tours.

Once they arrived there, they planned to freshen up and have breakfast before heading over to Montcresse, the château that was the family home of Jean Beauvais-Cresse. Only Tom, the two

women, and Alain would go there; this had been decided over dinner last night, when the five of them had gone to Le Relais-Plaza
for a meal. They had agreed that Mark would remain with Tom's
parents. As soon as the meeting with Jean had taken place, the
other four would return for lunch and then head back to Paris in
mid-afternoon.

Because it was so early in the morning, it seemed to Tom that
no one wanted to talk, and perhaps it was best that they didn't, he
decided. He slipped a disc into the player on the dashboard, and
turned the volume down to low. Soon the car was filled with the
background themes from great Hollywood movies, and it was
soothing, not at all intrusive.

Jessica's eyes were closed, but she was not dozing. She was wide
awake, simply feigning sleep in order to sink down into her diverse
thoughts.

She had been determined to come and see this man in the Loire
who looked so much like Lucien, but now she felt a bit queasy
about it.

On the other hand, Alain was with them, and this helped. In
fact, he had insisted on accompanying them, and she felt she owed
it to him. After all, he had helped her so much when Lucien had
disappeared. This aside, Alain knew Lucien as well as she did, and
if she were at all uncertain about the man's true identity, she had
Alain to turn to for a proper assessment.

Could it be Lucien? Was he alive and well and living in the
Loire? Perhaps. Certainly she had sometimes had a weird feeling
that Lucien was alive somewhere out there. She had even said that
to Alain on the day they had lunched together at Chez André, when
she had first arrived in Paris. That day she had been quite positive
that Alain knew no more than she did, and he had proved that once
again when she had gone to the Bonnal Gallery last Monday.

In the taxi from Le Grand Véfour, Alexa had told her about the
photograph album, Tom's reaction to the photograph of her and

Lucien standing at the edge of the Pont des Arts. And although she had been momentarily startled, it had not come as a great shock. In one sense, she had half expected to hear something like this over the years. Then again, Mark had put a bug in her ear in February when he had suggested that Lucien might have vanished on purpose.

Alain had pooh-poohed that over lunch, and then again at the gallery, when Alexa had told him about Jean Beauvais-Cresse. It was apparent he had never heard of the man, that he did not know him, and he was very dismissive when Alexa said Jean could be Lucien. But when he heard they were planning a trip to the Loire, he had pleaded to be included, and Jessica had agreed, knowing she owed him this because of the past and his friendship to her.

The past, she thought now. Seven years ago. I was twenty-four and so innocent at that time, even more naive when I met Lucien when I was twenty-two, just a country girl from Texas. But Lucien had not been overly sophisticated, simply a good-looking, pleasant young man who loved being an actor. He had had a great zest for life, and they had been so compatible. And he had made her feel good about herself, their relationship, life in general, and the future they planned . . . California here we come, they used to say in unison. That had been their aim. An interior design business for her, Hollywood movies for him . . .

Alexa had been wonderful to her last Monday, so kind and compassionate, understanding of her sudden dilemma: to go and confront this man, or not to go. Alexa had been very determined, had opted for going down there, pointing out she really had no alternative. Jessica had at once seen the sense in making the trip.

She wanted, no, needed, to close this chapter in her life . . . she could do that only by going to Château Montcresse. If the man who lived there with his wife and child were not Lucien, then no harm had been done, and perhaps she could close the book anyway.

But if it was Lucien, then she would finally have the answers to some very pertinent questions, the most important one being *WHY?*

She had voiced all this to Mark yesterday before they had gone to meet the others at Le Relais for dinner. He had encouraged the trip, and agreed with her. He had also asked her to allow him to come along. "I care about you, Jessica," he had said. "And I'd like to be there for you, in case you need me. I'm your friend, you know." She had smiled and squeezed his arm, and said she would be relieved if he went with them, genuinely meaning this.

————

Not long after he had left the motorway at the exit to Tours, Tom quickly circumvented the town, drove past Amboise, and took a secondary road going toward Loches. "We'll soon be there," he said at one moment, and everyone sat up, looking out of the car windows eagerly.

Fifteen minutes later Tom was slowing down and turning into a driveway through iron gates that stood open and welcoming. At the end of a short drive stood a lovely old manor house, typical of the area, made of the local Loire stone that was renowned for turning white as it aged over the years. The manor looked pale and elegant set against a backdrop of dark green trees with an azure sky above.

As Tom pulled up and braked outside the front door, it opened and his father came hurrying down the steps.

After embracing his son, who was a younger version of himself, Paul Conners hugged Alexa with great affection, and then Tom made the introductions all around.

"Come on, let's go inside and have breakfast," Paul said, leading the way into the circular front hall with a terra-cotta-tiled floor and white stone walls hung with antique tapestries.

Christiane Conners, Tom's mother, appeared at this moment, and once she had kissed Tom and Alexa, her son introduced their companions.

"Perhaps you would like to freshen up," Christiane said, turning to Alexa and Jessica, and then heading toward the staircase, beckoning to them. "And Paul and Tom, I'll leave you to look after Mark and Alain."

Christiane led the way up the curving staircase to the floor above, and showed them both into a pretty guest room decorated with a pale blue toile de Jouy used throughout. It covered the walls, the bed, and was hanging at the windows as draperies.

Jessica noticed it immediately and thought the room looked so fresh and airy, but she made no comment. She was preoccupied, nervous now that they had arrived in the area.

"You will find everything you need here, Alexa," Christiane said, waving her hand around the room and then indicating the bathroom.

"Thank you, Christiane." Alexa turned to Jessica. "Why don't you tidy up first, Jess, I want to talk to Tom's mother for a moment."

"Thanks," Jessica replied, and disappeared into the bathroom.

Once they were alone, Christiane rushed over to Alexa and hugged her. She had always liked Tom's parents, and she knew this feeling was mutual. They had made her feel welcome, had always been loving.

Finally releasing her, Christiane looked into her face and said softly, "I was so happy when I heard you were in Paris, *ma petite,* and that you and Tom were back together." A beautifully arched blond brow lifted, and she quickly asked, "You are, are you not?"

"Yes, we are," Alexa answered. "We're meant to be together, and I think Tom knows that now."

"I hope so, *chérie.* You are important for him, good for him. I know this . . . ah, *les hommes* . . . sometimes they can be . . . stupid." She shook her head. "But what would we do without them?"

When Jessica came out of the bathroom, Christiane looked at her intently, said, "Tom wished me to tell you about Jean Beauvais-Cresse, but there is not much to tell, Jessica."

"He's the mystery man, according to Tom," Jessica responded, sitting down on the chair opposite Christiane while they waited for Alexa.

"Mystery man?" Tom's mother repeated, and shook her head. *"Non, non."* She thought for a moment, before continuing. "I think of him as a *recluse*. We do not see much of him in public. Nor his wife. They keep . . . to themselves."

"Perhaps that's an indication of *something* peculiar," Alexa said as she came out of the bathroom. "I think so anyway."

"I hope we'll soon have some answers," Jessica muttered.

Christiane nodded. "Let us go downstairs and have a little refreshment. I am sure you are eager to be on your way to Montcresse." She now hurried out of the blue guest room, and the two young women followed hard on her heels.

Despite her preoccupation, the designer in Jessica surfaced a couple of times as she followed Tom's mother and Alexa down the stairs, across the entrance hall, and into an unusual circular room. This was at the back of the house, and had many windows; these looked out onto lawns, gardens, and a stand of trees. Beyond she could see a stretch of the river.

"How beautiful!" she exclaimed as she glanced around, noting the tasteful decorations, the mellow antiques, the displays of porcelain plates on the walls.

"This is the summer dining room," Christiane explained, ushering them toward the circular table in the middle of the room.

They sat down just as Tom, his father, and the other two men came into the room. "Sit anywhere you wish," Paul said. He took a seat next to Alexa, grasped her hand in his, and squeezed it.

Alexa squeezed back, smiled into his face. She thought: How handsome he is. Tom will look like this when he is sixty-five. *I've got to be with Tom. Always. I want to share my life with him.*

Paul said, "Penny for your thoughts, Alex?"

She laughed. "I couldn't possibly tell you."

"Then I'll tell you," he said with a small, knowing smile. Leaning closer, he whispered in her ear, "You want to be with him for the rest of your life."

Alexa stared at Paul Conners, squinting in the sunlight streaming in through the windows. "How did you know?"

"It's written all over your face, honey."

Christiane was pouring coffee, and Tom was offering a basket of breads to everyone, moving around the table slowly.

"What would you like, Alexa?" he asked when he finally stopped next to her chair.

"You," she mouthed silently as she looked upon him and took a croissant.

Tom kissed the top of her head, made no comment.

Paul focused on Alain and said, "Tom explained to me that you used to know Lucien Girard when Jessica did. At the time he lived in Paris."

"*Oui, oui,*" Alain said, nodding.

"And he was a nice guy then?"

"*Ah, bien sûr,*" Alain exclaimed. "A man of integrity. I find it hard to accept this theory that he . . . disappeared on purpose."

Mark interjected, "It wouldn't be the first time a man has done that. Or a woman, for that matter."

Paul nodded in agreement. "And there's usually a helluva good reason when this happens. I can't imagine what his family suffered, quite aside from Jessica's grief, of course."

"He told me he was an orphan, that his parents were dead," Jessica volunteered.

Alain added, "And he told me the same thing. No parents, no siblings."

"And seemingly no past," Mark remarked, staring at Paul pointedly.

"If you're intent on leading a double life, it's always best to keep the story and the details very simple. That way you can't make too many mistakes," Paul responded.

"That is true," Christiane murmured.

Alexa, studying Tom's mother, thought how lovely she looked, but then, she usually had in the past. Christiane Conners was one of those well-groomed Frenchwomen who could manage to look chic in a plain cotton shirt and pants, which is what Christiane was wearing this morning. She admired her for looking the way she did at her age, and she was glad Tom's mother was her ally.

Jessica had been listening to them all, quietly sipping her coffee, saying nothing very much. But once she thought everyone had finished, she said, "Do you think we can drive over there, Tom? I'm awfully nervous, and as long as I sit here, I'm prolonging the agony. . . ."

Tom and Alexa both leapt to their feet, and Tom said, "Of course we can go." Taking hold of Alexa's hand, he moved away from the table, telling his parents he would see them later. Alain did the same, then ushered Jessica out of the dining room.

Mark pushed back his chair, excused himself, and hurried out after Jessica. He caught up with her on the front steps, took hold of her arm, drew her toward him. Looking down into her face, he said, "Whatever happens over there doesn't really matter, Jess darling. One way or another, you'll finally have *closure.*"

Jessica tried to smile, but it faltered. "You're right, Mark, I know that. I'm just nervous, queasy."

He brought her into his arms, held her close, and said against her hair, "You're going to be all right, Jessica. I'm going to make damned sure of that."

CHAPTER THIRTY-ONE

Tom and Alain sat in the front of the Mercedes; Alexa and Jessica took the backseat. No one spoke on the way to Montcresse, but at one moment Alexa reached out, grabbed Jessica's hand, and held it tightly in hers, wanting to comfort and reassure her.

Jessica sat very still on the backseat, holding her breath, eager to get to the château. Already she was wishing the confrontation were over, and that they were on their way back to Paris. Confrontation, she said to herself. Who knew if there would even be one? Jean Beauvais-Cresse was more than likely a very nice man leading a quiet life with his family, who simply happened to bear a resemblance to Lucien Girard. An innocent bystander, in other words.

Tom broke the silence in the car when he said, "That's Montcresse straight ahead of us."

Jessica and Alexa strained to get a better glimpse.

What they saw was a truly grand château, standing proudly on a rise not far from the river Indre, another tributary of the Loire. Its white stone walls gleamed in the bright morning sunlight, while the black, bell-shaped roofs atop the numerous circular towers gave the massive edifice a fanciful air.

As Tom drove up the rise, Jessica noticed the well-kept grassy lawns edging the sand-colored gravel driveway, and behind the château there was a dense wood of tall, dark trees. Two more circular towers with bell-shaped roofs and thin spires flanked the drawbridge leading into the interior courtyard.

Tom slowed down as he rolled over the drawbridge, went under the arch and into the yard, heading toward the front door.

Jessica felt her stomach lurch, and for a second she thought she could not go through with this encounter. She almost told Tom to turn around and leave; she looked at Alexa, opened her mouth to speak, but no words came out.

At once, Alexa saw the expression of anxiety mingled with fear on Jessica's pale face, and she tightened her grip on Jessica's hand, murmured, "It'll be fine."

Still unable to say anything, Jessica merely nodded.

Tom parked close to the château's walls, a short distance away from the huge front door. Half turning in his seat, he said to the two women, "One of the staff might answer the door, and in that case I'd be invited inside. Should that happen, wait five minutes and then come looking for me. You'll be allowed inside if you say you're with me."

Now glancing at Alain, Tom went on. "You should take charge if I go inside, it'll be quicker and easier for you to deal with any staff member."

"Of course, Tom, don't worry," Alain answered.

Alexa asked, "But what if Jean answers the door?"

"I'll engage him in conversation for a few minutes, then I'll glance at the car, wave to you. At that moment you should come and join me . . . join us. Everything clear?"

"Yes," Alexa said, and Jessica nodded.

Tom alighted and walked down the cobbled courtyard, heading for the huge front door made of nail-embellished wood. When he came to a stop, he saw that it stood ajar. Nonetheless, he knocked and waited. When no one came, he pushed the door slightly, peered inside, and shouted, "Hello!"

A moment later an elderly gray-haired man wearing a striped apron over his pants, shirt, and waistcoat suddenly appeared in the entrance hall. He was carrying a silver tray, and he stepped forward when he saw Tom. He inclined his head. *"Bonjour, monsieur."*

"Bonjour. J'aimerais voir Monsieur le Marquis."

"Oui, oui, attendez une minute, s'il vous plaît."

These words had hardly left the man's mouth when Tom heard footsteps on the cobblestones, and he glanced down toward the stables.

Jean Beauvais-Cresse was walking toward him. He wore black riding boots, white jodhpurs, and a black turtleneck sweater. He raised a hand in recognition, and a split second later the two men were greeting each other and shaking hands.

Tom then went on. "I apologize for intruding like this, without telephoning first, but as we passed the château my clients asked me to stop the car. They were intrigued by Montcresse. You see, they're making a movie about Mary Queen of Scots and plan to shoot in the Loire. I've been showing them this area, since they're seeking possible locations for the upcoming film—"

"C'est pas possible," Jean cut in with a small, regretful smile. "Many people have wanted to film here in the past. But it doesn't work. The château's not the best place to shoot a film, I'm afraid."

"I see," Tom responded, and wanting to find a way to keep him talking, he improvised. "But what about outside? There are quite a lot of exterior scenes, and perhaps you would consider allowing them access to the property."

Unexpectedly, Jean Beauvais-Cresse seemed to hesitate all of a sudden, appeared to be considering this idea. At the same time, he moved forward, stepped inside the château, stood regarding Tom from the entrance hall. "Perhaps there might be a way to film on the estate," he said finally.

Tom was listening attentively, but out of the corner of his eye he saw Alexa, Alain, and Jessica alighting and walking toward him. Wishing to keep the other man totally engaged as they approached, Tom leaned forward slightly, and continued. "There would be a very good fee involved, and the crew would have instructions to be extremely careful on your land. Also, the production company is insured anyway."

"I understand. But I must think about it—" Jean broke off abruptly. Shock was registering on his narrow face, and he had paled. As if undone, he staggered slightly, leaned against the doorjamb, his light eyes wide with surprise and panic.

Jessica, who stood just behind Tom, now stepped forward, staring at Jean. Immediately, she recognized him, just as he had recognized her. It *was* him. A grayer, older version of Lucien Girard. There was no doubt in her mind.

Shaking inside, and just as undone as Jean was, she swallowed hard. "I often thought you must be alive somewhere out there in the world. . . ." Her eyes welled with tears.

Jean stared at her, then his gaze settled on Alain and finally Alexa. His eyes acknowledged them but he said nothing.

He shook his head slowly and directed his attention on Tom. "Your talk about filming intrigued me," he murmured. Sighing heavily, he opened the door wider. "You'd better come inside," he said.

————

Jessica was still shaking inside and her legs felt weak, but she managed to hold herself together as the four of them followed Jean across the huge stone hall. It was baronial, hung with dark tapestries and stags' heads; a huge chandelier dropped down from the high ceiling. Their footsteps echoed on the stone floor.

He led the way down three steps into a long, spacious room with French windows opening onto a terrace. Jessica did not pay much attention, only vaguely noticed the dark wood pieces, the faded fabrics, the worn antique Aubusson underfoot. There was an air of shabby elegance about it.

Jean paused in the center of the room and waved his hand at a grouping of chairs and sofas. "Please," he murmured. He did not sit himself, but moved away, went and stood near the stone fireplace.

Once the others were seated, he glanced at Tom and asked, "Did we know each other in Paris years ago?"

"No."

"How did you . . . make the connection?"

"My friend Alexa has a photograph of Jessica with you. When I mentioned your name, she said the man in the picture was some-one called Lucien Girard. Then she told me the story . . . of your disappearance."

"I see." He shifted on his feet, blinked several times.

No longer able to contain herself, Jessica leaned forward slightly, and asked in a tight voice, "*Why?* Why did you do it? Vanish the way you did, without a trace?"

He did not respond.

No one else spoke. The room was very quiet.

Outside, a light wind rustled through the trees, and in the dis-tance a bird trilled. Through the open French windows the scent of roses and other flowers floated inside, filling the air with sweet-ness. There was a sense of tranquillity in this long, narrow library, an air of timelessness, of gentleness.

But emotions were high.

Jessica exclaimed, "I think you owe me an explanation. And Alain. We tried so hard to find you, and when we couldn't, we thought you were dead. We grieved for you!" She shook her head, and tears gathered in her eyes. "I think I've been grieving for you right until this very moment." Her voice broke and she could not continue.

"I think you should tell Jessica why you disappeared, Lucien. You owe that to Jessica, if not to me," Alain interjected.

"Yes, it is true. I do owe you both an explanation." He sat down on a chair near the fireplace and took a deep breath. After a moment, he looked over at Jessica, and slowly began to speak.

"I said I was going to Monte-Carlo to work because I couldn't tell you the truth, Jessica."

"And what was the truth?" she asked, still tearful.

"That I was not really Lucien Girard. This name was my stage name . . . I was, I am, Jean de Beauvais-Cresse. But twelve years ago I left this house and went to live and work in Paris, after a bad quarrel with my father. He disapproved of my desire to be an actor, and washed his hands of me. In any case, my older brother, Philippe, was his favorite, and, of course, he was the heir to the title and the lands. Seven years ago, just before you graduated, Philippe was tragically killed in an accident. He was flying on a private plane to Corsica, to join his fiancée and her family, when the plane went down in a bad thunderstorm. Everyone on board was killed.

"When he received the terrible news of Philippe's death, my father had a stroke. My mother, who was an invalid, summoned me to return to Montcresse. I was needed here. I had a funeral to arrange, and other matters to attend to, as well as my mother and father to care for."

"But why didn't you tell me?" Jessica demanded. "I could have come with you, helped you."

"It was far too complicated. I did not have time for long explanations. I was suddenly needed immediately. Urgently. Anyway, I

believed I would be here in the Loire for only a week at the most."
Jean paused, leaned back in his chair, took a deep breath.

Scrutinizing him intently, Jessica thought he looked older than
thirty-five. His narrow face was lined and his fair hair was meager.
He had always been slender, but now he was really thin. To her, he
seemed undernourished, and it struck her that he had lost his
looks. And, not unnaturally, he was very nervous. Beads of sweat
lined his upper lip and his forehead. It was not overly warm in this
room, and she suddenly understood the extent of his unease with
them, with her in particular.

For his part, Jean de Beauvais-Cresse was fully aware of her
fixed scrutiny, and he flinched under it. His discomfort was pro-
found. Seeing her again had sent shock waves through him. She
had never looked more beautiful, and her allure for him was as potent as ever. He still loved her deeply. He had never stopped loving
her. He would love her until the day he died. She had been, still
was, the love of his life. But it was not meant to be, could not be.
Not anymore.

Jean filled with regret. A deep sense of loss overwhelmed him,
and his emotions ran high. And he had to steady himself, take hold
of his swimming senses. For one awful moment he thought he was
going to weep. Breathing deeply, taking hold of himself with steely
determination, not wishing to break down in front of them, he rose,
moved to the fireplace once more, took up a stance there.

Clearing his throat, he said, "As I was saying a moment ago, I
did not think I would be staying here for very long. Perhaps a week.
I truly did intend to tell you everything when I returned to Paris,
Jessica. Please believe that."

"And then what?" Jessica asked, her voice still shaking.

"I hoped we could continue as we were, make a life together.
Somehow. But then something else occurred, just after the funeral
of my brother."

Alain, frowning intently, asked quickly, "What happened?"

"I became ill. Extremely ill. I had been fighting what I thought was flu. A scratchy throat, aches and pains, night sweats, fever, were the symptoms. I mentioned this to my father's doctor the day after the funeral, when he came to Montcresse to see my parents. At once he insisted I go to his office for an examination—" Jean stopped, cleared his throat, seemed for a moment hesitant to continue.

Jessica's eyes were riveted on Jean, and she held her breath. Even before he spoke she knew he was about to tell them something quite terrible.

Jean continued. "Dr. Bitoun did not like what he found. He sent me immediately to Orléans, to see a cancer specialist, an oncologist. I had X-rays, a CAT scan, and an MRI. The doctor also took a biopsy of a node under my arm. Everyone's worst fears were confirmed when the results of the tests came back. I had Hodgkin's disease."

"But you were so young, only in your mid-twenties!" Jessica cried, her eyes wide with shock.

"That is true. It usually does strike young men in their twenties, sometimes even in their teen years," Jean answered, and went on to explain. "Hodgkin's disease is cancer of the lymphatic system, and once I was diagnosed, the oncologist at the clinic in Orléans hospitalized me at once, and started radiation treatment. Aside from—"

"But why didn't you call me?" Jessica interrupted heatedly. "I would have come to you at once. I loved you."

"I know, and I love—" He coughed behind his hand before saying, "I loved you too, Jessica. And because I loved you I decided it was better to . . . just disappear."

"But why?" she demanded. Her eyes filled again, and the tears trickled down her cheeks. "I loved you so much . . . with all my heart."

"I know," he said in a low, faltering voice. "However, I suddenly realized I had nothing to offer you. I believed I was going to die. I truly did not believe the treatments would work. Then again, I had an invalid mother, a stricken father, and the responsibility of running the estate . . . if I lived. It seemed . . . all too much to burden you with at the time. You were so young. And, as I just said, I did not think I would live for very long."

"But you did live," Alain said, staring hard at Jean.

Jean nodded. "I did, yes. After a number of agonizing treatments, I went into remission after about eight months. Even so, the prognosis was not encouraging. The oncologist warned me the cancer could come back; in fact, he led me to believe it would do so." He looked across at Jessica. "Marriage was no longer a possibility."

"But you *did* marry. And you have a child," she responded quietly, hurting inside.

"That is true, yes. I married three years ago. I had a childhood friend living nearby, and once I came out of the hospital she came here to Montcresse to help me handle things. Then my father suddenly died, and I inherited. My responsibilities increased. Sadly, my mother died a few months after my father. I was totally overwhelmed. Annick, my dear old friend, was my rock at the time. Slowly, we became involved, but I had no plans to marry."

"Then why did you marry her?" Jessica asked. "And not me? I would have come here. I, too, could have been your rock."

"Because to my utter surprise Annick became pregnant," Jean answered. "I had not thought this possible, because often the treatment for cancer renders a man . . . sterile. But Annick was pregnant all of a sudden. I cared for her. She loved me, wanted to marry me, and so I did the correct thing. Also, she was going to give me an heir to the title and the lands, someone to follow me when I died. She knew that I would probably not live to see the boy grow up, but she and I accepted that."

"How old is the child?" Alexa said, speaking for the first time.

Jean looked at her, a faint smile flickering on his mouth. "Three."

"And you are in remission now, are you?" Alain asked.

"No. I'm undergoing treatment again. Chemotherapy this time."

"I'm sorry," Alain responded. "I'm sorry it has come back."

Jessica, staring at him, her eyes still moist, said slowly, "I would have understood all this, I would have come to you, Lucien, I would, I really would. You were . . . my life."

Jean's light bluish-gray eyes filled with tears. He opened his mouth to reply but found he could not say a word, so choked was he.

Jessica, always so close to him, always so understanding of his thoughts and feelings, rose and walked across the room, her step firm. When she drew closer to him, Jean reached out to her.

As she came to a standstill in front of him, Jessica saw the tears on his cheeks, grief and sorrow in his eyes.

He was aware of no one else in the room but her. He took hold of her gently, brought her into his arms. She clung to him, rested her head against his chest, her own face wet with tears. And she forgot every other question she had meant to ask him. They no longer mattered.

Against the top of her head, he said in a low voice, "I thought I was doing the right thing. The best for you. Perhaps I was wrong."

When she did not respond, Jean murmured, "Forgive me, Jessica."

"I do," she whispered against his chest. "I do forgive you, Lucien." She blinked back fresh tears, endeavoring to compose herself. "I'll always think of you as Lucien, remember you as him."

"I know."

There was a sudden rustling noise, the sound of running feet, and as the two of them drew apart, a small boy came hurtling into the library through the French windows. *Papa! Papa! Je suis là!*

he cried, and then stopped when he saw that there were other people with his father.

Jean walked over to him, took hold of his hand, and led him over to Jessica. "This is my son . . . Lucien," Jean told her, looking deeply into her eyes.

She gazed back at Jean, nodding, understanding. Then she hunkered down in front of the child, touched his soft, round baby cheek with one finger, and smiled at him. *"Bonjour. Je suis Jessica,"* she said.

The boy smiled back at her. *"Bonjour,"* he answered in his high child's voice, his little pink face radiant with happiness and good health.

Swallowing her emotions, Jessica stood up, looked across at Alexa and the two men. "I think perhaps we should go," she said to them, and turning to Jean, she added, "Thank you for explaining . . . everything."

"And I believe you understand *everything*."

"I do."

Dropping his voice, he said, "So you are not married, Jessica."

"No."

He sighed, looked at her sadly. "I'm sorry. *C'est dommage.*"

"It's all right."

Jean escorted them out of the library, one hand on Jessica's shoulder, the other holding his son's hand as he crossed the stone hall to the front door. When they stepped out into the courtyard, he leaned into her, kissed her cheek.

"Au revoir, Jessica. *Bonne chance."*

"Good-bye."

He inclined his head.

She walked away from him, heading for the car. She heard the others taking their leave, hurrying after her. Jessica paused at the car; turning around, she looked back.

He stood where she had left him, near the door, holding the child's hand. With the other he blew a kiss to her, and then waved. So did Lucien.

She blew kisses back and waved to them, then got into the car, her heart full.

———

No one spoke as they drove away from Montcresse.

Alexa held Jessica's hand and looked at her several times. But once they had left the château behind, she finally asked, "Are you all right?"

"Oh, yes, I'm fine," Jessica replied in a fading voice. Clearing her throat, she went on speaking softly. "Now that I know what happened to Lucien I can be at peace with myself. I have closure, as I always knew I would."

"It was so sad," Alexa said. "My heart went out to him."

"I also felt sorry for him," Alain murmured, turning to look at them. "What a pity the cancer has come back. But perhaps . . . Well, let us hope he will go into remission again."

"I honestly think he truly believes he made the right choice. For you, Jessica. He thought he was protecting you," Tom told her.

"I know he did. But he did my thinking for me. That's not really fair." Jessica let out a deep sigh. "All these years I have been in love with a memory. A memory of Lucien, a memory of my first love. But *he* is different now. *I* am different now. I just wish he had trusted me. Trusted our love enough to tell me the truth seven years ago, when all these terrible things were happening to him."

"What would you have done?" Alexa ventured, looking at her intently.

"I would have gone to him immediately. There is no question in my mind about that," Jessica asserted.

"And would it have worked, do you think?" Tom asked.

"I don't know, I really don't. But I am relieved I did finally see him again. Now I can move on at last." But part of me will always love him, Jessica added to herself as she leaned back and closed her eyes. And part of me will always belong to him, as I know part of him belongs to me. He made that so very clear, just as he made it clear that he still loves me.

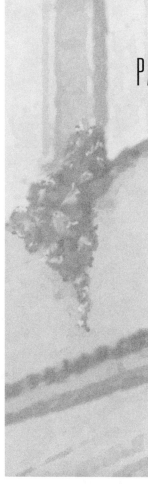

PART FOUR

Celebration

CHAPTER THIRTY-TWO

Kay sat staring at herself in the mirror, wondering if she needed just a touch more blush. It seemed to her that her face was paler than usual, and she wanted to look her best tonight.

Leaning back in the small chair, she now scrutinized herself from a distance, her eyes narrowing slightly, her head held on one side. Picking up the brush, she delicately stroked her cheekbones with it, and finally, satisfied with the effect, she turned her attention to her hair. It fell around her face in a tumble of auburn waves and curls; she mussed it a little more with her hands, combed the front, and sprayed it lightly. "There, that's the best I can do," she said out loud, again peering at herself in the dressing table mirror.

"You look beautiful, Kay," Ian said from behind her, placing a hand on her bare shoulder.

"Gosh, you surprised me!" she exclaimed, craning her neck to look up at him towering above her.

Smiling, he bent down, touched her cheek with his finger, then swiveled her shoulders so that she was again looking at herself in the mirror.

"Close your eyes," he instructed.

"Why?"

"Just do as I say."

"All right."

Once her eyes were tightly shut, Ian reached into the pocket of his robe and pulled out a necklace. Very carefully, he placed this around Kay's long, slender neck, fastened it, then said, "Now you can open your eyes."

When Kay did so, she gasped in surprise and delight. Around her neck her husband had placed the most beautiful diamond and topaz necklace she had ever seen. Loops of diamonds formed a lacy bib, and set along the front in the loops of the diamonds were eight large topaz stones.

"Ian, it's exquisite! I've never seen anything quite like it!" she exclaimed, gazing at him through the mirror. "Thank you, oh, thank you so much."

"I'm glad you like it, darling. I fell in love with it the moment I saw it, in just the same way I fell in love with you. Immediately, to be precise."

She laughed, and then her eyes widened as he handed her a small black velvet box.

"These will add the finishing touch," he said.

Again she gasped as she lifted the lid. Lying on the black velvet were a pair of topaz earrings, each large stone encircled by diamonds. "Ian, how extravagant you've been," she cried. "But they're so beautiful. Darling, thank you."

A wide smile spread across his face. He knew her happiness, excitement, and pleasure were genuine, and this gratified him. He wanted to please her, to let her know in every way possible how much he loved her. "Put them on," he said.

"Right away, sir," she answered, and clipped an earring on each ear, staring at herself. "They're just . . . *magnificent,*" she said.

"As is my beautiful wife."

"Again, thank you, for the compliment and these beautiful pieces. But it's not Christmas, nor is it my birthday."

"It doesn't have to be a special day for me to give you a present, does it?"

She laughed. "No. And you're quite incorrigible."

"I truly hope so." He stroked her shoulder, then said, "Do you remember when I went into Edinburgh that Saturday in February? The day before Fiona's birthday?"

"Yes, very well. You seemed a bit mysterious. Or maybe *vague* is a better word. Certainly you were rather closemouthed when you came back."

"I know. And actually I was mysterious. The reason being the necklace and earrings."

"Oh!" she said, staring at him through the mirror.

"I'd asked old Barnes, the manager of Codrington's, the jewelers, to keep his eyes open for a diamond necklace. Imagine my delight when he phoned to say he had a diamond and topaz necklace, very rare, very old, and would I like to see it." Ian paused, touched a strand of her auburn hair. "You can't imagine how those topaz stones match this," he said, and continued. "I really went into Edinburgh to look at the necklace, although I did need to buy something for my sister."

"And you've had those pieces all these months?"

He nodded. "Actually, Kay, I was going to give them to you for Christmas, but suddenly I realized that now would be as good a time as any. So I brought them with me on Thursday."

She nodded and rose, went to him, put her arms around his neck, and kissed him firmly on the mouth. "You are the most unique and wonderful husband a girl could ever want."

"Likewise, my pet." As he spoke, he untied the belt of her robe, slipped it off her shoulders. It fell to the floor, a pool of pale blue around her feet. He held her away from him, gazing at her. "Look at you, Kay. So beautiful."

Slipping off his own robe, Ian brought her into his arms, held her tightly, kissing the hollow of her neck, and then her breasts. Lifting his head he looked deeply into her eyes and said, "Come to bed with me. I promise I won't mess your face and hair."

She laughed lightly. "As if I really care. I can do it all again."

"We do have time," he murmured as he drew her toward the bed. "We don't have to meet Alexa and Tom until six forty-five."

They lay down together, clasped in each other's arms, their mouths meeting again. Kay let her tongue brush Ian's lips and then she opened her mouth slightly, tasting him, their tongues meeting. His kisses became more passionate, more intense, and his hands roamed over her delicately, touching, stroking, exploring. Her long, tapering fingers went into his hair, and then moved down to stroke his back his firm, muscular buttocks.

Kay felt him growing harder against her, and she rolled away from him, onto her back, and pulled him onto her. Pushing himself up on his hands, he looked down into her eyes and said softly, "I love you, Kay, with all my heart."

"Oh, Ian, Ian," she whispered, and she arched her body toward him. "I want you . . . I want to feel you inside me. Please, please."

Leaning over her, he kissed her on her mouth slowly, lingeringly, and then he lay on top of her, pushed his hands under her buttocks, and brought her closer. He entered her swiftly, and she groaned; instantly the two of them fell into a rhythm they had made their own long ago. As she moved her body against him, breathing harder, clutching at his shoulders, he felt as though he were going to explode. A moment later, she spasmed convulsively, and so did he, and they were carried along on a wave of rising passion, lost in their mutual ecstasy.

At last, when they lay still, their hard breathing slowing to normal, Ian raised himself up on an elbow, gazed down at her, moving a strand of hair away from her face. "Perhaps we just made that baby you want so badly," he murmured, a half smile playing around his wide and generous mouth. "But if we haven't, it doesn't matter. You do understand that now, don't you, darling?"

"Yes, I do." She returned his smile. "And as Dr. Boujon told me, I have to relax, and we have to just keep on trying. And as he mentioned, there are always ways he can help."

Ian laughed. "That won't be necessary, I'm sure of that. Don't forget, I'm a full-blooded Scotsman from the Highlands."

———

Fifteen minutes later, Kay was sitting at the dressing table again, smoothing a makeup sponge across her face, adding a little powder and blush. As she outlined her mouth with a lip pencil, she thought about the last five days. Ian had arrived in Paris unexpectedly, responding to her invitation to join her for Anya's birthday party tonight.

He had come a few days early, he explained, because he felt they needed a few days together, alone, away from Lochcraigie.

And on that first night, after they had made passionate love in her suite at the Meurice, she had found herself telling him about her visits to Dr. Boujon. There was nothing physically wrong with her; now that she knew this she had been able to confide her worries about not getting pregnant to her husband. The doctor had recommended that she do this, and it had been worth it.

After Ian had listened to her concerns about not conceiving, he had told her to stop worrying, that it didn't trouble him at this moment in time.

His kindness and understanding had given her the courage to tell him about her past . . . all the terrible things that had happened to her when she was a child. Ian had listened closely, and very quickly the expression of horror and shock on his face had turned to one of compassion mingled with love. And when she had finished at last, he took her in his arms and held her close, wanting to nurture and protect her. After a while he said, "That a man could take advantage of a child in that way is horrendous, so vile, it is inconceivable to me. However you coped with it I will never know, but you must have been a very brave little girl, and your mother must have been too."

Ian had touched her cheek gently and kissed her forehead, then looked deeply into her eyes. "But now you have me to look after you, Kay darling, and I'll never let anyone hurt you ever again."

She had held on to him tightly, loving him more than ever for being such a good man. She also understood that he had never changed toward her. All of that had been in her head. And later she had wondered why she had never trusted their love enough to tell him about her past before. She had no answer for herself. But at that moment, she vowed never to doubt him or his love for her ever again.

Now Kay rose from the dressing table, satisfied with her makeup and hair, and moved across the bedroom. Tall, slender, long-limbed, and elegant. She was already wearing stockings and high heels, and she took the champagne-colored chiffon dress from its hanger, stepped into it.

Suddenly, as if she had summoned him, Ian was standing there, hovering in the doorway, looking handsome in his tuxedo. "Shall I zip you up, my sweet?"

Turning, she smiled. "Thanks, Ian."

Once she had smoothed the dress down and adjusted it on her body, she swung around. "Do you like it?"

"It's wonderful on you, so . . . frothy and light, and the necklace and earrings are perfect with it."

"Thank you again for those beauties . . . and now I think we'd better go down to the bar. I'm sure the others are waiting."

———

Kay spotted Alexa the moment they entered the Bar Fontainebleau. She and Tom were seated at a table in a corner near the window, and she raised her hand and waved.

As Kay and Ian drew closer, she saw that Alexa was also wearing a chiffon dress; it looked as if it were cut on the bias and it was composed of variegated greens. To Kay it was the perfect choice. The mingled greens matched Alexa's eyes, set off her dark hair.

Tom jumped up and greeted them, and, once they were seated, the waiter brought them glasses of champagne. A moment after this, Jessica arrived with Mark Sylvester. Jessica had chosen to wear a pale blue organza gown delicately patterned with trailing darker blue flowers, and like Kay's and Alexa's, it was light and airy, floated gently around her as she moved.

As soon as Mark and Jessica drew to a standstill at the table, Alexa said with a light laugh, "Well, I see we all had the same idea about a June party in Paris, and what to wear."

Mark, his eyes roving over them, said, "You're going to be the belles of the ball."

"Oh, no!" Kay exclaimed, smiling, her eyes sparkling. "That role is reserved for Anya."

Alexa, glancing from Tom to Ian to Mark, exclaimed, "But one thing is certain, girls, we've got the most handsome men for our escorts."

"Thanks for the rather nice compliment, Alexa," Ian responded. He liked Kay's girlfriends, and the men in their lives, all of whom he had met last night. Tom had taken everyone to dinner at the beautiful L'Ambroisie in the Place des Vosges. It had been the kind of evening he had not had in a long time, and he had appreciated every moment of it.

But most of all he had enjoyed meeting Anya Sedgwick, and he had listened to her raptly as she extolled Kay's virtues, acclaimed her talent, and confided how much she loved his wife, "cherished her" was the way she had put it. He had been bursting with pride, and love for his wonderful Kay.

And her great-nephew Nicky had been charming, friendly, and highly amusing. While the fourth member of the quartet, Maria Franconi, had been such a knockout in her simple black dress and pearls, none of the other diners had been able to take their eyes off her.

Now Ian said, "I suppose Nicky and Maria are not coming for drinks with us. I rather got the impression they were going to collect Anya and take her to the party directly."

"Anya didn't want to be late," Alexa explained. "She wanted to be there first, to greet the guests as they arrived."

More flutes of champagne arrived at the table for Jessica and Mark, and the six of them now clinked glasses and toasted one another. And then they settled down to chat for a short while before leaving for Ledoyen.

CHAPTER THIRTY-THREE

Anya, flanked by Nicky and Maria, stood in the entrance foyer of Ledoyen, glancing about her.

A look of enchantment crossed her face, brought a sparkle to her blue eyes, a glow to her face. "Oh, Nicky, my darling boy, you've outdone yourself!" she exclaimed, turning to him, clutching his arm. "This is simply beautiful!"

He smiled with pleasure and gratification. "I'm glad you like it. I wanted you to feel . . . at home."

Anya laughed her light, tinkling laugh that was ageless, and took a step forward, her eyes everywhere. What Nicky had done was recreate the front façade of her black and white half-timbered manor house in Paris, with its trellis and ivy growing up part of the façade. This replica was actually a trompe l'oeil, the style of painting that gave an illusion of reality, like a photograph, and the giant canvas was attached to a long wall at one side of the foyer. This entire area had been designed to look like the cobbled courtyard of her house; the cherry tree in full bloom was there, with the four metal garden chairs standing underneath its laden branches. And her flower garden, enclosed within a white picket fence, took pride of place at the other side of the foyer.

Taking hold of her arm, Nicky said, "Come along, Anya, I've more surprises for you."

Still smiling broadly, Anya allowed herself to be propelled up the staircase. "Where are we going?" she asked, filled with curiosity and anticipation.

"For cocktails," Maria said, beaming at her.

Anya nodded, glanced at Maria out of the corner of her eye, thinking how marvelous she looked, slimmer than ever and elegant in a midnight-blue chiffon gown with a strapless top and a flowing skirt, her only jewelry a thin strand of tiny diamonds around her neck and diamond studs in her ears.

"Maria, you're simply exquisite," Anya murmured, momentarily awed by the girl's staggering beauty tonight.

"It's thanks to Nicky, he chose my dress. It's from Balmain," Maria said.

"Oh, it's not the dress I'm talking about, but you, my dear."

Maria flushed slightly, smiled with pleasure. "And you look wonderful in your signature red, Anya."

Anya said, "Well, you know I've always loved red. It makes me feel happy. Not that I need a color to do that for me tonight. I'd be happy whatever color I was wearing."

When they reached the landing of the second floor, Nicky took hold of Anya's hand and led her toward large double doors. He opened them, ushered her inside, and exclaimed, *"Voilà!"*

Anya gasped, truly surprised.

She stood staring at another replica, this time of the sitting room of her house in Provence, the house Hugo had bought for her years ago, and where they had spent so many happy times together. Nicky had used Provençal country furniture, many bright colors reminiscent of the real room, and in doing so had created a perfect copy. Waiters and waitresses, dressed in the local costumes of the area, stood around smiling, ready to serve drinks.

"Nicky, oh, Nicky" was all Anya could manage to say as he guided her through the room and into one that adjoined.

Now she found herself in a Russian dacha filled with rustic peasant furniture, and here, to make it completely authentic in mood, were waiters wearing scarlet and gold Cossack tunics, baggy pants tucked into black boots.

She stood stock-still, glancing around, endeavoring to take everything in, but Nicky would not permit her to linger long. He took her hand in his, moving her forward and into a third room.

Anya was startled, amazed, and touched all at the same time, and she experienced a rush of emotion. Here she stood, in the living room where she had grown up in London with her parents. Nicky had re-created it down to the last detail. Tears suddenly sprang into her eyes.

Turning to him, she asked a little tremulously, "How on earth did you manage this?"

"With your sister's help. Aunt Ekaterina was my marvelous partner in crime, so to speak. She had some old photographs of your parents' living room, which were a great help. But most important, she has a photographic memory, and it's not dimmed by age at all."

"I should hope not!" Anya exclaimed, blinking back her tears, walking around the room, noting the samovar, and the icons on velvet-skirted tables. Nicky had found so many objects similar to the things her mother had owned and loved, and all were arrayed here. There were photographs in old Fabergé frames . . . obviously borrowed from Katti . . . photographs of her parents, the Romanovs, her siblings . . . and of her when she was a young girl. And the color scheme of pale blue and gold was the one her mother had so loved. Even the furniture was similar to the pieces she had grown up with.

Slowly, she walked back to Nicky and embraced him. "Thank you, thank you," she said, her voice choked. "Thank you for bringing so many of my very cherished memories to life tonight."

A waiter rigged out as an English butler came forward with a tray of drinks, and the three of them took flutes of champagne. They clinked glasses and said cheers at the same time, and Nicky added, "I want you to have the most wonderful evening, Anya."

"I know I will, and what you've done is quite extraordinary."

He laughed. "There are still a few surprises in store for you, Anya."

"I can't believe you can top this! Such as what?" she probed.

"Oh, you'll just have to wait and see," he teased.

"Now, where do you want to greet your guests? Which room?" Nicky asked.

"I'm not sure, darling boy, each room is so very special."

"Perhaps we should wait in the first room, because everyone enters there," Maria suggested.

"Good idea, my sweet," Nicky said, and together the three of them walked back to the Provençal sitting room with its small tables covered with the cheerful red, green, and yellow tablecloths from Provence. Brown ceramic jugs filled with tall sunflowers stood on a long sideboard and the scent of lavender filled the air.

As they entered, one of the waitresses wearing a Provençal costume came over to them holding a tray, and Anya smiled when she saw all of her favorite things. Warm piroshki, the small Russian pastries filled with chopped meat, dollops of caviar atop tiny baked potatoes, smoked salmon on toast, and miniature English sausage rolls.

"Well," she exclaimed, "I can't resist these. I must sample one of each."

"I hoped you would," Nicky said. "I'll join you."

And then a few minutes later the guests began to arrive.

———

Anya was suddenly surrounded by family.

Her sister and brother-in-law, Katti and Sacha, and all the Lebedevs, kissing her, congratulating her. And then her brother, Vladimir, and his wife, Lili, and their children, so warm and loving. And behind them came her own children, Olga and Dimitri, and their families, hugging her, wishing her a happy birthday, their faces smiling and happy.

After them came the tribe of Sedgwicks, also full of love for her . . . and so many old friends from across the years followed, and the students who had passed through the school and remained close to her for over thirty years or more.

And then at last her special girls.

Her four favorites from the class of '94. Alexa, Jessica, Kay, and Maria. How beautiful they all looked as they now walked toward her, escorted by the men in their lives, handsome, elegant in their dinner jackets.

Alexa, Kay, and Jessica greeted her, and so did Tom, Ian, and Mark, and then with Nicky the three men stepped back so that she was left alone with the quartet.

"It goes without saying that you all look gorgeous!" Anya exclaimed, beaming at them. "And before we go any further, I want to thank you all for your gifts. Kay, this antique shawl is exquisite, I couldn't resist wearing it tonight. And as you see, it's the same red as my gown. And, Jessica, the icon is a prize, and it has pride of my place in my sitting room. And so does your lacquered box, Alexa. The painting of St. Petersburg on its lid is a little jewel. Thank you, thank you." Anya smiled at Maria, and finished. "As for your painting, Maria, it is absolutely extraordinary, and it is now hanging in my bedroom. I thank you so much for parting with it."

Maria blushed and smiled but remained silent.

Anya's eyes swept over them again, and she said softly, in the most intimate of voices, "I am so happy you all came to Paris early, so that we had time to visit and you had the chance to air your differences and make up. And I can see that you have."

"It's like old times," Alexa said. "We're here for each other. Forever. Through thick and thin. Aren't we, girls?"

They all agreed with her, and Kay said, "It doesn't seem like seven years at all, only yesterday that we were here at your school, Anya."

"You taught us so much, brought out and nurtured our talents, helped us to realize our aspirations and our dreams," Jessica told her. "You helped to make us what we are, Anya. And for that we'll be forever grateful."

Anya nodded. "You all came to Paris for some other reasons as well, I realize that. You had unfinished business . . . each one of you had a quest. And I'm so very happy you found what you were seeking. . . ." She focused on Alexa. "You and Tom got back together . . . permanently?"

Alexa nodded, her face glowing as she showed Anya her left hand. A diamond ring sparkled on it. "We got engaged tonight. Tom slipped the ring on my finger in the car as we were being driven over here."

"I'm so happy for you, Alexa darling. He's always been the only man for you."

Looking closely at Maria, Anya continued. "And you and Nicky seem to be ideally suited. . . ."

"Yes, we are, Anya, and Nicky wants us to marry. When he's free, after he is divorced. And I'm not going back to Milan. I'm going to live in Paris with Nicky, and I'm going to be an artist. No more textile designing for me," Maria announced.

Anya clapped her hands together softly. "Thank God for that, Maria. It would be such a waste of your talent if you kept your job at home. And congratulations to you too. I shall give the wedding for you when you marry. It will be my great pleasure. And, Kay, what about you? Everything seems to be working with you and your lovely Ian."

"It is, Anya, and as I told you, there's nothing wrong with me physically. There's no reason why I can't have a baby." Kay laughed lightly. "But Ian doesn't care. He says it's me he wants."

"And why wouldn't he feel that way? He's a lucky man to have you," Anya replied. Her eyes rested finally on Jessica, and she noticed yet again that there was still a wistfulness to her, a sadness in her eyes.

"I'm relieved you found Lucien, and that you had a chance to see him, Jessica," Anya began. "I know what a shock it was for you, but now I believe you can close this chapter, my dear. Finally, after all these years."

"Close the book, actually, Anya," Jessica answered. "It's not often a person gets a second chance in life . . . but I'm so very lucky because I have Mark. He thinks we have a future together, and I have a feeling he's right."

"I know he is. And he's a lovely man. Why, they're all lovely men. . . ."

———

A short while after this they all went downstairs to dinner.

Nicky and Maria escorted Anya, and as they led her into the dining room she was unexpectedly blinded by tears.

The room had been transformed into the most beautiful English garden she had ever seen. Masses of flowering plants were banked high around the room. Orange trees in tubs decorated corners. Stone fountains sprayed arcs of shimmering water up into the air. There were stone statues and stone sundials in strategic places, and bowers and arches of fresh roses entwined with ivy leaves. And each table was skirted in pale pink with low bowls of pink roses in the center, and votive candles flickered brightly . . . hundreds of tiny lights around the room that added to the magic.

"Oh, Nicky," Anya said, and was unable to say another word. She shook her head and clutched his arm as he led her forward to the main table, where she was to sit with her immediate family. "Thank you, thank you, darling," she whispered hoarsely, still choked as he pulled out her chair for her.

"It was my pleasure, my very great pleasure, Anya," he said, and moved away, holding Maria's hand as they went to join the others at their intimate table for eight.

I'm so very lucky, a most fortunate woman, Anya thought as she sipped her water, waiting for the table to fill up with her children and her beloved sister, Katti. What a life I've had. Eighty-five wonderful years. Love and happiness. Pain and suffering. And quite a lot of grief. But I've always come through my troubles. I've endured. Perhaps that's what life is all about. Enduring. Being a survivor.

And my four girls are survivors. Anya turned in her chair, focused her eyes on the dance floor. The table next to hers had emptied, and its occupants were on the dance floor. . . .

Maria was in Nicky's arms. He was moving her slowly around the room, whispering in her ear.

Kay's head was against Ian's shoulder, her expression dreamy, and he had a look of absolute contentment in his eyes.

Jessica was holding on to Mark very tightly, and her face was no longer quite so sad. She was looking up at him and laughing, her eyes sparkling.

Alexa and Tom were not dancing at all, merely swaying to the music. At one moment he looked down at her and kissed her lightly on the lips. "Let's get married as soon as possible," he said softly. "I can't wait for you to be my wife. I love you so much."

"And I love you, Tom. For always," Alexa said, and she held him closer to her. All she wanted was to share that humdrum life of his, as he called it. She smiled a small, secret smile. Humdrum indeed, she thought.

Anya, still watching them, wished she knew what they were saying to each other. And then she laughed out loud. Of course they were telling each other beautiful things, making promises, making commitments . . . just as she had done so many years ago. First with Michel Lacoste and then with Hugo Sedgwick.

Love, she thought. There's nothing like it in this world. It's the only thing that really matters in the end.

CINNAMON KISS

CINNAMON KISS

WALTER MOSLEY

Weidenfeld & Nicolson
London

First published in the United States by Little Brown & Co. in 2005

First published in Great Britain in 2005
by Weidenfeld & Nicolson, a division of
the Orion Publishing Group Ltd
Orion House
5 Upper Saint Martin's Lane
London
WC2H 9EA

A CIP catalogue record for this book is available
from the British Library

ISBN 0 29784854 2

This book proof printed by Antony Rowe Ltd, Chippenham, Wiltshire

www.orionbooks.co.uk

For Ossie Davis,
our shining king

Cinnamon Kiss

1

So it's real simple," Mouse was saying. When he grinned the diamond set in his front tooth sparkled in the gloom.

Cox Bar was always dark, even on a sunny April afternoon. The dim light and empty chairs made it a perfect place for our kind of business.

". . . We just be there at about four-thirty in the mornin' an' wait," Mouse continued. "When the mothahfuckahs show up you put a pistol to the back of the neck of the one come in last. He the one wit' the shotgun. Tell 'im to drop it —"

"What if he gets brave?" I asked.

"He won't."

"What if he flinches and the gun goes off?"

"It won't."

"How the fuck you know that, Raymond?" I asked my lifelong

friend. "How do you know what a finger in Palestine, Texas, gonna do three weeks from now?"

"You boys need sumpin' for your tongues?" Ginny Wright asked. There was a leer in the bar owner's voice.

It was a surprise to see such a large woman appear out of the darkness of the empty saloon.

Ginny was dark-skinned, wearing a wig of gold-colored hair. Not blond, gold like the metal.

She was asking if we needed something to drink but Ginny could make a sexual innuendo out of garlic salt if she was talking to men.

"Coke," I said softly, wondering if she had overheard Mouse's plan.

"An' rye whiskey in a frozen glass for Mr. Alexander," Ginny added, knowing her best customer's usual. She kept five squat liquor glasses in her freezer at all times — ready for his pleasure.

"Thanks, Gin," Mouse said, letting his one-carat filling ignite for her.

"Maybe we should talk about this someplace else," I suggested as Ginny moved off to fix our drinks.

"Shit," he uttered. "This my office jes' like the one you got on Central, Easy. You ain't got to worry 'bout Ginny. She don't hear nuttin' an' she don't say nuttin'."

Ginny Wright was past sixty. When she was a young woman she'd been a prostitute in Houston. Raymond and I both knew her back then. She had a soft spot for the younger Mouse all those years. Now he was her closest friend. You got the feeling, when she looked at him, that she wanted more. But Ginny satisfied herself by making room in her nest for Raymond to do his business.

On this afternoon she'd put up her special sign on the front

4

door: CLOSED FOR A PRIVATE FUNCTION. That sign would stay up until my soul was sold for a bagful of stolen money.

Ginny brought our drinks and then went back to the high table that she used as a bar.

Mouse was still grinning. His light skin and gray eyes made him appear wraithlike in the darkness.

"Don't worry, Ease," he said. "We got this suckah flat-footed an' blind."

"All I'm sayin' is that you don't know how a man holding a shotgun's gonna react when you sneak up behind him and put a cold gun barrel to his neck."

"To begin wit'," Mouse said, "Rayford will not have any buck-shot in his shooter that day an' the on'y thing he gonna be thinkin' 'bout is you comin' up behind him. 'Cause he know that the minute you get the drop on 'im that Jack Minor, his partner, gonna swivel t' see what's what. An' jest when he do that, I'ma bop old Jackie good an' then you an' me got some heavy totin' to do. They gonna have a two hunnert fi'ty thousand minimum in that armored car — half of it ours."

"You might think it's all good and well that you know these guys' names," I said, raising my voice more than I wanted. "But if you know them then they know you."

"They don't know me, Easy," Mouse said. He looped his arm around the back of his chair. "An' even if they did, they don't know you."

"You know me."

That took the smug smile off of Raymond's lips. He leaned forward and clasped his hands. Many men who knew my murder-ous friend would have quailed at that gesture. But I wasn't afraid. It's not that I'm such a courageous man that I can't know fear in the face of certain death. And Raymond "Mouse" Alexander was certainly death personified. But right then I had problems that went far beyond me and my mortality.

"I ain't sayin' that you'd turn me in, Ray," I said. "But the cops know we run together. If I go down to Texas and rob this armored car with you an' Rayford sings, then they gonna know to come after me. That's all I'm sayin'."

I remember his eyebrows rising, maybe a quarter of an inch. When you're facing that kind of peril you notice small gestures. I had seen Raymond in action. He could kill a man and then go take a catnap without the slightest concern.

The eyebrows meant that his feelings were assuaged, that he wouldn't have to lose his temper.

"Rayford never met me," he said, sitting back again. "He don't know my name or where I'm from or where I'll be goin' after takin' the money."

"And so why he trust you?" I asked, noticing that I was talking the way I did when I was a young tough in Fifth Ward, Houston, Texas. Maybe in my heart I felt that the bravado would see me through.

"Remembah when I was in the can ovah that manslaughter thing?" he asked.

He'd spent five years in maximum security.

"That was *hard* time, man," he said. "You know I never wanna be back there again. I mean the cops would have to kill me before I go back there. But even though it was bad some good come out of it."

Mouse slugged back the triple shot of chilled rye and held up his glass. I could hear Ginny hustling about for his next free drink.

"You know I found out about a very special group when I was up in there. It was what you call a syndicate."

"You mean like the Mafia?" I asked.

"Naw, man. That's just a club. This here is straight business. There's a brother in Chicago that has men goin' around the country scopin' out possibilities. Banks, armored cars, private poker games — anything that's got to do wit' large amounts of cash, two hunnert fi'ty thousand or more. This dude sends his boys in to make the contacts and then he give the job to somebody he could trust." Mouse smiled again. It was said that that diamond was given to him by a rich white movie star that he helped out of a jam.

"Here you go, baby," Ginny said, placing his frosty glass on the pitted round table between us. "You need anything else, Easy?"

"No thanks," I said and she moved away. Her footfalls were silent. All you could hear was the rustle of her black cotton trousers.

"So this guy knows you?" I asked.

"Easy," Mouse said in an exasperated whine. "You the one come to me an' said that you might need up t' fi'ty thousand, right? Well — here it is, prob'ly more. After I lay out Jack Minor, Rayford gonna let you hit him in the head. We take the money an' that's that. I give you your share that very afternoon."

My tongue went dry at that moment. I drank the entire glass of cola in one swig but it didn't touch that dryness. I took an ice cube into my mouth but it was like I was licking it with a leather strip instead of living flesh.

"How does Rayford get paid?" I asked, the words warbling around the ice.

"What you care about him?"

"I wanna know why we trust him."

Mouse shook his head and then laughed. It was a real laugh, friendly and amused. For a moment he looked like a normal person instead of the supercool ghetto bad man who came off so hard that he rarely seemed ruffled or human at all.

"The man in Chi always pick somebody got somethin' t' hide. He gets shit on 'em and then he pay 'em for their part up front. An' he let 'em know that if they turn rat they be dead."

It was a perfect puzzle. Every piece fit. Mouse had all the bases covered, any question I had he had the answer. And why not? He was the perfect criminal. A killer without a conscience, a warrior without fear — his IQ might have been off the charts for all I knew, but even if it wasn't, his whole mind paid such close attention to his profession that there were few who could outthink him when it came to breaking the law.

"I don't want anybody gettin' killed behind this, Raymond."

"Nobody gonna die, Ease. Just a couple'a headaches, that's all."

"What if Rayford's a fool and starts spendin' money like water?" I asked. "What if the cops think he's in on it?"

"What if the Russians drop the A-bomb on L.A.?" he asked back. "What if you drive your car on the Pacific Coast Highway, get a heart attack, and go flyin' off a cliff? Shit, Easy. I could 'what if' you into the grave but you got to have faith, brother. An' if Rayford's a fool an' wanna do hisself in, that ain't got nuthin' to do with what you got to do."

Of course he was right. What I had to do was why I was there. I didn't want to get caught and I didn't want anybody to get killed, but those were the chances I had to take.

"Lemme think about it, Ray," I said. "I'll call you first thing in the morning."

2

I walked down the small alleyway from Cox Bar and then turned left on Hooper. My car was parked three blocks away because of the nature of that meeting. This wasn't grocery shopping or parking in the lot of the school I worked at. This was serious business, business that gets you put in prison for a child's lifetime.

The sun was bright but there was a slight breeze that cut the heat. The day was beautiful if you didn't look right at the burned-out businesses and boarded-up shops — victims of the Watts riots not yet a year old. The few people walking down the avenue were somber and sour looking. They were mostly poor, either unemployed or married to someone who was, and realizing that California and Mississippi were sister states in the same union, members of the same clan.

I knew how they felt because I had been one of them for more than four and a half decades. Maybe I had done a little more with my life. I didn't live in Watts anymore and I had a regular job. My live-in girlfriend was a stewardess for Air France and my boy owned his own boat. I had been a major success in light of my upbringing but that was all over. I was no more than a specter haunting the streets that were once my home.

I felt as if I had died and that the steps I was taking were the final unerring, unalterable footfalls toward hell. And even though I was a black man, in a country that seemed to be teetering on the edge of a race war, my color and race had nothing to do with my pain.

Every man's hell is a private club, my father used to tell me when I was small. *That's why when I look at these white people sneerin' at me I always smile an' say, "Sure thing, boss."*

He knew that the hammer would fall on them too. He forgot to say that it would also get me one day.

I drove a zigzag side street path back toward the west side of town. At every intersection I remembered people that I'd known in Los Angeles. Many of those same folks I had known in Texas. We'd moved, en masse it seemed, from the Deep South to the haven of California. Joppy the bartender, dead all these years, and Jackson the liar; EttaMae, my first serious love, and Mouse, her man and my best friend. We came here looking for a better life — the reason most people move — and many of us believed that we had found it.

. . . You put a pistol to the back of the neck of the one come in last . . .

I could see myself, unseen by anyone else, with a pistol in my hand, planning to rob a big oil concern of its monthly payroll. Nearly twenty years of trying to be an upright citizen making an honest wage and it all disappears because of a bucketful of bad blood.

With this thought I looked up and realized that a woman pushing a baby carriage, with two small kids at her side, was in the middle of the street not ten feet in front of my bumper. I hit the brake and swerved to the left, in front of a '48 wood-paneled station wagon. He hit his brakes too. Horns were blaring.

The woman screamed, "Oh Lord!" and I pictured one of her babies crushed under the wheel of my Ford.

I jumped out the door, almost before the car came to a stop, and ran around to where the dead child lay in my fears.

But I found the small woman on her knees, hugging her children to her breast. They were crying while she screamed for the Lord.

An older man got out of the station wagon. He was black with silver hair and broad shoulders. He had a limp and wore metal-rimmed glasses. I remember being calmed by the concern in his eyes.

"Mothahfuckah!" the small, walnut-shell-colored woman shouted. "What the fuck is the mattah wit' you? Cain't you see I got babies here?"

The older man, who was at first coming toward me, veered toward the woman. He got down on one knee even though it was difficult because of his bum leg.

"They okay, baby," he said. "Your kids is fine. They fine. But let's get 'em out the street. Out the street before somebody else comes and hits 'em."

The man led the kids and their mother to the curb at Florence and San Pedro. I stood there watching them, unable to move. Cars were backed up on all sides. Some people were getting out to see what had happened. Nobody was honking yet because they thought that maybe someone had been killed.

The silver-haired man walked back to me with a stern look in his eye. I expected to be scolded for my careless behavior. I'm sure I saw the reprimand in his eyes. But when he got close up he saw something in me.

"You okay, mister?" he asked.

I opened my mouth to reply but the words did not come. I looked over at the mother, she was kissing the young girl. I noticed that all of them — the mother, her toddler son, and the six- or seven-year-old girl — were wearing the same color brown pants.

"You bettah watch out, mister," the older man was saying. "It can get to ya sometimes but don't let it get ya."

I nodded and maybe even mumbled something. Then I stumbled back to my car.

The engine was still running. It was in neutral but I hadn't engaged the parking brake.

I was an accident waiting to happen.

For the rest of the ride home I was preoccupied with the image of that woman holding her little girl. When Feather was five and we were at a beach near Redondo she had taken a tumble down a small hill that was full of thorny weeds. She cried as Jesus held her, kissing her brow. When I came up and lifted her into my arms she said, "Don't be mad at Juice, Daddy. He didn't make me fall."

I pulled to the curb so as not to have another accident. I sat there with the admonition in my ears. *It can get to ya sometimes but don't let it get ya.*

3

When I came in the front door I found my adopted son, Jesus, and Benita Flag sitting on the couch in the front room. They looked up at me, both with odd looks on their faces.

"Is she all right?" I asked, feeling my heart do a flip-flop.

"Bonnie's with her," Jesus said.

Benita just nodded and I hurried toward Feather's room, down the small hallway, and through my little girl's door.

Bonnie was sitting there dabbing the light-skinned child's brow with isopropyl alcohol. The evaporation on her skin was meant to cool the fever.

"Daddy," Feather called weakly.

I was reminded of earlier times, when she'd shout my name and then run into me like a small Sherman tank. She was a daddy's girl. She'd been rough and full of guffaws and squeals.

But now she lay back with a blood infection that no one on the North American continent knew how to cure.

"The prognosis is not good," Dr. Beihn had said. "Make her comfortable and make sure she drinks lots of liquid . . ."

I would have drained Hoover Dam to save her life.

Bonnie had that strange look in her eye too. She was tall and dark skinned, Caribbean and lovely. She moved like the ocean, surging up out of that chair and into my arms. Her skin felt hot, as if somehow she was trying to draw the fever out of the girl and into her own body.

"I'll go get the aspirin," Bonnie whispered.

I released her and took her place in the folding chair next to my Feather's pink bed. With my right hand I held the sponge against her forehead. She took my left hand in both of hers and squeezed my point finger and baby finger as hard as she could.

"Why am I so sick, Daddy?" she whined.

"It's just a little infection, honey," I said. "You got to wait until it works its way outta your system."

"But it's been so long."

It had been twenty-three days since the diagnosis, a week longer than the doctor thought she'd survive.

"Did anybody come and visit you today?" I asked.

That got her to smile.

"Billy Chipkin did," she said.

The flaxen-haired, bucktoothed white boy was the fifth and final child of a family that had migrated from Iowa after the war. Billy's devotion to my foundling daughter sometimes made my heart swell to the point that it hurt. He was two inches shorter than Feather and came to sit at her side every day after school. He brought her homework and gossip from the playground.

Sometimes, when they thought that no one was looking,

they'd hold hands while discussing some teacher's unfair punish-ments of their unruly friends.

"What did Billy have to say?"

"He got long division homework and I showed him how to do it," she said proudly. "He don't know it too good, but if you show him he remembers until tomorrow."

I touched Feather's brow with the backs of three fingers. She seemed to be cool at that moment.

"Can I have some of Mama Jo's black tar?" Feather asked.

Even the witch-woman, Mama Jo, had not been able to cure her. But Jo had given us a dozen black gummy balls, each wrapped up in its own eucalyptus leaf.

"If her fevah gets up past one-oh-three give her one'a these here to chew," the tall black witch had said. "But nevah more than one in a day an' aftah these twelve you cain't give her no mo'."

There were only three balls left.

"No, honey," I said. "The fever's down now."

"What you do today, Daddy?" Feather asked.

"I saw Raymond."

"Uncle Mouse?"

"Yeah."

"What did you do with him?"

"We just talked about old times."

I told her about the time, twenty-seven years earlier, when Mouse and I had gone out looking for orange monarch butter-flies that he intended to give his girlfriend instead of flowers. We'd gone to a marsh that was full of those regal bugs, but we didn't have a proper net and Raymond brought along some moonshine that Mama Jo made. We got so drunk that both of us had fallen into the muddy water more than once. By the end of the day Mouse had caught only one butterfly. And that night when we got to Mabel's house, all dirty from our antics, she took one look at the orange-and-black monarch in the glass jar and set him free.

"He just too beautiful to be kept locked up in this bottle," she told us.

Mouse was so angry that he stormed out of Mabel's house and didn't talk to her again for a week.

Feather usually laughed at this story, but that afternoon she fell asleep before I got halfway through.

I hated it when she fell asleep because I didn't know if she'd wake up again.

WHEN I GOT BACK to the living room Jesus and Benita were at the door.

"Where you two goin'?" I asked.

"Uh," Juice grunted, "to the store for dinner."

"How you doin', Benita?" I asked the young woman.

She looked at me as if she didn't understand English or as if I'd asked some extremely personal question that no gentleman should ask a lady.

Benny was in her mid-twenties. She'd had an affair with Mouse which broke her heart and led to an attempted suicide. Bonnie and I took her in for a while but now she had her own apartment. She still came by to have a home-cooked meal now and then. Bonnie and she had become friends. And she loved the kids.

Lately it had been good to have Benny around because when Bonnie and I needed to be away she'd stay at Feather's side.

Jesus would have done it if we asked him to, but he was eighteen and loved being out on his homemade sailboat, cruising up and down the Southern California coast. We hadn't told him how sick his sister actually was. They were so close we didn't want to worry him.

"Fine, Mr. Rawlins," she said in a too-high voice. "I got a job in a clothes store on Slauson. Miss Hilda designs everything she sells. She said she was gonna teach me."

"Okay," I said, not really wanting to hear about the young woman's hopeful life. I wanted Feather to be telling me about her adventures and dreams.

When Benny and Jesus were gone Bonnie came out of the kitchen with a bowl full of spicy beef soup.

"Eat this," she said.

"I'm not hungry."

"I didn't ask if you were hungry."

Our living room was so small that we only had space for a love seat instead of a proper couch. I slumped down there and she sat on my lap shoving the first spoonful into my mouth.

It was good.

She fed me for a while, looking into my eyes. I could tell that she was thinking something very serious.

"What?" I asked at last.

"I spoke to the man in Switzerland today," she said.

She waited for me to ask what he said but I didn't. I couldn't hear one more piece of bad news about Feather.

I turned away from her gaze. She touched my neck with four fingertips.

"He tested the blood sample that Vicki brought over," she said. "He thinks that she's a good candidate for the process."

I heard the words but my mind refused to understand them. What if they meant that Feather was going to die? I couldn't take the chance of knowing that.

"He thinks that he can cure her, baby," Bonnie added, understanding the course of my grief. "He has agreed to let her apply to the Bonatelle Clinic."

"Really?"

"Yes."

"In Montreux?"

"Yes."

"But why would they take a little colored girl in there? Didn't you say that the Rockefellers and Kennedys go there?"

"I already told you," Bonnie explained. "I met the doctor on an eight-hour flight from Ghana. I talked to him the whole time about Feather. I guess he felt he had to say yes. I don't know."

"What do we have to do next?"

"It's not free, honey," she said, but I already knew that. The reason I'd met with Mouse was to raise the cash we might need if the doctors agreed to see my little girl.

"They'll need thirty-five thousand dollars before the treatments can start and at least fifteen thousand just to be admitted. It's a hundred and fifty dollars a day to keep her in the hospital, and then the medicines are all unique, made to order based upon her blood, sex, age, body type, and over fifteen other categories. There are five doctors and a nurse for each patient. And the process may take up to four months."

We'd covered it all before but Bonnie found solace in details. She felt that if she dotted every *i* and crossed every *t* then everything would turn out fine.

"How do you know that you can trust them?" I asked. "This could just be some scam."

"I've been there, Easy. I visited the hospital. I told you that, baby."

"But maybe they fooled you," I said.

I was afraid to hope. Every day I prayed for a miracle for Feather. But I had lived a life where miracles never happened. In my experience a death sentence was just that.

"I'm no fool, Easy Rawlins."

The certainty of her voice and her stare were the only chances I had.

"Money's no problem," I said, resolute in my conviction to go down to Texas and rob that armored car. I didn't want Rayford or his partner to die. I didn't want to spend a dozen years behind bars. But I'd do that and more to save my little girl.

I went out the back door and into the garage. From the back shelf I pulled down four paint cans labeled Latex Blue. Each was sealed tight and a quarter filled with oiled steel ball bearings to give them the heft of full cans of paint. On top of those pellets, wrapped in plastic, lay four piles of tax-free money I'd come across over the years. It was my children's college fund. Twelve thousand dollars. I brought the money to Bonnie and laid it on her lap.

"What now?" I asked.

"In a few days I'll take a flight with Vicki to Paris and then transfer to Switzerland. I'll take Feather and bring her to Dr. Renee."

I took a deep breath but still felt the suffocation of fear.

"How will you get the rest?" she asked me.

"I'll get it."

4

Jesus, Feather, and I were in a small park in Santa Monica we liked to go to when they were younger. I was holding Feather in my arms while she laughed and played catch with Jesus. Her laughter got louder and louder until it turned to screams and I realized that I was holding her too tightly. I laid her out on the grass but she had passed out.

"You killed her, Dad," Jesus was saying. It wasn't an indictment but merely a statement of fact.

"I know," I said as the grasses surged upward and began swallowing Feather, blending her with their blades into the soil underneath.

I bent down but the grasses worked so quickly that by the time my lips got there, there was only the turf left to kiss.

I felt a buzzing vibration against my lips and jumped back, trying to avoid being stung by a hornet in the grass.

Halfway out of bed I realized that the buzzing was my alarm clock.

It felt as if there was a crease in my heart. I took deep breaths, thinking in my groggy state that the intake of air would somehow inflate the veins and arteries.

"Easy."

"Yeah, baby?"

"What time is it?"

I glanced at the clock with the luminescent turquoise hands. "Four-twenty. Go back to sleep."

"No," Bonnie said, rising up next to me. "I'll go check on Feather."

She knew that I was hesitant to go into Feather's room first thing in the morning. I was afraid to find her dead in there. I hated her sleep and mine. When I was a child I fell asleep once and awoke to find that my mother had passed in the night.

I went to the kitchen counter and plugged in the percolator. I didn't have to check to see if there was water and coffee inside. Bonnie and I had a set pattern by then. She got the coffee urn ready the night before and I turned it on in the morning.

I sat down heavily on a chrome and yellow vinyl dinette chair. The vibrations of the hornet still tickled my lips. I started thinking of what would happen if a bee stung the human tongue. Would it swell up and suffocate the victim? Is that all it would take to end a life?

Bonnie's hand caressed the back of my neck.

"She's sleeping and cool," she whispered.

The first bubble of water jumped up into the glass knob at the top of the percolator. I took in a deep breath and my heart smoothed out.

Bonnie pulled a chair up beside me. She was wearing a white

lace slip that came down to the middle of her dark brown thighs. I wore only briefs.

"I was thinking," I said.

"Yes?"

"I love you and I want to be with you and only you."

When she didn't say anything I put my hand on hers.

"Let's get Feather well first, Easy. You don't want to make these big decisions when you're so upset. You don't have to worry — I'm here."

"But it's not that," I argued.

When she leaned over to nuzzle my neck the coffee urn started its staccato beat in earnest. I got up to make toast and we ate in silence, holding hands.

After we'd eaten I went in and kissed Feather's sleeping face and made it out to my car before the sun was up.

I PULLED INTO the parking lot at five-nineteen, by my watch. There was an orangish-yellow light under a pile of dark clouds rising behind the eastern mountains. I used my key to unlock the pedestrian gate and then relocked it after I'd entered.

I was the supervising senior head custodian of Sojourner Truth Junior High School, an employee in good standing with the LAUSD. I had over a dozen people who reported directly to me and I was also the manager of all the plumbers, painters, carpenters, electricians, locksmiths, and glaziers who came to service our plant. I was the highest-ranking black person on the campus of a school that was eighty percent black. I had read the study plans for almost every class and often played tutor to the boys and girls who would come to me before they'd dream of asking their white teachers for help. If a big boy decided to see if he could intimidate a small woman teacher I dragged him down to the *main* office, where the custodians congregated, and let him know, in no uncertain terms, what would happen to him if I were to lose my temper.

I was on excellent terms with Ada Masters, the diminutive and wealthy principal. Between us we had the school running smooth as satin.

I entered the main building and started my rounds, going down the hallways looking for problems.

A trash can had not been emptied by the night custodian, Miss Arnold, and there were two lights out in the third-floor hallway. The first floor needed mopping. I made meaningless mental notes of the chores and then headed down to the lower campus.

After checking out the yards and bungalows down there I went to the custodians' building to sit and think. I loved that job. It might have seemed like a lowly position to many people, both black and white, but it was a good job and I did many good things while I was there. Often, when parents were having trouble with their kids or the school, I was the first one they went to. Because I came from the South I could translate the rules and expectations of the institution that many southern Negroes just didn't understand. And if the vice principals or teachers overstepped their bounds I could always put in a word with Miss Masters. She listened to me because she knew that I knew what was what among the population of Watts.

"*Ain't* is a valid negative if you use it correctly and have never been told that it isn't proper language," I once said to her when an English teacher, Miss Patterson, dropped a student two whole letter grades just for using *ain't* one time in a report paper.

Miss Masters looked at me as if I had come from some other planet and yet still spoke her tongue.

"You're right," she said in an amazed tone. "Mr. Rawlins, you're right."

"And you're white," I replied, captive to the rhyme and the irony.

We laughed, and from that day on we had weekly meetings where she queried me about what she called my *ghetto pedagogy*.

They paid me nine thousand dollars a year to do that service. Not nearly enough to float a loan for the thirty-five-plus thousand I needed to maybe save my daughter.

I owned two apartment buildings and a small house with a big yard, all in and around Watts. But after the riots, property values in the black neighborhoods had plummeted. I owed more on the mortgages than the places were worth.

In the past few days I had called John and Jackson and Jewelle and the bank. No one but Mouse had come through with an idea. I wondered if at my trial they would take into account all of my good deeds at Truth.

AT ABOUT A QUARTER to seven I went out to finish my rounds. My morning man, Ace, would have been there by then, unlocking the gates and doors for the students, teachers, and staff.

Halfway up the stairs to the upper campus I passed the midway lunch court. I thought I saw a motion in there and took the detour out of habit. A boy and girl were kissing on one of the benches. Their faces were plastered together, his hand was on her knee and her hand was on his. I couldn't tell if she was urging him on or pushing him off. Maybe she didn't know either.

"Good morning," I said cheerily.

Those two kids jumped back from each other as if a powerful spring had been released between them. She was wearing a short plaid skirt and a white blouse under a green sweater. He had the jeans and T-shirt that almost every boy wore. They both looked at me speechlessly — exactly the same way Jesus and Benita had looked.

My shock was almost as great as those kids'. Eighteen-year-old Jesus and Benita in her mid-twenties . . . But my surprise subsided quickly.

"Go on up to your lockers or somethin'," I said to the children.

As they scuttled off I thought about the Mexican boy I had adopted. He'd been a man since the age of ten, taking care of me and Feather like a fierce and silent mama bear. Benita was a lost child and here my boy had a good job at a supermarket and a sailboat he'd made with his own hands.

Thinking of Feather dying in her bed, I couldn't get angry with them for hurrying after love.

The rest of the campus was still empty. I recognized myself in the barren yards and halls and classrooms. Every step I took or door I closed was an exit and a farewell.

"GOOD MORNING, Mr. Rawlins," Ada Masters said when I appeared at her door. "Come in. Come in."

She was sitting on top of her desk, shoes off, rubbing her left foot.

"These damn new shoes hurt just on the walk from my car to the office."

We never stood on ceremony or false manners. Though white and very wealthy, she was like many down-to-earth black women I'd known.

"I'm taking a leave of absence," I said and the crease twisted my heart again.

"For how long?"

"It might be a week or a month," I said. But I was thinking that it might be ten years with good behavior.

"When?"

"Effective right now."

I knew that Ada was hurt by my pronouncement. But she and I respected each other and we came from a generation that did not pry.

"I'll get the paperwork," she said. "And I'll have Kathy send you whatever you have to sign."

"Thanks." I turned to leave.

"Can I be of any help, Mr. Rawlins?" she asked my profile.

She was a rich woman. A very rich woman if I knew my clothes and jewelry. Maybe if I was a different man I could have stayed there by borrowing from her. But at that time in my life I was unable to ask for help. I convinced myself that Ada wouldn't be able to float me that kind of loan. And one more refusal would have sunk me.

"Thanks anyway," I said. "This is somethin' I got to take care of for myself."

Life is such a knotty tangle that I don't know even today whether I made the right decision turning away from her offer.

5

I had changed the sign on my office door from EASY
RAWLINS — RESEARCH AND DELIVERY to simply INVESTIGA-
TIONS. I made the switch after the Los Angeles Police Department had granted me a private detective's license for my part in
keeping the Watts riots from flaring up again by squelching the
ugly rumor that a white man had murdered a black woman in
the dark heart of our boiler-pot city.

I went to my fourth-floor office on Central and Eighty-sixth to
check the answering machine that Jackson Blue had given me.
But I found little hope there. Bonnie had left a message saying
that she'd called the clinic in Montreux and they would allow
Feather's admission with the understanding that the rest of the
money would be forthcoming.

Forthcoming. The people in that neighborhood had heart disease and high blood pressure, cancer of every type, and deep

self-loathing for being forced to their knees on a daily basis. There was a war waging overseas, being fought in great part by young black men who had no quarrel with the Vietnamese people. All of that was happening but I didn't have the time to worry about it. I was thinking about a lucky streak in Vegas or that maybe I should go out and rob a bank all on my own.

Forthcoming. The money would be forthcoming all right. Rayford would have a gun at the back of his neck and I'd be sure to have a fully loaded .44 in my sweating hand.

There was one hang-up on the tape. Back then, in 1966, most folks weren't used to answering machines. Few people knew that Jackson Blue had invented that device to compete with the downtown mob's control of the numbers business. The underworld still had a bounty on his head.

The row of buildings across the street were all boarded up — every one of them. The riots had shut down SouthCentral L.A. like a coffin. White businesses had fled and black-owned stores flickered in and out of existence on a weekly basis. All we had left were liquor stores for solace and check-cashing storefronts in place of banks. The few stores that had survived were gated with steel bars that protected armed clerks.

At least here the view matched my inner desolation. The economy of Watts was like Feather's blood infection. Both futures seemed devoid of hope.

I couldn't seem to pull myself from the window. That's because I knew that the next thing I had to do was call Raymond and tell him that I was ready to take a drive down south.

The knock on the door startled me. I suppose that in my grief I felt alone and invisible. But when I looked at the frosted glass I knew who belonged to that silhouette. The big shapeless nose and the slight frame were a dead giveaway.

"Come on in, Saul," I called.

He hesitated. Saul Lynx was a cautious man. But that made sense. He was a Jewish private detective married to a black woman. They had three brown children and the enmity of at least one out of every two people they met.

But we were friends and so he opened the door.

Saul's greatest professional asset was his face — it was almost totally nondescript even with his large nose. He squinted a lot but if he ever opened his eyes wide in surprise or appreciation you got a shot of emerald that can only be described as beautiful.

But Saul was rarely surprised.

"Hey, Easy," he said, giving a quick grin and looking around for anything out of place.

"Saul."

"How's Feather?"

"Pretty bad. But there's this clinic in Switzerland that's had very good results with cases like hers."

Saul made his way to my client's chair. I went behind the desk, realizing as I sat that I could feel my heart beating.

Saul scratched the side of his mouth and moved his shoulder like a stretching cat.

"What is it, Saul?"

"You said that you needed work, right?"

"Yeah. I need it if it pays."

Saul was wearing a dark brown jacket and light brown pants. Brown was his color. He reached into the breast pocket and came out with a tan envelope. This he dropped on the desk.

"Fifteen hundred dollars."

"For what?" I asked, not reaching for the money.

"I put out the word after you called me. Talked to anybody who might need somebody like you on a job."

Like you meant a black man. At one time it might have angered me to be referred to like that but I knew Saul, he was just trying to help.

"At first no one had anything worth your while but then I heard from this cat up in Frisco. He's a strange guy but . . ." Saul hunched his shoulders to finish the sentence. "This fifteen hundred is a down payment on a possible ten grand."

"I'll take it."

"I don't even know what the job is, Easy."

"And I don't need to know," I said. "Ten thousand dollars will put me in shootin' range of what I need. I might even be able to borrow the rest if it comes down to it."

"Might."

"That's all I got, Saul — might."

Saul winced and nodded. He was a good guy.

"His name is Lee," he said. "Robert E. Lee."

"Like the Civil War general?"

Saul nodded. "His parents were Virginia patriots."

"That's okay. I'd meet with the grand wizard of the Ku Klux Klan if this is how he says hello." I picked up the envelope and fanned my face with it.

"I'll be on the job too, Easy. He wants to do it with you answering to me. It's no problem. I won't get in your way."

I put the envelope down and extended that hand. For a moment Saul didn't realize that I wanted to shake with him.

"You can ride on my back if you want to, Saul. All I care about is Feather."

I WENT HOME late that afternoon. While Bonnie made dinner I sat by Feather's side. She was dozing on and off and I wanted to be there whenever she opened her eyes. When she did come awake she always smiled for me.

Jesus and Benny came over and had dinner with Bonnie. I didn't eat. I wasn't hungry. All I thought about was doing a good job for the man named after one of my enemies by descendants of my enemies in the land of my people's enslavement. But none of that mattered. I didn't care if he hated me and my kind. I didn't care if I made him a million dollars by working for him. And if he wanted a black operative to undermine black people, well . . . I'd do that too — if I had to.

AT THREE IN THE MORNING I was still at Feather's side. I sat there all night because Saul was coming at four to drive with me up the coast. I didn't want to leave my little girl. I was afraid she might die in the time I was gone. The only thing I could do was sit there, hoping that my will would keep her breathing.

And it was lucky that I did stay because she started moaning and twisting around in her sleep. Her forehead was burning up. I hurried to the medicine cabinet to get one of Mama Jo's tar balls.

When I got back Feather was sitting up and breathing hard.

"Daddy, you were gone," she whimpered.

I sat beside her and put the tar ball in her mouth.

"Chew, baby," I said. "You got fever."

She hugged my arm and began to chew. She cried and chewed and tried to tell about the dream where I had disappeared. Remembering my own dream I kept from holding her too tightly.

In less than five minutes her fever was down and she was asleep again.

*   *   *

AT FOUR Bonnie came into the room and said, "It's time, honey."

Just when she said these words there was a knock at the front door. Feather sighed but did not awaken. Bonnie put her hand on my shoulder.

I felt as if every move and gesture had terrible importance. As things turned out I was right.

"I gave her some of Mama Jo's tar," I said. "There's only two left."

"It's okay," Bonnie assured me. "In three days we'll be in Switzerland and Feather will be under a doctor's care twenty-four hours a day."

"She's been sweating," I said as if I had not heard Bonnie's promise. "I haven't changed the sheets because I didn't want to leave her."

Saul knocked again.

I went to the door and let him in. He was wearing brown pants and a russet sweater with a yellow shirt underneath. He had on a green cap made of sewn leather strips.

"You ready?" he asked me.

"Come on in."

We went into the kitchen, where Saul and Bonnie kissed each other's cheeks. Bonnie handed me my coat, a brown shopping bag filled with sandwiches, and a thermos full of coffee.

"I got some fruit in the car," Saul said.

I looked around the house, not wanting to leave.

"Do you have any money, Easy?" Bonnie asked me.

I had given her the fifteen-hundred-dollar invitation.

"I could use a few bucks I guess."

Bonnie took her purse from the back of the chair. She rummaged around for a minute, but she had so much stuff in there that she couldn't locate the cash. So she spilled out the contents on our dinette table.

There was a calfskin clasp-purse but she never kept money there. She had cosmetic cases and a jewelry bag, two paperback books, and a big key ring with almost as many keys as I carried at Truth. Then came a few small cloth bags and an enameled pin or stud. The pin was the size of a quarter, decorated with the image of a white-and-red bird in flight against a bronze background.

If I wasn't already used to the pain I might have broken down and died right then.

"Easy," Bonnie was saying.

She proffered a fold of twenties.

I took the money and headed for the door.

"Easy," Bonnie said again. "Aren't you going to kiss me good-bye?"

I turned back and kissed her, my lips tingling as they had in the dream where the hornet was hiding in Feather's grassy grave.

6

A thin coating of freshly fallen snow hid the ruts in the road and softened the bombed-out buildings on the outskirts of Düsseldorf. The M1 rifle cradled in my arms was fully loaded and my frozen finger was on the trigger. At my right marched Jeremy Wills and Terry Bogaman, two white men that I'd only met that morning.

"Don't get ahead, son," Bogaman said.

Son.

"Yeah, Boots," Wills added. "Try and keep up."

Boots.

General Charles Bitterman had ordered forty-one small groups of men out that morning. Among them were thirteen Negroes. Bitterman didn't want black men forming into groups together. He'd said that we didn't have enough experience, but we all thought that he didn't trust us among the German women we might come across.

"I'm a sergeant, Corporal," I said to Wills.

"Sergeant Boots," he said with a grin.

Jeremy Wills was a fair-looking lad. He had corn-fed features and blond hair, amber-colored eyes, and big white teeth. To some lucky farm girl he might have been a good catch but to me he was repulsive, uglier than the corpses we ran across on the road to America's victory. My numb finger tightened and I gauged my chances of killing both soldiers before Bogaman, who was silently laughing at his friend's joke, could turn and fire.

I hadn't quite decided to let them live when a bullet lifted Wills's helmet and split his skull in two. I saw into his brain before he hit the ground. It was only then that I became aware of the machine-gun reports. When I started firing back Bogaman screamed. He had been hit in the shoulder, chest, and stomach. I fell to the ground and rolled off the road into a ditch. Then I was scuttling on all fours, like a lizard, into the meager shelter of the leafless woods.

Machine-gun fire ripped the bark and the frozen turf around me. I had gone more than fifty yards before I realized that somewhere along the way I'd dropped my rifle. In my mind at the time (and in the dream I was having) I imagined that my hatred for those white men had brought on the German attack.

The rattling roar of their fire proved to me that the Germans were desperate. I didn't think they could see me but they kept firing anyway.

Kids, I thought.

I took out my government-issue .45 and crawled around to the place where I had seen the flashes from their gun. I moved through the sound-softening snow hardly feeling the cold along my belly. I had no hatred for the Germans who tried to kill me out there on the road. I didn't feel that I had to avenge the deaths of the men who had so recently despised and disrespected me. But I knew that if I let the machine gunners live, sooner or later they might get the drop on me.

The Nazis wanted to kill me. That's because the Nazis knew that I was an American even if Bogaman and Wills did not.

I went maybe four hundred yards more through the woods and then I slithered across the road, making it back to the clump of branches that camouflaged the nest. I jumped up without thinking and began firing my pistol, holding it with both hands. I hit the first man in the eye and the second in the gut. They were completely surprised by the attack. I noticed, even in the two short seconds it took me to kill them, that their uniforms were makeshift and their hands were wrapped in rags.

The third soldier in the nest leaped at me with a bayonet in his hand. The impact of his attack knocked the pistol from my grasp. We fell to the ground, each committed to the other's death. I grabbed his wrist with one hand and pressed with all my might. The milky-skinned, gray-eyed youth grimaced and used all of his Aryan strength in an attempt to overwhelm me. But I was a few years older and that much more used to the logic of senseless violence. I grabbed the haft of his bayonet with my other hand while he wasted time hitting me with his free fist. By the time he realized that the tide was turning against him it was too late. He now used both hands to keep the blade from his chest but still it moved unerringly downward. As the seconds crept by, real fear appeared in the teenage soldier's eyes. I wanted to stop but there was no stopping. There we were, two men who had never known each other, working toward that young man's death. He spoke no English, could not beg in words I might understand. After maybe a quarter of a minute the blade passed through his coat and into his flesh, but then it got caught on one of his breastbones. I almost lost heart then but what could I do? It was him or me. I leaned forward with all my weight and the German steel broke the German's bone and plunged deep into his heart.

The most terrible thing was his last gasp, a sudden hot gust of breath into my face. His eyes opened wide as if to see some way out of the finality in his body — and then he was dead.

I jumped up from my sleep in Saul's Rambler. A sign at the side of the road read THE ARTICHOKE CAPITAL OF THE WORLD.

"Bad dream?" Saul asked me.

It was a dream, but everything in it had happened more than twenty years before. It was real. That German boy had died and there wasn't a thing either one of us could do to stop it.

"Yeah," I said. "Just a dream."

"I guess I should tell you a little about this guy Lee," Saul said. "He's not known to the public at large but in certain circles he's the most renowned private detective in the world."

"The world?"

"Yes sir. He does work in Europe and South America and Asia too."

I noticed that he didn't mention Africa. People rarely did when talking about the world in those days.

"Yes sir," Saul Lynx said again. "He has entrée to every law enforcement facility and many government offices. He's a connoisseur of fine wines, women, and food. Speaks Chinese, both Mandarin and Cantonese, Spanish, French, and English, which means that he can converse with at least one person in almost every town, village, or hamlet in the world. He's extremely well read. He thinks that he is the better of every, and any, man regardless of race or rank. And that means that his racism includes the whole human race."

"Sounds like a doozy," I said. "What's he look like?"

"I don't know."

"What do you mean you don't know? I thought that you'd done work for him before."

"I have. But I never met him face-to-face. You see, Bobby Lee doesn't like to sully himself with operatives. He has this woman named Maya Adamant who represents him to most clients and to almost all the PIs that do his legwork. She's one of the most beautiful women I've ever seen. He spends most of his time hidden away in his mansion on Nob Hill."

"Have you ever talked to him, in Chinese or otherwise?" I asked.

Saul shook his head.

"Have you seen his picture?"

"No."

"How do you even know that this man exists?"

"I've met people who've met him — clients mainly. Some of them liked to talk about his talents and eccentricities."

"You should meet with a man you work for," I said.

"People work for Heinz Foods and Ford Motor Company and never meet them," Saul argued.

"But they employ thousands. This dude is a small shop. He needs to at least say hello."

"What difference would that make, Easy?" Saul asked.

"How can you work for a man don't even have the courtesy to come out from his office and nod at you?"

"I received an envelope yesterday morning with twenty-five hundred dollars in it," he said. "I get a thousand dollars just to deliver you your money and take a drive up to Frisco. Sometimes I work two weeks and don't make half that."

"Money isn't everything, Saul."

"It is when your daughter is at death's door and only money can buy her back."

I could see that Saul regretted his words as soon as they came out of his mouth. But I didn't say anything. He was right. I didn't have the luxury of criticizing that white man. Who cared if I ever met him? All I needed was his long green.

7

A beautiful day in San Francisco is the most beautiful day on earth. The sky is blue and white, Michelangelo at his best, and the air is so crystal clear it makes you feel that you can see more detail than you ever have before. The houses are wooden and white with bay windows. There was no trash in the street and the people, at least back then, were as friendly as the citizens of some country town.

If I hadn't had Feather, and that enameled pin, on my mind I would have enjoyed our trip through the city.

On Lower Lombard we passed a peculiar couple walking down the street. The man wore faded red velvet pants with an open sheepskin vest that only partially covered his naked chest. His long brown hair cascaded down upon broad, thin shoulders. The woman next to him wore a loose, floral-patterned dress with nothing underneath. She had light brown hair with a dozen yellow flowers twined into her irregular braids. The two were walking, barefoot and slow, as if they had nowhere to be on that Thursday afternoon.

"Hippies," Saul said.

"Is that what they look like?" I asked, amazed. "What do they do?"

"As little as possible. They smoke marijuana and live a dozen to a room, they call 'em crash pads. And they move around from place to place saying that owning property is wrong."

"Like communists?" I asked. I had just finished reading *Das Kapital* when Feather got weak. I wanted to get at the truth about our enemies from the horse's mouth but I didn't have enough history to really understand.

"No," Saul said, "not communists. They're more like dropouts from life. They say they believe in free love."

"Free love? Is that like they say, 'That ain't my baby, baby'?"

Saul laughed and we began the ascent to Nob Hill.

Near the top of that exclusive mount is a street called Cushman. Saul took a right turn there, drove one block, and parked in front of a four-story mansion that rose up on a slope behind the sidewalk.

The walls were so white that it made me squint just looking at them. The windows seemed larger than others on the block and the conical turrets at the top were painted metallic gold. The first floor of the manor was a good fifteen feet above street level — the entrance was barred by a wrought iron gate.

Saul pushed a button and waited.

I looked out toward the city and appreciated the view. Then I felt the pang of guilt, knowing that Feather lay dying four hundred miles to the south.

"Yes?" a sultry woman's voice asked over an invisible intercom.

"It's Saul and Mr. Rawlins."

A buzzer sounded. Saul pulled open the gate and we entered onto an iron platform. The elevator vestibule was carved into the rock beneath the house. As soon as Saul closed the gate the platform began to move upward toward an opening at the first-floor level of the imposing structure. As we moved into the aperture a panel above us slid aside and we ascended into a large, well-appointed room.

The walls were mahogany bookshelves from floor to ceiling — and the ceiling was at least sixteen feet high. Beautifully bound books took up every space. I was reminded of Jackson Blue's beach house, which had cheap shelves everywhere. His books for the most part were ratty and soiled, but they were well read and his library was probably larger.

Appearing before us as we rose was a white woman with tanned skin and copper hair. She wore a Chinese-style dress made of royal blue silk. It fitted her form and had no sleeves. Her eyes were somewhere between defiant and taunting and her bare arms had the strength of a woman who did things for herself. Her face was full and she had a black woman's lips. The bones of her face made her features point downward like a lovely, earthward-bound arrowhead. Her eyes were light brown and a smile flitted around her lips as she regarded me regarding her beauty.

She would have been tall even if she were a man — nearly six feet. But unlike most tall women of that day, she didn't let her shoulders slump and her backbone was erect. I made up my mind then and there that I would get on naked terms with her if it was at all possible.

She nodded and smiled and I believe she read the intentions in my gaze.

"Maya Adamant," Saul Lynx said, "this is Ezekiel Rawlins."

"Easy," I said, extending a hand.

She held my hand a moment longer than necessary and then moved back so that we could step off of the platform.

"Saul," she said. "Come in. Would you like a drink?"

"No, Maya. We're in kind of a hurry. Easy's daughter is sick and we need to get back as soon as possible."

"Oh," she said with a frown. "I hope it's not serious."

"It's a blood condition," I said, not intending to be so honest. "Not quite an infection but it really isn't a virus either. The doctors in L.A. don't know what to do."

"There's a clinic in Switzerland . . . ," she said, searching for the name.

"The Bonatelle," I added.

Her smile broadened, as if I had just passed some kind of test. "Yes. That's it. Have you spoken to them?"

"That's why I'm here, Miss Adamant. The clinic needs cash and so I need to work."

Her chest expanded then and an expression of delight came over her face.

"Come with me," she said.

She led us toward a wide, carpeted staircase that stood at the far end of the library.

Saul looked at me and hunched his shoulders.

"I've never been above this floor before," he whispered.

THE ROOM ABOVE was just as large as the one we had left. But where the library was dark with no windows, this room had a nearly white pine floor and three bay windows along each wall.

There were maybe a dozen large tables in this sun-drenched space. On each was a battle scene from the Civil War. In each tableau there were scores of small, hand-carved wooden figurines engaged in battle. The individual soldiers — tending cannon, engaged in hand-to-hand combat, down and wounded, down and dead — were compelling. The figurines had been carved for maximum emotional effect. On one table there was a platoon of Negro Union soldiers engaging a Confederate band.

"Amazing, aren't they?" Maya asked from behind me. "Mr. Lee carves each one in a workroom in the attic. He has studied every aspect of the Civil War and has written a dozen monographs on the subject. He owns thousands of original documents from that period."

"One wonders when he has time to be a detective with all that," I said.

For a moment there was a deadness in Maya's expression. I felt that I had hit a nerve, that maybe Bobby Lee really was a figment of someone's imagination.

"Come into the office, Mr. Rawlins. Saul."

We followed her past the miniature scenes of murder and mayhem made mythic. I wondered if anyone would ever make a carving of me slaughtering that young German soldier in the snow in suburban Düsseldorf.

MAYA LED US through a hand-carved yellow door that was painted with images of a naked island woman.

"Gauguin," I said as she pushed the gaudy door open. "Your boss does paintings too?"

"This door is an original," she said.

"Whoa" came unbidden from my lips.

The office was a nearly empty, windowless room with cherry floors. Along the white walls were a dozen tall lamps with frosted glass globes around the bulbs. These lamps were set before as many floor-to-ceiling cherry beams imbedded in the plaster walls. All the lights were on.

In the center of the room was an antique red lacquered Chinese desk that had four broad-bottomed chairs facing it, with one behind for our absentee host.

"Sit," Maya Adamant said.

She settled in one of the visitors' chairs and Saul and I followed suit.

"We're looking for a woman," she began, all business now.

"Who's we?" I asked.

This brought on a disapproving frown.

"Mr. Lee."

"That's a *he* not a *we*," I said.

"All right," she acquiesced. "Mr. Lee wants —"

"Do you own this house, Miss Adamant?"

Another frown. "No."

"Easy," Saul warned.

I held up my hand for his silence.

"You know, my mother, before she died, told me that I should never enter a man's house without paying my respects."

"I'll be sure to tell Mr. Lee that you said hello," she told me.

"It was a double thing with my mother," I said, continuing with my train of thought. "On the one hand you didn't want a man thinking that you were in his domicile doing mischief with his property or his wife —"

"Mr. Lee is not married," Maya put in.

"And on the other hand," I went on, "being of the darker persuasion, you wouldn't want to be treated like a nigger or a slave."

"Mr. Lee doesn't meet with anyone who works for him," she informed me.

"Come on, Easy," Saul added. "I told you that."

Ignoring my friend, I said, "And I don't work for anyone I don't meet with."

"You've taken his money," Maya reminded me.

"And I drove four hundred miles to tell him thank you."

"I really don't see the problem, Mr. Rawlins. I can brief you on the job at hand."

"I could sit with you on a southern beach until the earth does a full circle, Miss Adamant. And I'm sure that I'd rather speak to you than to a man named after the number one Rebel general. But you have your orders from him and I got my mother's demands. My mother is dead and so she can't change her mind."

In my peripheral vision I could see Saul throw his hands up in the air.

"I can't take you to him," Maya said with finality.

I stood up from my fine Chinese chair saying, "And I can't raise the dead."

I made ready to leave, knowing that I was being a fool. I needed that money and I knew how powerful white men could act. But still I couldn't help myself. Hell, there was an armored car waiting for me in the state of Texas.

Thinking about the robbery, everything that could go wrong came back to me. So, standing there before my chair, I was torn between walking out and apologizing.

"Hold up there," a man's voice commanded.

I turned to see that a panel in the wall behind the lacquered desk had become a doorway.

A man emerged from the darkness, a very short man.

"I am Robert E. Lee," the little man said.

8

He wasn't over five feet tall. He might not have made the full sixty inches. He wore navy blue pants and a black coat cut in the fashion of a nineteenth-century general's jacket. He had short black hair and wispy sideburns, a completely round head, and the large dark eyes of a baby who had wisdom past its years.

He marched up to the chair behind the desk and sat with an air that could only be described as pompous.

It was obvious that he had been watching us since we entered the office. I suspected that he had probably been monitoring our conversation from the moment we entered the house. But the little general wasn't embarrassed by this exposure. He touched something on his desk and the portal behind him slid shut.

"It's like the house of the future at Disneyland," I said.

"I've never been," he said with an insincere smile plastered to his lips.

"You should go sometime. Might give you some tips."

"You've met me, Mr. Rawlins," Robert E. Lee said. "We've had mindless banter. Is that enough for your mother?"

An instant rage rose up in my heart. I had never loved anyone in life as much as I did my mother — at least not until the birth of my blood daughter and then when Jesus and Feather found their way into my home. The idea that this arrogant little man would refer to my mother in that tone made me want to slap him. But I held myself in check. After all, I had mentioned my mother's admonition and Feather needed my best effort if she was going to live.

"So why am I here?" I asked.

"You'd need a practicing existentialist to answer a question like that," he said. "All I can do is explain the job at hand. Mr. Lynx . . ."

"Yes sir," Saul said. "May I say that it's an honor to meet you."

"Thank you. Do you vouch for Mr. Rawlins?"

"He's among the best, sir. And he is the best in certain parts of town, especially if that town is Los Angeles."

"You realize that you will be held accountable for his actions?"

Lee referred to me as if I weren't there. A moment before, that would have angered me, but now I was amused. His effort was petty. I turned to Maya Adamant and winked.

"I'd trust Ezekiel Rawlins with my life," Saul replied. There was deep certainty in his voice.

"I'm my own man, Mr. Lee," I said. "If you want to work with me, then fine. If not I have things to do in L.A."

"Or in Montreux," he added, proving my suspicions about the eavesdropping devices throughout the house.

"The job," I prodded.

Lee pressed his lips outward and then pulled them in. He looked at me with those infant orbs and came to a decision.

"I have been retained by a wealthy man living outside Danville to discover the whereabouts of a business associate who went missing five days ago. This associate has absconded with a briefcase that contains certain documents that must be returned as soon as possible. If I can locate this man and return the contents of that briefcase before midnight of next Friday I will receive a handsome fee and you, if you are instrumental in the acquisition of that property, will receive ten thousand dollars on top of the monies you've already been paid."

"Who's the client?" I asked.

"His name is unimportant," Lee replied.

I knew from the way he lifted his chin that my potential employer meant to show me who was boss. This was nothing new to me. I had tussled with almost every boss I'd ever had over the state of my employment and the disposition of my dignity.

And almost every boss I'd ever had had been a white man.

"What's in the briefcase?"

"White papers, printed in ink and sealed with red wax."

I turned my head to regard Saul. Beyond him, on the far wall, next to a lamp, was a small framed photograph. I couldn't make out the details from that distance. It was the only decoration on the walls and it was in an odd place.

"Is your client the original owner of these white papers, printed in ink and sealed with red wax?"

"As far as I know my client is the owner of the briefcase in question and its contents."

Lee was biding his time, waiting for something. In my opinion he was acting like a buffoon but those eyes made me wary.

"What is the name of the man who stole the briefcase?"

Lee balked then. He brought his fingers together, forming a triangle.

"I'd like to know a little bit more about you before divulging that information," he said.

I sat back and turned my palms upward. "Shoot."

"Where are you from?"

"A deep dark humanity down in Louisiana, a place where we never knew there was a depression because we never had the jobs to lose."

"Education?"

"I read Mann's *Magic Mountain* last month. The month before that I read *Invisible Man*."

That got a smile.

"H. G. Wells?"

"Ellison," I countered.

"You fought in the war?"

"On both fronts."

Lee frowned and cocked his head. "The European and Japanese theaters?" he asked.

I shook my head and smiled.

"White people took their shots at me," I said. "Most of them were German but there was an American or two in the mix."

"Married?"

"No," I said with maybe a little too much emphasis.

"I see. Are you a licensed PI, Mr. Rawlins?"

"Yes sir, I am."

Holding out a child's hand, he asked, "May I see it?"

"Don't have it with me," I said. "It's in a frame on the wall in my office."

Lee nodded, stopped to consider, and then nodded again — listening to an unseen angel on his right shoulder. Then he rose, barely taller standing than he was seated.

"Good day," he said, making a paltry attempt at a bow.

Now I understood. From the moment I flushed him out of hiding he intended to dismiss my services. What I couldn't understand was why he didn't let me leave when I wanted to the first time.

"Fine with me." I stood up too.

"Mr. Lee," Maya said then. She also rose from her chair. "Please, sir."

Please. The conflict wasn't between me and Lee — it was a fight between him and his assistant.

"He's unlicensed," Lee said, making a gesture like he was tossing something into the trash.

"He's fully licensed," she said. "I spoke with Mayor Yorty himself this morning. He told me that Mr. Rawlins has the complete support of the LAPD."

I sat down.

There was too much information to sift through on my feet. This woman could get the mayor of Los Angeles on the phone, the mayor knew my name, and the Los Angeles cops were willing to say that they trusted me. Not one of those facts did I feel comfortable with.

Lee sighed.

"Mr. Lynx has always been our best operative in Los Angeles," Maya said, "and he brought Mr. Rawlins to us."

"How long ago did you first come to us, Mr. Lynx?" Lee asked.

"Six years ago, I guess."

"And you never tried to extort your way into my presence?"

Saul didn't say anything.

"And why should I put a man I don't know on a case of this much importance?" Lee asked Maya.

"Because he's the only man for the job and therefore he's the best," she said confidently.

"Why don't you call Chief Parker and get him to find the girl?" Lee said.

"To begin with, he's a public official and this is a private matter." I felt that her words carried hidden meaning. "And you know as well as I do that white policemen in white socks and black shoes are never going to find Cargill."

Lee stared at his employee for a moment and then sat down. Maya let out a deep breath and lowered, catlike, into her chair.

Saul was looking at us with his emerald eyes evident. For a deadpan like Saul this was an expression of bewilderment.

Lee was regarding his own clasped hands on the red lacquered desk. I got the feeling that he didn't lose many arguments with the people he deigned to meet. It would take a few moments for him to swallow his pride.

"The man we're looking for is named Axel Bowers," Lee said at last. "He's a liberal lawyer living in Berkeley, from a wealthy family. He has a storefront practice in San Francisco, where he and an associate attempt to help miscreants evade the law. He's the one who stole from my client."

"What's the catch?" I asked.

"Bowers had a colored servant named Philomena Cargill, generally known as Cinnamon — because of the hue of her skin, I am told. This Cinnamon worked for Bowers as a housekeeper at first, but she had some education and started doing secretarial and assistant work also.

"When my client realized that Bowers had stolen from him he

called his home to demand the return of his property. Miss Cargill answered and said that Bowers had left the country.

"The client came to me but by the time my people got there Miss Cargill had fled also. It is known that she came to Berkeley from Los Angeles, that she was raised near Watts. It is also known that she and Axel were very close, unprofessionally so.

"What I need for you to do is find Miss Cargill and locate Bowers and the contents of the briefcase."

"So you want Bowers too?" I asked.

"Yes."

"Why? Doesn't sound like you're planning to prosecute."

"Do you accept the task as I have presented it?" he asked in return.

"I'd like to know where these people live in San Francisco and Berkeley," I said.

"Neither of them is in the Bay Area, I can assure you of that," the little Napoleon said. "Bowers is out of the country and Cargill is in Los Angeles. We've tried to contact her family but all attempts have failed."

"She might have friends here who know where she went," I suggested.

"We are pursuing that avenue, Mr. Rawlins. You are to go to L.A. and search for the girl there."

"Girl," I repeated. "How old is she?"

Lee glanced at Maya.

"Early twenties," the knockout replied.

"Anything else?" Lee asked.

"Family?" I said. "Previous address, photograph, distinguishing habits or features?"

"You're the best in Los Angeles," Lee said. "Mr. Lynx assures

us of that. Maya will give you any information she deems necessary. Other than that, I'm sure you will find the answers to all of
your questions and ours. Do you accept?"

"Sure," I said. "Why not? Philomena Cargill also known as
Cinnamon, somewhere on the streets of L.A."

Robert E. Lee rose from his chair. He turned his back on us
and made his way through the hole in the wall. The panel closed
behind him.

I turned to Maya Adamant and said, "That's one helluva boss
you got there."

"Shall we go?" was her reply.

9

F irst I want to check something out," I said.

I crossed the room, approaching the small out-of-the-way frame. It was a partially faded daguerreotype-like photograph, imprinted on a pane of glass. It looked to be the detective's namesake. The general was in full uniform. He had, at some point during the exposure, looked down, maybe at a piece of lint on his magnificent coat. The result was the image of a two-headed man. The more tangible face stared with grim conviction at the lens while the other was peering downward, unaware of history.

I was intrigued by the antique photograph because of its vulnerability. It was as if the detective wanted to honor the past general in both victory and defeat.

"Shall we go, Mr. Rawlins?" Maya Adamant said again.

I realized that she was worried about Lee getting mad if he saw me getting too intimate with his sanctorum.

"Sure."

IN THE LIBRARY Maya gave me a business card.

"These are my numbers," she said, "both at home and at work."

Saul had been forgotten. He'd merely been their, or was it her, pipeline to a Watts connection.

"What's the disagreement between you and your boss?" I asked.

"I don't know what you're talking about."

"Sure you do. He went through that whole song and dance about getting rid of me because he wanted you to beg him. What's that all about?"

"You would be better served, Mr. Rawlins, by using your detecting skills to find Philomena Cargill."

There was an almost physical connection between us. It was like we'd known each other in a most fundamental way — so much so that I nearly leaned forward to kiss her. She saw this and moved her head back half an inch. But even then she smiled.

We went down to the library. I gave her my office phone number.

"When will you be there?" she asked me.

"Doesn't matter."

"You have a secretary?"

"Electronic," I said, more for her master than for her.

"I don't understand."

"I got a tape recorder attached to my phone. It records a message and plays it back when I get in."

* * *

OUTSIDE THE SUN was dazzling. A cool breeze blew over Nob Hill.

"What the hell was that all about?" Saul said as soon as we were back at his car.

"What?"

"I don't know. You choose. Making Lee come out to talk to you. Looking at Maya like that."

"You got to admit that Miss Adamant is a good-looker."

"I have to admit that you need this job."

"Listen, Saul. I won't work for a guy that refuses to meet me face-to-face. You know what'll happen if the cops come breakin' down my door and I can't even say that I ever talked to the man."

"I brought you there, Easy. I wouldn't put you in jeopardy like that."

"*You* wouldn't. I know that because I know you. But hear me, man, that black son'a yours will be out on his own one day. And when he is he will tell you that every other white man he meets will sell an innocent black man down the river before he will turn on a white crook."

That silenced my friend for a moment. I had waited years to be able to slip that piece of intelligence into his ear.

"Well what did you think about Lee?" he asked.

"I don't trust him."

"You think he's bent?"

"I don't know about that but he seems like the kinda fool get you down a dark alley and then forget to send your backup."

"Forget? Bobby Lee doesn't forget a thing. He's one of the smartest men in the world."

"That might be," I replied, "but he thinks he's even smarter than what he is. And you and I both know that if a man is too proud then he's gonna fall. And if I'm right under him . . ."

Saul respected me. I could see in his eye that he was halfway convinced by my argument. Now that he'd met Lee he had reservations of his own.

"Well," he said, "I guess you got to do it anyway, right? I mean that's your little girl."

I nodded and gazed southward at a huge bank of fog descending on the city.

"I guess we better be getting back," Saul said.

"You go on. I'm gonna stick around town and see about these people here."

"But all they need you to do is find Philomena Cargill."

"I don't know that she's in L.A. Neither does Lee."

SAUL HAD TO GET BACK home. He was due to meet with a client the next morning. I had him drop me off at a Hertz rental car lot.

It only took them an hour and a half to call Los Angeles to validate my BankAmericard.

"You always call the bank to check out a credit card?" I asked the blue-suited and white salesman.

"Certainly," he replied. He had a fat face, thinning hair, and a slender frame.

"Seems to defeat the purpose of a credit card."

"You can never be too careful," he told me.

"I look at it the other way around," I said. "The way I see it you can never be careful enough."

The salesman squinted at me then. He understood that I was making fun of him — he just didn't get the joke.

*   *   *

AN OAKLAND PHONE BOOK at the Hertz office told me that
Axel Bowers lived on Berkeley's Derby Street. The Bay Area
street map in my glove compartment put it a block or so up from
Telegraph. I drove my rented Ford across the Bay Bridge and
parked a block away from the alleged thief's house.

Derby was a major education for me. Everything about that
block was in transition. But not the way neighborhoods usually
change. It wasn't black folks moving in and whites moving out or
a downward turn in the local economy so that homes once filled
with middle-class families were turning into rooming houses for
the working poor.

This neighborhood was transforming as if under a magic spell.

The houses had gone from the standard white and green, blue,
and yellow to a wide range of pastels. Pinks, aquas, violets, and
fiery oranges. Even the cars were painted like rainbows or with
rude images or long speeches etched by madmen. Music of every
kind poured from open windows. Some women wore long tie-dyed
gowns like fairy princesses and others wore nearly nothing at all.
Half of the men were shirtless and almost all of them had long
hair like women. Their beards went untrimmed. American flags
were plastered into windows and tacked to walls in a decidedly
unpatriotic manner. Many of the young women carried babies.

It was the most integrated neighborhood I had ever seen.
There were whites and blacks and browns and even one or two
Asian faces.

It seemed to me that I had wandered into a country where
war had come and all the stores and public services had been
shut down; a land where the population was being forced into a
more primitive state.

I stopped in front of one big lavender house because I heard something and someone that I recognized. "Show Me Baby," the signature blues song of my old friend Alabama Slim, was blasting from the front door. 'Bama was crooning from the speakers. 'Bama. I didn't think that there were ten white people in the United States who knew his work. But there he was, singing for a street filled with hairy men and women of all races in a country that was no longer the land of his birth.

BOWERS'S HOUSE, a single-story wood box, was the most normal-looking one on the block. Its plank walls were still white, but the trim was a fire-engine red and the front door was decorated with a plaster mosaic set with broken tiles, shards of glass, marbles, trinkets, and various semiprecious stones: rough garnets, pink quartz, and turquoise.

I rang the bell and used the brass skull knocker but no one answered. Then I went down the side of the house, toward the back. There I came across a normal-looking green door that had a pane of glass set in it. Through this window I could see a small room that had a broom leaning in a corner and rubber boots on the floor. A floral-pattern apron hung from a peg on the wall.

I knocked. No answer. I knocked again. When nobody came I took off my left shoe, balled my fist in it, and broke the window.

"Hey, man! What you doin'?" a raspy voice called from up toward the street.

I was unarmed, which was either a good or a bad thing, and caught red-handed. The strange character of the neighborhood had made me feel I could go unnoticed, doing whatever I needed to get the job done. That was a mistake a black man could never afford to make.

I turned to see the man who caught me. He walked the slender, ivy-covered corridor with confidence — as if he were the owner of the house.

He was short, five six or so, with greasy black hair down to his shoulders. Most of his face was covered by short, bristly black hairs. He had on a blood-red shirt that was too large for his thin frame and black jeans. He wore no shoes but his feet were dirty enough to be mistaken for leather. His dark eyes glittered in their sockets. Golden earrings dangled from his ears in a feminine way that made me slightly uncomfortable.

"Yes?" I asked pleasantly, as if addressing an officer of the law.

"What you doin' breakin' into Axel's house?" the sandpaper-toned hippie asked.

"A guy named Manly hired me to find Mr. Bowers," I said. "He called on me because my cousin, Cinnamon, works for him."

"You Philomena's cousin?" the crazy-looking white man asked.

"Yeah. Second cousin. We were raised not six blocks from each other down in L.A."

"So why you breakin' in?" the man asked again. He looked deranged but his question was clear and persistent.

"Like I said. This guy Manly, over in Frisco, asked me to find Bowers. Cinnamon is missing too. I decided to take his money and to see if anything was wrong."

The small man looked me up and down.

"You could be Philomena's blood," he said. "But you know Axel's a friend'a mine and I can't just let you walk in his house like this."

"What's your name?" I asked.

"Dream Dog," he replied without embarrassment or inflection. It was just as if he had said Joe or Frank.

"I'm Dupree," I said and we shook hands. "I'll tell you what, Dream Dog. Why don't you come in with me? That way you can see that I'm just looking to find out where they are."

When the man smiled I could see that he was missing two or three teeth. But instead of making him ugly the spaces reminded me of a child playing pirate with pasted-on whiskers and a costume that his mother made from scraps.

10

"You know about karma, brother?" Dream Dog asked as I snaked my hand down to turn the lock on the doorknob.

"Hindu religion," I said, remembering a talk I'd had with Jackson Blue in which he explained how much he disagreed with the Indian system of the moral interpretation of responsibility.

You know, the undersized genius had said, *ain't no way in the world that black folks could'a done enough bad to call all them centuries'a pain down on our heads.*

Dream Dog smiled. "Yeah. Hindu. All about what you do an' how it comes back to you."

"Is this apron Cinnamon's?" I asked.

We were in the door.

"Sure is. But you know she wasn't really a maid or nuthin' like that. She had a business degree from Berkeley and wanted to get on Wall Street. Oh yeah, that Philomena got her some spunk."

"I knew she was in school," I said. "The whole family is very proud of her. That's why they're so worried. Did she tell you where she was going?"

"Uh-uh," Dream Dog said while he gauged my words.

The utility room led into a long kitchen that had a lengthy butcher block counter with a copper sink on one side and a six-burner stove-oven on the other. It was a well-appointed kitchen with copper pots hanging from the walls and glass cabinets filled with all kinds of canned goods, spices, and fine china. It was very neat and ordered, even the teacup set tidily in the copper sink spoke to the owner's sense of order.

Dream Dog opened a cabinet and pulled down a box of Oreo cookies. He took out three and then placed the box back on the shelf.

"Axel keeps 'em for me," he said. "My mom can't eat 'em on account'a she's got an allergy to coconut oil and sometimes they use coconut oil in these here. But you know I love 'em. An' Axel keeps 'em for me on this shelf right here."

There was a reverence and pride in Dream Dog's words — and something else too.

THE LIVING ROOM had three plush chaise lounges set in a square with one side missing. The backless sofas stood upon at least a dozen Persian rugs. The carpets had been thrown with no particular design one on top of the other and gave the room a definitely Arabian flavor. The smell of incense helped the mood as did the stone mosaics hung upon the walls. These tiled images were obviously old, probably original, coming from Rome and maybe the Middle East. One was of a snarling, long-tongued wolf harrying a naked brown maiden; another one was a scene of a bacchanal with men, women, children, and dogs drinking, dancing, kissing, fornicating, and leaping for joy.

In each of the four corners was a five-foot-high Grecian urn glazed in black and brown-red and festooned with the images of naked men in various competitions.

"I love these couches, man," Dream Dog said to me. He had stretched out on the middle lounger. "They're worth a lotta money. I told Axel that somebody might come in and steal his furniture while he was outta town, and that's when he asked me to look out for him."

"He outta town a lot?"

"Yeah. For the past year he been goin' to Germany and Switzerland and Cairo. You know Cairo's in Egypt and Egypt is part of Africa. I learned that from a brother talks down on the campus before they have the Congo drum line."

"You think he's in Cairo now?" I asked.

"Nah, he's always down at the campus on Sunday talkin' history before the drum line."

"Not the guy at school," I said patiently, "Axel."

Dream Dog bounced off the couch and held an Oreo out to me.

"Cookie?"

I'm not much for sweets but even if I had a sugar tooth the size of Texas I wouldn't have eaten from his filthy claws.

"Watchin' my weight," I said.

On a side table, set at the nexus where two of the loungers met, were two squat liquor glasses. Both had been filled with brandy but the drinks had evaporated, leaving a golden film at the bottom of each glass. Next to the glasses was an ashtray in which a lit cigarette had been set and left to burn down to its filter. There was also a photograph of a man, his arms around an older woman, with them both looking at the camera.

"Who's this?" I asked my companion.

"That's Axel and his mom. She died three years ago," Dream Dog said. "His father passed away from grief a year and a half later."

The younger Bowers couldn't have been over twenty-five, maybe younger. He had light brown hair and a handsome smile. You could tell by his clothes and his mother's jewelry that there was money there. But there was also sorrow in both their smiles and I thought that maybe a poor childhood in southern Louisiana wasn't the worst place that a man could come from.

"I told him that he should open the drapes too," Dream Dog was saying. "I mean God gives sunlight to warm you and to let you see."

"Where's the bedroom?" I asked.

"Axel's cool though," my new friend said as he led me through a double-wide door on the other side of the room. "He comes from money and stuff, but he knows that people are worth more than money and that we got to share the wealth, that a ship made outta gold will sink . . ."

He flipped a wall switch and we found ourselves in a wide, wood-paneled hallway. Down one side of the hall were Japanese woodprints framed in simple cherrywood. Each of these prints (which looked original) had the moon in one aspect or another as part of the subject. There were warriors and poets, fishermen and fine ladies. Down the other side were smaller paintings. I recognized one that I'd seen in an art book at Paris Minton's Florence Avenue Bookshop. It was the work of Paul Klee. Upon closer examination I saw that all of the paintings on that side of the wall were done by him.

"I paint some too," Dream Dog said when I stopped to examine the signature. "Animals mostly. Dogs and cats and ducks. I told Axel that he could have some of my drawings when he got tired'a this stuff."

It was a large bedroom. The oversized bed seemed like a raft on a wide river of blue carpet. The sheets and covers were a jaundiced yellow and the windows looked out under a broad redwood that dominated the backyard.

A newspaper, the *Chronicle,* was folded at the foot of the bed. The date was March 29.

There were whiskey glasses at the side of the unmade bed. They also had the sheen of dried liquor. The pillows smelled sweetly, of a powerful perfume. I had the feeling that vigorous sex had transpired there before the end, but that might have been some leftover feeling I had about Maya Adamant.

The room was so large that it had its own dressing nook. I thought that this was a very feminine touch for a man, but then maybe the previous owners had been a couple and this was the woman's corner.

There was an empty briefcase next to the cushioned brown hassock that sat there between three mirrors. Next to the handle was a shiny brass nameplate that had the initials ANB stamped on it.

There was a bottle of cologne on the little dressing table; it smelled nothing like those pillows.

"Axel entertain a lot?" I asked my hippie guide.

"Oh man," Dream Dog said. "I seen three, four women in here at the same time. Axel gets down. And he shares the wealth too. Sometimes he calls me in and we all get so high that nobody knows who's doin' what to who — if you know what I mean."

I did not really know and felt no need for clarification.

The dressing table had three drawers. One contained two plastic bags of dried leaves, marijuana by the smell of them. Another drawer held condoms and various lubricants. The bottom drawer held a typed letter, with an official heading, from a man named Haffernon. There was also a handwritten envelope with Axel's name scrawled on it. There was no stamp or address or postmark on that letter.

"I'm going to take these letters," I said to my escort. "Maybe I can get to Axel or Cinnamon through somebody here."

"But you're gonna leave the dope?" Dream Dog sounded almost disappointed.

"I'm not a thief, brother."

The little white man smiled and I realized that his attitude toward me was different from that of most whites. He was protecting his friend from invasion, but this had nothing to do with my being black. That was a rare experience for me at that time.

There was an empty teacup on the dressing table too. It was also dried up. From the smell I knew that it had been a very strong brew.

11

When we were back out on the sidewalk I felt as if a weight had been taken off of me. Something about the house, how it seemed as if it were frozen into a snapshot, made me feel that something sudden and violent had occurred.

"You spend a lot of time with Bowers?" I asked the hippie.

"He gives these big old dinners and your cousin's always there with some other straights from over in Frisco. Axel buys real good wine in big bottles and has Hannah's Kitchen make a vegetarian feast."

Dream Dog was around thirty, but he looked older because of the facial hair and skin weathered by many days and nights outside.

I was smoking Parliaments at that time. I offered him one and he took it. I lit us both up and we stood there on Derby surrounded by all kinds of hippies and music and multicolored cars.

"We trip a lot," Dream Dog said.

"What's that?"

"Drop acid."

"What kind of acid?" I asked.

"LSD. Where you from? We drop acid. We trip."

"Oh," I said. "I see. You do drugs together."

"Not drugs, man," Dream Dog said with disdain. "Acid. Drugs close down your mind. They put you to sleep. Acid opens your crown chakra. It lets God leak in — or the devil."

I didn't know very much about psychedelics back then. I'd heard about the "acid test" that they gave at certain clubs up on Sunset Strip but that wasn't my hangout. I knew my share of heroin addicts, glue sniffers, and potheads. But this sounded like something else.

"What happens when you drop?" I asked.

"Trip," he said, correcting my usage.

"Okay. What happens?"

"This one time it was really weird. He played an album by Yusef Lateef. *Rite of Spring* but in a jazz mode. And there was this chick there named Polly or Molly . . . somethin' like that. And we all made love and ate some brownies that she was sellin' door-to-door. I remember this one moment when me and Axel were each suckin' on a nipple and I felt like I was a baby and she was as big as the moon. I started laughin' and I wanted to go off in the corner but I had to crawl because I was a baby and I didn't know how to walk yet."

Dream Dog was back in the hallucination. His snaggletoothed grin was beatific.

"What did Axel do?" I asked.

"That's when his bad trip started," Dream Dog said. His smile faded. "He remembered something about his dad and that made him mad. It was his dad and two of his dad's friends. He called them vulture-men feeding off of carrion. He ran around the ashram swinging this stick. He knocked out this tooth'a mines right here." Dream Dog flipped up his lip and pointed at the gap.

"Why was he so mad?" I asked.

"It's always somethin' inside'a you," the hippie explained. "I mean it's always there but you never look at it, or maybe on the trip you see what you always knew in a new way.

"After he knocked me down Polly put her arms around him and kissed his head. She kept tellin' him that things were gonna be fine, that he could chase the vultures away and bury the dead . . ."

"And he calmed down?"

"He went into a birth trip, man. All the way back to the fetus in the womb. He went through the whole trip just like as if he was being born again. He came out and started cryin' and me and Polly held him. But then she an' me were holdin' each other and before you know it we're makin' love again. But by then Axel was sitting up and smiling. He told us that he had been given a plan."

"What plan?"

"He didn't say," Dream Dog said, shaking his head and smiling. "But he was happy and we all went to sleep. We slept for twenty-four hours and when we woke up Axel was all calm and sure. That was when he started doin' all'a that travelin' and stuff."

"How long ago was that?" I asked.

"A year maybe. A little more."

"Around the time his father died?" I asked.

"Now that you say it . . . yeah. His father died two weeks before — that's why we did acid."

"And where is this Polly or Molly?"

"Her? I dunno, man. She was goin' from door to door sellin' brownies. Axel an' me were ready to trip and we asked her if she wanted to join in. Axel told her that if she did he'd buy all'a her brownies."

"But I thought you said that you were at this other place. Asham?"

"Ashram," Dream Dog said. "That's the prayer temple that Axel built out behind the trees in his backyard. That's his holy place."

"Where do you live?" I asked Dream Dog.

"On this block mainly."

"Which house?"

"There's about five or six let me crash now and then. You know it depends on how they're feelin' and if I got some money to throw in for the soup."

"If I need to find you is there somebody around here that might know how to get in touch?" I asked.

"Sadie down in the purple place at the end of the block. They call her place the Roller Derby 'cause of the street and because so many people crash there. She knows where I am usually. Yeah, Sadie."

Dream Dog's gaze wandered down the street, fastening upon a young woman wearing a red wraparound dress and a crimson scarf. She was barefoot.

"Hey, Ruby!" Dream Dog called. "Wait up."

The girl smiled and waved.

"One more thing," I said before he could sprint away.

"What's that, Dupree?"

"Do you know where Axel's San Francisco office is?"

"The People's Legal Aid Center. Just go on down to Haight-Ashbury and ask anyone."

I handed Dream Dog a twenty-dollar bill and proffered my hand. He smiled and pulled me into a fragrant hug. Then he ran off to join the red-clad Ruby.

The idea of karma was still buzzing around my head. I was thinking that maybe if I was nice to Dream Dog, someone somewhere would be kind to my little girl.

I WALKED AROUND the block after Dream Dog was gone. I didn't want him or anybody else to see me investigate the ashram, so I came in through one of the neighbors' driveways and into the backyard of Axel Bowers.

It was a garden house set behind two weeping willows. You might not have seen it even looking straight at it because the walls and doors were painted green like the leaves and lawn.

The door was unlocked.

Axel's holy place was a single room with bare and unfinished pine floors and a niche in one of the walls where there sat a large brass elephant that had six arms. Its beard sprouted many half-burned sticks of incense. Their sweet odor filled the room but there was a stink under that.

A five-foot-square bamboo mat marked the exact center of the floor but beyond that there was no other furniture.

All of the smells, both good and bad, seemed to emanate from the brass elephant. It was five feet high and the same in width. At its feet lay a traveling trunk with the decals of many nations glued to it.

Somebody had already snapped off the padlock, and so all I had to do was throw the trunk open. Because of the foul odor that cowered underneath the sweet incense I thought that I'd find a body in the trunk. It was too small for a man but maybe, I thought, there would be some animal sacrificed in the holy ashram.

Failing an animal corpse, I thought I might find some other fine art like the pieces that graced the house.

The last thing I expected was a trove of Nazi memorabilia.

And not just the run-of-the-mill pictures of Adolf Hitler and Nazi flags. There was a dagger that had a garnet-encrusted swastika on its hilt, and the leather-bound copy of *Mein Kampf* was signed by Hitler himself. The contents of the trunk were all jumbled, which added to the theory that someone had already searched it. Bobby Lee said that he'd sent people to look for Philomena — maybe this was their work.

There was a pair of leather motorcycle gloves in the trunk. I accepted this providence and donned the gloves. I'd made sure to touch as few surfaces as possible in the house but gloves were even better.

A box for a deck of cards held instead a stack of pocket photographs of a man I did not recognize posing with Mussolini and Hitler, Göring and Hess. The man had an ugly-looking scar around his left eye. That orb looked out in stunned blindness. For a moment I remembered the boy I killed in Germany after he had slaughtered the white Americans who'd made fun of me. I also remembered the concentration camp we'd liberated and the starved, skeletal bodies of the few survivors.

The putrid odor was worse inside the trunk but there was no evidence of even a dead rat. There were a Nazi captain's uniform and various weapons, including a well-oiled Luger with three clips of ammo. There was also, hidden inside a package that looked like it contained soap, a thick stack of homemade pornographic postcards. They were photographs of the same heavyset man who had posed with the Nazi leaders. Now he was in various sexual positions with young women and girls. He had a very large erection and all of the pictures were of him penetrating women from in front or behind. One photo centered on a teenage girl's face — she was screaming in pain as he lowered on her from overhead.

I took the Luger and the clips of ammo, then I tried to move the trunk but I could see that it was anchored to the floor somehow. I got down on my knees and sniffed around the base of the trunk — the smell was definitely coming from underneath.

After looking around the base I decided to pull away the carpet that surrounded the trunk. There I saw a brass latch. I lifted this and the trunk flipped backward, revealing the corpse of a man crushed into an almost perfect rectangle — the size of the space beneath the trunk.

The man's head was facing upward, framed by his forearms.

It was the face of the young man hugging his mother — Axel Bowers.

12

I had seen my share of dead bodies. Many of them had died under violent circumstances. But I had never seen anything like Axel Bowers. His killer treated the body like just another thing that needed to be hidden, not like a human being at all. The bones were broken and his forehead was crushed by the trunk coming down on it.

The smell was overwhelming. Soon the neighbors would begin to detect it. I wondered if the person who had searched the trunk had found Axel. Not necessarily; if they'd been there a few days before, there might not have been a smell yet, so they'd have had no reason to suspect there was a secret compartment.

It was a gruesome sight. But even then, in the presence of such awful violence and evil intent, I thought about Feather lying in her bed. I felt like running from there as fast as I could.

But instead I forced myself to wait and think about how even this horror might help her.

The knife was worth nothing and I didn't think that I had the kind of contacts to sell Hitler's signature. For that matter the signature might have been a fake.

I considered taking a couple of the Klec paintings from the house, but again I didn't know where to sell them. And if I got caught trying to fence stolen paintings I could end up in jail before getting the money I needed.

For a while I thought about burning down the ashram. I wanted to get rid of the evidence of the murder so that I wouldn't be implicated by Dream Dog or some other hippie on the block.

I even went so far as to get a can of gasoline from the garage. I also took tapered candles from the house to use as a kind of slow-burning fuse. But then I decided that fire would call attention to the murder instead of away from it. And what if the flames spread and killed someone in a nearby house?

The stench made my eyes tear and my gorge rise. I had wiped off the places I had touched in the ashram and the house. Dream Dog would think twice before giving information about breaking into Axel's place. Besides, he didn't know my name.

At some point I realized that I was finding it hard to leave. There was something in me that wanted to help Axel find some peace. The humiliation of his interment made me uncomfortable. Maybe it was the memory of the German boy I killed or the fragility of my adopted daughter's life. Maybe it was something deeper that had been instilled in me when I was a child among the superstitious country people of Louisiana.

Finally I decided that the only thing I could do for Axel was to make him a promise.

"I can't give you a proper burial, Mr. Bowers," I said. "But I swear that if I find out who did this to you I will do my best to make sure that they pay for their crime. Rest easy and go with the faith you lived with."

Those words spoken, I lowered the trunk and stole away from the white man's home, luckier to be a poor black man in America than Axel Bowers had been with his white skin and all his wealth.

I DROVE DOWN Telegraph into Oakland and the black part of town. There I found a motel called Sleepy Time Inn. It was set on a hillside, with the small stucco rooms stacked like box stairs for some giant leading up toward the sky.

Melba, the night clerk, gave me the top room for eighteen dollars in cash. They didn't take credit cards at Sleepy Time. When I looked at the cash I remembered that enameled pin in Bonnie's purse. For a moment I couldn't hear what Melba was saying. I could see her mouth moving. She was a short woman with skin that was actually black. But the rest of her features were more Caucasian than Negroid. Thin lips and round eyes, hair that had been straightened and a Roman nose.

". . . parties in the rooms," she was saying.

"What?"

"We don't want any carousing or parties in the rooms," she repeated. "You can have a guest but these rooms are residential. We don't want any loud crowds."

"Only noise I make is snoring," I said.

She smiled, indicating that she believed me. That simple gesture almost brought me to tears.

THE TELEVISION had a coin slot attached to it. It cost a quarter per hour to watch. If Feather was there with me she'd be begging for quarters to see her shows and to get grape soda from the machine down below. I put in a coin and switched channels until I came across *Gigantor,* her favorite afternoon cartoon. Letting the cartoon play, it felt a little like she was there with me.

That calmed me down enough to think about the mess I'd fallen into.

The man Robert E. Lee was looking for had been murdered. The initials on the empty briefcase in his room might have belonged to him or to somebody related to him. But then again, maybe he'd switched briefcases after removing the papers from the one Lee said he'd stolen.

At any other time I would have taken the fifteen hundred and gone home to Bonnie. But there was no more going home for me, and even if there was, Feather needed nearer to thirty-five thousand than fifteen hundred.

I couldn't call Lee. He might pull me off the case if he knew Axel was dead. And there was still Cinnamon — Philomena — to find. Maybe she knew where the papers were. I had to have those papers, because ten thousand dollars was a hard nut to crack.

I read one of the letters I'd taken from Axel's bureau. It was typewritten under the business heading of Haffernon, Schmidt, Tourneau and Bowers — a legal firm in San Francisco.

```
Dear Axel:
   I have read your letter of February 12 and
I must say that I find it intriguing. As far
as I know, your father had no business deal-
ings in Cairo during the period you indicated
and this firm certainly has not. Of course,
I'm not aware of all your father's personal
business dealings. Each of the partners had
```

his own portfolio from before the formation
of our investment group. But I must say that
your fears seem far-fetched, and even if they
weren't, Arthur is dead. How can an inquiry
of this sort have any productive outcome?
Only your family, it seems, will have a price
to pay.

   At any rate, I have no information to bring
to bear on the matter of the briefcase you
got from his safe-deposit box. Call me if you
have any further questions, and please consider your actions before rushing into anything.

Yours truly,
Leonard Haffernon, Esq.

Something happened with Axel's father, something that could
still cause grief for the son and maybe others. Maybe Haffernon
knew something about it. Maybe he killed Axel because of it.

   Lee had told me that Axel had stolen a briefcase, but this letter indicated that he received it legally. It could have been another case . . .

   The handwritten letter was a different temperature. There
was no heading.

Really, Axel. I can see no reason for you to follow this
line of questioning. Your father is dead. Anyone that
had anything to do with this matter is either dead or
so old that it doesn't make any difference. You cannot
judge them. You don't know how it was back then. Think
of your law offices in San Francisco. Think of the good
you have done, will be able to do. Don't throw it all

away over something that's done and gone. Think of your
own generation. I'm begging you. Please do not bring
these ugly matters to light.

                                                    N.

Whoever N was, he or she had something to hide. And that
something was about to be exposed to the world by Axel Bowers.

If I had had a good feeling about Bobby Lee I would have
taken the letters and reconnaissance to him. But we didn't like
each other and I couldn't be sure that he wouldn't take what I
gave him and cut me out of my bonus. My second choice was to
tell Saul but he would have been torn in allegiance between me
and the Civil War buff. No. I had to go this one alone for a while
longer.

Later that evening I was asking the operator to make a collect
call to a Webster exchange in West Los Angeles.

"Hello?" Bonnie said into my ear.

"Collect call to anyone from Easy," the operator said quickly
as if she feared that I might slip a message past her and hang up.

"I'll accept, operator. Easy?"

I tried to speak but couldn't manage to raise the volume in my
lungs.

"Easy, is that you?"

"Yeah," I said, just a whisper.

"What's wrong?"

"Tired," I said. "Just tired. How's Feather?"

"She sat up for a while and watched *Gigantor* this afternoon,"
Bonnie said hopefully, her voice full of love. "She's been trying to
stay awake until you called."

I had to exert extraordinary self-control not to put my fist
through the wall.

"Did you get the job?" she asked.

"Yeah, yeah. I got it all right. There's a few snags but I think I can work 'em if I try."

"I'm so happy," she said. It sounded as if she really meant it. "When you went out to meet with Raymond I was afraid that you'd do something you'd regret."

I laughed. I was filled with regrets.

"What's wrong, Easy?"

I couldn't tell her. My whole life I'd walked softly around difficulties when I knew my best defense was to keep quiet. I needed Bonnie to save my little girl. Nothing I felt could get in the way of that. I had to maintain a civil bearing. I had to keep her on my side.

"I'm just tired, baby," I said. "This case is gonna be a ballbreaker. Nobody I can trust out here."

"You can trust me, Easy."

"I know, baby," I lied. "I know. Is Feather still awake?"

"You bet," Bonnie said.

I had installed a long cord on the telephone so that the receiver could reach into Feather's room. I heard the shushing sounds of Bonnie moving through the rooms and then her voice gently talking to Feather.

"Daddy?" she whispered into the line.

"Hi, babygirl. How you doin'?"

"Fine. When you comin' home, Daddy?"

"Tomorrow sometime, honey. Probably just before you go to sleep."

"I dreamed that I was lookin' for you, Daddy, but you was gone and so was Juice. I was all alone in a tiny little house and there wasn't a TV or phone or nothing."

"That was just a dream, baby. Just a dream. You got a big house and lots of people who love you. Love you." I had to say the words twice.

"I know," she said. "But the dream scared me and I thought that you might really be gone."

"I'm right here, honey. I'm comin' home tomorrow. You can count on that."

The phone made a weightless noise and Bonnie was on the line again.

"She's tired, Easy. Almost asleep now that she's talked to you."

"I better be goin'," I said.

"Did you want to talk about the job?" Bonnie asked.

"I'm beat. I better get to bed," I said.

Just before I took the receiver from my ear I heard Bonnie say, "Oh."

13

The Haight, as it came to be called, was teeming with hip-pie life. But this wasn't like Derby. Most of the people on that Berkeley block still had one foot in real life at a job or the university. But the majority of the people down along Haight had completely dropped out. There was more dirt here, but that's not what made things different. Here you could distinguish different kinds of hippies. There were the clean-cut ones who washed their hair and ironed their hippie frocks. There were the dirty bearded ones on Harley-Davidson motorcycles. There were the drug users, the angry ones. There were the young (very young) runaways who had come here to blend in behind the free love philosophy. Bright colors and all that hair is what I remember mainly.

A young man wearing only a loincloth stood in the middle of a busy intersection holding up a sign that read END THE WAR. No-body paid much attention to him. Cars drove around him.

"Hey, mister, you got some spare change?" a lovely young raven-haired girl asked me. She wore a purple dress that barely made it to her thighs.

"Sorry," I said. "I'm strapped."

"That's cool," she replied and walked on.

Psychedelic posters for concerts were plastered to walls. Here and there brave knots of tourists walked through, marveling at the counterculture they'd discovered.

I was reminded of a day when a mortar shell in the ammunition hut of our base camp in northern Italy exploded for no apparent reason. No one was killed but a shock ran through the whole company. All of a sudden whatever we had been doing or thinking, wherever we had been going, was forgotten. One man started laughing uncontrollably, another went to the mess tent and wrote a letter to his mother. I kept noticing things that I'd never seen before. For instance, the hand-painted sign above the infirmary read HOSPItAL, all in capital letters except for the *t*. That one character was in lower case. I had seen that sign a thousand times but only after the explosion did I really look at it.

The Haight was another kind of explosion, a stunning surge of intuition that broke down all the ways you thought life had to be. In other circumstances I might have stayed around for a while and talked to the people, trying to figure out how they got there.

But I didn't have the time to wander and explore.

I'd gotten the address of the People's Legal Aid Center from the information operator. It had been a storefront at one time where a family named Gnocci sold fresh vegetables. There wasn't even a door, just a heavy canvas curtain that the grocer raised when he was open for business.

The store was open and three desks sat there in the recess. Two professional women and one man talked to their clients.

The man, who was white with short hair, wore a dark suit with a white shirt and a slate-blue tie. He was talking to a fat hippie mama who had a babe in arms and a small boy and girl clutching the hem of her Indian printed dress.

"They're evicting me," the woman was saying in a white Texan drawl I knew and feared. "What they expect me to do with these kids? Live in the street?"

"What is the landlord's name, Miss Braxton?" the street lawyer asked.

"Shit," she said and the little girl giggled.

At that moment the boy decided to run across the sidewalk, headed for the street.

"Aldous!" the hippie mama yelled, reaching out unsuccessfully for the boy.

I bent down on reflex, scooping the child up in my arms as I had done hundreds of times with Feather when she was smaller, and with Jesus before that.

"Thank you, mister. Thank you," the mother was saying. She had lifted her bulk from the lawyer's folding chair and was now taking the grinning boy from my arms. I could see in his face that he wasn't what other Texans would call a white child.

The woman smiled at me and patted my forearm.

"Thank you," she said again.

Her looking into my eyes with such deep gratitude was to be the defining moment in my hippie experience. Her gaze held no fear or condescension, even though her accent meant that she had to have been raised among a people who held themselves apart from mine. She didn't want to give me a tip but only to touch me.

I knew that if I had been twenty years younger, I would have been a hippie too.

"May I help you?" a woman's voice asked.

She was of medium height with a more or less normal frame, but somewhere in the mix there must have been a Teutonic Valkyrie because she had the figure of a Norse fertility goddess. Her eyes were a deep ocean blue and though her face was not particularly attractive there was something otherworldly about it. As far as clothes were concerned she was conservatively dressed in a cranberry dress that went down below her knees and wore a cream-colored woolen jacket over that. There was a silver strand around her neck from which hung a largish pearl with a dark nacre hue. Her glasses were framed in white.

All in all she was a Poindexter built like Jayne Mansfield.

"Hi. My name is Ezekiel P. Rawlins." I held out a hand.

A big grin came across her stern face but somehow the mirth didn't make it to her eyes. She shook my hand.

"How can I help you?"

"I'm a private detective from down in L.A.," I said. "I've been hired to find a woman named Philomena Cargill . . . by her family."

"Cinnamon," the woman said without hesitation. "Axel's friend."

"That's Axel Bowers?"

"Yes. He's my partner here."

She looked around the storefront. I did too.

"Not a very lucrative business," I speculated.

The woman laughed. It was a real laugh.

"That depends on what you see as profit, Mr. Rawlins. Axel and I are committed to helping the poor people of this society get a fair shake from the legal system."

"You're both lawyers?"

"Yes," she said. "I got my degree from UCLA and Axel got his across the Bay in Berkeley. I worked for the state for a while but

I didn't feel very good about that. When Axel asked me to join him I jumped at the chance."

"What's your name?" I asked.

"Oh. Excuse my manners. My name is Cynthia Aubec."

"French?"

"I was born in Canada," she said. "Montreal."

"Have you seen your partner lately?" I asked.

"Come on in," she replied.

She turned to go through another canvas flap, this one standing as a door to the back room of the defunct grocery.

There were two desks at opposite ends of the long room we entered. It was gloomy in there, and the floors had sawdust on them as if it were still a vegetable stand.

"We keep sawdust on the floor because the garage next door sometimes uses too much water and it seeps under the wall on our floor," she said, noticing my inspection.

"I see."

"Have a seat."

She switched on a desk lamp and I was gone from the hippie world of Haight Street. I wasn't in modern America at all. Cynthia Aubec, who was French Canadian but had no accent, lived earlier in the century, walking on sawdust and working for the poor.

"I haven't seen Axel for over a week," she said, looking directly into my gaze.

"Where is he?"

"He said that he was going to Algeria but I can never be sure."

"Algeria? I met a guy who told me that Axel was all over the world. Egypt, Paris, Berlin . . . Now you tell me he's in Algeria. There's got to be some money somewhere."

"Axel's family supports this office. They're quite wealthy. Actually his parents are dead. Now I guess it's Axel's money that runs our firm. But it was his father who gave us our start." She was still looking at me. In this light she was more Mansfield than Poindexter.

"Do you know when he might be back?"

"No. Why? I thought you were looking for Cinnamon."

"Well . . . the way I hear it Philomena and Axel had a thing going on. Actually that's why I'm here."

"I don't understand," she said with a smile that was far away from Axel and Philomena.

"Philomena's parents are racists," I explained, "not like you and me. They don't think that blacks and whites should be mixing. Well . . . they told Philomena that she was out of the family because of the relationship she had with your partner, but now that she hasn't called in over two months they're having second thoughts. She won't talk to them and so they hired me to come make their case."

"And you're really a private detective?" she asked, cocking one eyebrow.

I took out my wallet and handed her the license. I hadn't shown it to Lee out of spite. She glanced at it but I could see that she stopped to read the name and identify the photo.

"Why don't you just go to Cinnamon's apartment?" Cynthia suggested.

"I was told that she was living with Axel on Derby. I went there but no one was around."

"I have an address for her," Cynthia told me. Then she hesitated. "You aren't lying to me are you?"

"What would I have to lie about?"

"I wouldn't know." Her smile was suggestive but her eyes had not yet decided upon the nature of the proposal.

"No ma'am," I said. "I just need to find Philomena and tell her that her parents are willing to accept her as she is."

Cynthia took out a sheet of paper and scrawled an address in very large characters, taking up the whole page.

"This is her address," she said, handing me the leaf. "I live in Daly City. Do you know the Bay Area, Mr. Rawlins?"

"Not very well."

"I'll put my number on the back. Maybe if you're free for dinner I could show you around. I mean — as long as you're in town."

Yes sir. Twenty years younger and I'd have bushy hair down to my knees.

14

Philomena's apartment was on Avery Street, at Post, in the Fillmore District, on the fourth floor of an old brick building that had been christened The Opal Shrine. A sign above the front door told me that there were apartments available and that I could inquire at apartment 1a. There was no elevator so I climbed to the fourth floor to knock at the door of apartment 4e, the number given me by Cynthia Aubec.

There was no answer so I went back down to the first floor and tried the super's door.

He was a coffee-brown man with hair that might have been dyed cotton. He was smiling when he opened the door, a cloud of marijuana smoke attending him.

"Yes sir?" he said with a sly grin. "What can I do for you?"

"Apartment four-e."

"Fo'ty fi'e a mont', gas an' 'lectric not included. Got to clean it out yo' own self an' it's a extra ten for dogs. You can have a cat for free." He smiled again and I couldn't help but like him.

"I think I used to know a girl lived there. Cindy, Cinnamon . . . somethin'."

"Cinnamon," he said, still grinning like a coyote. "That girl had a butt on her. An' from what I hear she knew how to use it too."

"She move?"

"Gone's more like it," he said. "First'a the mont' came and the rent wasn't in my box. She ain't come back. I'ont know where she is."

"You call the cops?"

"Are you crazy? Cops? The on'y reason you call a cop is if you white or already behind bars."

I did like him.

"Can I see it?" I asked.

He reached over to his left, next to the door, and produced a brass key tethered to a multicolored flat string.

I took the key and grinned in thanks. He grinned *you're welcome*. The door closed and I was on my way back upstairs.

PHILOMENA CARGILL had left the apartment fully furnished, though I was sure that the super had emptied it of all loose change, jewelry, and other valuables. Most of the possessions I was interested in were still there. She had a bookcase filled with books and papers and a pile of *Wall Street Journal*s on the floor next to the two-burner stove. There was a small diary tacked up on the wall next to the phone and a stack of bills and some other mail on the kitchen table.

I pulled a chair up to the table and looked out of the window onto Post Street. San Francisco was much more of a city than

L.A. was back in '66. It had tall buildings and people who walked when they could and who talked to each other.

There was a ceramic bear on the table. He was half filled with crystallized honey. There was a teacup that had been left out. In it were the dried dregs of jasmine tea — nothing like the flavor left on Axel's dressing table.

There were also two dog-eared books out, *The Wealth of Nations* and *Das Kapital*. On the first page of Marx's opus she had written, *Marx seems to be at odds with himself over the effect that capitalism has on human nature. On the one hand he says that it is the dialectical force of history that forms the economic system, but on the other he seems to feel that certain human beings (capitalists) are evil by nature. But if we are pressed forward by empirical forces, then aren't we all innocent? Or at least equally guilty?* I was impressed by her argument. I had had similar thoughts when reading about the Mr. Moneybags capitalist in Marx's major work.

She had a big pine bed and all her plates, saucers, and cups were made from red glass. The floor was clean and her clothes, at least a lot of them, still hung in the closet. That bothered me. It was as if she just didn't come home one day rather than moved out.

The trash can was empty.

The bathroom cabinet was filled with condoms and the same lubricant used by Bowers.

He'd died instantly, between lighting a cigarette and the first drag. She had seemingly disappeared in the same way.

I decided to search the entire apartment from top to bottom. The super, I figured, was downstairs with his joint. I didn't have to worry about him worrying about me.

The more I explored the more I feared for the bright young woman's safety. I found a drawer filled with makeup and soaps.

She had a dozen panties and four bras in her underwear drawer. There were sewing kits and cheap fountain pens, sanitary napkins and sunglasses — all left behind.

Luckily there was no brass elephant grinning at me from the closet, no trunk filled with pornography and the accoutrements of war.

After about an hour I was convinced that Philomena Cargill was dead. It was only then that I began to sift through her mail. There were bills from various clothing stores and utilities, a bank statement that said she had two hundred ninety-six dollars and forty-two cents to her name. And there was a homemade postcard with the photograph of a smiling black woman on it. I knew the woman — Lena Macalister. She was standing in front of the long-closed Rose of Texas, a restaurant that had had some vogue in L.A. in the forties and fifties.

Dear Phil,

Your life sounds so exciting. New man. New job. And maybe a little something that every woman who's really a woman wants. My hopes and prayers are with you darling. God knows the both of us could use a break.

Tommy had to leave. He was good from about nine at night to daybreak. But when the sun came up all he could do was sleep. And you know I don't need no man resting on my rent. Don't worry about me though. You just keep on doing what you're doing.

Love,

L

It was certainly a friendly card. That gave me an idea. I went through Philomena's phone bill picking out telephone numbers with 213 area codes. I found three. The first number had been disconnected.

The second was answered by a woman.

"Westerly Nursing Home," she said. "How may we be of service?"

"Hi," I said, stalling for inspiration. "I'm calling on behalf of Philomena Cargill. She had a sudden case of appendicitis —"

"Oh that's terrible," the operator said.

"Yes. Yes, but we got it in time. I'm a PN here and the doctor told me to call because Miss Cargill was supposed to visit her aunt at Westerly but of course now you see . . ."

"Of course. What did you say was her aunt's name?"

"I just know her name," I said. "Philomena Cargill."

"There's no Cargill here, Mr. . . ."

"Avery," I said.

"Well, Mr. Avery, there's no Cargill, and I'm unaware of any Philomena Cargill who comes to visit. You know we have a very select clientele."

"Maybe it was her husband's relative," I conjectured. "Mr. Axel Bowers."

"No. No. No Bowers either. Are you sure you have the right place?"

"I thought so," I said. "But I'll go back to the doctor. Thank you very much for your help."

"YEEEEES?" the male voice of the last number crooned.

"Philomena please," I said in a clipped, sure tone.

"Who's this?" the voice asked, no longer playful.

"Miller," I said. "Miller Jones. I'm an employee of Bowers up here and he wanted me to get in touch with Cinnamon. He gave me this number."

"I don't know you," the voice said. "And even if I did, I haven't seen Philomena in months. She's in Berkeley."

"She was," I said. "To whom am I speaking?"

The click of the phone in my ear made me grimace. I should have taken another tack. Maybe claimed to have found some lost article from her apartment.

I sat in the college student's kitchen chair and stared at the street. This was an ugly job and it was likely to get uglier. But that was okay. I was feeling ugly, ugly as a sore on a dead man's forehead.

I left the apartment, taking the two books she'd been reading and Lena's postcard. I took them out to my rented Ford and then went back to return the key. I knocked, knocked again, called out for the super, and then gave up. He was either unconscious, otherwise engaged, or out. I slipped the key under the door wrapped in a two-dollar bill.

15

Haffernon, Schmidt, Tourneau and Bowers occupied the penthouse of a modern office building on California Street. There was a special elevator car dedicated solely to their floors.

"May I help you?" a white-haired matron, who had no such intention, asked me. Her nameplate read THERESA PONTE.

She was very white. There was a ring with a large garnet stone on her right hand. The gem looked like a knot of blood that had congealed upon her finger. A cup of coffee steamed next to her telephone. She was wearing a gray jacket over a yellow blouse, seated behind a magnificent mahogany desk. Behind her was a mountain of fog that was perpetually descending upon but rarely managing to reach the city.

"Leonard Haffernon," I said.

"Are you delivering?"

I was wearing the same jacket and pants that I'd had on for two days. But I'd made use of the iron in my motel room and I didn't smell. I wore a tie and I'd even dragged a razor over my chin. I held no packages or envelopes.

"No ma'am," I said patiently. "I have business with him."

"Business?"

"Yes. Business."

She moved her head in a birdlike manner, indicating that she needed more of an explanation.

"May I see him?" I asked.

"What is your business?"

From a door to my left emerged a large strawberry blond man. His chest was bulky with muscles under a tan jacket. Maybe one of those sinews was a gun. I had Axel's Luger in my belt. I thought of reaching for it and then I thought of Feather.

A moment of silence accompanied all that thinking.

"Tell him that I've come about Axel Bowers," I said. "My name is Easy Rawlins and I'm looking for someone named Cargill."

"Cargill who?" the receptionist asked.

"This is not the moment at which you should test your authority, Theresa," I said.

The combination of vocabulary, grammar, and intimacy disconcerted the woman.

"There a problem?" the Aryan asked.

"Not with me," I said to him while looking at her.

She picked up the phone, pressed a button, waited a beat, and then said, "Let me speak to him." Another beat and she said, "A man called Rawlins is here about Axel and someone named Cargill." She listened then looked up at me and said, "Please have a seat."

The big boy came to stand next to my chair.

My heart was thundering. My mind was at an intersection of many possible paths. I wanted to ask that woman what she was thinking when she asked me if I was a delivery boy when obviously I was not. Was she trying to be rude or did my skin color rob her of reason? I wanted to ask the bodyguard why he felt it necessary to stand over me as if I were a prisoner or a criminal when I hadn't done anything but ask to see his boss. I wanted to yell and pull out my gun and start shooting.

But all I did was sit there staring up at the white ceiling.

I thought about that coat of paint upon the plaster. It meant that at one time a man in a white jumpsuit had stood on a ladder in the middle of that room running a roller or maybe waving a brush above his head. That was another room but the same, at another time when there was no tension but only labor. That man probably had children at home, I decided. His hard work turned into food and clothing for them.

That white ceiling made me happy. After a moment I forgot about my bodyguard and the woman who couldn't see the man standing in front of her but only the man she had been trained to see.

"Mr. Rawlins?" a man said.

He was tall, slender, and very erect. The dark blue suit he wore would have made the down payment on my car. His scarlet tie was a thing of beauty and the gray at his temples would remind anyone of their father — even me.

"Mr. Haffernon?" I rose.

The bodyguard stiffened.

"That will be all, Robert," Haffernon said, not even deigning to look at his serf.

Robert turned away without complaint and disappeared behind the door that had spawned him.

"Follow me," Haffernon said.

He led me back past the elevator and through a double door. Here we entered into a wide hallway. The floors were bright ash and the doors along the way were too. These doors opened into anterooms where men and women assistants talked and typed and wrote. Beyond each assistant was a closed door behind which, I imagined, lawyers talked and typed and wrote.

At the end of the hall were large glass doors that we went through.

Haffernon had three female assistants. One, a buxom forty-year-old with horn-rimmed glasses and a flouncy full-length dress, came up to him reading from a clipboard.

"The Clarks had to reschedule for Friday, sir. He's had an emergency dental problem. He says that he'll need to rest after that."

"Fine," Haffernon said. "Call my wife and tell her that I will be coming to the opera after all."

"Yes sir," the woman said. "Mr. Phillipo decided to leave the country. His company will settle."

"Good, Dina. I can't be interrupted for anything except family."

"Yes sir."

She opened a door behind the three desks and Haffernon stepped in. In passing I caught the assistant's eye and gave her a quick nod. She smiled at me and let her head drift to the side, letting me know that the counterculture had infiltrated every pore of the city.

HAFFERNON HAD A BIG DESK under a picture window but he took me into a corner where he had a rose-colored couch with a matching stuffed chair. He took the chair and waved me onto the sofa.

"What is your business with me, Mr. Rawlins?" he asked.

I hesitated, relishing the fact that I had this man by the short hairs. I knew this because he had told Dina not to bother him for anything but the blood of blood. When powerful white men like that make time for you there's something serious going on.

"What problem did Axel Bowers come to you with?" I asked.

"Who are you, Mr. Rawlins?"

"Private detective from down in L.A.," I said, feeling somehow like a fraud but knowing I was not.

"And what do Axel's . . . problems, as you call them, have to do with your client?"

"I don't know," I said. "I'm looking for Axel and your name popped up. Have you seen Mr. Bowers lately?"

"Who are you working for?"

"Confidential," I said with the apology in my face.

"You walk in here, ask me about the son of one of my best friends and business associates, and refuse to tell me who wants to know?"

"I'm looking for a woman named Philomena Cargill," I said. "She's a black woman, lover of your friend's son. He's gone. She's gone. It came to my attention that you and he were in negotiations about something that had to do with his father. I figured that if he was off looking into that problem that you might know where he was. He, in turn, might know about Philomena."

Haffernon sat back in his chair and clasped his hands. His stare was a spectacle to behold. He had cornflower-blue eyes and black brows that arced like descending birds of prey.

This was a white man whom other white men feared. He was wealthy and powerful. He was used to getting his way. Maybe if I hadn't been fighting for my daughter's life I would have felt the weight of that stare. But as it was I felt safe from any threat he could make. My greatest fear flowed in a little girl's veins.

"You have no idea who you're messing with," he said, believing the threatening gaze had worked.

"Do you know Philomena?" I asked.

"What information do you have about me and Axel?"

"All I know is that a hippie I met said that Axel has been spending time in Cairo. That same man said that Axel had asked you about his father and Egypt."

His right eye twitched. I was sure that there were Supreme Court justices who couldn't have had that effect on Leonard Haffernon. I lost control of myself and smirked.

"Who do you work for, Mr. Rawlins?" he asked again.

"Are you a collector, Mr. Haffernon?"

"What?"

"That hippie told me that Axel collected Nazi memorabilia. Daggers, photographs. Do you collect anything like that?"

Haffernon stood then.

"Please leave."

I stood also. "Sure."

I sauntered toward the door not sure of why I was being so tough on this powerful white man. I had baited him out of instinct. I wondered if I was being a fool.

OUTSIDE HIS OFFICE I asked Dina for a pencil and paper.

I wrote down my name and the phone of my motel and handed it to her. She looked up at me in wonder, a small smile on her lips.

"I wish it was for you," I said. "But give it to your boss. When he calms down he might want to give me a call."

16

I ate a very late lunch at a stand-up fried clam booth on Fisherman's Wharf. It was beautiful there. The smell of the ocean and the fish market reminded me of Galveston when I was a boy. At any other time in my life those few scraps of fried flour over chewy clam flesh would have been soothing. But I didn't want to feel good until I knew that Feather was going to be okay. She and Jesus were all I had left.

I went to a pay phone and made the collect call.

Benny answered and accepted.

"Hi, Mr. Rawlins," she said, a little breathless.

"Where's Bonnie, Benita?"

"She went out shoppin' for a wheelchair to take Feather with. Me an' Juice just hangin' out here an' makin' sure Feather okay. She sleep. You want me to wake her up?"

"No, honey. Let her sleep."

"You wanna talk to Juice?"

"You know, Benita, I really like you," I said.

"I like you too, Mr. Rawlins."

"And I know how messed up you were when Mouse did you like he did."

She didn't say anything to that.

"And I care very deeply about my children . . ." I let the words trail off.

For a few moments there was silence on the line. And then in a whisper Benita Flag said, "I love 'im, Mr. Rawlins. I do. He's just a boy, I know, but he better than any man I ever met. He sweet an' he know how to treat me. I didn't mean to do nuthin' wrong."

"That's okay, girl," I said. "I know what it is to fall."

"So you not mad?"

"Let him down easy if you have to," I said. "That's all I can ask."

"Okay."

"And tell Feather I had to stay another day but that I will bring her back a big present because I had to be late."

We said our good-byes and I went to my car.

ON THE WAY BACK to the motel I picked up a couple of newspapers to keep my mind occupied.

Vietnam was half of the newspaper. The army had ordered the evacuation of the Vietnamese city of Hue, where they were on the edge of revolt. Da Nang was threatening revolution and the Buddhists were demonstrating against Ky in Saigon.

Jimmy Hoffa was on the truck manufacturers for the unions and some poor schnook in Detroit had been arrested for bank robbery when the tellers mistook his car for the robber's getaway car. He was a white guy on crutches.

I found that I couldn't concentrate on the stories so I put the paper down. I could feel the fear about Feather rising in my chest.

In order to distract myself I tried to focus on Lee's case. The man he wanted to talk to was dead. The papers the dead man had were gone — I had no idea where to. Cinnamon Cargill was probably dead also. Or maybe she was the killer. Maybe they were tripping together and he died, by accident, and she pressed him into the space below the brass elephant.

I had the telephone numbers of an old folks' home for rich people and a secretive man whose voice was effeminate, and I had a postcard.

All in all that was a lot, but there was nothing I could do about it until the morning. That is unless Haffernon called. Haffernon knew about the trouble Axel was in. He might even have known about the young man's death.

I took out the Nazi Luger I'd stolen from the dead man's treasure chest and placed it on the night table next to the bed.

Then I sat back thinking about the few good years that I'd had with Bonnie and the kids. We had family picnics and long tearful nights helping the kids through the pain of growing up. But all of that was done. A specter had come over us and the life we'd known was gone.

I tried to think about other things, other times. I tried to feel fear over the payroll robbery that Mouse wanted me to join in on. But all I could think about was the loss in my heart.

At eleven o'clock I picked up the phone and dialed a number.

"Hello?" she said.

"Hi."

"Mr. Rawlins? Is that you?"

"You're a lawyer, right, Miss Aubec?"

"You know I am. You were at my office this morning."

"I know that's what you said."

"I am a lawyer," she said. There was no sleep in her voice or annoyance at my late-night call.

"How does the law look on a man who commits a crime when he's under great strain?"

"That depends," she said.

"On what?"

"Well . . . what is the crime?"

"A bad one," I said. "Armed robbery or maybe murder."

"Murder would be simpler," she said. "You can murder someone in the heat of the moment, but a robbery is quite another thing. Unless the property you stole just fell into your lap the law would look upon it as a premeditated crime."

"Let's say that it's a man who's about to lose everything, that if he didn't rob that bank someone he loved might die."

"The courts are not all that sympathetic when it comes to crimes against property," Cynthia said. "But you might have a case."

"In what situation?"

"Well," she said. "Your level of legal representation means a lot. A court-appointed attorney won't do very much for you."

I already knew about the courts and their leanings toward the rich, but her honesty still was a comfort.

"Then of course there's race," she said.

"Black man's not gonna get an even break, huh?"

"No. Not really."

"I didn't think so," I said. And yet somehow hearing it said out loud made me feel better. "How does a young white girl like you know all this stuff?"

"I've sent my share of innocent men to prison," she said. "I worked in the prosecutor's office before going into business with Axel."

"I guess you got to be a sinner to know a sin when you see it."

"Why don't you come over," she suggested.

"I wouldn't be very good company."

"I don't care," she said. "You sound lonely. I'm here alone, wide awake."

"You know a man named Haffernon?" I asked then.

"He was Axel's father's business partner. The families have been friends since the eighteen hundreds."

"Was?"

"Axel's father died eighteen months ago."

"What do you think of Haffernon?"

"Leonard? He was born with a silver spoon up his ass. Always wears a suit, even when he's at the beach, and the only time he ever laughs is when he's with old school friends from Yale. I can't stand him."

"What did Axel think of him?"

"Did?"

"Yeah," I said coolly even though I could feel the sweat spread over my forehead. "Before today, right?"

"Axel has a thing about his family," Cynthia said, her voice clear and trusting still. "He thinks that they're all like enlightened royalty. They *did* put money into our little law office."

"But Haffernon's not family," I said. "He didn't put any money into your office did he?"

"No."

"No what?"

"He didn't give us any money. He doesn't have much sympathy for poor people. He's not related to Axel either — by blood anyway. But the families are so close that Axel treats him like an uncle."

"I see." Calm was returning to my breath and the sweat had subsided.

"So?" Cynthia Aubec asked.

"So what?"

"Are you coming over?"

I felt the question as if it were a fist in my gut.

"Really, Cynthia, I don't think it's a good idea for me tonight."

"I understand. I'm not your type, right?"

"Honey, you're *the* type. A figure like you got on you belongs in the art museum and up on the movie screen. It's not that I don't want to come, it's just a bad time for me."

"So who is this man who might commit a crime under pressure?" she asked, switching tack as easily as Jesus would the single sail of his homemade boat.

"Friend'a mine. A guy who's got a lot on his mind."

"Maybe he needs a vacation," Cynthia suggested. "Time away with a girl. Maybe on a beach."

"Yeah. In a few months that would be great."

"I'll be here."

"You don't even know my friend," I said.

"Would I like him?"

"How would I know what you'd like?"

"From talking to me do you think I'd like him?"

That got me to laugh.

"What's so funny?" Cynthia asked.

"You."

"Come over."

I began to think that it might be a good idea. It was late and there was nothing to hold me back.

There came a knock at the door. A loud knock.

"What's that?" Cynthia asked.

"Somebody at the door," I said, reaching for the German automatic.

"Who?"

"I gotta call you back, Cindy," I said, making the contraction on her name naturally.

"I live on Elm Street in Daly City," she said and then she told me the numbers. "Come over anytime tonight."

There was another knock.

"I'll call," I said and then I hung up.

"Who is it?" I shouted at the door.

"The Fuller Brush man," a sensual voice replied.

I opened the door and there stood Maya Adamant wrapped in a fake white fur coat.

"Come on in," I said.

I had made all the connections before the door was closed.

"So the Nazis brought you out of Mr. Lee's den."

She moved to the bed, then turned to regard me. The way she sat down could not have been learned in finishing school.

"Haffernon called Lee," she said. "He was very upset and now Lee is too. I was out on a date when he called my answering service and they called the club. You're supposed to be in Los Angeles looking for Miss Cargill."

I perched on the edge of the loungelike orange chair that came with my room. I couldn't help leering. Maya's coat opened a bit, exposing her short skirt and long legs. My talk with Cynthia had prepared me to appreciate a sight like that.

"There was no reason for me to think that Philomena had left the Bay Area," I said. "And even if she did she needn't have gone down south. There's Portland and Seattle. Hell, she could be in Mexico City."

"We didn't ask you about Mexico City."

"If you know where she is why do you need me?" I asked.

I forced my eyes up to hers. She smiled, appreciating my will power with a little pout.

"What is this about Nazi memorabilia?" she asked.

"I met a guy who told me that Axel collected the stuff. I just figured that Haffernon might know about it."

"So you've guessed that Leonard Haffernon is our client?"

"I don't guess, Miss Adamant. I just ask questions and go where they lead me."

"Who have you been talking to?" Her nostrils flared.

"Hippies."

She sighed and shifted on the bed. "Have you found Philomena?"

"Not yet," I said. "She left her apartment in an awful hurry though. I doubt she took a change of underwear."

"It would have been nice to meet you under other circumstances, Mr. Rawlins."

"You're right about that."

She stood up and smiled at my gaze.

"Are you ready to go back to L.A.?"

"First thing in the morning."

"Good."

She walked out the door. I watched her move on the stairs. It was a pleasurable sight.

There was a car waiting for her on the street. She got into the passenger's side. I wondered who her companion was as the dark sedan glided off.

I WENT TO BED consciously not calling Bonnie or Cynthia or Maya. I pulled up the covers to my chin and stared at the window until the dawn light illuminated the dirty glass.

17

That morning I headed out toward the San Francisco airport. Just at the mouth of the freeway on-ramp, with the entire sky at their backs, two young hippies stood with their thumbs out. I pulled to the side of the road and cranked down the window.

"Hey man," a sixteen- or seventeen-year-old red-bearded youth said with a grin. "Where you headed?"

"Airport."

"Could you take us that far?"

"Sure," I said. "Hop in."

The boy got in the front seat and the girl, younger than he was, a very blond slip of a thing, got in the back with their backpacks.

She was the reason I had stopped. She wasn't that much older than Feather. Just a child and here she was on the road with her man. I couldn't pass them by.

When I drove up the on-ramp a blue Chevy honked at me and then sped past. I didn't think that I'd cut him off so I figured he was making a statement about drivers who picked up hitchhikers.

"Thanks, man," the hippie boy said. "We been out there for an hour an' all the straights just passed us by."

"Where you headed?" I asked.

"Shasta," the girl said. She leaned up against the seat between me and her boyfriend. I could see her grinning into my eyes through the rearview mirror.

"That's where you live?"

"We heard about this commune up there," the boy said. He smelled of patchouli oil and sweat.

"What's that?"

"What's what?" he asked.

"Commune. What's that?"

"You never heard of a commune, man?" the boy asked.

"My name's Easy," I said. "Easy Rawlins."

"Cool," the girl crooned.

I suppose she meant my name.

"Eric," the boy said.

"Like the Viking," I said. "You got the red hair for it."

He took this as a compliment.

"I'm Star," the girl said. "An' a commune is where everybody lives and works together without anybody owning shit or tellin' anybody else how to live."

"Kinda like the kibbutz or the Russian farms," I said.

"Hey man," Eric said, "don't put that shit on us."

"I'm not puttin' anything on you," I replied. "I'm just trying to understand what you're saying by comparing it with other places that sound like your commune."

"There's never been anything like us, man," Eric said, filled with the glory of his own dreams. "We're not gonna live like you people did. We're gettin' away from that nine-to-five bullshit. People don't have to own everything. The wild lands are free."

"Yeah," Star said. Her tone was filled with Eric's love for himself. "At Cresta everybody gets their own tepee and a share in what everybody else has."

"Cresta is the name for your commune?"

"That's right," Eric said with such certainty that I almost laughed.

"Why don't you come with us?" Star asked from the backseat.

I looked up and into her eyes through the rearview mirror. There was a yearning there but I couldn't tell if it was hers or mine. Her simple offer shocked me. I could have kept on driving north with those children, to their hippie farm in the middle of nowhere. I knew how to raise a garden and build a fire. I knew how to be poor and in love.

"Watch it!" Eric shouted.

I had drifted into the left lane. A car's horn blared. I jerked my rented car back just in time. When I looked up into the mirror, Star was still there looking into my eyes.

"That was close, man," Eric said. Now his voice also contained the pride of saving us. I was once an arrogant boy like him.

"I can't," I said into the mirror.

"Why not?" she asked.

"How old are you?"

"Fifteen . . . almost."

"I got a daughter just a few years younger than you. She's real sick. Real sick. I got to get her to a doctor in Switzerland or she'll die. So no woods for me quite yet."

"Where is your daughter?" Star asked.

"Los Angeles."

"Maybe it's the smog killin' her," Eric said. "Maybe if you got her out of there she'd be okay."

Eric would never know how close he'd come to getting his nose broken in a moving car. It was only Star's steady gaze that saved him.

"I had a friend once," I said. "Him and me were something like you guys. We used to ride the rails down in Texas and Louisiana."

"Ride the rails?" Eric said.

"Jumping into empty boxcars, trains," I said.

"Like hitchin'," Eric said.

"Yeah. One night in Galveston we went out on a tear —"

"What's that?" Star asked.

"A drinking binge. Anyway the next day I woke up and Hollister was nowhere to be seen. He was completely gone. I waited a day or two but then I had to move on before the local authorities arrested me for vagrancy and put me on the chain gang."

I could see that Eric was now seeing me in a new light. But I didn't care about that young fool.

"What happened to your friend?" Star asked.

"Twenty years later I was driving down in Compton and I saw him walking down the street. He'd gotten fat and his hair was thinning but it was Hollister all right."

"Did you ask him what happened?" Eric asked.

"He'd met a girl after I'd passed out that night. They spent the night together and the next couple'a days. They drank the whole time. One day Holly woke up and realized that at some point they'd gotten married — he didn't even remember saying I do."

"Whoa," Eric said in a low tone.

"Did they stay together?" Star wanted to know.

"I went back with Hollister to his house and met her there. They had four kids. He was a plumber for the county and she baked pies for a restaurant down the street. You know what she told me?"

"What?" both children asked at once.

"That on the evening she'd met Holly I had picked her up at the local juke joint. We'd hit it off pretty good but I drank too much and passed out. When Holly came into the lean-to where we were stayin', Sherry, that was his wife's name, asked him if he would walk her home. That was when they got together."

"He took your woman?" Eric said indignantly.

"Not mine, brother," I said. "That lean-to was our own private little commune. What was mine was me, and Sherry had her own thing to give."

Eric frowned at that, and I believed that I was the first shadow on his bright notions of communal life. That made me smile.

I let them out at the foot of the off-ramp I had to take to get to the airport.

While Eric was wrestling the backpacks out of the backseat Star put her skinny arms around my neck and kissed me on the lips.

"Thanks," she said. "You're really great."

I gave her ten dollars and told her to stay safe.

"God's looking after me," she said.

Eric handed her a backpack then and they crossed the road.

18

After leaving my Hertz car at their airport lot I went to the ticket counter. The flight from San Francisco to Los Angeles on Western Airlines was $24.95.

They took my credit card with no problem.

While waiting for my flight I called home and got Jesus. I gave him the flight number and told him to be there to pick me up.

He didn't ask any questions. Jesus would have crossed the Pacific for me and never asked why.

In a small airport store — where they sold candy bars, newspapers, and cigarettes — I bought a large brown teddy bear for $6.95.

I sat in the bulkhead aisle seat next to a young white woman who wore a rainbow-print dress that came to about midthigh. She was a beauty but I wasn't thinking about her.

I buckled my seat belt and unfolded the morning paper.

Ky had given in to Buddhist pressure and agreed to have free elections in South Vietnam. The bastion of democracy, the United States, however, said publicly that it still backed the dictator.

A couple who were going to lose a baby they were trying to adopt had attempted suicide. They didn't die but their baby did.

I put that paper away.

The captain told us to fasten our seat belts and the stewardess showed us how it was done. The engine on the big 707 began to roar and whine.

"Hello," the young woman said.

"Hi." I gave her just a glance.

"My name is Candice." She held out a hand.

It would have been impolite for me to ignore her gesture of friendship.

"Easy Rawlins."

"Do you fly often, Mr. Rawlins?"

"Every now and then. My girlfriend's a stewardess for Air France."

"I don't. This is only my second flight and I'm scared to death."

She wouldn't let go of my hand. I squeezed and said, "We'll make it through this one together."

We held hands through the takeoff and for five minutes into the ascent. Every now and then she increased the pressure. I matched the force of her grip. By the time we were at full altitude she had calmed down.

"Thank you," she said.

"No problem."

I picked up the paper again but the words scrambled away from my line of vision. I was thinking about Dream Dog and karma, then about Axel Bowers and the humiliating treatment he'd received after his death. I thought about that white girl who just needed somebody to hold on to regardless of his color.

Maybe the hippies were right, I thought. Maybe we should all go outside in our underwear and protest the way of the world.

THE YOUNG WOMAN and I didn't speak another word to each other. There was no need to.

When I got out of the gate in L.A., Jesus was there waiting for me.

"Hi, Dad," he said and shook my hand.

He'd driven my car to the airport and I let him drive going back home. He took La Cienega where I would have taken the freeway but that was okay by me.

"Feather had fever again this morning," he said. "Bonnie gave her Mama Jo's medicine and it came down."

"Good," I said, trying to hide my fear.

"Is she gonna die, Dad?"

"Why you say that?"

"Bonnie told Benny why she had to stay and look after Feather and Benny told me. Is she gonna die?"

There never was a brother and sister closer than Jesus and Feather. I had taken him out of a bad situation when he was an infant, and when I brought Feather into our home he took to her like a mother hen.

"I don't know," I said. "Maybe."

"But if Bonnie takes her to Switzerland they might save her?"

"Yeah. They saved other people with infections like hers."

"Do you want me to go with them?"

"No. The doctors can help. What I need is the money to pay those doctors."

"I could sell my boat."

That boat was everything to Jesus.

"No, son. I think I got a line on a moneymaker. It's gonna be okay."

I had planned to talk to him about Benita and the difference in their ages. But when he offered to give his boat up for Feather I couldn't imagine what there was I had to tell him.

BONNIE HAD PACKED a large traveling suitcase for Feather. It seemed as if she'd taken every toy, doll, dress, and book that Feather owned. When I got there they were ready to go to the airport.

There was a bright chrome and red canvas wheelchair in the living room.

Bonnie came out and kissed me, and even though I tried to put some tenderness into the caress she leaned away and gave me an odd stare.

"What's wrong?"

"If I was to tell you the things I'd seen in the last two days you wouldn't be asking me that," I said truthfully.

Bonnie nodded, still frowning.

"Could you put the suitcase into the trunk?" she asked. "The wheelchair folds up and can go on top."

I knew that they had to get to the airport soon and so I got to work. Jesus helped me figure out that the wheelchair had to go in the backseat.

When I got back in the house Feather was screaming. I ran into her room to find her struggling with Bonnie.

"I want you to carry me, Daddy," she pleaded.

"It's okay," I said and I took her up in my arms.

*   *   *

BONNIE DROVE, Feather slept on my lap, and I stared out the window, wondering how long it would take to drive down to Palestine, Texas. I knew that my work for Lee would be a dead end. Axel was dead. Philomena was probably dead. The papers were long gone. I had gotten a Luger and fifteen hundred dollars in the deal. I could use the German pistol to press against Rayford's willing neck.

FEATHER WOKE UP when we pulled into the employees' lot at the airport. She was happy to have a wheelchair and she raced ahead of us at the special employee entrance to TWA. They had to go to San Francisco first and then transfer to the polar flight to Paris. I saw them to the special entrance for the crew.

A woman I recognized met us there — Giselle Martin.

"Aunt Giselle," Feather cried.

Giselle was a friend of Bonnie's. She was tall and thin, a brunette with a delicate porcelain beauty that you'd miss if you didn't take time with it. They worked together for Air France. She was there to help with Feather.

"Allo, ma chérie," the French flight attendant said to my little girl. "These big strong men are going to carry you up into the plane."

Two brawny white men were coming toward us from a doorway to the terminal building.

"I want Daddy to take me," Feather said.

"It is the rules, ma chérie," Giselle said.

"That's okay, honey," I said to Feather. "They'll carry you up and then I'll come buckle you in."

"You promise?"

"I swear."

The workmen took hold of the chair from the front and back.

Feather grabbed on to the armrests, looking scared. I was scared too. I watched them go all the way up the ramp.

I was about to follow when Bonnie touched my arm and asked, "What's wrong, Easy?"

I had planned for that moment. I thought that if we found ourselves alone and Bonnie wondered at my behavior, I'd tell her all the grisly details of Axel Bowers's death. I turned to her, but when she looked into my eyes, as so many women had in the past few days, I couldn't bring myself to lie.

"I read a lot, you know," I said.

"I know that." Her dark skin and almond eyes were the most beautiful I had ever seen. Two days ago I had wanted to marry her.

"I read the papers and all about anything I have an interest in. I read about a group of African dignitaries getting the Senegalese award of service that was symbolized by a bronze pin with a little design enameled on it — a bird in red and white . . ."

There was no panic on Bonnie's face. The fact that I knew that she had recently received such an important gift from a suitor only served to sadden her.

"He was the only one who could get Feather into that hospital, Easy . . ."

"So there's nothing between you?"

Bonnie opened her mouth but it was her turn not to lie.

"Thank him for me . . . when you see him," I said.

I walked past her and up into the plane.

"WILL YOU COME and see me in the Alps, Daddy?" Feather asked as I buckled her seat belt.

The plane was still empty.

"I'll try. But you know Bonnie'll be there to look after you. And before you know it you'll be all better and back home again."

"But you'll try and come?"

"I will, honey."

I walked past Bonnie as she came up the aisle.

Neither of us spoke.

What was there to say?

19

From the terminal building I could make out the white bow in Feather's hair through a porthole in the plane. And even though she looked out now and then she never saw me waving. Her skin had been warm when I buckled her in but her eyes weren't feverish. Bonnie had Mama Jo's last ball of medicine, I'd made sure of that. Bonnie wouldn't let Feather die no matter who her heart belonged to.

The passengers filed on. Final boarding was announced. The jet taxied away and finally, after a long delay, it nosed its way above the amber layer of smog that covered the city.

I stayed at the window watching as a dozen jets lined up and took off.

"Mister?"

She was past sixty with blue-gray hair and a big red coat made from cotton — the Southern California answer to the eastern overcoat. There was concern on her lined white face.

"Yes?" My voice cracked.

"Are you all right?"

That's when I realized that tears were running from my eyes. I tried to speak but my throat closed. I nodded and touched the woman's shoulder. Then I staggered away amid the stares of dozens of travelers.

I DIDN'T TURN the ignition key right away.

"Snap out of it, Easy," a voice, only partly my own, said. "You know once a man break down the wreck ain't far off. You don't have no time to wallow. You don't have it like some rich boy can feel sorry for hisself."

I drove on surface streets with no destination in mind. Even the next day I couldn't have recalled the route I'd taken. But my instinct was to head in the direction of my office.

I was on Avalon, crossing Manchester, when I heard two horns. I looked up just as my car slammed into a white Chrysler. The next thing I did was to check out the traffic light — it was against me. I had been distracted and a fool for the past few days, but something told me to take that German pistol out of my pocket and hide it under my seat before I did anything else.

I jumped out of my car and ran to the boatlike Chrysler.

There was a middle-aged black couple in the front seat. The man, who wore a brown suit, was clutching his arm and the woman, who was easily twice the man's size, was bleeding freely from a cut over her left eye.

"Nate," she was saying. "Nate, are you okay?"

The man held his left arm between the elbow and shoulder.

I opened the door.

"Let's get you outta there, man," I said.

"Thank you," he mouthed, his face twisted with the pain.

When I got him set up against the hood of his car I went around to the passenger's side. It was then that I heard the first siren, a distant cry.

"Is my husband okay?" the woman asked.

She and Nate both had very dark skin and large facial features. Her mouth was wide and so were her nostrils. The blood was coming down but she didn't seem to notice.

"Just a hurt arm," I said. "He's standing up on the other side."

I took off my shirt and tore it in half, then I pressed the material against her wound.

"Why you pushin' on my head?"

"You're bleeding."

"I am?" she said, the growing panic crowding her words.

When she looked down at her hands her eyes, nostrils, and mouth all grew to extraordinary proportions.

She screamed.

"Alicia!" Nate called. He was shambling around the front of the car.

A lanky woman came up to steady him.

There were people all around but most of them stayed back.

Three sirens wailed not far away.

"It's okay, ma'am," I was saying. "I stopped the bleeding now."

"Am I bleedin'?" she asked. "Am I bleedin'?"

"No," I said. "I stopped it with this bandage."

"All right now, back away!" a voice said.

Two white men dressed all in white except for their shoes ran up.

"Two, Joseph," one man said. "A stretch for each."

"Got it," the other man said.

The nearest ambulance attendant took the torn shirt from my hands and began speaking to the woman.

"What's your name, lady?" he asked.

"Alicia Roman."

"I need you to lie down, Alicia, so that I can get you into the ambulance and stop this cut from bleeding."

There was authority in the white man's voice. Alicia allowed him to lower her onto the asphalt. The other attendant, Joseph, came up with a stretcher. This he put down beside her.

The lanky woman was helping Nate to the back of the ambulance. She was plain looking and high brown, like a polished pecan. There was no expression on her face. She was just doing her part.

I looked down at my hands. Alicia's blood had trailed over my palms and down my forearms. The blood had splattered onto my T-shirt too.

"Are you hurt?" a man asked me.

It was a policeman who came up from the crowd. I saw three other policemen directing traffic and keeping pedestrians out of the street.

"No," I said. "This is her blood."

"Were you in their car?" The cop was blond but he had what white people call swarthy skin. The racial blend hadn't worked too well on him. I remember thinking that the top of his head was in Sweden but his face reflected the Maghreb.

"No," I said. "I ran into them."

"They ran the light?"

"No. I did."

A surprised look came into his face.

"Come over here," he said, leading me to the curb.

He made me touch my nose then walk a straight line, turn around, and come back again.

"You seem sober," he told me.

The ambulance was taking off.

"Are they gonna be okay?" I asked.

"I don't know. Put your hands behind your back."

THEY TOOK AWAY my belt, which was a good thing. I was so miserable in that cell that I might have done myself in. Jesus wasn't home. Neither was Raymond or Jackson, Etta or Saul Lynx. If I stayed in jail until the trial Feather might be kicked out of the clinic and die. I wondered if Joguye Cham, Bonnie's African prince, would help my little girl. I'd be the best man at their wedding if he did that for me.

I finally got Theodore Steinman at his shoe shop down the street from my house. I told him to keep calling EttaMae.

"I'll come down and get you, Ezekiel," Steinman said.

"Wait for Etta," I told him. "She does this shit with Mouse at least once every few months."

"CIGARETTE?" my cellmate asked.

I didn't know if he was offering or wanting one but I didn't reply. I hadn't uttered more than three sentences since the arrest. The police were surprisingly gentle with me. No slaps or insults. They even called me mister and corrected me with respect when I turned the wrong way or didn't understand their commands.

The officer who arrested me, Patrolman Briggs, even dropped by the cell to inform me that Nate and Alicia Roman were doing just fine and were both expected to be released from the hospital that day.

"Here you go," my cellmate said.

He was holding out a hand-rolled cigarette. I took it and he lit it. The smoke in my lungs brought my mind back into the cell.

My benefactor was a white man about ten years my junior, thirty-five or -six. He had stringy black hair that came down to his armpits and sparse facial hair. His shirt was made from various bright-colored scraps. His eyes were different colors too.

"Reefer Bob," he said.

"Easy Rawlins."

"What they got you for, Easy?"

"I ran into two people in their car. Ran a red light. You?"

"They found me with a burlap sack in a field of marijuana up in the hills."

"Really? In the middle of the day?"

"It was midnight. I guess I should'a kept the flashlight off."

I chuckled and then felt a tidal wave of hysterical laughter in my chest. I took a deep draw on the cigarette to stem the surge.

"Yeah," Reefer Bob was saying. "I was stupid but they can't keep me."

"Why not?"

"Because the bag was empty. My lawyer'll tell 'em that I was just looking for my way outta the woods, that I'm a naturalist and was looking for mushrooms."

He grinned and I thought about Dream Dog.

"Good for you," I said.

"You wanna get high, Easy?"

"No thanks."

"I got some reefer in a couple'a these cigarettes here."

"You know, Bob," I said. "The cops put spies in these cells. And they'd love nothing more than to catch you with contraband in here."

"You a spy, Easy?" he asked.

"No. A spy would never let you know."

"You blowin' my mind, man," he said. "You blowin' my mind."

He crawled into the lower bunk in our eight-by-six cell. I laid on my stomach in the upper bed and stared out of the criss-crossed bars of steel. I thought back to midday, when I'd buckled Feather into her seat.

Axel Bowers was far off in my mind.

I felt that somehow I'd been defeated by my own lack of heart.

GUARDS CAME DOWN the hallway at midnight exactly. The jail was dark but they had flashlights to show them the way. When they came into the cell Reefer Bob yelled, "He killed Axel. He told me when he thought I wasn't listening. He killed him and then stuffed him up in a elephant's ass."

They told me to get up and I obeyed. They asked me if I needed handcuffs and I shook my head.

We walked down the long aisle toward a faraway light.

When we reached the room I realized that this was the day of my execution. They strapped me into the gas chamber chair. On the wall there was the stopwatch that Jesus used to have to time his races when he was in high school.

I had one minute left to live when they closed the door to the chamber.

A hornet was buzzing at the portal of the door. It flew right at my eyes. I shook my head around trying to get the stinger away from my face. When it finally flew off I looked back at the stop-watch: I only had three seconds left to live.

20

Rawlins!" The guard's shout jarred me awake.
I'd dozed off for only a few moments.

"Yo!" I hopped down to the concrete floor.

Bob was huddled into a ball in the back corner of his bunk. I wondered if he really thought I was a spy. If so he'd flush the dope into our corroded tin toilet. I might have saved him three years of hard time.

ETTAMAE HARRIS was in the transit room when they got me there.

She was a big woman but no larger that day than she had been back when we were coming up in the late thirties in Fifth Ward, Houston, Texas. Back then she was everything I ever wanted in a woman except for the fact that she was Mouse's wife.

She hugged me and kissed my forehead while I was buckling my belt.

Etta didn't utter more than three words in the jailhouse. She didn't talk around cops. That was an old habit that never died with her. In her eyes the police were the enemy.

She wasn't wrong.

Out in front of the precinct building LaMarque Alexander, Raymond and Etta's boy, sat behind the wheel of his father's red El Dorado. He was a willowy boy with his father's eyes. But where Mouse had supremely confident bravado in his mien his son was petulant and somewhat petty. Even though he was pushing twenty he was still just a kid.

By the time Raymond was his son's age he had already killed three men — that I knew of.

I tumbled into the backseat. Etta climbed in the front and turned around to regard me.

"Your office?" she asked.

"Yeah."

It was only a few blocks from the precinct. LaMarque pulled away from the curb.

"How's college, LaMarque?" I asked the taciturn boy.

"Okay."

"What you studyin'?"

"Nuthin'."

"He's learnin' about electronics and computers, Easy," Etta said.

"If he wants to know about computers he should talk to Jackson Blue. Jackson knows everything about computers."

"You hear that, LaMarque?"

"Yeah."

When he pulled up in front of my office building at Eighty-sixth and Central, Etta said, "Wait here till I come back down."

"But I was goin' down to Craig's, Mom," he complained.

EttaMae didn't even answer him. She just grunted and opened her door. I jumped out and helped her. Then together we walked up the stairs to the fourth floor.

I ushered her into my office and held my client's chair for her.

Only when we were both settled did Etta feel it was time to talk.

"How's your baby doin'?" she asked.

"Bonnie took her to Europe. They got doctors over there worked with these kinds of blood diseases."

Etta heard more in my tone and squinted at me. For my part I felt like I was floating on a tidal wave of panic. I stayed very still while the world seemed to move around me.

Etta stared for half a minute or so and then she broke out with a smile. The smile turned into a grin.

"What you smirkin' 'bout?" I asked.

"You," she said with emphasis.

"Ain't nuthin' funny 'bout me."

"Oh yes there is."

"How do you see that?"

"Easy Rawlins," she said, "if you wandered into a minefield you'd make it through whole. You could sleep with a girl named Typhoid an' wake up with just sniffles. If you fell out a windah you could be sure that there'd be a bush down on the ground t' break yo' fall. Now it might be a thorn bush but what's a few scratches up next to death?"

I had to laugh. Seeing myself through Etta's eyes gave me hope out there in the void. I guess I was lucky compared to all those I'd known who'd died of disease, gunshot wounds, lynching, and alcohol poisoning. Maybe I did have a lucky star. Dim — but lucky still and all.

"How's that boy Peter?" I asked.

Peter Rhone was a white man whom I'd saved from the LAPD when they needed to pin a murder on somebody his color. His only crime was that he loved a black woman. That love had killed her. And when it was all over Peter had a breakdown and Etta took him in.

"He bettah," she said, the trace of a grin still on her lips. "I got him livin' out on the back porch. He do the shoppin' an' any odd jobs I might need."

"An' Mouse doesn't mind?"

"Naw. The first day I brought him home he called Raymond Mr. Alexander. You know Ray always been a sucker for a white boy with manners."

We both laughed.

Etta reached into her purse and pulled out the Luger that had been under the seat of my Ford. She put it on the desk.

"Primo got your car out the pound. He left his Pontiac parked out back." She brought out a silver key and placed it next to the pistol. "He said that he'll have your Ford ready in two weeks."

I had friends in the world. For a moment there I had more than an inkling that things would turn out okay.

Etta stood up.

"Oh yeah," she said. "Here."

She reached into her purse and came out with a roll of twenty-dollar bills.

"Raymond told me to give you this."

I took the money even though I knew he'd see it as a down payment on the heist he wanted me to join him in.

* * *

THE '56 PONTIAC PRIMO left for me was aqua-colored with red flames painted down the passenger's side and across the hood. It wasn't the kind of car I could shadow with but at least it had wheels.

Sitting upright in the passenger's seat was the teddy bear I'd bought in San Francisco. It had been forgotten in our rush to the airport. Primo must have found it along with the pistol.

When I got home there was a note from Benny on the kitchen table. She and Jesus were going to Catalina Island for two days. They were going to camp on the beach but there was a number for the harbormaster of the dock where they were staying. I could call him if there was an emergency.

I showered and shaved, shined my shoes, and made a pan of scrambled eggs and diced andouille sausages. After eating and a good scrubbing I felt ready to try to find any trail that Cinnamon Cargill might have left. I dressed in black slacks and a peach-colored Hawaiian shirt and sat down to the phone.

"HELLO?" She answered the phone after three rings.

"Alva?" I said.

"Oh." There was a brief pause.

I knew what her hesitation meant. I had saved her son from being killed in a police ambush a few years before. At that time she had been married to John, one of my oldest and closest friends.

In order to save Brawly I'd had to shoot him in the leg. The doctors said that he'd have that limp for the rest of his life.

"Hello, Mr. Rawlins." I'd given up getting her to call me Easy.

"I need to speak to Lena Macalister. She's a friend of yours isn't she?"

More silence on the line. And then: "I don't usually give out my friends' numbers without their permission, Mr. Rawlins."

"I need her address, Alva. This is serious."

We both knew that she couldn't refuse me. Her boy had survived to shuffle in the sun because of me.

She hemmed and hawed a few minutes more but then came across with the address.

"Thanks," I said when she finally relented. "Say hi to Brawly for me."

She hung up the phone in my ear.

I was going toward my East L.A. hot rod when the next-door neighbor, Nathaniel Pulley, hailed me.

"Mr. Rawlins."

He was a short white man with a potbelly and no muscle whatsoever. His blond hair had kept its color but was thinning just the same. Nathaniel was the assistant manager of the Bank of Palms in Santa Monica. It was a small position at a minuscule financial institution but Pulley saw himself as a lion of finance. He was a liberal and in his largesse he treated me as an equal. I'm sure he bragged to his wife and children about how wonderful he was to consider a janitor among his friends.

"Afternoon, Nathaniel," I said.

"There was a guy here asking for you a few hours ago. He was scary looking."

"Black guy?"

"No. White. He wore a jacket made out of snakeskin I think. And his eyes . . . I don't know. They looked mean."

"What did he say?"

"Just if I knew when you were coming back. I asked him if he had a message. He didn't even answer. Just walked off like I wasn't even there."

Pulley was afraid of a car backfiring. He once told me that he couldn't watch westerns because the violence gave him nightmares. Whoever scared him might have been an insurance agent or a door-to-door salesman.

I was taken by his words, though, *Like I wasn't even there*. Pulley was a new neighbor. He'd only been in that house for a year or so. I'd been there more than six years — settled by L.A. standards. But I was still a nomad because everybody around me was always moving in or moving out. Even if I stayed in the same place my neighborhood was always changing.

"Thanks," I said. "I'll look out for him."

We shook hands and I drove off, thinking that nothing in the southland ever stayed the same.

21

My first destination was the Safeway down on Pico. I got ground round, pork chops, calf's liver, broccoli, cauliflower, a head of lettuce, two bottles of milk, and stewed tomatoes in cans. Then I stopped at the liquor store and bought a fifth of Johnnie Walker Black.

After shopping I drove back down to South L.A.

Lena Macalister lived in a dirty pink tenement house three blocks off Hooper. I climbed the stairs and knocked on her door.

"Who is it?" a sweet voice laced with Houston asked.

"Easy Rawlins, Lena."

A chain rattled, three locks snapped back. The door came open and the broad-faced restaurateur smiled her welcome as I had seen her do many times at the Texas Rose.

"Come in. Come in."

She was leaning on a gnarled cane and her glasses had lenses with two different thicknesses. But there was still something stately about her presence.

The house smelled of vitamins.

"Sit. Sit."

The carpet was blue and red with a floral pattern woven in. The furniture belonged in a better neighborhood and a larger room. On the wall hung oil paintings of her West Indian parents, her deceased Tennessee husband, and her son, also dead. The low coffee table was well oiled and everything was drenched in sunlight from the window.

When I set the groceries down on the table I realized that I'd forgotten the scotch in the backseat of my car.

"What's this?" she asked, pointing at the bag.

"Your name came up recently and I realized that I had to ask you a couple'a questions. So I thought, as long as I was comin', you might need some things."

"Aren't you sweet."

She backed up to the stuffed chair, made sure of where she was standing, and let herself fall.

"Let's put them away later," she said with a deep sigh. "You know it takes a lot outta me these days just to answer the door."

"You sick?"

"If you call getting old sick, then I sure am that." She smiled anyway and I let the subject drop.

"How long has it been since you closed the Rose?"

"Eight years," she said, smiling. "Those were some days. Hubert and Brendon were both alive and working in the kitchen. We had every important black person in the country, in the world, coming to us for dinner."

She spoke as if I were a reporter or a biographer coming to get down her life story.

"Yeah," I said. "That was somethin' else."

Lena smiled and sighed. "The Lord only lets you have breath for a short time. You got to take it in while you can."

I nodded, thinking about Feather and then about Jesus out on some beach with Benita.

"Alva called. Why are you coming to see me, Mr. Rawlins?"

While inhaling I considered lying. I held the breath for a beat and then let it go.

"I think Philomena Cargill is in trouble. Some people hired me to find her up in Frisco, and even though I didn't, what I did find makes me think that she might need some help."

"Why are these people looking for Cindy?" Lena asked.

"Her boss walked off with something that didn't belong to him. At least that's what they told me. He disappeared and then, a little while later, she did too."

"And why are you coming to me?"

"I found a postcard from you in Philomena's apartment."

"You broke into her place?"

"No. As a matter of fact that's one of the reasons I'm worried about her. They had her place up for rent. She'd left everything behind."

I let these words sink in. Lena lifted her gaze above the glasses as if to get a better view of my heart. I have no idea what her nearly blind eyes saw.

"I don't know where she is, Easy," Lena said. "The last I heard she was in San Francisco working for a man named Bowers."

"Are her parents here?"

"When her father died her mother moved to Chicago to live with a sister."

"Brothers? Sisters?"

"Her brothers are both in the service, Vietnam. Her sister married a Chinese man and they moved to Jamaica."

There was something Lena wasn't telling me.

"What's she like — Cinnamon?"

"Reach over in that drawer in the end table," she said, waving in that general direction.

The drawer was filled with papers, ballpoint pens, and pencils.

"Under all that," she said. "It's a frame."

The small gilded frame held a three-by-five photo of a pretty young woman in a graduation cap and gown. She was smiling like I would have liked my daughter to do on her graduation day. The photograph was black-and-white but you could almost see the reddish hue to her skin through the shading. There was a certainty in her eyes. She knew what she was seeing.

"She's the kind of woman that men hate because she's not afraid to be out there in a man's world. Broke all'a the records at Jordan High School. Made it to the top of her class at University of California at Berkeley. Ready to fly, that child is . . ."

"She honest?"

"Let me tell you something, young man," Lena said. "The reason I know her is that she worked in my restaurant in the last two years. She was just a girl but sharp and true. She loved to work and learn. I wished my own son had her wits. After the restaurant closed she came to see me every week to learn from what I knew. She was no crook."

"Did she have any close friends down here?"

"I didn't know her friends. She saw boys but they were never serious. The young men around here don't value a woman with brains and talent."

"Do you know how I can find her?" I asked, giving up subtlety.

"No."

Maybe I thought she was lying because all I could see was the opaque reflective surface of her glasses.

"If you hear from her will you tell her that I'm looking for the documents Bowers took?"

"What documents?"

"All I know is that he took some papers that have red seals on them. But I'm not worried about them as much as I'm worried about Miss Cargill's safety."

Lena nodded. If she did know where Philomena was she'd be sure to give her the message. I wrote down my home and office numbers. And then I helped Lena put away the groceries.

Her refrigerator was empty except for two hard-boiled eggs.

"With my legs the way they are it's hard for me to get out shopping very much," she said, apologizing for her meager fare.

I nodded and smiled.

"I come down to my office at least twice a week, Lena. I can always make a supermarket run for you."

She patted my forearm and said, "Bless you."

There are all kinds of freedom in America — free speech, the right to bear arms — but when the years have piled up so high on their back that they can't stand up straight anymore, many Americans find out they also have the freedom to starve.

AT A PHONE BOOTH down the street from Lena's house I looked up a number and then made a call.

"Hello?" a man answered.

"Billy?"

"Hey, Easy. She ain't here."

"You know when she'll be in?"

"She at work, man."

"On Saturday?"

"They pay her to sit down in her office when the band comes in for practice. She opens up the music building at nine and then closes it at three. Not bad for time and a half."

"Okay," I said. "I'll go over and see her there."

"Bye, Easy. Take care."

Jordan High School had a sprawling campus. There were over three thousand students enrolled. I came in through the athletic gate and made my way toward the boiler room. That's where Helen McCoy made her private office. She was the building supervisor of the school, a position two grades above the one I'd just left.

Helen was short and redheaded, smart as they come, and tougher than most men. I had seen her kill a man in Third Ward one night. He'd slapped her face and then balled up a fist. When she pressed five inches of a Texas jackknife into his chest he sat down on the floor — dying as he did so.

"Hi, Easy," she said with a smile.

She was sitting at a long table next to the boiler, writing on a small white card. There was a large stack of blank cards on her left and a smaller stack on the right. The right-side cards had already been written on.

"Party?" I asked.

"My daughter Vanessa's gettin' married. These the invitations. You gettin' one."

I sat down and waited.

When Helen finished writing the card she sat back and smiled, indicating that I had her attention.

"Philomena 'Cinnamon' Cargill," I said. "I hear she was a student here some years ago."

"Li'l young," Helen suggested.

"It's my other job," I said. "I'm lookin' for her for somebody."

"Grapevine says you quit the board."

"Sabbatical."

"Don't shit me, Easy. You quit."

I didn't argue.

"Smart girl, that Philomena," Helen said. "Lettered in track and archery. Gave the big speech at her graduation. She was wild too."

"Wild how?"

"She wasn't shy of boys, that one. One time I found her in the boys' locker room after hours with Maurice Johnson. Her drawers was down and her hands was busy." Helen grinned. She'd been wild herself.

"I was told that her father died and her mother left for Chicago," I said. "You know anybody else she might be in touch with?"

"She had a school friend named Raphael Reed. He was funny, if you know what I mean, so he never got jealous of her runnin' around."

"That all?"

"All I can think of."

"You think you could go down and pull Reed's records for me?"

Helen considered my request.

"We known each other a long time haven't we, Easy?"

"Sure have."

"You the one got me this job."

"And you moved up past me in grade in two years."

"I don't have no job on the side to distract me," she said.

I nodded, submitting to her logic.

"You know I ain't s'posed t' give the public information on students or faculty."

"I know that."

She laughed then. "I guess we all do things we ain't s'posed to do sometimes."

"Can't help it," I agreed.

"Wait here," she said, patting the table with her knife hand. "I'll be back in a few minutes."

22

I told Raphael's mother — a small, dark woman with big, brown, hopeful eyes — that I was Philomena Cargill's uncle and that I needed to talk to her son about a pie-baking business that my niece and I were starting up in Oakland. All I hoped for was a phone number, but Althea was so happy about the chance for a job for her son that she gave me his address too.

This brought me to a three-story wooden apartment building on Santa Barbara Boulevard. It was a wide building that had begun to sag in the middle. Maybe that's why the landlord painted it bright turquoise, to make it seem young and sprightly.

I walked up the sighing stairs to 2a. The door was painted with black and turquoise zebra stripes and the letters RR RR were carved into the center.

The young man who answered my knock wore only black jeans. His body was slender and strong. His hair was long (but not hippie long) and straightened — then curled. He wasn't very tall, and the sneer on his lips was almost comical.

"Yeeees?" he asked in such a way that he seemed to be suggesting something obscene.

I knew right then that this was the young man who'd hung up on me, the one I'd called from Philomena's apartment.

"Raphael Reed?"

"And who are you?"

"Easy Rawlins," I said.

"What can I do for you, Easy Rawlins?" he asked while appraising my stature and style.

"I think that a friend of yours may have been the victim of foul play."

"What friend?"

"Cinnamon."

It was all in the young man's eyes. Suddenly the brash flirtation and sneering façade disappeared. Now there was a man standing before me, a man who was ready to take serious action depending on what I said next.

"Come in."

It was a studio apartment. A Murphy bed had been pulled down from the wall. It was unmade and jumbled with dirty clothes and dishes. A black-and-white portable TV with bent-up rabbit-ear antennas sat on a maple chair at the foot of the bed. There was no sofa, but three big chairs, upholstered with green carpeting, were set in a circle facing each other at the center of the room.

The room smelled strongly of perfumes and body odors. This scent of sex and sensuality was off-putting on a Saturday afternoon.

"Come on out, Roget," Raphael said.

A door opened and another young man, nearly a carbon copy of the first, emerged. They were the same height and had the same hairstyle. Roget also wore black jeans, no shirt, and a sneer. But where Raphael had the dark skin of his mother, Roget was the color of light brown sugar and had freckles on his nose and shoulders.

"Sit," Raphael said to me.

We all went to the chairs in a circle. I liked the configuration but it still felt odd somehow.

"What about Philomena?" Raphael asked.

"Her boss disappeared," I said. "A man named Adams hired me to find him. He also told me that Philomena had disappeared a couple of days later. I went to her apartment and found that she'd moved out without even taking her clothes."

Raphael glanced at his friend, but Roget was inspecting his nails.

"So what?"

"You're her friend," I said. "Aren't you worried?"

"Who says I'm her friend?"

"At Jordan you two shared notes on boys."

"What the hell do you mean by that?" he asked.

I realized that I had gone too far, that no matter how much it seemed that these young men were homosexuals, I was not allowed to talk about it.

"Just that she had a lot of boyfriends," I said.

Roget made a catty little grunt. It was the closest he came to speaking.

"Well," Raphael said, "I haven't even spoken to her since the day she graduated."

"Valedictorian wasn't she?"

"She sure was," Raphael said with some pride in his tone.

"Is Roget here a friend'a hers?"

"What?"

"She did call here didn't she?" I asked.

"You the niggah called the other day," Raphael said. "I thought I knew your voice."

"Look, man. I'm not tryin' to mess with you or your friends. I don't care about anything but finding Bowers for the man hired me. I think that Philomena is in trouble, because why else would she leave her place without taking her clothes and personal things? If you know where she is tell her that I'm looking for her."

"I don't know where she is."

"Take my number. If she calls give it to her."

"I don't need your number."

I wondered if my daughter could die because of this petulant boy. The thought made me want to slap him. But I held my temper.

"You're makin' a mistake," I said. "Your friend could get hurt — bad."

Raphael's lips formed a snarl and his head reared back, snakelike — but he didn't say a word.

I got up and walked out, glad that I'd left my new stolen Luger at home.

23

I drove home carefully, making sure to check every traffic light — twice.

Once in my house I gave in to a kind of weariness. It's not that I was tired, but there was nothing I could do. I'd done all I could about Philomena Cargill. And even though I'd chummed the waters for her I doubted that she was alive to take the bait.

Bonnie was off, probably with Joguye Cham, her prince.

And Feather would die unless I made thirty-five thousand dollars quickly. She might die anyway. She might already be dead.

I hadn't had a drink in many years.

Liquor took a toll on me. But Johnnie Walker was still in the backseat of the car and I went to my front door more than once, intent on retrieving him.

And why not take up the bottle again? There was no one to disapprove. Oblivion called to me. I could navigate the tidal wave of my life on a full tank; I'd be a black Ulysses singing with the stars.

It was early evening when I went out the front door and to my borrowed car. I looked in the window at the slender brown bag on the backseat. I wanted to open the door but I couldn't. Because even though there was no trace of Feather she still was there. Looking at the backseat I thought about her riding in the backseat of my Ford. She was laughing, leaning up against the seat as the young hippie Star had done, telling me and Jesus about her wild adventures on the playground and in the classroom. Sometimes she made up stories about her and Billy Chipkin crossing Olympic and going up to the County Art Museum. There, she'd say, they had seen pictures of naked ladies and kings.

I remembered her sitting by my side in the front seat reading *Little Women,* snarling whenever I interrupted her with questions about what she wanted for dinner or when she was going to pick up her room.

Dozens of memories came between me and that door handle. I got dizzy and sat down on the lawn. I put my head in my hands and pressed all ten fingers hard against my scalp.

"Go back in the house," the voice that was me and not me said. "Go back an' do it until she's in her room dreamin' again. Then, when she safe, you can have that bottle all night long."

The phone rang at that moment. It was a weak jingle, almost not there. I struggled to my feet, staggering as if Feather were already healed and I was drunk on the celebration. My pants were wet from the grass.

The weak bleating of the phone grew loud when I opened the door.

"Hello."

"So what's it gonna be, Ease?" Mouse asked.

It made me laugh.

"I got to move on this, brother," he continued. "Opportunity don't wait around."

"I'll call you in the mornin', Ray," I said.

"What time?"

"After I wake up."

"This is serious, man," he told me.

Those words from his lips had been the prelude to many a man's death but I didn't care.

"Tomorrow," I said. "In the mornin'." And then I hung up.

I turned on the radio. There was a jazz station from USC that was playing twenty-four hours of John Coltrane. I liked the new jazz but my heart was still with Fats Waller and Duke Ellington — that big band sound.

I turned on the TV. Some detective show was on. I don't know what it was about, just a lot of shouting and cars screeching, a shot now and then, and a woman who screamed when she got scared.

I'd been rereading *Native Son* by Richard Wright lately so I hefted it off the shelf and opened to a dog-eared page. The words scrambled and the radio hummed. Every now and then I'd look up to see that a new show was on the boob tube. By midnight every light in the house was burning. I'd switched them on one at a time as I got up now and then to check out various parts of the house.

I was reading about a group of boys masturbating in a movie theater when the phone rang again. For a moment I resisted answering. If Mouse had gotten mad I didn't know if I could placate him. If it was Bonnie telling me that Feather was dead I didn't know that I could survive.

"Hello."

"Mr. Rawlins?" It was Maya Adamant.

"How'd you get my home number?"

"Saul Lynx gave it to me."

"What do you want, Miss Adamant?"

"There has been a resolution to the Bowers case," she said.

"You found the briefcase?"

"All I can tell you is that we have reached a determination about the disposition of the papers and of Mr. Bowers."

"You don't even want me to report on what I've found?" I asked.

This caused a momentary pause in my dismissal.

"What information?" she asked.

"I found Axel," I said.

"Really?"

"Yes, really. He came down to L.A. to get away from Haffernon. Also to be nearer to Miss Cargill."

"She's down there? You've seen her?"

"Sure have," I lied.

Another silence. In that time I tried to figure Maya's response to my talking to Cinnamon. Her surprise might have been a clue that she knew Philomena was dead. Then again . . . maybe she'd been given contradictory information . . .

"What did Bowers say?" she asked.

"Am I fired, Miss Adamant?"

"You've been paid fifteen hundred dollars."

"Against ten thousand," I added.

"Does that mean you are withholding intelligence from Mr. Lee?"

"I'm not talking to Mr. Lee."

"I carry his authority."

"I spent a summer unloading cargo ships down in Galveston back in the thirties," I said. "Smelled like tar and fish, and you know I was only fifteen — with a sensitive nose. My back hurt carryin' them cartons of clothes and fine china and whatever else the man said I should carry for thirty-five cents a day. I had his authority but I was just a day laborer still and all."

"What did Axel say?"

"Am I fired?"

"No," she said after a very long pause.

"Let Lee call me back and say that."

"Robert E. Lee is not a man to fool with, Mr. Rawlins."

"I like it when you call me mister," I said. "It shows that you respect me. So listen up — if I'm fired then I'm through. If Lee wants me to be a consultant based on what I know then let him call me himself."

"You're making a big mistake, Easy."

"Mistake was made before I was even born, honey. I came into it cryin' and I'll go out hollerin' too."

She hung up without another word. I couldn't blame her. But neither could I walk away without trying to make my daughter's money.

I SAUTÉED chopped garlic, minced fresh jalapeño, green pepper, and a diced shallot in ghee that I'd rendered myself. I added some ground beef and, after the meat had browned, I put in some cooked rice from a pot in the refrigerator. That was my meal for the night.

I fell asleep on the loveseat with every light in the house on, the television flashing, and John Coltrane bleating about his favorite things.

24

I moved the trunk in front of the big brass elephant. Underneath was the crushed, cubical body of Axel Bowers. I watched him, worrying once again about the degradation of his carcass. I told him that I was sorry and he moved his head in a little semicircle as if trying to work out a kink in his neck. With his hands he lifted his head, raising it up from the hole. It took him a long while to crawl out of the makeshift grave — and longer still to straighten out all of the bloody, cracked, and shattered limbs. He looked to me like a butterfly just out of the cocoon, unfolding its wet wings.

All of that work he did without noticing me. Pulling on his left arm, turning his foot around until the ankle snapped into place, pressing his temples until his forehead was once more round and hard.

He was putting his fingers back into alignment when he happened to look up and notice me.

"I'm going to need a new hip," he said.

"What?"

"The hip bones don't reform like other bones," he said. "They need to be replaced or I won't be able to walk very far."

"Where you got to go?" I asked.

"There's a Nazi hiding in Egypt. He's going to assassinate the president."

"The president was assassinated three years ago," I said.

"There's a new president," Axel assured me. "And if this one goes we'll be in deep shit."

The phone rang.

"You going to get that?" Axel asked.

"I should stay with you."

"Don't worry, I can't go anywhere. I'm stuck right here on my broken hips."

The phone rang.

I wandered back through the house. In the kitchen Dizzy Gillespie had taken Coltrane's place. He was standing in front of the sink with his cheeks puffed out like a bullfrog's, blowing on that trumpet. The front door was open and *The Mummy* was playing outside. The movie was now somehow like a play being enacted in the street. On the sidewalks all the way up to the corners, extras and actors with small roles were smoking cigarettes and talking, waiting to come onstage to do their parts.

Egypt, I thought and the phone rang.

I came back in the house but the phone wasn't on its little table. Above, on the bookshelf, Bigger Thomas was strangling a woman who was laughing at him.

"You can't kill me," she said. "I'm better than you are. I'm still alive."

The phone rang again.

I returned to the brass elephant to tell Axel something but he was back in his hole, crushed and debased.

"My hips were my downfall," he said.

"You can make it," I told him. "Lots of people live in wheel-chairs."

"I will not be a cripple."

The phone rang and he disappeared.

I opened my eyes. *The Mummy,* with Boris Karloff, was play-ing on TV. Coltrane had not been replaced, and every light in the house was still on.

I wondered about the coincidence of a movie about a corpse rising from the dead in Egypt and Axel's trips to that country.

The phone rang.

"Somebody must really wanna talk," I said to myself, thinking that the phone must have rung nearly a dozen times.

I went to the podium and picked up the receiver.

"Hello."

"Why are you looking for me?" a woman's voice asked.

"Philomena? Is that you?"

"I asked you a question."

My lips felt numb. Coltrane hit a discordant note.

"I thought you were dead," I said. "You didn't even take any underwear as far as I could tell. What woman leaves without a change of underwear?"

"I am alive," she said. "So you can stop looking for me."

"I'm not lookin' for you, honey. It's your boyfriend Axel an' them papers he stole."

"Axel's gone."

"Dead?"

"Who said anything about dead? He's gone. Left the country."

"Just up and left his house without tellin' anybody? Not even Dream Dog?"

"Who are you working for, Mr. Rawlins?"

"Call me Easy."

"Who are you working for?"

"I don't know."

"What do you mean you don't know?"

"A man I know came to me with fifteen hundred dollars and said that another man, up in Frisco, was willing to pay that and more for locating Axel Bowers. That man said he was working for somebody else but he didn't tell me who. After I looked around I found out that you and Axel were friends, that you disappeared too. So here I am with you on the phone, just a breath away."

"You weren't that far wrong about me, Easy," the woman called Cinnamon said.

"What exactly was I right about?"

"I think there is a man trying to kill me. A man who wants the papers that Axel has."

"What's this man's name?" I asked, made brave by the ano-nymity of the phone lines.

"I don't know his name. He's a white man with dead eyes."

"He wear a snakeskin jacket?" I asked on a hunch.

"Yes."

"Where are you?"

"Hiding," she said. "Safe."

"I'll come to you and we'll try and work this thing out."

"No. I don't want your help. What I want is for you to stop looking for me."

"Nothing would make me happier than to let this drop, but

I'm in it now. All the way in it," I said, thinking about Axel's hip bones. "So either we get together or I talk to the man pays my salary."

"He's probably the one trying to have me killed."

"You don't know that."

"Axel told me. He said that people would kill for those papers. Then that man . . . he . . ."

"He what?"

She hung up the phone.

I held on to the receiver for a full minute at least. Sitting there I thought again about my dream, about the corpse trying to re-suscitate himself. Philomena had described a killer who had been at my doorstep. All of a sudden the prospect of robbing an armored car delivery didn't seem so dangerous.

I had a good laugh then. There I was all alone in the night with killers and thieves milling outside in the darkness.

I rooted my .38 out of the closet and made sure that it was loaded. The Luger was a fine gun but I had no idea how old its ammo was. I went around the house turning off lights.

In bed I was overcome by a feeling of giddiness. I felt as if I had just missed a fatal accident by a few inches. In a little while Bonnie's infidelity and Feather's dire illness would return to dis-turb my rest, but right then I was at peace in my bed, all alone and safe.

Then the phone rang.

I had to answer it. It might be Bonnie. It might be my little girl wanting me to tell her that things would be fine. It could be Mouse or Saul or Maya Adamant. But I knew that it wasn't any of them.

"Hello."

"I'm at the Pixie Inn on Slauson," she said. "But I'm very tired. Can you come in the morning?"

"What's the room number?"

"Six."

"What size dress you wear?" I asked.

"Two," she said. "Why?"

"I'll see you at seven."

I hung up and wondered at the mathematics of my mind. Why had I agreed to go to her when I'd just been thankful for a peaceful heist?

"'Cause you the son of a fool and the father of nothing," the voice that had abandoned me for so many years said.

25

I couldn't sleep anymore that night.

At four I got up and started cooking. First I fried three strips of bacon. I cracked two eggs and dropped them into the bacon fat, then I covered one slice of whole wheat bread with yellow mustard and another one with mayonnaise. I grated orange cheddar on the eggs after I flipped them, put the lid on the frying pan, and turned off the gas flame. I made a strong brew of coffee, which I poured into a two-quart thermos. Then I made the eggs and bacon into a sandwich that I wrapped in wax paper.

Riding down Slauson at five-fifteen with the brown paper bag next to me and Johnnie Walker in the backseat, I tried to come up with some kind of plan. I considered Maya and Lee, dead Axel and scared Cinnamon — and the man in the snakeskin jacket. There was no sense to it; no goal to work toward except making enough money to pay for Feather's hospital bill.

I parked across the street from the motel. It was of a modern design, three stories high, with doors that opened to unenclosed platforms. Number 6 was on the ground floor. Its door opened onto the parking lot. I supposed that Philomena wanted to be able to jump out the back window if need be.

I sat in my car wondering what I should ask the girl.

What should I tell her? Should it be truth?

When my Timex read six-eighteen the door of number 6 opened. A tall woman wearing dark slacks and a long white T-shirt came out. Even from that distance I could see that she was braless and barefoot. Her skin had a reddish hue and her hair was long and straightened.

She walked to the soda machine near the motel office, put in her coins, and then bent down to get the soda that fell out. The streets were so quiet that I heard the jumbling glass.

She walked back to the door, looked around, then went inside.

A minute later I was walking toward her door.

I listened for a moment. There was no sound. I knocked. Still no sound. I knocked again. Then I heard a shushing sound like the slide of a window.

"It's me, Philomena," I said loudly. "Easy Rawlins."

It only took her half a minute to come to the door and open it.

Five nine with chiseled features and big, dramatic eyes, that was Philomena Cargill. Her skin was indeed cinnamon red. Lena's photograph of her had faithfully recorded the face but it hadn't given even a hint of her beauty.

I held out the paper bag.

"What's this?"

"An egg sandwich an' coffee," I said.

While she didn't actually grab the bag she did take it with eager hands.

She went to one of the two single beds and sat with the sack on her lap. After closing the door I put the cloth bag I'd brought on the bed across from her and sat next to it.

There were three lamps in the room. They were all on but the light was dim at best.

Philomena tore open the sandwich and took a big bite out of it.

"I'm a vegetarian usually," she said with her mouth full, "but this bacon is good."

While she ate I poured her a plastic cup full of coffee.

"I put milk in it," I said as she took the cup from me.

"I don't care if you put vinegar in it. I need this. I left my house with only forty dollars in my purse. It's all gone now."

She didn't speak again until the cup was drained and the sandwich was gone.

"What's in the other bag?" she asked. I believe she was hoping for another sandwich.

"Two dresses, some panties, and tennis shoes."

She came to sit on the other side of the bag, taking out the clothes and examining them with an expert feminine eye.

"The dress is perfect," she said. "And the shoes'll do. Where'd you get these?"

"My son's girlfriend left them. She's a skinny thing too."

When Cinnamon smiled at me I understood the danger she represented. She was more than pretty or lovely or even beautiful. There was something regal about her. I almost felt like bowing to show her how much I appreciated the largesse of her smile.

"They say that Hitler was a vegetarian too," I said and the smile shriveled on her lips.

"So what?"

"Why don't you tell me, Philomena?"

After regarding me for a moment she said, "Why should I trust you?"

"Because I'm on your side," I said. "I don't want any harm coming to you and I'll work to see that no one else hurts you either."

"I don't know any of that."

"Sure you do," I said. "You talked to Lena about me. She gave you my number. She told you that I've traded tough favors down around here for nearly twenty years."

"She also said that she's heard that people you've helped have wound up hurt and even dead sometimes."

"That might be, but any girl bein' followed by a snakeskin killer got to expect some danger," I countered. "I'd be a fool if I told you everything'll work out fine and you'd be a fool to believe it. But if you all mixed up with murder then you need somebody like me. It don't matter that you got a business degree from UC Berkeley and a boyfriend got Paul Klee paintings hangin' on his walls. If somethin' goes wrong you the first one they gonna look at. An' if a white killer wanna kill somebody a black woman will be the first on his list. 'Cause you know the cops will ask if you had a boyfriend they could pin it on, an' if you don't they'll call you a whore and close the book."

Philomena listened very carefully to my speech. Her royal visage made me feel like some kind of minister to the crown.

"What do want from me?" she asked.

"What papers did Axel steal?"

"He didn't steal anything. He found those papers in a safe-deposit box his father had. He kept them with memorabilia he had from Germany. When Mr. Bowers died, he left the key to Axel."

"If that's so then why did Haffernon tell the man who hired me that Axel stole the papers from him?"

"Who hired you?"

I told her about Robert Lee and his Amazon assistant. She had never heard of either one.

"Haffernon and Mr. Bowers and another man were partners before the war. They worked in chemicals," Philomena said.

"Who was their partner?"

"A man named Tourneau, Rega Tourneau. They did some bad things, illegal things during the war."

"What kind of things?"

"Treason."

"No." I was still a good American back in those days. It was almost impossible for me to believe that American businessmen would betray the country that had made them rich.

"The papers are Swiss bearer bonds issued in 1943 for work done by the Karnak Chemical Company in Cairo," Philomena said. "And even though the bonds themselves are only endorsed by the banks there's a letter from top Nazi officials that details the expectations that the Nazis had of Karnak."

"Whoa. And Axel wanted to cash the bonds?"

"No. He didn't know what he wanted exactly, but he knew that something should be done to make amends for his father's sins."

"But Haffernon doesn't want to pay the price," I said. "What about this Tourneau guy?"

"I don't know about him. Axel just said that he's out of it."

"Dead?"

"I don't know."

"What did his father's company do for the Nazis?" I asked.

"They developed special kinds of explosives that the Germans used for construction in a few of their slave labor camps."

"And what do you get outta all'a this?" I asked.

"Me? I was just helping him."

"No. I don't hardly know you at all, girl, but I do know that you look out for number one. What's Axel gonna do for you?"

Cinnamon let her left shoulder rise, ceding a point that was hardly worth the effort.

"He had friends in business. He was going to set me in a job somewhere. But he would have done that even if I hadn't tried to help."

I was suddenly aware of a slight dizziness.

"But it didn't hurt," I said. "You could work all you wanted."

"What?" she asked.

I realized that the last part of what I said didn't make sense.

I blinked, finding it hard to open my eyes again.

I shook my head but the cobwebs went nowhere.

"Philomena."

"Yes?"

"Would you mind if I just laid out here a minute? I haven't got much sleep lookin' for you and I'm tired. Real tired."

Her smile was a thing to behold.

"Maybe I could rest too," she said. "I've been so scared alone in this room."

"Let's get a short nap and then we can finish talkin' in a while." I lay back on the bed as I spoke.

She said something. It seemed like a really long sentence but I couldn't make out the words. I closed my eyes.

"Uh-huh," I said out of courtesy and then I was asleep.

26

In the dream I was kissing Bonnie. She whispered something sweet and kissed my forehead, then my lips. I tried to hold myself back, to tell her how angry I was. But every time her lips touched mine my mouth opened and her tongue washed away all my angry words.

"I need you," she told me and I had to strain to hold back the tears.

She pressed her body against mine. I held her so tight that she pulled away for a moment, but then she was kissing me again.

"Thank God," I whispered. "Thank God."

I reached down into her panties and she moaned.

But when I felt her cold hand on my erection I realized that it wasn't Bonnie. It wasn't Bonnie because it wasn't a dream and Bonnie was in Switzerland.

Who was in my bed? Nobody. Another deeply felt kiss. I was in a motel room . . . with Cinnamon Cargill.

I raised up, pushing her away as I did so. Her T-shirt was up to her midriff. My erection was standing straighter than it had in some while. She reached out and stroked it lightly with two fingers. The groan came from my lips against my will.

I stood up, pushed the urgent cock back behind the zipper.

Cinnamon sat up and smiled.

"I was scared," she explained. "I just lay down next to you and went to sleep."

What could I say?

"I guess you must have kissed me in your sleep," she said. "It was nice."

"Yeah." I wondered if it was me who cast the first kiss. "I'm sorry about that."

"Nothing to be sorry about. It's natural. I have protection."

Even her sexy nonchalance was imperial.

"Where'd you get that?" I asked her. "You left with nothing."

"I always have a backup in my wallet," she said, sounding decidedly like a man.

"Let's go get some breakfast," I said.

A shadow of disappointment darkened her features for a moment and then she pulled on her pants, which she'd dropped on the floor next to my bed.

I WANTED BREAKFAST even though it was two in the afternoon. Philomena and I had slept for almost eight hours before we started making out.

Brenda's Burgers had everything I needed: an all-day breakfast menu and a booth at the back of her tiny diner where you could talk without being overheard. It was a small restaurant with pitted floors and mismatched furniture. The cook and waiter was a dark-skinned mustachioed man with mistrustful eyes.

I ordered fried ham and buttermilk biscuits. Philomena wanted a steak with collard greens, mashed potatoes, and salad.

"I thought you were vegetarian?" I asked.

"Need to keep up my strength," she replied.

I was a little off because the erection hadn't gone all the way down. My heart was thrumming and every time she smiled I wanted to suggest going back to her room and finishing off what we had started.

"What's wrong?" she asked me.

"Nuthin'. Why you ask?"

"You seem kind of nervous."

"This is just the way I am," I said.

"Okay."

"Tell me about the man in the snakeskin jacket," I said, watching the cook eye us from behind the kitchen window.

"He came to Axel's house one day last week. I was in the hallway that led to the bedroom but I could see them through a crack in the double doors."

"They didn't know you were there?"

"Axel knew but the other guy didn't. He told Axel that he needed the papers his father left. Axel told him that they'd been given to a third party who would make them public upon his death."

Watching her, listening to her story made me sweat. Maybe it was the heat from the kitchen but I didn't think so. Neither did I feel my temperature came from anything having to do with sex.

"Did he threaten Axel?"

"Yes. He said, 'A man can get hurt if he doesn't know when to fold.'"

"He's right about that," I said, wanting to stave off the details of Axel's murder.

"He was a frightening man. Axel was scared but he stood up to him."

"What happened then?"

"The man left."

"He didn't . . . hurt Axel?"

"No. But he put the fear of God into him. He told me to get out of there, not even to go home. He gave me the money he had in his pocket and said to go down to L.A. until he figured out what to do."

"Why you?" I asked. "He wasn't after you."

"Axel and I were close." There was a brazen look on Cinnamon's face, as if she were daring me to question her choice of lovers.

"So you have the papers," I said.

She didn't deny it.

"Those papers can get you killed," I said.

"I've been trying to call Axel for days," she said, agreeing with me in her tone. "I called his cousin but Harmon hadn't heard from him and there's no answer at his house."

"How about his office?"

"He never tells them anything."

"How many people know where you are now?" I asked.

"No one."

"What about Lena?"

"I call her every other day or so but I don't tell her where I am."

"And Raphael?"

That was the first time I'd surprised her.

"How did you . . . ?"

"I'm a real live detective, honey. Finding out things is what I do."

"No. I mean I've talked to Rafe but I didn't tell him where I was staying."

"Have you seen anybody you know or have they seen you?"

"I don't think so."

"Are you willing to trade those papers for your life?" I asked.

"Axel made me promise to turn them in if anything happened," she said.

"Axel's dead," I said.

"You don't know that."

"Yes I do and you know it too," I told her. "This is big money here. You learn more outta this than five PhDs at Harvard could ever tell ya. Axel messed with some big men's money and now he's dead. If you wanna live you had better think straight."

"I . . . I have to think about this. I should at least try to find Axel once more."

I didn't want to implicate myself in the particulars of Axel's demise. So I reached into my pocket and peeled off five of Mouse's twenties. I palmed the wad and handed it to her under the table. At first she thought I was trying to hold her hand. She clutched at my fingers and then felt the bills.

"What's this?"

"Money. Pay for your room and some food. But don't go out much. Try to hide your face if you do. You got my office number too?"

She nodded.

"I'll call you tonight or at the latest tomorrow morning. You got to decide though, honey."

She nodded. "You want to come back to the room with me?"

"I'll walk you but then I got to get goin'. Got to get a bead on how we get you outta this jam."

Her shoulder heaved again, saying that a roll in the hay would have been nice but okay.

I knew she was just afraid to be alone.

I MADE IT to my office a little bit before four.

There were three messages on the machine. The first was from Feather.

"Hi, Daddy. Me an' Bonnie got here after a loooong time on three airplanes. Now I'm in a house on a lake but tomorrow they're gonna take me to the clinic. I met the doctor and he was real nice but he talks funny. I miss you, Daddy, and I wish you would come and see me soon. . . . Oh yeah, an' Bonnie says that she misses you too."

I turned off the machine for a while after that. In my mind every phrase she used turned over and over. Bonnie saying that she missed me, the doctor's accent. She sounded happy, not like a dying girl at all.

I was so distracted by these thoughts that I didn't hear him open the door. I looked up on instinct and he was standing there, not six feet from where I sat head in hands.

He was a white man, slender and tall, wearing dark green slacks and a jacket of tan and brown scales. His hat was also dark green, with a small brim. His skin was olive-colored and his pale eyes seemed to have no color at all.

"Ezekiel Rawlins?"

"Who're you?"

"Are you Ezekiel Rawlins?"

"Who the fuck are you?"

There was a moment there for us to fight. He was peeved at me not answering his question. I was mad at myself for not hearing him open the door. Or maybe I hadn't closed it behind me. Either way I was an idiot.

But then Snakeskin smiled.

"Joe Cicero," he said. "I'm a private operative too."

"Detective?"

"Not exactly." His smile had no humor in it.

"What do you want?"

"Are you Ezekiel Rawlins?"

"Yeah. Why?"

"I'm looking for a girl."

"Try down on Avalon near Florence. There's a cathouse behind the Laundromat."

"Philomena Cargill."

"Never heard of her."

"Oh yeah. You have. You talked to her and now I need to do the same thing."

I remembered the first day I opened the office two years earlier. I'd had a little party to celebrate the opening. All of my friends, the ones who were still alive, had come. Mouse was there drinking and eating onion dip that Bonnie'd made. He waited until everyone else had gone before handing me a paper bag that held a pistol, some chicken wire, and a few U-shaped tacks.

"Let's put this suckah in," he said.

"In what?"

"Under the desk, fool. You know you cain't be workin' wit' these niggahs down here without havin' a edge. Shit, some mothahfuckah come in here all mad or vengeful an' there you are without a pot to piss in. No, brothah, we gotta put this here gun undah yo' desk so that when the shit hit the fan at least you got a even chance."

I slid my hand around the smooth butt of the .25 caliber gift.

"I don't know no Cargill," I said. "Who says that I do?"

Cicero made an easy move with his hand and I came out with my gun. I pointed it at his head just in case he was wearing something bulletproof on his chassis.

The threat just made him smile.

"Nervous aren't you, son?" he said. "Well . . . you should be."

"Who said I know this woman?"

"You have twenty-four hours, Mr. Rawlins," he replied. "Twenty-four or things will get bad."

"Do you see this gun?" I asked him.

He grinned and said, "Family man like you has to think about his liabilities. Me, I'm just a soldier. Knock one down and two take his place. But you — you have Feather and Jesus and whatshername, Bonnie, yeah Bonnie, to think about."

With that he turned and walked out the door.

I'd met men with eyes like his before — killers, every one of them. I knew that his threats were serious. I would have shot him if I could have gotten away with it. But my floor had five other tenants and not one of them would have lied to save my ass.

Two minutes after Joe Cicero walked out the door I went to the hall to make sure that he was gone. I checked both stairwells and then made sure to lock my own door behind me.

27

The second phone message was from Mouse.

"I called it off, Easy," he said in a subdued voice. "I fig-ure you don't want it bad enough an' I already got a business t' run. Call me when you get a chance."

The last message was from Maya Adamant.

"Mr. Rawlins, Mr. Lee is willing to come to an agreement about your information. And where he cannot see paying you the full amount, he's willing to compromise. Call me at my home number."

Instead I called the harbormaster at the Catalina marina and left a message for my son. Then the international operator con-nected me with a number Bonnie had left.

"Hello?" a man said. His voice was very sophisticated and European.

"Bonnie Shay," I uttered in the same muted tones that Mouse had used.

"Miss Shay is not in at the moment. Is there a message?"

I almost hung up the phone. If I were a younger man I would have.

"Could you write this down please?" I asked Joguye Cham.

"Hold a minute," he said. Then, after a moment, he said, "Go on."

"Tell her that there's a problem at the house. It could be dangerous. Tell her not to go there before calling EttaMae. And say that this has nothing to do with our talk before she left. It's business and it's serious."

"I have it," he said and then he read it back to me. He got every word. His voice had taken on an element of concern.

I disconnected the line and took a deep breath. That was all the energy I could expend on Bonnie and Joguye. I didn't have time to act the fool.

I dialed another number.

"Saul Lynx investigations," a woman's voice answered.

It was Saul's business line in his home.

"Doreen?"

"Hi, Easy. How're you?"

"If blessings were pennies I wouldn't even be able to buy one stick of gum."

Doreen had a beautiful laugh. I could imagine her soft brown features raising into that smile of hers.

"Saul's in San Diego, Easy," she said, and then, more seriously, "He told me about Feather. How is she?"

"We got her into a clinic in Switzerland. All we can do now is hope."

"And pray," she reminded me.

"I need you to give Saul a message, Doreen. It's very important."

"What is it?"

"You got a pencil and paper?"

"Right here."

"Tell him that the Bowers case has gone sour, rancid, that I had a visit from Adamant and a man came here that, uh . . . Just tell Saul that I need to talk to him soon."

"I'll tell him when he calls, Easy. I hope everything's okay."

"Me too."

I pressed the button down with my thumb and the phone rang under my hand. Actually it vibrated first and then rang. I remember because it got me thinking about the mechanism of my phone.

"Yeah?"

"Dad, what's wrong?" Jesus asked. "Is Feather okay?"

"She's fine," I said, glad to be giving at least one piece of good news. "But I need you to leave Catalina right now and go down to that place you dock near San Diego."

"Okay. But why?"

"I crossed a bad guy and he knows where we live. Bonnie and Feather are safe in Europe but I don't know if he got into the house and read Benny's note. So go to San Diego and don't come home until I tell you to. And don't tell anybody, anybody, where you're going."

"Do you need help, Dad?"

"No. I just need time. And you stayin' down there will give it to me."

"I'll call EttaMae if I need to talk to you?"

"You know the drill."

I ERASED ALL THE MESSAGES and then disconnected the answering machine so that Cicero wouldn't be able to break in and listen to my news. I left the building by a little-used side entrance and walked around the block to get to my car. I drove straight from there over to Cox Bar.

Ginny told me that Mouse hadn't been around yet that day and so he'd probably be there soon. I took a seat in the darkest corner nursing a Pepsi.

The denizens of Cox Bar drifted in and out. Grave men and now and then a wretched woman or two. They came in quietly, drank, then left again. They hunched over tables murmuring empty secrets and recalling times that were not at all what they remembered.

At other occasions I had felt superior to them. I'd had a job, a house in West L.A., a beautiful girlfriend who loved me, two wonderful children, and an office. But now I was one step away from losing all of that. All of it. At least most of the people at Cox Bar had a bed to sleep in and someone to hold them.

After an hour I gave up waiting and drove off in my souped-up Pontiac.

ETTAMAE AND MOUSE had a nice little house in Compton. The yard sloped upward toward the porch, where they had a padded bench and a redwood table. In the evenings they sat outside eating ham hocks and greeting their neighbors.

Etta's sepia hue and large frame, her lovely face and iron-willed gaze, would always be my standard for beauty. She came to the screen door when I knocked. She smiled in such a way that I knew Mouse wasn't home. That's because she knew, and I did too, that if there had been no Raymond Alexander we would have been married with a half-dozen grown kids. I had always been her second choice.

When I was a young man that was my sorrow.

"Hi, Easy."

"Etta."

"Come on in."

The entrance to their small house was also the dining room. There were stacks of paper on the table and clothes hung on the backs of chairs.

"'Scuse the mess, honey. I'm jes' doin' my spring cleanin'."

"Where's Mouse, Etta?"

"I don't know."

"When you expect him?"

"No time soon."

"He left for Texas?"

"I don't know where he went . . . after I kicked his butt out."

I wasn't ready for that. Every once in a while Etta would kick Mouse out of the house. I had never figured out why. It wasn't for anything he'd done or even anything that she suspected. It was almost as if spring cleaning included getting rid of a man.

The problem was I needed Raymond, and with him being gone from the house he could be anywhere.

"Hello, Mr. Rawlins," a man said from the inner door to the dining room.

The white man was tall, and even though he was in his mid-thirties his face belonged on a boy nearer to twenty. Blue eyes, blond hair, and the fairest of fair skin — that was Peter Rhone, a man I'd cleared of murder charges after the riots that decimated Watts. He'd met Etta at a funeral I gave for the young black woman, Nola Payne, who had been his lover. Gruff EttaMae was so moved by the pain this white man felt over the loss of a black woman that she offered to take him in.

His wife had left him. He had no one else.

He wore jeans and a T-shirt and the saddest face a man can have.

"Hey, Pete. How's it goin'?"

He sighed and shook his head.

"I'm trying to get on my feet," he said. "I'll probably go back to school to learn auto mechanics or something like that."

"I got a friend livin' in a house I own on One-sixteen," I said. "Primo. He's a mechanic. If I ask him I'm sure he'll show you the ropes."

Rhone had been a salesman brokering advertising deals with companies that didn't have offices in Los Angeles. But he had a new life now, or at least the old life was over and he was waiting on Etta's porch for the new one to kick in.

"Don't take my boy away from me so quick, Easy," Etta said. "You know he earns his keep just workin' round the house here."

Peter flashed a smile. I could see that he liked being kept on the back porch by EttaMae.

"You know where I can find Mouse?" I asked.

"No," Etta said.

Peter shook his head.

"Well okay then," I said. "I got to find him, so if he calls tell him that. And if Bonnie or Jesus call just tell 'em to stay away until I say they can come back."

"What's goin' on, Easy?" Etta asked, suddenly suspicious.

"I just need a little help on somethin'."

"Be careful now," she said. "I kicked him out but that don't mean I want him in a casket."

"Etta, how you expect somebody like me to be a threat to him?" I asked even though I had once nearly gotten her man killed.

"You the most dangerous man in any room you in, Easy," she said.

I didn't argue with her assessment because I suspected that she might be right.

28

There was a place called Hennie's on Alameda. It took up the third floor of a building that occupied an entire block. That building once housed a furniture store before the riots depleted its stock. Hennie's wasn't a bar or a restaurant; it wasn't a club or private fraternity either — but it was any one of those things and more at different times of the week. It had a kitchen in the back and round folding tables in the hall. One evening Hennie's would host a recital for some church diva from a local choir; later that same night there might be a high-stakes poker game for gangsters in from St. Louis. There had been retirement parties for aldermen and numbers runners there. It was an all-purpose room for a select few.

You never went to Hennie's unless you'd been invited. At least I never did. For some people the door was always open. Mouse was one of them.

Marcel John stood at the downstairs alley door that led up to Hennie's. Marcel was a big man with a heavyweight's physique and an old woman's face. He had a countenance of sad kindliness but I knew that he'd killed half a dozen men for money before coming to work for Hennie. He wore an old-fashioned brown woolen suit with a gold watch chain in evidence. A purple flower drooped in his lapel.

"Marcel," I said in greeting.

He raised his head in a half-inch salutation, watching me with those watery grandmother eyes.

"Lookin' for Mouse," I said.

I'd said those words so many times in my forty-six years that they might have been an incantation.

"Not here."

"He needs to be found."

Marcel's wide nostrils flared even further as he tried to get the scent of my purpose. He took in a deep breath and then nodded. I walked past him into the narrow stairway that went upward without a turn, to the third-floor entrance on the other side of the building.

When I neared the top the ebony wood door swung open and Bob the Baptist came out to meet me.

Bob the Baptist's skin was toasted gold. His features were neither Caucasian nor Negroid. Maybe his grandmother had been an Eskimo or a Hindu deity. Bob was always grinning. And I knew that if he hadn't gotten the signal from Marcel he would have been ready to shoot me in the forehead.

"Easy," Bob said. "What's your business, brother?"

"Lookin' for Mouse."

"Not here." Bob, who was wearing loose white trousers and a blue box-cut shirt, twisted his perfect lips to add, *Oh well, see you later.*

"He needs finding," I said, knowing that even the self-important employees of Hennie's wouldn't want to cross Raymond Alexander.

He had to let me in but he didn't have to like it.

"You armed?" he asked, the godlike grin wan on his lips.

"Yes I am," I said.

He sniffed, considering if I was a threat, decided I was not, and moved aside.

Hennie's was mostly one big room that took up nearly the entire floor. It was empty that day. As I walked from Bob's post to the other side my footfalls echoed, announcing my approach.

Hennie was sitting at a small round table against the far wall. There was a brandy snifter in front of him, also the *Los Angeles Examiner,* opened to the sports page. He had a half-smoked cigar smoldering in a cut crystal ashtray.

He was a dapper soul, wearing a dark blue suit, an off-white satin shirt, and a red tie held down by a pearl tack. The shirt was so bright that it seemed to flare from his breast. His hair was close-cropped and his skin was black as an undertaker's shoes.

"I'm readin' the paper," he said, not inviting me to sit. He didn't even look up to meet my eye.

"You see Mouse in there?" I took out my pack of Parliaments and produced a cigarette, which I proceeded to light.

"Raymond didn't leave me any messages for you, Easy Rawlins."

"The message is for him," I said.

He finally looked up.

"What is it?" Hennie's eyes had no sparkle to them whatsoever, giving the impression that he had seen such bad times that all of his hope had died.

"It's for Mouse," I said.

Hennie stared at me for a few seconds and then called out, "Melba!"

"Yes, Daddy," a high-toned woman's voice called back.

She came into a doorway about ten feet away.

"Bring me the phone."

"Yes, Daddy."

Melba belonged with that crew. Her skin was the color of a reddish-brown plantain. Her breasts were small but her butt was quite large. She balanced precariously on high heels that were on their way to becoming stilts. The black dress was midthigh and she walked with a circular movement which made even that pedestrian activity seem like dancing.

She brought a black phone on an extremely long cord. If she'd wanted to she could have dragged it all the way to Bob the Baptist's chair.

She offered the phone to Hennie.

He declined, saying, "Dial Raymond."

She did so, though she seemed to have some difficulty maintaining her balance and dialing at the same time.

The moments lagged by.

"Mr. Alexander?" she asked in her child's voice. "Hold on, I got Daddy on the line."

She handed the receiver to Hennie. He took it while staring at my forehead.

"Raymond? . . . I got Easy Rawlins here sayin' that you need findin'. . . . Uh-huh . . . uh-huh. . . . You got that thing covered for Julius? . . . All right then. Talk to you."

He handed the receiver back to Melba and she sashayed away.

"You know the funeral parlor down on Denker?" Hennie asked me.

"Powell's?"

"Yeah. There's a red house next door that got a garage behind it. Raymond's in the apartment above that."

"Thank you," I said taking in a deep draft of smoke.

"And don't come here no more if I don't ask ya," he added.

"So you sayin' that if I'm lookin' for Raymond don't ask you?" I asked innocently.

And Hennie winced. I liked that. I liked it a lot.

I DROVE from Hennie's to Powell's funeral parlor. I marched down the driveway to the garage next door. But there I stopped. The door was ajar and those stairs were daring me to come on. It was twilight and the world around me was slowly blending into gray. Going to Mouse over this problem would, I knew, create problems of its own. With no exaggeration Mouse was one of the most dangerous individuals on the face of the earth.

And so I stopped to consider.

But I didn't have a choice.

Still, I took the stairs one at a time.

The apartment door was also partly open. That was a bad sign.

I heard women's voices inside. They were laughing and cooing.

"Raymond?" I said.

"Come on in, Easy."

The sitting room was the size of a tourist-class cabin on an ocean liner. The only place to sit comfortably was a plush red couch. Mouse had the middle cushion and two large, shapely women took up the sides.

"Well, well, well. There you are at last. Where you been?"

"Gettin' into trouble," I said.

Mouse grinned.

"This is Georgette," he said, waving a hand at the woman on his right. "Georgette, this Easy Rawlins."

She stood up and stuck out her hand.

"Hi, Easy. Pleased to meet you."

She was tall for a woman, five eight or so, the color of tree bark. She hadn't made twenty-five, which was why the weight she carried seemed to defy the pull of gravity. For all her size her waist was slender, but that wasn't her most arresting feature. Georgette gave off the most amazing odor. It was like the smell of a whole acre of tomato plants — earthy and pungent. I took the hand and raised it to my lips so that I could get my nose up next to her skin.

She giggled and I remembered that I was single.

"And this here is Pinky," Mouse said.

Pinky's body was similar to her friend's but she was lighter skinned. She didn't stand up but only waved her hand and gave me a half smile.

I hunkered down on the coffee table that sat before the couch.

"How you all doin'?" I asked.

"We ready to party tonight — right, girls?" Mouse said.

They both laughed. Pinky leaned over and gave Raymond a deep soul kiss. Georgette smiled at me and moved her butt around on the cushion.

"What you up to, Easy?" Mouse asked.

He planned to have a party with just him and the two women. At any other time I would have given some excuse and beaten a hasty retreat. But I didn't have the time to waste. And I knew that I had to explain to Mouse why I didn't go on the heist with him before I could ask for help.

"I need to talk to you, Ray," I said, expecting him to tell me I had to wait till tomorrow.

"Okay," he said. "Girls, we should have some good liquor for this party. Why'ont you two go to Victory Liquors over on Santa Barbara and get us some champagne?"

He reached into his pocket and came out with two hundred-dollar bills.

"Why we gotta go way ovah there?" Pinky complained. "There's a package sto' right down the street."

"C'mon, Pinky," Georgette said as she rose again. "These men gotta do some business before we party."

When she walked past me Georgette held her hand out — palm upward. I kissed that palm as if it were my mother's hand reaching out to me from long ago. She shuddered. I did too.

Mouse had killed men for lesser offenses but I was in the frame of mind where danger was a foregone conclusion.

After the women were gone I turned to Raymond.

He was smiling at me.

"You dog," he said.

29

S orry 'bout the job, Ray."
    I moved over to the couch. He slid to the side to give
me room.

"That's okay, Ease. I knew it wasn't your thing. But you
wanted money an' that Chicago syndicate's been my cash cow."

"Did I cause you a problem with them?"

"They ain't gonna fuck wit' me," Mouse said with a sneer.

He sat back and blew a cloud of smoke at the ceiling. He
wore a burgundy satin shirt and yellow trousers.

"What's wrong then?" I asked.

"What you mean?"

"I don't know. Why you send those girls off?"

"I was tired anyway. You wanna get outta here?"

"What about Pinky and Georgette?"

"T'ont know. Shit . . . all they wanna do is laugh an' drink up my liquor."

"An' you wanna talk?"

"I ain't got nuthin' t' laugh about."

Living my life I've come to realize that everybody has different jobs to do. There's your wage job, your responsibility to your children, your sexual urges, and then there are the special duties that every man and woman takes on. Some people are artists or have political interests, some are obsessed with collecting seashells or pictures of movie stars. One of my special duties was to keep Raymond Alexander from falling into a dark humor. Because whenever he lost interest in having a good time someone, somewhere, was likely to die. And even though I had pressing business of my own, I asked a question.

"What's goin' on, Ray?"

"You have dreams, Easy?"

I laughed partly because of the dreams I did have and partly to put him at ease.

"Sure I do. Matter'a fact dreams been kickin' my butt this last week."

"Yeah? Me too." He shook his head and reached for a fifth of scotch that sat at the side of the red sofa.

"What kinda dreams?"

"I was glass," he said after taking a deep draft.

He looked up at me. I would have thought that wide-eyed vulnerability was fear in another man's face.

"Glass?"

"Yeah. People would walk past me an' look back because they saw sumpin' but they didn't know what it was. An' then, then I bumped inta this wall an' my arm broke off."

"Broke off?" I said as a parishioner might repeat a minister's phrase — for emphasis.

"Yeah. Broke right off. I tried to catch it but my other hand was glass too an' slippery. The broke arm fell to the ground an' shattered in a million pieces. An' the people was just walkin' by not even seein' me."

"Damn," I said.

I was amazed not by the content but by the sophistication of Mouse's dream. I had always thought of the diminutive killer as a brute who was free from complex thoughts or imagination. Here we'd known each other since our teens and I was just now seeing a whole other side of him.

"Yeah," Mouse warbled. "I took a step an' my foot broke off. I fell to the ground an' broke all to pieces. An' the people jes' walked on me breakin' me down inta sand."

"That's sumpin' else, man," I said just to keep him in the conversation.

"That ain't all," he declared. "Then, when I was crushed inta dust the wind come an' all I am is dust blowin' in the air. I'm everywhere. I see everything. You'n Etta's married an' LaMarque is callin' you Daddy. People is wearin' my jewelry an' drivin' my car. An' I'm still there but cain't nobody see me or hear me. Ain't nobody care."

In a moment of sudden intuition I realized then the logic behind Etta's periodic banishment of Mouse. She knew how much he needed her, but he was unaware, and so she'd send him away to have these dreams and then, when he came back again, he'd be pleasant and appreciative of her worth — never knowing exactly why.

"You know, Easy," he said. "I been wit' two women every night since I walked out on Etta. An' I can still go all night long. Got them girls callin' in languages they didn't know they could talk. But even if I sleep on a bed full'a women I still have them dreams."

"Maybe you should give Etta another chance," I suggested. "I know she misses you."

"She do?" he asked me with all of the innocence of the child he never was.

"Yes sir," I said. "I saw her just today."

"Well," Mouse said then. "Maybe I'll make her wait a couple'a days an' then give her a break."

I doubted if Mouse connected the dream with Etta even though she came into the conversation so easily. But I could see that he was getting better by the moment. The prospect of a homecoming lifted his dark mood.

For a while he regaled me with stories of his sexual prowess. I didn't mind. Mouse knew how to tell a story and I had to wait to ask for my favor.

Half an hour later the door downstairs banged against the wall and the loud women started their raucous climb up the stairs.

"I better be goin', Ray," I said. "But I need your help in the mornin'."

I stood up.

"Stay, Easy," he said. "Georgette likes you an' Pinky gets all jealous when she got to share. Stay, brothah. An' then in the mornin' we take care'a this trouble you in."

Before I could say no the women came in the door.

"Hi, Ray," Pinky said. She had two champagne bottles under each arm. "We got a bottle for everybody."

Georgette lit up when she saw that I was still there. She perched on the table in front of me and put her hands on my knees.

Raymond smiled and I shook my head.

"I got to be goin'," I said.

BUT THE EVENING wore on and I was still there. I had nowhere to go. Mouse popped three corks and the ladies laughed. He was a great storyteller. And I rarely heard him tell the same story twice.

After midnight Pinky started kissing Ray in earnest. Georgette and I were on the couch with them, sitting very close. We were talking to each other, whispering really, when Georgette looked over and gave a little gasp.

I turned and saw that Pinky had worked Ray's erection out of his pants and was pulling on it vigorously. He was leaning back with closed eyes and a big smile on his lips.

"Let's go in the other room and give 'em some privacy," Georgette whispered in my ear.

The bedroom was small too, only large enough to accommodate a king-size bed and a single stack of maple drawers.

I closed the door and when I turned to face Georgette she kissed me. It was as passionate an embrace as I had ever known. Our tongues were speaking to each other. Hers telling me that I had her full attention and everything within her power to give. And mine telling her that I was desperately in need of someone to give me life and hope.

I put my hand under her coral blouse and laid the hot palm at the base of her neck. She groaned and so did Pinky in the next room.

Georgette reached for the lamp and turned it off.

"Turn it back on," I said.

She did.

I sat on the bed and stood her between my knees. Then I

191

started on the buttons of her blouse. She stood still, breathing lightly as I drew the silky top down and dropped it to the floor. She moved then, attempting to sit next to me, but I grabbed onto her forearms, making it clear that she was to stay where she was. I moved close to get my arms around to unhook the black bra she wore.

Her nipples were long, hard things. I licked them very lightly and she held my head, moving it the way she wanted my tongue to move.

The black miniskirt was tight around her butt, and taking it off while kissing her hard nipples I pulled the pink panties down too. Her pubic hair was broad and dense. I buried my face in it to get the full scent of that field of tomatoes. If I had any notion of stopping, it evaporated then.

Georgette was a large woman. And even though she was slim of waist her belly protruded a bit. Her navel was a deep hole, dark against even her dark skin. Tentatively I poked my tongue inside.

She gasped and jumped back, holding both hands in front of her stomach.

"Come back here," I said.

Georgette shook her head with a pleading look on her face.

Pinky started yelping in the next room.

"Come back here," I said again.

"It's too sensitive," she said.

I held out a hand and she allowed me to draw her near. I positioned her between my knees again and moved slowly toward the belly button.

This time I stuck my tongue all the way in so I could feel the rough skin at the bottom. I moved the tip of my tongue around and she shuddered, holding my head for support.

After a few seconds she cried, "Stop!"

I moved my head back and looked up into her eyes.

"This is like food to me, Georgette," I said. "Do you understand? Food for me."

She replied by pressing my face against her stomach. My tongue lanced out again and she screamed.

After another minute she moved my face back.

"Can I lay down now, baby?" she asked.

I moved to the side and she got down on her back.

We did things that night that I had never done with any woman. She did things to me that even now make me tremble with fervor and humiliation.

We fell asleep in each other's arms, still kissing, still rubbing.

But when I jolted awake, I found myself alone.

I stumbled to the toilet and then back into the living room. Mouse was laid out naked on the couch with his hands crossed over his chest like a dead king on display for the public to mourn. Pinky was gone.

30

Sensing me, Mouse roused from his slumber. He opened his eyes and frowned. Then he sat up and moved his head in a circle. His neck bones cracked loudly.

"Mornin', Easy."

"Ray."

"The girls gone?"

"I guess so."

"Good. Now we can take care'a business an' not have to mess with them."

He stood up and stomped into the bedroom toward the toilet.

I sat down and fell asleep in that position.

The flush of the toilet jolted me awake.

When Raymond came back in he'd put on black slacks and a black T-shirt — his work clothes.

"Place ain't got no kitchen," he said. "If you want coffee we gotta go to Jelly's down the street."

"What time they open?" I asked.

"What time you got?"

"Twenty past five."

"Let's go."

WE WALKED the few blocks down Denker. The sun was a crimson promise behind the San Bernardino Mountains.

"What you got, Easy?" Mouse asked when we were halfway to the doughnut shop.

"Man up in Frisco hired me to find a black girl named Cinnamon. I went to her boyfriend's house and found him dead —"

"Damn," Mouse said. "Dead?"

"Yeah. Then I came back down to L.A. I found the girl but she told me about a dude in a snakeskin jacket she thinks killed him. That day a man in a snakeskin jacket come around askin' at my house for me."

"He find Bonnie an' the kids?"

"She and Feather are in Switzerland and Jesus is out on his boat." I decided not to mention that Ray's ex-girlfriend was with my son.

"Good."

"So the guy shows up at my office. Says his name is Joe Cicero. He's a stone killer, I could see it in his eyes. He threatened my family."

"You fight him?"

"I took out the gun you gave me and he left."

"Why'idn't you shoot him?"

"There was other people around. I didn't think they'd lie for me."

Mouse shrugged at my excuse, neither agreeing nor disagreeing with the logic I offered. We'd arrived at the doughnut place. He pushed the glass door open and I followed him in.

Jelly's seating arrangement was a long counter in front of which stood a dozen stools anchored in a concrete shelf. Behind the counter were eight long slanted shelves lit by fluorescent lights. These shelves were crowded with every kind of doughnut.

A brown woman stood at the edge of the counter smoking a cigarette and staring off into space.

"Millie," Mouse said in greeting.

"Mr. Alexander," she replied.

"Coffee for me an' my friend." He took a seat nearest the door and I sat next to him. "What you eatin', Ease?"

"I'll take lemon filled."

"Two lemon an' two buttermilk," Mouse said to Millie.

She was already pouring our coffees into large paper cups.

I needed the caffeine. The way I figured it Georgette and I hadn't gotten to sleep until past three.

Our doughnuts came. We fired up cigarettes and drank coffee. Millie refilled our cups and then moved to the far end of the counter. I could tell that she was used to giving my friend his privacy.

"Thanks for talkin' to me last night, Easy," Mouse said.

"Sure." I wasn't used to gratitude from him.

"How you spell that guy's name?"

"The Roman is C-I-C-E-R-O but he didn't spell it for me."

"I'ma use a pay phone in back to ask around," he said. "Sit tight."

"Early to be callin' people isn't it?"

"Early for a man workin' for somebody else. But a self-employed man gotta get up when the cock crow." With that he walked toward the back of the shop and through a green doorway.

I sat there smoking and thinking about Joe Cicero. It didn't really make sense that he worked for Lee, because why would Lee fire me and then put a man on my tail? But there seemed to be a divide between Lee and his assistant. Maybe she had put Cicero on me. But again, why not just let me work for Lee and bring them what information I got? She was my only contact with the man.

A cool breeze blew on my back. I turned to see an older black man come in. His clothes were rumpled as if he had slept in them and he gave off an odor of dust as he went past. He sat two seats down from me and gestured to Millie (who never smiled) and murmured his order.

I put out my cigarette and thought about Haffernon. Maybe he hired Cicero. That could be. He was a powerful man. Then there was Philomena. But she had said that she was afraid of the snakeskin killer. That made me grin. The day I started believing what people told me would probably be the day I died.

The man next to me said something to the waitress. *Nice day,* I think.

And didn't Philomena say something about a cousin? And of course there was Saul. Maybe he knew more than he was letting on. Maybe he stumbled across something and was trying to get around me. No. Not Saul. At least not yet.

"They havin' a festival down Watts," I overheard the man saying to Millie. She didn't answer or maybe she whispered a reply or nodded.

Of course anyone who was involved in the business deal in Egypt might have hired Cicero. Anyone interested in those bearer bonds.

"So you too lofty to talk to me, huh?" the man was saying to Millie.

His anger caught my attention and so I glanced in his direction. Millie was at the far end of the counter and the rumpled man was staring at me.

"Excuse me?" I said.

"You too lofty to speak?" he asked.

"I didn't know you were talkin' to me, man," I said. "I thought you were speaking to the woman."

"Yeah," he said, not really replying, "I gots all kindsa time at sea with men from every station. Just 'cause my clothes is old don't mean I'm dirt."

"I didn't mean to say that . . . I was just thinkin'."

"In the merchant marines I seen it all," he said. "War, mutiny, an' so much money you choke a fuckin' elephant wit' it. I got chirren all over the world. In Guinea and New Zealand. I got a wife in Norway so china white an' beautiful she'd make you cry."

My mind was primed to wonder. I just moved it over to think about this man and all of his children and all of his women.

"Easy Rawlins," I said. I held out my hand.

"Briny Thomas." He took my hand and held on to it while peering into my eyes. "But you know the most important thing I ever learned in all my travels?"

"What's that?"

"The only law that matters is yo' own troof. You stick to what you think is right and when the day is done you will be satisfied."

Mouse was coming out from the green doorway.

I pulled my hand away from Briny.

Raymond stopped between us.

"Move on down the row, man," he said to the merchant marine. "Go on."

The old man had a good sense of character. He didn't even think twice, just picked up his coffee and moved four seats down.

"You should'a kilt that mothahfuckah, Easy. You should'a kilt him."

"Cicero?"

"My people tell me he's a bad man — a very bad man. Called him a assassin. Did work for the government, they said, an' then went out on his own."

Mouse had been frowning while telling me about Cicero but then, suddenly, he smiled.

"This gonna be goooood. Man like that let you know what you made of."

"Flesh and blood," I said.

"That ain't good enough, brother. You need some iron an' gunpowder an' maybe a little luck to get ya past a mothahfuckah like this here."

Raymond was happy. The challenge of Joe Cicero made him feel alive. And I have to say that I wasn't too worried either. It's not that I took a government-trained assassin lightly. But I had other work to do and my survival wasn't the most important thing on the list. If I died saving Feather then it was a good trade. So I smiled along with my friend.

Over his shoulder I saw Briny lift his coffee in a toast.

This gesture also gave me confidence.

31

After six cups of coffee, four doughnuts apiece, and half a pack of cigarettes, we made our way back to Mouse's pied-à-terre. He took the bedroom this time and I stretched out on the couch. That was a little shy of seven.

I didn't get up again until almost eleven.

It was a great sleep. To begin with there was no light in the cabinlike living room, and the couch was both soft and firm, filled as it was with foam rubber. No one knew where I was and I had Mouse to ride with me when I finally had to go out in the world. I had to believe that Feather's doctors would keep her alive and Bonnie didn't enter my thoughts at all. It's not that I was over her, but there's only so much turmoil that a heart can keep focused on.

Bonnie was a problem that had to come later.

While I was getting dressed I heard the toilet flush. Mouse

slept more lightly than a pride of lions. He once told me that he could hear a leaf thinking about falling from a tree.

He came out wearing a blue dress shirt under a herringbone jacket. His slacks were black. I went through to the restroom. There I shaved and washed the stink from my body with a washrag because Mouse's hideaway didn't have a shower or a tub.

At the door, on the way out, he asked me, "You armed?"

"I got a thirty-eight in my pocket, a Luger in my belt, and that twenty-five you gave me in the band of my sock."

He gave me an approving nod and led the way down the stairs.

IN 1966, L.A.'s downtown was mostly brick and mortar, plaster and stone. There were a few new towers of steel and glass but mostly squat red and brown buildings made up the business community.

I needed to gather some financial information and the best way to do that, I knew, was at the foot of the cowardly genius — Jackson Blue.

Jackson had left his job at Tyler after going out on a maintenance call to Proxy Nine Insurance Group, a consortium of international bank insurers. Jackson had come in to fix their computer's card reader and then (almost as an afterthought, to hear him tell it) he revamped the way they conducted their daily business. Their president, Federico Bignardi, was so impressed that he offered to double Jackson's salary and put him in charge of their new data processing department.

I drove down to about a block from Jackson's office and went to a phone booth. I was looking up the number in the white pages while Mouse leaned up against the door.

"Easy," he said in warning.

I looked up in time to see the police car rolling up to the curb.

I had found Jackson's company's number but I only had one coin. I didn't drop the dime, reasoning that I might have to make the call later on, from jail.

The other reason I held back was because I had to pay very close attention to events as they unfolded. There was always the potential for gunplay when you mixed Raymond Alexander and the police in the same bowl. He saw them as his enemy. They saw him as their enemy. And neither side would hesitate to take the other one down.

As the two six-foot white cops (who might have been brothers) stalked up to us, each with a hand on the butt of his pistol, I couldn't help but think about the cold war going on inside the borders of the United States. The police were on one side and Raymond and his breed were on the other.

I came out of the phone booth with my hands in clear sight. Raymond grinned.

"Good morning," one of the white men said. To my eyes only his mustache distinguished him from his partner.

"Officer," Mouse allowed.

"What are you doing here?"

"Calling a Mr. Blue," I said.

"Mr. Blue?" the policeman countered.

"He's a friend'a ours," I replied to his partial question. "He's a computer expert but we're here to ask him about bearer bonds."

"Bonds?" the cop with the hairless lip said.

"Yeah," Mouse said. "Bonds."

The way he said the word made me think of chains, not monetary instruments.

"And what do you need to know about bonds for?" one of the cops, I can't remember which one, asked.

My job was to make those cops feel that Raymond and I had a legitimate reason to be there at that phone booth on that street corner. Most Americans wouldn't understand why two well-dressed men would have to explain why they were standing on a public street. But most Americans cannot comprehend the scrutiny that black people have been under since the days we were dragged here in bondage. Those two cops felt fully authorized to stop us with no reason and no warrant. They felt that they could question us and search us and cart us off to jail if there was the slightest flaw in how we explained our business.

Even with all the urgency I felt at that moment I had a small space to hate what those policemen represented in my life.

But I could hate as much as I wanted: I still didn't have the luxury to defy their authority.

"I'm a private detective, Officer," I said. "Working for a man named Saul Lynx. He's got an office on La Brea."

"Detective?" No Mustache said. He was a king of the one-word question.

I took the license from my shirt pocket. Seeing this state-issue authorization so disconcerted them that they went back to their car to natter on their two-way radio.

"Bonds?" Mouse asked.

"Yeah. The man I told you about had gotten some Swiss bonds. Maybe it was Nazi money. I don't know."

"How much money?" he asked.

Why hadn't I asked that question of Cinnamon? The only answer that came to me was Cinnamon's kiss.

The cops came back and handed me my license.

"Checks out," one of them said.

"So may we continue?" I asked.

"Who are you investigating?"

"It's a private investigation. I can't talk about it."

And even though I don't remember which cop I was talking to, I do remember his eyes. There was hatred in them. Real hate. It's a continual revelation when you come to understand that the only thing you can expect in return for your own dignity is hatred in the eyes of others.

"BLUE," Jackson answered when the Proxy Nine operator transferred my call.

"I'm down here with Mouse, Jackson," I said. "We need to talk."

I could feel his hesitation in the silence on the line. That was often the way with poor people who had finally crawled out of hardship and privation. The only thing one of your old friends could do would be to pull you back down or bleed you dry. If it was anybody but me he would have made up some excuse. But Jackson was too deeply indebted to me for even his ungrateful nature to turn a deaf ear to my call.

"McGuire's Steak House down on Grant," he said in clipped words. "Meet you there at one-fifteen."

It was twelve fifty-five. Raymond and I walked to McGuire's at a leisurely pace. He was in a good mood, looking forward to getting back with Etta.

"You don't mind that white boy stayin' there while you gone?" I asked near the time of our meeting.

"Naw, man. I look at him like he the pet Etta never had. You know — a white dog."

There was something very ugly in the words and the way he said them. But ugly was the life we lived.

*   *   *

THE MAÎTRE D' frowned when we entered the second-floor restaurant but he changed his attitude when I mentioned Jackson Blue.

"Oh, Mr. Blue," he said in a slight French accent. "Yes, he is waiting for you."

With a snap of his fingers he caught the attention of a lovely young white woman wearing a black miniskirt and T-shirt top.

"These are Mr. Blue's guests," he said and she smiled at us like we were distant cousins that she was meeting for the first time.

The door she led us to opened on a private dining room dominated by a round table that could seat eight people comfortably.

Jackson stood up nervously when we walked in. He wore an elegant gray suit and sported the prescriptionless glasses that he claimed made him seem less threatening to white folks.

I didn't see how anyone could be intimidated by Jackson in the first place. He was short and thin with almost jet skin. His mouth was always ready to grin and he'd jump at the sound of a door slamming. But from the moment he put on those glasses white people all over L.A. started offering him jobs. I often thought that when he donned those frames he became another mild-mannered person. But what did I know?

"Jackson," Mouse hailed.

Jackson forced a grin and shook the killer's hand.

"Mouse, Easy, how you boys doin'?"

"Hungry as a mothahfuckah," Mouse said.

"I ordered already," Jackson told him. "Porterhouse steaks and Beaujolais wine."

"All right, boy. Shit, that bank treatin' you fine."

"Insurance company," Jackson corrected.

"They insure banks, right?" Mouse asked.

"Yeah. So, Easy, what's up?"

"Can I sit down first, Jackson?"

"Oh yeah, yeah, yeah, yeah. Sit, sit, sit."

The room was round too, with pastoral paintings on the wall. Real oil paintings and a vase with silk roses on a podium next to the door.

"How's life treatin' you, Jackson?"

"All right, I guess."

"Seems better than that. This is a fine place and they know your name at the door."

"Yeah . . . I guess."

I realized then that Jackson had been holding in tension. His face let go and there were traces of grief around his eyes and mouth.

"What's wrong, man?" I asked.

"Nuthin'."

"Is it Jewelle?"

"Naw, she fine. She managin' a motel down in Malibu."

"So what is it?"

"Nuthin'."

"Come on, Jackson," Mouse said then. "Easy an' me got serious business, so get on wit' it here. You look like the doctor just give you six months."

For a moment I thought the bespectacled genius was going to break down and cry.

"Well," he said, "if you have to know, it's a computer tape."

"You messed it up or somethin'?"

"Naw. I mean it's messed up all right. It's the TXT tape they drop on my desk ev'ry mornin' at three twenty-five."

"What's a TXT tape?" I asked.

"Transaction transmissions from all around the world . . . financial transactions."

"What about it?"

"Proxy got a hunnert banks for clients in the United States alone an' twice that in European banks. They transfer stock investments for special customers for less than a broker do."

"So what?" I asked.

"It's anywhere from three hunnert thousand to four million dollars in transactions every day."

That got a long whistle from Mouse.

Jackson began to sweat.

"Yeah," Jackson said. "Every time I look at that thing my heart starts to thunderin'. It's like if some fine-assed girl took off her clothes and jump in yo' bed an' then say, 'I know you won't take advantage'a me, now will you?'"

Mouse laughed. I did too.

"Listen, Jackson," I said. "I need to know about Swiss bearer bonds."

"What kind?"

I told him all that I learned from Cinnamon.

"Yeah," he said in a way that I knew he was still thinking about that tape. "Yeah, if you bring me one I should be able to work up a pedigree. The people I work with use bonds like that all the time. I got access to everything they do. If a bearer bond got a special origin I could prob'ly sniff it out."

Our steaks came soon after that. Mouse ate like two men. Jackson didn't even touch his food. After the meal was over Jackson took the check. I had known him nearly thirty years and that was the first time he ever willingly paid for a meal.

We made small talk for a while. Mouse caught Jackson up on what our mutual friends were doing. Who was up, who was dead. After forty-five minutes or so Jackson looked at his watch and said that he had to get back to work.

At the door Mouse took him by the arm.

"You like that little girl Jewelle?" he asked.

"Love her," Jackson said.

"How 'bout yo' car an' clothes an' this here job?"

"Great. I never been so happy. Shit, I do stuff most people don't even know that they don't know about."

"Then why you so hot and bothered over a few dollars on a tape? Fuck that tape, man. That money ain't gonna suck yo' dick. Shit, if you happy then keep on doin' what you doin' an' don't let the niggah in you run riot."

Raymond's words transformed Jackson as he heard them. He gave a little nod and the hopelessness in his eyes faded a little.

"Yeah, you right," he said. "You right."

"Damn straight," Mouse said. "We ain't dogs, man. We ain't have to sniff after them. Shit. You an' me an' Easy here do things our mamas an' papas never even dreamed they could do."

I appreciated being included in the group but I realized that Mouse and Jackson were living on a higher plane. One was a master criminal and the other just a genius, but both of them saw the world beyond a paycheck and the rent. They were beyond the workaday world. I wondered at what moment they had left me behind.

32

I dropped Mouse off at his apartment on Denker. He told me that he was going to look into Cicero, his habits and friends.

"If you lucky, Ease," he told me, "the mothahfuckah be dead by the time you see me again."

Most other times I would have tried to calm Mouse down. But I had looked into Joe Cicero's eyes deeply enough to know, all other things being equal, that he was the killer and I was the prey.

SAUL LYNX AND DOREEN lived on Vista Loma in View Park at that time. Their kids had a yard to play in and colored neighbors who, on the whole, didn't mind the interracial marriage.

Doreen came to the door with a toddler crying in her arms.

"Hi, Easy," she said.

We had a pretty good relationship. I respected her husband and didn't have any problem with their union.

"Saul call yet, honey?"

"No. I mean . . . he called once but George answered it and he didn't call me. I was hanging clothes on the line out back."

I could see my disappointment register on her face.

"I'm sure that he'll call soon though," she said. "He calls every evening about six."

It was just past three.

"Do you mind if I come back at about five-thirty or so? I really have to talk to Saul."

"Sure, Easy. Can I help you?"

"I don't think so, honey."

"How's it going with Feather?"

"I'll catch you in a couple'a hours," I said. I didn't have the heart to talk about Feather one more time.

WHEN CINNAMON DIDN'T ANSWER my knock I figured that either she was dead or out eating. If she'd been killed, there wouldn't be anything to learn from her body. If she'd had the bonds they'd be gone, and so the only thing I could gain by breaking in would be another possible murder charge. So I decided to sit at a bus stop bench across the street and wait until she returned or it was time for me to go talk to Saul.

While waiting I thought about my plan of action. Survival was the priority. I had to believe that Joe Cicero wanted to kill Cinnamon and anyone else that got in his way. Therefore he had to go — one way or another. The police wouldn't help me. I had no evidence against him. Axel Bowers was dead but I couldn't prove who had killed him. All I could do would be to tell the cops where his body was hidden — and that would point a finger at me.

Money was the next thing on my mind. I needed to pay for Feather. It was then that I remembered Maya Adamant's last call.

There was a phone booth down the street from the Pixie Inn. I called my old friend the long-distance operator and asked for another collect call.

"Lee investigations," Maya answered.

"I have a collect call for anyone from Easy Rawlins. Do you accept the charges?"

"Yes, operator," she said a little nervously.

"How much?" I asked.

"You were supposed to call me yesterday — at my house."

"I'm callin' you now." I wondered if Bobby Lee had his phones bugged too. Maya was probably thinking the same.

"Where are you?"

"Down the street from the apartment where Cinnamon Cargill is staying."

"What's that address?"

"How much?" I asked again.

"Three thousand dollars for the addresses of Cargill and Bowers."

"It's the same address," I said.

"Okay."

I couldn't tell if she knew about Bowers's death so I decided to try another approach.

"Tell me about Joe Cicero," I said.

"What about him?" she asked at about half the volume of her regular voice.

"Did you put him on me?"

"I don't know what you're talking about, Mr. Rawlins. I know the name and the reputation of the man Joe Cicero but I have never had any dealings with him."

"No? Then what was Joe Cicero doin' at my office askin' about Cinnamon Cargill?"

"I have no idea. But you'd be smart to look out for a man like that. He's a killer, Mr. Rawlins. The best thing you could do would be to give Mr. Lee the information he wants, take the money, and then leave town for a while."

I had to smile. Usually when I was working I was the one who did the manipulating of people's fears. But here Maya was trying to maneuver me.

"Thirty thousand dollars," I said.

"What?"

"Thirty grand and I give you everything you want. But it gots to be thirty and it gots to be today. Tomorrow it goes up to thirty-five."

"A dead man has no use for money, Ezekiel."

"You'd be surprised, Maya."

"Why would you think that Mr. Lee would be willing to pay such an outrageous figure?"

"First, I don't think Mr. Lee knows a thing about this conversation. Second, I don't know the exact amount on those bearer bonds —"

"What bearer bonds?"

"Don't try an' mess wit' me, girl. I know about the bonds because I've talked to Philomena. So like I was sayin' . . . I don't know exactly how much they're worth but I'm willing to wager that even after the thirty grand you and Joe Cicero will have enough left over to make me look like a bum."

"I have no business with Cicero," she said.

"But you know about the bonds."

"Call me this evening on my home phone," she said. "Call me then and we'll talk."

*   *   *

TWENTY MINUTES LATER Cinnamon walked up to her motel door. She was carrying a brown supermarket bag. It made me
like her more to see that she was conserving her money, buying
groceries instead of restaurant meals.

"Miss Cargill," I called from across the street.

She turned and waved to me as if I were an old friend.

She used her key on the lock and walked in, leaving the door
open for me. She was taking a box of chocolate-covered doughnuts from the bag when I came in.

"Have you heard anything about Axel?" were the first words
she said.

"Not yet. I had a visit from your friend in the snakeskin jacket
though."

There was fear in her eyes, no mistaking that. But that didn't
make her innocent, just sensible.

"What did he say?"

"He wanted to know where you were."

"And what did you tell him?"

"I pointed a gun at his eyeball and all he did was shrug. It's a
bad man who's not even afraid of a gun in his face."

"Did you shoot him?" she whispered.

"Somebody else asked me that," I replied. "I sure hope that
you're not like him."

"Did you shoot him?"

"No."

The fear crept over her face like night over a broad plain.

"What are you gonna do, Philomena?"

"What do you mean?"

"Nobody is interested in you. It's those bonds they want, and
that letter."

"I promised Axel that I'd hold them for him."

"Have you been calling him?" I asked.

"Yes. But he's nowhere to be found."

"Does he know how to get in touch with you?"

"Yes. Yes, he has Lena's number."

"What does that tell you, Philomena?" I asked, knowing that her boyfriend was long dead.

"But how can I be sure?"

"Those bonds are like a bull's-eye on you, girl," I said. "You need to use them to deal yourself out of danger."

I didn't feel guilty that getting those bonds might also net me thirty thousand dollars. I was trying to save Philomena's life too. You couldn't put a price tag on that.

"I don't know," she said sadly, hanging her head. She sat down on the bed. "I promised Axel to make sure the world knew about those bonds if he failed."

"What for?"

"Because they were wrong to do that work. Axel felt that it was a blight on him to live knowing that his father dealt with the Nazis."

"But his father's dead and he is too, probably. What good will it do you to join them?"

She clasped her hands together and began rocking back and forth.

Something about this motion made me think about her San Francisco apartment. That reminded me of something else.

"Who do you know in the Westerly Nursing Home?"

She looked up at me. There was no knowledge behind her eyes. She shook her head and stopped rocking.

"You called there from your home phone."

"I didn't. Maybe Axel did. He stayed over sometimes. If he used my phone he'd pay for it later."

I stared into those lovely eyes a moment longer.

"I don't know anyone in a nursing home," she said.

Whether she did or didn't, I couldn't tell. I moved on.

"Listen," I said. "Think about how much those bonds will be worth to you dead. Think it over. Talk with whoever you trust. I'm gonna write a number down on this paper here on the desk."

"What is it?"

"It's the phone number and address of a friend of mine — Primo. He lives in a house down on One-sixteen. Call him, go to him if you're scared. I'll be back later on tonight. But remember, if you want to get on with your life you got to work this thing out."

33

I got to Saul's at a quarter to six. Doreen and I sat in the living room surrounded by their three kids. Their eight-year-old daughter, Miriam, was listening to a pink transistor radio that hung from her neck on a string necklace, also pink. She had brown hair that drooped down in ringlets and green eyes, a gift from her father. George, the five-year-old, had the TV on and he was jumping around on a threadbare patch of carpet, acting out some swashbuckling derring-do. Simon, the toddler, was wandering back and forth between his sister and brother, making sounds that wouldn't be understood for another six months or so.

"So how long will Feather have to be in the clinic?" Doreen asked.

"Might be as long as six months."

"Six months?" Miriam cried. "I could go visit her if she's lonely."

"It's in Switzerland," I explained to the good girl.

"We could go to 'itzerland," George said, bravely swinging his imaginary sword.

"It's way far away in the Valley," Miriam told her brother.

"I know that," George said. "We could still go."

"Can we go, Mom?" Miriam asked Doreen.

"We'll see."

It was then that the phone rang.

"Daddy!" George yelled.

"No, George," Doreen said but the boy leaped for the phone on the coffee table.

Doreen put out her hand and George bounced backward, falling on his backside. As Doreen was saying hello, George began to howl. I saw her mouth Saul's name but I couldn't hear what she was saying because Simon was crying too and Miriam was shouting for them both to be quiet.

Doreen gestured toward the kitchen. I knew they had an extension in there and so I went on through, closing the door behind me.

"Hello!" I yelled. "I got it, Doreen!"

When she hung up the sound of the crying subsided somewhat.

"Easy," Saul said. "What's wrong?"

"I got a visit from a guy yesterday," I said. "He knew that I was working on the Lee case. He told me to give him what I knew or he'd kill me and my family too."

"What was this guy's name?"

"Cicero."

"Joe Cicero?"

"You know him?"

"Don't go home, Easy. Don't go to your office or your job. Call this number." He gave me an area code and a number, which I wrote down on a notepad decorated with pink bunnies. "I'll be there as soon as I can. Put my wife back on the line."

When I went back into the TV room the children had quieted down.

"Saul wants to talk to you, Doreen," I said and she took up the phone.

"Daddy!" George cried.

"Dada," Simon echoed.

Miriam watched her mother's eyes. So did I.

We both saw Mrs. Lynx's expression change from attentive interest to fear. Instead of answering she kept nodding her head. She reached for her pocketbook on the coffee table.

"I wanna talk to Daddy," George complained.

Doreen gave him one stern look and he shut right up.

"Okay," Doreen said. "All right. I will. Be careful, Saul."

She hung up the phone and stood in one fluid movement.

"Holiday time," she said in a forced happy voice. "We're all going to Nana's cabin in Mammoth."

"Yah," George cried.

Simon laughed but Miriam had a grim look on her face. She was getting older and understood that something was wrong.

"Saul said that he'd be at the meeting place by nine tonight," Doreen told me. "He's in San Diego but he said that he'd drive straight there."

"What meeting place? He just gave me a number."

"Call it and they will tell you where to go."

"Is Daddy okay, Mommy?" Miriam asked.

"He's fine, sweetie. Tonight he's going to meet with Mr. Rawlins and then he's coming up to the cabin where we can go fishing and swimming."

"But I have my clarinet lesson tomorrow," Miriam said.

"You'll have to take a makeup," Doreen explained.

The two boys were capering around, celebrating the holiday that had befallen their family.

I LEFT DOREEN packing suitcases and keeping the children on track.

On the way down to the Pixie Inn I tried not to get too far ahead of myself. Saul's reaction to just a name increased my fears. I decided that Cinnamon had to be moved to a place where I knew that she'd be safe.

I parked down the block this time, just being cautious. There was a Mercedes-Benz parked on the motel lot. I didn't like that. I liked it even less when I saw the words *Fletcher's Mercedes-Benz of San Francisco* written on the license plate frame.

The door of Cinnamon's room was ajar. I nudged it open with my toe.

He was lying facedown, the six-hundred-dollar suit now just a shroud. I turned him over with my foot. Leonard Haffernon, Esquire, was quite dead. The bullet had entered somewhere at the base of the skull and exited through the top of his head.

The exit wound was the size of a silver dollar.

A wave of prickles went down my left arm. Sweat sprouted from my palms.

His valise was on the bed. Its contents had been turned out. There was some change and a toenail clipper, a visitor's pass to a San Francisco bank, and a silver flask. Any papers had been taken. The only potential perpetrator in evidence, once more, was me.

For a brief moment I was frozen there like a bug in a sudden frost. I was trying to glean from Haffernon's face what had occurred. Did Cinnamon kill him and run?

Probably.

But why? And why had he been there?

A horn honked out on the street. That brought me back to my senses. I walked out of that room and into the parking lot, then down the street to my loud car and drove away.

34

I drove for fifteen minutes, looking in the rearview mirror every ten seconds, before stopping at a gas station on a block of otherwise burned-out buildings. There was a phone booth next to the men's toilet at the back.

"Etta, is that you?" I asked when she answered on the ninth ring.

"Is it my number you dialed?"

"Have you heard from Raymond?"

"And how are you this evenin', Mr. Rawlins? I'm fine. I was layin' up in the bed watchin' *Doctor Kildare*. How 'bout you?"

"I just stumbled on a dead white man never saw it comin'."

"Oh," Etta said. "No, Ray haven't called."

"Shit."

"Primo did though."

"When?"

"'Bout a hour. He said to tell you that a guy came by an' left sumpin' for ya."

"What guy?"

"He didn't say."

"What did he leave?"

"He didn't say that either. He just said to tell you. You in trouble, Easy?"

"Is the sky blue?"

"Not right now. It's evenin'."

"Then wait a bit. It'll be there."

Etta chuckled and so did I. She was no stranger to violent death. She'd once shot a white man, a killer, in the head because he was about to shoot me. If we couldn't laugh in the face of death there'd be precious little humor for most black southerners.

"You take care, Easy."

"Tell Mouse I need his advice."

"When I see him."

I SPED OVER to Primo's place worried about having given his number to Philomena. Primo was a tough man, a Mexican by birth. He had spent his whole life traveling back and forth across the border and south of there. On one trip through Panama he'd met Flower, his wife. They lived in a house I owned and had more than a dozen kids. They took in stray children too, and animals of all kinds. Any grief I brought to them would cause pain for a thousand miles.

But Primo was sitting out in the large yard. He was laid back in a lawn chair, drinking a beer and watching six or seven grandchildren play in the diminishing light. Flower was up on the porch with a baby in her arms. I wondered if it was her baby or just a grandchild.

As I approached, half a dozen dogs ran at me growling and crying, wagging their tails and baring their fangs.

"Hi-ya!" Primo shouted at the animals.

The children ran forward, grabbing the dogs and pulling them back. A pure-bred Dalmatian eluded his child handler and jumped on me, pressing my chest with his forepaws.

"That's my guard dog," Primo said.

He put out a hand, which I shook as the dog licked my forearm.

"Love thy neighbor," I said.

Primo liked my sense of humor. He laughed out loud.

"Flower," he called. "Your boyfriend is here."

"Send him to my bedroom when you finish twisting his ears," she responded.

"I wish I had time to sit, man," I said.

"But you want them papers." Primo finished my sentence.

"Papers?"

All the children, dogs, and adults crowded through the front door and into the house. There was shouting and laughing and fur floating in the air.

While Primo went into the back room looking for my delivery, Flower came very close to me. She stared in my face without saying anything.

She was a very black, beautiful woman. Her features were stern, almost masculine, most of the time, but when she smiled she honored the name her father had blessed her with.

At that moment she had on her serious face.

"How is she, Easy?"

"Very sick," I said. "Very sick."

"She will live," Flower told me. "She will live and you will have a beautiful granddaughter from her."

I touched Flower's face and she took my hand in hers.

The dogs stopped barking and the children hushed. I looked up and saw Primo standing there, smiling at me.

"Here it is," he said, handing me a brown envelope large enough to contain unfolded pages of typing paper.

"Who left this?"

"A black boy. Funny, you know?"

Raphael.

"What did he say?"

"That this was what you wanted and he hopes you do what's right."

I stood there thinking with all the brown children and red-tongued dogs panting around me.

"Stay and eat," Flower said.

"I got to go."

"No. You are hungry. Sit. It will only take a few moments and then you will have the strength to do whatever it is you're doing."

THAT WAS A TOUGH PERIOD in my life. There's no doubt about it. I was on the run in my own city, homeless if I wanted to live. Feather's well-being was never far from my heart, but the road to her salvation was being piled with the bodies of dead white men. And you have to understand the impact of the death of a white man on a black southerner like me. In the south if a black man killed a white man he was dead. If the police saw him on the street they shot first and asked questions . . . never. If he gave himself up he was killed in his cell. If the constable wasn't a murdering man then a mob would come and lynch the poor son of a bitch. And failing all that, if a black man ever made it to trial and was convicted of killing a white man — even in self-defense, even if it was to save another white man — that convict would spend the rest of his days incarcerated. There would be no parole, no commutation of sentence, no extenuating circumstances, no time off for good behavior.

There was no room in my heart except for hope that Feather would live. Hovering above that hope was the retribution of the white race for my just seeing two of their dead sons.

But even with all of that trouble I have to take time to recall Flower's simple meal.

She gave me a large bowl filled with chunks of pork loin simmered in a pasilla chili sauce. She'd boiled the chilies without removing the seeds so I began to sweat with the first bite. There was cumin and oregano in the sauce and pieces of avocado too. On the side I had three homemade wheat flour tortillas and a large glass of lightly sweetened lemonade.

I felt like a condemned man but at least my last meal was a feast.

AFTER I ATE I made noises about leaving, but Primo told me that I could use his den to take care of any business I needed to attend to.

In the little study I settled into his leather chair and opened the envelope left by Raphael.

There were twelve very official sheets of parchment imprinted with declarations in French, Italian, and German. Each page had a large sum printed on it and a red wax seal embossed at one corner or another. There was a very fancy signature at the bottom of each document. I couldn't make out the name.

And there was a letter, a note really, written in German and signed H. W. Göring. In the text of the note the name H. Himmler appeared. The note was addressed to R. Tourneau. I didn't need to know what the letter said. At any other time I would have burned it up and moved on with my life. But there was too much I didn't understand to discard such an important document.

I had what Lee wanted but I didn't trust that Maya would pass on the information. I didn't know how much the bonds were worth but I did know that they were said to be Swiss and that my daughter was in a Swiss hospital.

I called Jackson and gave him all the information I could about the bonds. He asked a few questions, directing me to codes and symbols that I would never have noticed on my own.

"It'd be better if I could check 'em myself, Ease," Jackson said at one point.

But remembering his quandary over the TXT tape on his desk, I said, "I better hold on to these here, Jackson. There's some bloodthirsty people out there willing to do anything to get at 'em."

Jackson backed down and I made my second call.

He answered the phone on the first ring.

"Easy?"

"Yeah. Who's this?"

"Christmas Black," the man said. I couldn't tell one thing about him. Not his age or his race.

"I'm up in Riverside," Black said, "on Wayfarer's Road. You know it?"

"Can't say that I do."

He gave me precise instructions that I wrote down.

"What do you have to do with all this?" I asked.

"I'm just a layover," he said. "A place to gather the troops and regroup."

After talking to Christmas I called EttaMae and left the particulars with her.

"Tell Mouse to come up when he gets the chance," I said.

"What makes you think I'll be talkin' to him anytime soon?"

"Is the sky blue?" I asked.

35

I took Highway 101 toward Riverside. The fact that I had a destination relaxed me some. The thousands of dollars in Swiss bonds on the seat beside me gave me heart. Haffernon's body and Cinnamon's involvement with his death were on my mind. And then there was the Nazi high command.

Like most Americans I hated Adolf Hitler and his crew of bloodthirsty killers. I hated their racism and their campaign to destroy any people not their own. In '45 I was a concentration camp liberator. My friends and I killed a starving Jewish boy by feeding him a chocolate bar. We didn't know that it would kill him. How could we?

Even as a black American I felt patriotic about the war and my role in it. That's why I found it so hard to comprehend wealthy and white American businessmen trading with such villains.

Between Feather and Bonnie, Haffernon and Axel, Cinnamon and Joe Cicero, it was a wonder that I didn't go crazy. Maybe I did, a little bit, lose control at the edges.

CHRISTMAS BLACK had given me very good directions. I skirted downtown Riverside and took a series of side streets until I came to a graded dirt road that was still a city street. The houses were a little farther apart than in Los Angeles. The yards were larger and there were no fences between them. Unchained dogs snapped at my tires as I drove past.

After a third of a mile or so I came to the dead end of Wayfarer's Road. Right where the road terminated stood a small white house with a yellow light shining over the doorway. It was the embodiment of peace and domesticity. You'd expect your aged, widowed grandmother to live behind that door. She'd have pies and a boiled ham to greet you.

I knocked and a child called out in some Asian language.

The door swung inward and a tall black man stood there.

"Welcome, Mr. Rawlins," he said. "Come in."

He was six foot four at least but his shoulders would have been a good fit for a man six inches taller. His skin was medium brown and there was a whitish scar beneath his left eye. The brown in his eyes was lighter than was common in most Negroes. And his hair was as close-cropped as you can get without being bald.

"Mr. Black?"

He nodded and stepped back for me to enter. A few steps away stood a small Asian girlchild dressed in a fancy red kimono. She bowed respectfully. She couldn't have been more than six years old but she held herself with the poise and attitude of the woman of the house. Just seeing her I knew that there was no wife or girlfriend in the black man's life.

"Easy Rawlins, meet Easter Dawn Black," Christmas said.

"Pleased to meet you," I said to the child.

"It is an honor to have you in our home, Mr. Rawlins," Easter Dawn said with solemnity.

To her right was a door open onto a bedroom, probably hers. On the other side was a cavernous sitting room that had a very western, almost cowboy feel to it. The girl gestured toward the sitting room and I followed her direction.

Behind Easter was a bronze mirror. In the reflection I could see the satisfaction in Christmas's face. He was proud of this little girl who could not possibly have been of his blood.

Feather came into my mind then and I tripped on the Indian blanket used as a throw rug. I would have fallen but Black was quick. He rushed forward and grabbed my arm.

"Thanks," I said.

The sitting room had a fifteen-foot ceiling, something you would never have expected upon seeing the seemingly small house from the road. Beyond that room was a kitchen with a loft above it, neither room separated by walls.

"Sit," Black said.

I sat down on one of the two wood-framed couches that he had facing each other.

He sat opposite me and flashed a brief smile.

"Tea?" Easter asked me.

"No thank you," I said.

"Coffee?"

"Naw. I would never get to sleep then."

"Ice water?"

"Are you going to keep on offering me drinks till you find one I want?" I asked her.

That was the first time she smiled. The beauty of her beaming face hurt me more than Bonnie and a dozen African princes ever could.

"Beer?" she asked.

"I'll take the water, honey."

"Daddy?"

"Whiskey and lime, baby."

The child walked away with perfect posture and regal bearing. I had no idea where she could have come from or how she got there.

"Adopted daughter," Black said. "I got her when she was a tiny thing."

"She's a beautiful princess," I said. "I have a girl too. Nothing like this one but I'm sure they'd be the best of friends."

"Easter Dawn doesn't have many friends. I'm schooling her here at home. You can't trust strangers with the people you love."

This felt like a deeply held secret that Christmas was letting me in on. I began to think that his bright eyes might have the light of madness behind them.

"Where you from?" I asked because he had no southern accent.

"Massachusetts," he said. "Newton, outside of Boston. You ever been there?"

"Boston once. I had a army buddy took me there after we were let go in Baltimore, after the war. Your family from there?"

"Crispus Attucks was one of my ancestors," Black said, nodding but not in a prideful way. "He was the son of a prince and a runaway slave. But most importantly he was a soldier."

There was a finality to every sentence he spoke. It was as if he was also royalty and not used to ordinary conversation.

"Attucks, huh?" I said, trying to find my way to a conversation. "That's the Revolutionary War there."

"My family's menfolk have been in every American war," he said, again with a remoteness that made him seem unstable. "Eighteen-twelve, Spanish-American, of course the Civil War. I myself have fought in Europe, and against Japan, the Koreans, and the Vietnamese."

"Here, Mr. Rawlins," Easter Dawn said. She was standing at my elbow holding a glass of water in one hand and her father's whiskey in the other.

Judging from her slender brown face and flat features I suspected that Easter had come from Black's last campaign.

She carried her father's whiskey over to him.

"Thanks, honey," he said, suddenly human and present.

"Easter here come from Vietnam?" I asked.

"She's my little girl," he said. "That's all we care about here."

Okay.

"What was your rank?" I asked.

"After a while it didn't matter," he said. "I was a colonel in Nam. But we were working in groups of one. You have no rank if there's nobody else there. Covered with mud and out for blood, we were just savages. Now how's a savage rate a rank?"

He shone those mad orbs at me and I believe that I forgot all the problems I came to his door with. Easter Dawn went to his side and leaned against his knee.

He looked down at her, placing a gigantic hand on her head. I could tell that it was a light touch because she pressed back into the caress.

"War has changed over my lifetime, Mr. Rawlins," Christmas Black said. "At one time I knew who the enemy was. That was clear as the nose on your face. But now . . . now they send us out to kill men never did anything to us, never thought one way or the other about America or the American way of life. When I realized that I was slaughtering innocent men and women I knew that the soldiering line had to come to an end with me."

Christmas Black could never hang out with the guys on a street corner. Every word he said was the last word on the subject. I liked the man and I knew he was crazy. The thing I didn't know was why I was there.

36

I was nursing my water, trying to think of some reply to a man who had just confessed to murder and gone on to his quest for redemption.

Lucky for me there came a knock at the door.

"It's Uncle Saul," Easter Dawn said. She didn't exactly shout but you could hear the excitement in her voice. She didn't exactly run either but rather rushed toward the front of the house.

"E.D.," Christmas said with authority.

The girl stopped in her tracks.

"What did I tell you about answering that door?" her father asked.

"Never open the door without finding out who it is," she said dutifully.

"Okay then."

She hurried on, followed by her father. I trailed after them.

"Who is it!" Easter Dawn shouted at the door.

"It's the big bad wolf," Saul Lynx replied in a playful voice he reserved for children.

The door flew open and Saul came in carrying a box wrapped in pink paper.

Easter Dawn put both hands behind her back and gripped them tightly to keep from jumping at him. He bent down and picked her up with one arm.

"How's my girl?"

"Fine," she said, obviously trying hard to restrain herself from asking what was in the box.

Christmas came up to them and put a hand on Saul's shoulder.

"How you doin'?" the black philosopher-king asked.

"Been better," Saul said.

By this time the girl had moved around until she had snagged the box.

"Is it for me?" she pleaded.

"You know it is," Saul said and then he put her down. "Hey, Easy. I see you made it."

"That reminds me," I said. "I gave Ray this address too. He should be by a little bit later."

"Who's that?" our host asked.

"Friend'a mine. Good guy in a pinch."

"Let's go in," Christmas said.

Easter ran before us, opening the present as she went.

SAUL SAT next to the war veteran and I sat across from them with my water.

"Joe 'Chickpea' Cicero" were the first words out of Saul's mouth. "The most dangerous man that anybody can think of. He's a killer for hire, an arsonist, a kidnapper, and he's also a torturer —"

"What's that mean?" I asked.

"It's widely known that if someone has a secret that you need to get at, all you have to do is hire Chickpea. He promises an answer to your question within seventy-two hours."

I glanced at Christmas. If he was frightened it certainly didn't show on his face.

"He's bad," Black agreed. "But not as bad as his rep. It's like a lot of white men. They can only see excellence in one of their own."

Excellence, I thought.

"That might be," Saul said. "But he's plenty dangerous enough for me."

Easter Dawn brought in a beer, which she offered to her Uncle Saul.

"Thanks, honey," Saul said.

"Easter, this is man talk," Christmas told the girl.

"But I wanted to show Mr. Rawlins my new doll," she said.

"Okay. But hurry up."

Easter ran out and then back again with a tallish figurine of an Asian woman standing on a platform and stabilized by a metal rod.

"You see," she said to me. "She has eyes like mine."

"I see."

The doll wore an elaborate black-and-gold robe that had a dragon stitched into it.

"That's a dragon lady," Saul told her, "the most important woman in the whole clan."

The child's eyes got bigger as she studied her treasure.

"You're spoiling her with all those dolls," Christmas said.

I was thinking about the assassin.

"No he's not, Daddy," Easter said.

"How many do you have now?"

"Only nine, and I have room for a lot more on the shelves you made me."

"Go on now and play with them," her unlikely father said. "I'll come say good night in an hour."

Decorum regained, Easter left the room and the men went back to barbarism.

"What's Cicero got to do with this?" Christmas asked.

"I don't know." Saul was wearing a tan suit with a brown T-shirt.

Christmas Black raised his head as if he'd heard something. A moment later there was a knock at the door.

"Stay in your room, E.D.," Christmas called.

We all went to the door together.

I had my hand on the .38 in my pocket.

Black pulled the door open and there stood Raymond.

"Christmas Day," Mouse hailed.

"Silent Knight," our host replied.

They shook hands and gave each other nods filled with mutual respect. I was impressed because Mouse's esteem was an event more rare than a tropical manifestation of the northern lights.

On our way back to the couches I felt my load lighten. With Raymond and someone he considered an equal on our side I didn't think that anyone would be too much for us.

I revealed as much of the story as I dared to. I told them about the state of Axel's house but not about finding his corpse. For that I relied on their imaginations when they heard about the meeting between Chickpea and Axel. I told them about Maya's calls and about finding Haffernon in Philomena's room. I told them about the existence of the bonds and the letter, but not that I had them.

"How much the bonds worth?" Raymond wanted to know.

"I don't know," I said. "Thousands."

"You think this Haffernon's the top man?" Christmas asked.

"Maybe. It's hard to tell. But if Haffernon was the boss, then who killed him? He is the one hired Lee. I'm sure of that."

"Lee has at least twenty operatives at his beck and call," Saul said.

"And if anybody's behind Haffernon," I added, "they'll have a whole army at their disposal."

"What's the objective, gentlemen?" Christmas asked.

"Kill 'em all," Mouse said simply.

Christmas's lower lip jutted out maybe an eighth of an inch. His head bobbed about the same distance.

"No." That was me. "We don't know which one of them it is."

"But if we do kill 'em all then the problem be ovah no mattah which one it was."

Christmas laughed for the first time.

Saul gave a nervous grin.

I said, "There's still the money, Ray."

"Money don't mean much if they put you in the ground, Ease."

"I can't go out killing people for no reason," Saul said.

"There's a reason," Christmas replied. "They suckered you in and now your life's on the line. The cops wouldn't touch this one and if they did they'd put you in jail. There's your reason."

"Yeah," I said, because once you invited men like Christmas and Mouse into the room Death had to have a seat at the table too. "But not before we find out what's what."

"An' how you plan to do that, Easy?" Mouse asked.

"We go to the horse's ass. We go to Robert E. Lee. He's the one brought us in. He should be able to find out what the problem is."

"What if he's the problem?" Christmas asked.

"Then we'll have to be smart enough to fool him into showing us that fact. The real problem is getting to him. I got the feelin' that Maya doesn't want that conversation to come about."

"That's easy," Saul told us. "Call him now, when she's not at work."

AFTER A SMALL STRATEGY discussion Saul dialed the number. It rang five times, ten. He wanted to hang up but I wouldn't let him. After at least fifty rings Lee answered his business phone.

"It's Saul Lynx, Mr. Lee. I'm calling you at this late hour because I have some fears that Maya may not be trustworthy. . . . The way I feel right now, sir, I wouldn't want to work for you again. . . . But you have to understand we believe . . . Mr. Rawlins and I believe that Axel Bowers was murdered and that Mr. Haffernon was too. . . . Yes . . . Easy has talked with Maya a few times since that initial meeting and he told her that he located Miss Cargill and that he'd spoken to Axel. Did she tell you about that? . . . I assume that she hasn't. . . . Sir, we need to meet . . . No, not at your house . . . Not in San Francisco. . . . There's a bar called Mike's on Slauson in Los Angeles. Easy and I want to meet you there."

There was a lot of argument about the meeting but Lee finally gave in. The way we figured it, if there was a problem between Maya and Lee he would have some inkling of it beyond our insinuations. If he doubted her loyalty he'd have to take the meeting.

As if she could read the vibrations in the air Easter Dawn made tea and brought it to us just when the call was over. Her father didn't chastise her for leaving her room.

I took the child on my lap and she sat there comfortably, listening to the men.

"I'll go with you and Raymond back to L.A.," Saul said.

"No. Go to your family, man. Ray and me can see to this."

"What about you?" Christmas asked Mouse.

"Naw, man. It ain't no war. Just one white boy think he bad. If I cain't take that then I'm past help."

Easter brought out her dolls after that and we all told her how beautiful they were. She basked in the attention of the four men and Christmas was glad for her. After he put her to bed we all left. Mouse asked Christmas could he leave his red El Dorado there for a few days. He wanted to be able to strategize with me on the ride.

When we approached my flashy Pontiac I felt that I was leaving something, a fellowship that I'd not known before. Maybe it was just sadness at leaving a home when I was homeless.

37

In the front yard Saul came up to us, shook Mouse by the hand, and then drew me away.

"Easy, I know I got you into this mess," he said. "Maybe I should come along."

"No, Saul, no. Neither you or me got the stomach for a man like this killer. Really Mouse would be better on this alone."

"Well then why don't you grab Jesus and come up and stay with us at the cabin?"

"Because EttaMae would kill me if I let her husband get shot out there. It already happened one time. I got to cover his back and you got to go to your family."

Saul gave me his hangdog stare. He was a homely man, there's no doubt about that. I held out a hand and he grabbed on to it.

"I'm sorry," he said.

"Don't be. I asked you for the job and you came through for

me. If I'm very lucky I'll come out of this alive and with the money for Feather's doctors. If I'm just plain old lucky I'll just get the money."

Saul nodded and turned to leave. I touched his arm.

"Why'd you want me to come out here?" I asked him. I thought I knew but I wanted to see what he had to say.

"I did Christmas a favor once. He's the kind of guy that takes a debt seriously. I wanted you to know him if you got into a bind. He'll do whatever it takes to make things right."

IT WAS LATE on the highway ride home. After my accident and two near misses I was paying close attention to the road and the speedometer. Mouse and I smoked with the windows down and the chilly breezes whipping around us.

After quite a while I asked, "So what's that Christmas Black's story?"

"What you mean?" Mouse asked. He understood my question; he was just naturally cagey.

"Is that his real name?"

"I think it is. All the kids in his family named after holidays. I think that's what he told me once."

"What's his story?" I asked again.

"He a terror," Mouse said.

"What's that supposed to mean?"

"He kilt a whole town once."

"A what?"

"Whole town. Men, women, chirren. All of 'em. Every last one." Mouse sneered thinking about it. "He kilt the dogs and the water buffaloes an' burnt down all the houses an' half the trees an' crops. Mothahfuckah kilt every last thing 'cept a couple'a chickens an' one baby girl."

"In Vietnam?"

"I guess it was. He didn't give the town a name. Maybe it was Cambodia or Laos maybe. Shit, the way he tell it, it could'a been anywhere. They just put that boy in a plane an' give him a parachute an' a duffel bag full'a guns an' bombs. Wherever he land people had to die."

"How do you know him?"

"Met once down in Compton. There was some guys thought they was bad messin' wit' a friend'a his. The dudes called themselves my friends an' so I looked into it. When I fount out what they was doin' I jes' smiled at Christmas. He taught 'em a lesson an' we went out to eat sour pork an' rice."

I was sure that there was more to the story but Raymond didn't brag about his crimes much anymore.

"So he left the army after killin' that village?"

"Yeah. I guess if you do sumpin' like that it's a li'l hard to live wit'. For him."

"You wouldn't take it hard if you had to kill like that?"

"I wouldn't never have to kill like that, Easy. I ain't never gonna be in no mothahfuckah's army, jumpin' out no plane, killin' li'l brown folk. If I kill a town it'a be for me. An' if it's for me then I'ma be fine wit' it."

I rolled up my window then, the chill of Raymond's words being enough for me.

For a long while I remained silent, even in my mind.

When we got to L.A. I asked Raymond where he was going.

"Home," he said.

"With Etta and LaMarque?"

"What other home you evah hear me talk about?"

That was how I learned that his exile was over.

"You know what to do at Mike's?"

"What, now I'm stupid too?"

"Come on, Ray. You know how serious I am about this."

"Sure I know what to do. When you get there we gonna be ready for Mr. Lee."

I dropped him off at maybe three in the morning. He gave me the keys for his place on Denker. I went there, scaled the stairs, and climbed into bed, fully dressed. The sheets smelled of Georgette. I inhaled her tomato garden bouquet and was suddenly awake. Not the wakefulness of a man aroused by the memory of a woman. Georgette's scent had aroused me but I had Christmas Black's story in my mind.

I was so close to death at that time that my senses were attuned to its intricacies. My country was sending out lone killers to murder women and children in far-flung nations. While I slept in the security of Mouse's hideaway innocent people were dying. And the taxes I paid on my cigarettes and the taxes they took out of my paycheck were buying the bullets and gassing up the bombers.

It was a state of mind, sure, but that didn't mean that I was wrong. All those years our people had struggled and prayed for freedom and now a man like Christmas, who came from a whole line of heroes, was just another killer like all those white men had been for us.

Is that what we labored for all those years? Was it just to have the right to step on some other poor soul's neck? Were we any better than the white men who lynched us in the night if we killed Easter Dawn's mother and father, sister and brother, cousins and friends? If we could kill like that, everything that we fought for would be called into question. If we became the white men we hated and who hated us, then we were nowhere, nowhere at all.

The sorrow in my heart finally came to rest on Feather. I thought about her dying and so I picked up the phone and called the long-distance operator.

"Allo?" Bonnie said in the French accent that came out whenever she was on the job in either Europe or Africa.

"It's me."

"Oh . . . hi, baby."

"Hey . . . how's Feather doin'?"

"The doctors say that she's very, very sick." She paused for a moment to hold back the grief. I took in a great gulp of air. "But they believe that with the proper transfusions and herbs, they can arrest the infection. And you don't have to worry about the money for a few months. They'll wait that long."

"Thank Mr. Cham for that," I said with hardly any bitterness in the words.

"Easy."

"Yeah?"

"We have to talk, honey."

"Yes. Yes we do. But right now I got my hands full with tryin' to get Feather's hospital bills paid without havin' medical bills of my own."

"I, I got your message," she said, not identifying the man who answered the phone. "Is everything okay?"

"All you got to do is call EttaMae before you come back to the house. There's a man I got to talk to first."

"It's been hard on me too, Easy. I had to do what I've done just to get —"

"Is Feather there?"

"No. She's in the hospital, in a room with three other children."

"There a phone in there?"

"Yes."

"Can I have the number?"

"Easy."

"The number, Bonnie. Whatever we feelin' it cain't touch what's goin' on with her."

"HELLO?"

"It's your daddy, sugar," I said.

"Daddy! Daddy! Where are you?"

"At Uncle Raymond's. How are you, baby?"

"The nurses are so nice, Daddy. And the other girls with me are very sick, sicker than me. And they don't speak English but I'm learning French 'cause they're just too tired to learn a new language. One girl is named Antoinette like the queen and one is Julia . . ."

She sounded so happy but after a short while she was tired again.

"HELLO?"

"It's me, Jackson."

"Easy, do you know what time it is?"

It was four forty-seven by my watch.

"Were you asleep?" I asked. Jackson Blue was a night owl. He'd party until near dawn and then read Voltaire for breakfast.

"No, but Jewelle is."

"Sorry. You made any progress on those bonds?"

"I put the numbers through a telex in the foreign department. They good to go, man. Good to go."

"How much?"

"The one you told me about is eight thousand four hunnert eighty-two dollars and thirty-nine cent. That's before fees."

A hundred thousand dollars, maybe a little more. I couldn't

see Haffernon putting his life on the line for money like that. So it had to be the letter.

"Jackson."

"Yeah, Ease?"

"You ever hear of a guy name of Joe Cicero? They call him Chickpea."

"Never heard of him but he got to be a literate son of a bitch."

"Why you say that?"

"'Cause the first Cicero, the Roman statesman, was called Chickpea. That's what Cicero means, only in the old Latin they had hard c's so you called it 'Kikero.'"

"Yeah. He got a kick all right."

38

I dreamed that I was a dead man in a coffin underground. Down there nobody could get to me but I could see everything. Feather was playing in the yard, Jesus and Benny had a child that looked like me. Bonnie lived with Joguye Cham on a mountaintop in Switzerland that somehow overlooked the continent of Africa. Across the street from the cemetery there was a jail and in it were all the people, living and dead, who had ever tried to harm my loved ones.

I'd fallen asleep on my back with my hands on my thighs. I woke up in the same position. I was completely rested and happy that Mouse's dreams infected mine.

It was after two. I had no job so the calendar and the clock lost meaning to me. It was like when I was a youngblood, running the streets hunting down love and the rent.

My passion had cooled in that imagined grave. The cold earth had leached out the pain and rage in my heart. Feather had a chance and I had a hundred thousand dollars in pay-on-demand bonds. Maybe I'd lost my woman. But, I reasoned, that was like if a man had come awake after a bad accident. The doctors tell him that he's lost an arm. It's a bad thing. It hurts and maybe he sheds tears. But the arm is gone and he's still there. That's some kind of luck.

MIKE'S BAR was in a large building occupying what had once been a mortuary. It had one large room and four smaller ones for private parties and meetings. In the old days, before I ever moved to L.A., the undertakers had a speakeasy behind their coffin repository. Mourners would come in grieving and leave with new hope.

Mouse knew about the old-time club because people liked talking to him. So we took the private room that used to store coffins and he secreted himself behind the hidden door. From there he could spy on the meeting with Lee.

This plan had a few points to recommend it. First, if Lee got hinky Mouse could shoot him through the wall. Also Mouse had a good ear. Maybe Lee would say something that he understood better than I. But the best thing was to have Mouse at that meeting without Lee seeing him; there might come a day when Raymond would have to get close to Lee without being recognized.

I got to the bar at six-twenty, ten minutes before the meeting was to take place. Sam Cooke was singing on the jukebox about the chain gang. Mike, a terra-cotta-colored man, stood statuelike behind his marble-top bar.

"Easy," he called as I came in the door.

I looked around for enemies but all I saw were men and

women hunched over small tables, drinking and talking under a haze of tobacco smoke.

"He in there," Mike told me when I settled at the bar.

"He say anything?"

"Nope. Just that you was comin' an' that a tiny little white man was comin' too. Told me that there might be another white guy in snakeskin, that if I saw him to give him a sign."

"When the little white guy gets here make sure he's alone," I said. "If he is then send him in."

"I know the drill," Mike said.

Mouse had done the bartender a favor some years before. Mike once told me that he was living on borrowed time because of what Raymond had done.

"Any favor he ask I gotta do," Mike had said. "You got to die one day."

I remembered those last words as I walked into the small room that had once held a few dozen coffins.

IT WAS A BRIGHT ROOM with a square pine table that had been treated with oak stain. The chairs were all of one general style, but if you looked closely you could see they weren't an exact match. Mouse was bunged up in the back wall, behind white plasterboard. I wondered if Lee would appreciate the poetry of our deception. He had watched me from behind a similar wall in his own house.

Raymond didn't talk to me. This was business.

I lit a cigarette and let it burn between my fingers while searching the room for living things. There were no plants in the sunless chamber, of course. But neither was there a solitary fly or mosquito, roach or black ant. The only visible, audible life in that room was me. It was more solitary than a coffin because at least in the ground you had gnawing worms for company.

There came a knock and before I could reply the door swung open. Red-skinned Mike stuck his head in and said, "He's cool, Easy." Then he moved back and Robert E. Lee entered.

Lee wore a big mohair overcoat and a black, short-brimmed Stetson. He looked from side to side and then stepped up to the table. His footsteps were loud for such a small man.

"Have a seat," I said.

"Where's Saul?"

"Hiding."

"From you?"

I shook my head. "Me'n Saul are friends. He's hiding from our enemies."

"Saul told me that he'd be here."

"You're here, man. Have a seat and let's talk some business."

He knew he would have to hear me out. But the white man hesitated, pretending that he was weighing the pros and cons of my request.

"All right," he said finally. Then he pulled out the chair opposite me and perched on the edge.

"I got the bonds," I said. "Bowers is most likely dead. So's Haffernon."

"Haffernon was my employer," Lee told me. "Turn over what you've got and we'll both walk away."

"What about my ten thousand?"

"I have no more employer," he said by way of explanation.

"Then neither do I."

"What do you want from me, Rawlins?"

"To make a deal. I get a piece of the action and you call Cicero off my ass."

"Cicero? Joe Cicero?"

The honesty of his fear made me understand that the situation was far more complex than I thought.

"I'd never do business with a man like that," Lee said with incantatory emphasis, like he was warding off an evil spell I'd cast.

"How do you know the guy if you don't work with him?" I asked. "I mean he's not in the kind of business that advertises."

"I know of him from the newspapers and some of my friends in the prosecutor's office. He was tried for the torture and murder of a young socialite from Sausalito. Fremont. Patrick Fremont."

"Well he's been runnin' around lookin' for that briefcase you hired me to find. He told me that he killed Haffernon and Axel and that me and my family are the next ones on his list."

"That's your problem," Lee said. He shifted as if he might stand and run.

"Come on, man. You the one hired me. All I got to do is tell Chickpea that you the one got the bonds, that Maya picked 'em up someplace. Then he be on your ass."

"Saul said something about Maya on the phone," Lee said. "Do you know anything about that?"

"A few days ago she fired me," I said.

"Nonsense."

"Then she hired me again when I told her that I'd found Philomena but refused to share my information."

"How can I believe anything you say, Mr. Rawlins? First you tell me that Joe Cicero is after the bonds, then you say that my client and your quarry are dead, that you have the bonds we were after, and that Maya has betrayed me. But you don't offer one shred of evidence."

"You never told me about no bonds, Bobby Lee," I said, falling into the dialect that gave me strength.

"Maybe you heard about them."

"Sure I did . . . from the woman had 'em — Philomena Cargill. She gave 'em to me to keep Cicero from makin' her dearly departed."

Somewhere in the middle of the conversation Lee had changed from a self-important ass to something much closer to a detective — I could see it in his eyes.

"So you have these bonds?" he asked.

"Sure do."

"Give them to me."

"I don't have 'em here, an' even if I did you'd have to take 'em. Because you didn't tell me about half the shit I was gettin' into."

"Detectives take chances."

"An' if I take 'em," I said, "then you gonna take 'em too."

"You can't threaten me, Rawlins."

"Listen, babe, you just named after a dead general. With the shit I got I could threaten Ike himself."

It was the certainty in my voice that tipped him to my side.

"You say Maya fired you?"

"Said that you'd concluded the case and that my services would no longer be needed."

"But she didn't tell you about the bonds?"

"No," I said. "All she said was that we were through and that I could keep the money I already had."

"I need proof," Lee said.

"There was a murder at the Pixie Inn motel this afternoon. The man found there is Haffernon."

"Even if that's so it doesn't prove anything," Lee said. "You could have killed him yourself."

"Fine. Go on then. Leave. I tried to warn you. I tried."

Lee remained seated, watching me closely.

"I know some federal officials that could look into Cicero," he said. "They could get him out of the action until the case is resolved. And if we can pin these murders on him . . ."

"You sayin' that we could be partners?"

"I need proof about Maya," he said. "She's been with me for many years. Many years."

"When it's over we could set her up," I offered. "Agree to give her the bonds or put her with Cinnamon and record what she says. I think those two would like each other. But I need you to do somethin' about Cicero. That mothahfuckah make a marble statue sweat."

Lee smiled. That gave me heart about him. In my many years I had come to understand that humor was the best test for intelligence in my fellow man. The fact that Lee gained respect for me because of a joke gave me hope that he would come to sensible conclusions.

"He really came to you?" Lee asked.

"Right up in my office. Told me to give up Cinnamon or else my family would be dead."

"He mentioned her name?"

I nodded. "Philomena Cargill."

"And you have the bonds?"

"Sure do."

"How many?"

"Twelve."

"Was there anything else with them?"

"They were in a brown envelope. No briefcase or anything."

"Was there anything attached?"

"Like what?" I was holding back a little to see how much he was willing to give.

"Nothing," he said. "So what do we do now?"

"You go home. Gimme a way to get in touch with you and I will in two days. In that time figure out what you need on Maya and talk to who you need to about J.C."

"And what do you do?"

"Keep from gettin' killed the best I can, sit on those bonds while they accrue interest."

He gave me a private phone number that only he answered.

He rose and so did I. We shook hands.

He was sweating under that heavy coat. He was probably armed under there. I would have been.

39

Thirty seconds after Lee left, a section of the wall to my left wobbled and then moved back. Mouse came out through the crack wearing a red suit and a black shirt. He was smiling.

"You didn't tell me you had the bonds, Ease."

"Sure I did. The same time I told Lee."

The smile remained on Raymond's face. He never minded a man holding his cards close to the vest. All that mattered to him was that in the end he got his proper share of the pot.

"What you think?" I asked as we emerged into the barroom.

"I like that dude. He got some nuts on him. An' he smart too. I know that 'cause a minute after he walked in I figgered I'd have to shoot the mothahfuckah in the head he mess around."

That was sixty seconds after Lee had left the room. We made

it halfway to the bar. Mouse ordered scotch and I was about to ask for a Virgin Mary when six or seven cracks sounded outside.

"What was that?" Mike shouted.

I looked at Raymond. He had his long barreled .41 caliber pistol in his hand.

Then two explosions thundered from the street. Shotgun blasts.

I headed for the door, pulling the pistol from my pocket as I went. Mouse was ahead of me. He threw the door open, moving low and to his left. A motor revved and tires squealed. I saw a car (I couldn't place the model) fishtailing away.

"Easy!" Mouse was leaning over Robert Lee, ripping open his overcoat and shirt.

There was a sawed-off shotgun next to the master detective's right hand and blood coming freely from the right side of his neck. When Mouse tore the shirt I could see the police-issue bulletproof vest with at least five bullet holes.

Mouse grinned. "Oh yeah. Head shot the only way to go."

He clasped his palm on the neck wound. Lee looked up at us, gasping. He was going into shock but wasn't quite there yet.

"She betrayed me," he said.

"Get the car, Easy. This boy needs some doctor on him."

I SAT WITH LEE in the backseat while Mouse drove Primo's hot rod. I had the general's namesake's head and shoulders propped up on my lap while holding his own torn shirt against the wound.

"She betrayed me," Lee said again.

"Maya?"

"I told her that I was coming to see Saul."

"Did you say why?"

His eyes were getting glassy. I wasn't sure that he heard me.

"She doesn't know, but if what you said, you said, you said . . ."

"Hold on, Bobby. Hold on."

"She knew. She knew where we were meeting. I didn't tell her what Saul said. I didn't, but she betrayed me to that snake, that snake Cicero."

He never closed his eyes but he passed out still and all. I couldn't get another word out of him.

IT WAS A SLOW NIGHT in the emergency room. Lee was the only gunshot wound in the place. Maybe it was because of that, or maybe it was his being white that got him such quick service that day. They had him in a hospital bed and hooked up to three machines before I had even finished filling out the paperwork.

Five minutes after that the cops arrived.

When I saw the three uniforms come in I turned to Mouse, intent on telling him to ditch his gun. But he was nowhere to be seen. Mouse knew that those cops were coming before they did. He was as elusive in the street as Willie Pepp had been in the ring.

"Are you the man that brought him in?" the head cop, a silver-haired sergeant, asked me right off.

The other uniforms performed a well-rehearsed flanking maneuver.

"Sure did. Easy Rawlins. We were meeting at Mike's Bar and he'd just left. I heard shots and ran out . . . found him lying on the ground. There was a car racin' off but I can't even say for sure what color it was."

"There was a report of a sawed-off shotgun on the ground. Who did that belong to?"

"I have no idea, Officer. I saw the gun but I left it . . . for evidence."

I was too cool for that man. He was used to people being agitated after a shooting.

"You say you were having a drink with the victim?" he asked.

"I said I was having a meeting with him."

"What kind of meeting?"

"I'm a detective, Sergeant. Private. Mr. Lee — that's the victim — he's a detective too."

I handed him my license. He studied the card carefully, made a couple of notes in a black leather pocket notebook, and then handed it back.

"What were you working on?"

"A security background check on a Maya Adamant. She's an operative who works with him from time to time."

"And why did you flee the scene?"

"You ever been shot in the neck, Sergeant?"

"What?"

"I hope not, but if ever that should happen I'm sure that you would want somebody to take you to a doctor first off. 'Cause you know, man, ain't no police report in the world worth bleedin' to death out on Slauson."

The sergeant wasn't a bad guy. He was just doing his job.

"Did you see the shooter?" he asked.

"No sir. Just what I said about the car."

"Did the victim . . ."

"Lee," I said.

"Did he say anything?"

"No."

"Did the shooter get shot?"

"I don't know."

"They found blood halfway up the block," the sergeant said. "That's why I ask."

He peered into my face. I shook my head, hoping that Joe Cicero was dying somewhere.

A young white doctor with a pointy nose came up to us.

"Your friend is going to be fine," he told me. "No major vascular damage. The shot went through."

"Can I speak to him?" the policeman asked the doctor.

"He's in shock and under sedation," the doctor said. He wouldn't meet the policeman's eye. I wondered what secrets he had to hide. "You won't be able to talk to him until morning."

Blocked there the cop turned back to me.

"Can you tell me anything else, Rawlins?"

I could have told him to call me mister but I didn't.

"No, Sergeant. That's all I know."

"Do you think this woman you're investigating might have something to do with it?"

"I couldn't say."

"You say you were investigating her."

"My findings were inconclusive," I said, falling out of dialect.

The cop stared at me a moment more and then gave up.

"I have your information. We may be calling you."

I nodded and the police took the doctor somewhere for his report.

EVERYTHING CALMED DOWN after half an hour or so. The police left, the doctor went on to other patients. Mouse was long gone.

I stayed around because I knew that someone wanted Lee dead, and so while he was unconscious I thought I'd watch over him. This wasn't as selfless an act as it might have seemed. I still needed the haughty little detective to run interference with Cicero. I didn't know if Lee had actually seen Cicero shoot at him, if Lee had shot him, and, if he had, if the wound would ultimately be fatal. I had to play it as if Cicero was still in the game and as deadly as ever.

The only thing worth reading in the magazine rack in the waiting room was a science fiction periodical called *Worlds of Tomorrow*. I found a story in it called "Under the Gaddyl." It was a tale about man's future, the white man's future, where all of white humanity was enslaved under an alien race — the Gaddyl. The purpose of the main character, a freed slave, was to emancipate his people. I read the story in a kind of wonderment. Here white people all over the country understood the problems that faced me and mine but somehow they had very little compassion for our plight.

I was thinking about that when a shadow fell over my page. I knew by the scent who it was.

"Hello, Miss Adamant," I said without looking up.

"Mr. Rawlins."

She took the seat next to me and leaned over, seemingly filled with concern.

"He knows you set him up. He told the cops that," I said.

"What are you talking about?"

"He knows that you sent Cicero down to blow him away."

"But I . . . I didn't."

She was good.

"If you don't know nuthin' about tonight then what the fuck you doin' here? How the hell you know to find him in this emergency room?"

"I came down because I knew you or Saul would tell him about our conversations. I wanted to talk to him, to explain."

"So you were outside the bar?" I asked. "Watchin' your boss get shot down?"

"No. I was at the Clarendon Hotel. I heard on the news about the shooting. I knew where the meeting was."

"What about Cicero?" I asked.

Her face went blank. I could tell that this was her way of going inward and solving some problem. I was the problem.

"He called me," she said.

"When?"

"After you came to see us. He wanted to talk to Mr. Lee but I told him that all information had to go through me. He said that we had interests in common, that he wanted to find Philomena Cargill and a document that Axel had given her."

"And what did you say?"

"I told him that I didn't know where she was."

If she could have, Maya would have stopped right there. But I moved my hands around in a helpless manner like Boris Karloff's Frankenstein's monster did just after he murdered the little girl.

"He said that he wanted to meet with you and did I know where you were," she added.

"Me?"

"He said that if anybody could find Philomena that you could."

"How did he know about me?" I asked.

"He didn't say."

"You didn't tell him?"

"No."

"How did he know how to call you in the first place?"

"I don't know."

"Did you tell anyone that I was working for you?" I asked.

"No."

"Did your boss?"

"I do all the talking about business," she said with a hint of contempt in her voice.

"And so you told Cicero where I was?"

"I didn't know. But when Mr. Lee said that he was coming down to meet Saul I called Cicero. I had been trying to get in touch with Mr. Lynx but he didn't answer his phones. I told Cicero where Saul would be, thinking that he might help him find you."

"And what would you get out of that?"

"Cicero has a reputation," she replied.

"Yeah," I said. "Assassin. Torturer."

"That may be. But he is always known to meet his side of a bargain. I told him what I wanted for the information and he agreed."

"You wanted the bonds," I said.

"Yes."

I didn't say anything, just stared at her.

"That little bastard pays me seven dollars an hour with no benefits. He makes more than a quarter million a year," she said in defense from my gaze, "and I do almost everything. I'm on duty twenty-four hours a day. He calls me home from vacations. He makes me talk to everybody, do the books, do all the business. I make all of the major decisions while he sits behind his desk and plays with his toy soldiers."

"Sounds like a good enough reason to kill him," I said.

"No. If I got the bonds I could cash them in and set up a retirement fund. That's all I wanted."

"Is that why you and Lee were feuding when Saul and I were there?"

"Yes. Mr. Lee didn't want to take the case but . . . but I hoped to be able to get hold of the bonds, and so I had talked him into it. He was looking for a way out of it, he didn't like the smell of Haffernon. When you demanded to meet him he almost let it go."

"So why would Cicero want to kill Lee?"

"I don't know but I would suspect that whatever job he was working on, Lee's death had to be part of it."

"Maybe yours too," I suggested.

She blanched at the notion.

40

After our chat I asked Maya to come up with me to the nurses' station. There I introduced her to the pointy-nosed doctor and to Mrs. Bernard, the bespectacled head nurse.

"This is Miss Maya Adamant," I said. "She'll tell you that she's a friend of Mr. Lee's, but the police suspect her in his shooting. They don't have proof, but you probably shouldn't let her run around here unsupervised."

The stunned look on their faces was worth it.

Maya smiled at them and said, "It's a misunderstanding. I work for Mr. Lee. At any rate I'll wait until he's conscious and then you can ask him if he wants to talk to me."

THE MORNING WAS CHILLY but I didn't feel so bad.

I missed having Bonnie to call. For the past few years I'd been able to talk to her about anything. That had been a new experience for me. Never before could I fully trust another human being. If it was five in the morning and I'd been out all night I could call her and she'd be there as fast as she could. She never asked why but I always explained. Being with her made me understand how lonely I'd been for all my wandering years. But being alone again made me feel that I was back in the company of an old friend.

I was worried about Feather's survival but she had sounded good on the phone and there was already new blood flowing in her veins.

Blood and money were the currencies I dealt in. They were inseparable. This thought made me feel even more comfortable. I figured that if I knew where I stood then I had a chance of getting where I was going.

I PARKED ACROSS THE STREET from Raphael Reed's apartment building a little after seven. I had coffee in a paper cup. The brew was both bitter and weak but I drank it to stay awake. Maybe Cinnamon was with the young men. I could hope.

Sitting there I went over the details I had. I knew more about Lee's case than anyone, but still there were big holes. Cicero was definitely the killer, but who held his reins? He couldn't have been a player in the business. He could have worked for anybody: Cinnamon, Maya, even Lee, or maybe Haffernon. Maybe Bowers hired him back in the beginning. It would be good to know the answers if the police came to see me.

Near nine Raphael's friend Roget came out the front door of the turquoise building. He carried a medium-sized suitcase. He could have had a change of underwear in there, could have been going to visit his mother, but I was intrigued. And so when the high-yellow freckled boy climbed into a light blue Datsun I turned over my own engine.

He led me all the way to Hollywood before parking in front of a boxy four-story house on Delgado. He walked up the driveway and into the backyard. After a moment I followed.

He went to the front door of a small house back there. He knocked and was admitted by someone I couldn't see. I went back to the car. When I sat down exhaustion washed over me. I lay back on the seat for just a moment.

Two hours later the sun on my face woke me up.

The blue Datsun was gone.

SHE WAS WEARING a T-shirt, that's all. The soft outline of her nipples pressed against the white cotton. The dark color pressed against it too.

After answering my knock she didn't know whether to smile or to run.

"What do you want from me now?" she asked. "I gave you the bonds."

"Can I come in?"

She backed away and I entered. It was yet another cramped cabinlike room. The normal-sized furniture crowded the small space. There was a couch and a round table upon which sat a portable TV. A radio on the window shelf played Mozart. Her musical taste shouldn't have surprised me but it did.

On the table was an empty glass jar that once held nine Vienna sausages, a half-drunk tumbler of orange juice, and a depleted bag of barbecue potato chips.

"You want something to drink?" she asked me.

"Water be great," I said.

She went through a tiny doorway. I heard the tap turn on and off and she returned with an aqua-colored plastic juice tumbler filled with water.

I drank it down in one gulp.

"You want more?"

"Let's talk," I said.

She sat down on one end of the golden sofa. I took the other end.

"What do you want to know?"

"First — who knows you're here?"

"Just Raphael and Roget. Now you."

"Do they gossip?"

"Not about this. Raphael knows someone's after me and Roget does whatever Raphael says."

"Why'd you kill Haffernon?" It was an abrupt and brutal switch calculated to knock her off track. But it didn't work.

"I didn't," she said evenly. "I found him there and ran but I didn't kill him. No. Not me."

What else could she say?

"How does that work?" I asked. "You find a dead man in your own room but don't know how he got killed?"

"It's the truth."

I shook my head.

"You look tired," she said, sympathy blending in with her words.

"How'd Haffernon get to your room?"

"I called him."

"When?"

"Right after I met you. I called him and told him that I wanted to get rid of the bonds. I asked him would he buy them off me for face value."

"And what about the letter?"

"He'd get that too."

"When was this meeting supposed to happen?"

"Today. This afternoon."

"So how does he show up dead on your floor yesterday?"

"After the last time I talked to you I realized that Haffernon could just send that man in the snakeskin jacket to kill me and take the bonds, so I went to Raphael and asked him to take the bonds to your friend."

"Why?"

"Because even though I hardly know you, you seem to be the most trustworthy person I've met, and anyway . . ." Her words trailed off as better judgment took the wheel.

"Anyway what?"

"I figured that you wouldn't know what to do with the bonds and so I didn't have to worry about you cashing them."

That made me laugh.

"What's so funny?"

I told her about Jackson Blue, that he was willing at that moment to cash them in. I could see the surprise on her face.

"My Uncle Thor once told me that for every one thing you learn you forget something else," I said.

"What's that supposed to mean?"

"That while they were teaching you all'a that smart white world knowledge at Berkeley you were forgetting where you came from and how we survived all these years. We might'a acted stupid but you know you moved so far away that you startin' to think the act is true."

Cinnamon smiled. The smile became a grin.

"Tell me exactly what happened with Haffernon," I said.

"It's like I said. I called him and made an appointment for him to meet me at the motel —"

"At what time?"

"Today at four," she said. "Then I got nervous and went to give the bonds to Raphael to give to your friend —"

"What time was that?"

"Right after I talked to you. I got back by about five. That's when I saw him on the floor. He'd been early, real early."

"But who could have killed him if you didn't?"

"I don't know," she said. "It wasn't me. But when I talked to him he said that he wasn't the only interested party, that what Axel planned to do would sink many innocent people."

I thought about the bullet that killed Haffernon. It had entered at the base of the skull and gone out through the top. He was a tall man. In all probability either a very short man or a woman had done him in.

"Did you give your real name at the motel?"

"No. I didn't. I called myself Mary Lornen. That's the names of two people I knew up north."

Proof is a funny thing. For policemen and for lawyers it depends on tangible evidence: fingerprints, eyewitnesses, irrefutable logic, or self-incrimination. But for me evidence is like morning mist over a complex terrain. You see the landscape and then it's gone. And all you can do is try to remember and watch your step.

The fact that Philomena had delivered those bonds to Primo meant something. It gave me doubts about her guilt. While I was having these thoughts Philomena moved across the couch.

"Kiss me," she commanded.

41

Cinnamon's kiss was a spiritual thing. It was like the sudden and unexpected appeasement between the east and west. A barrier fell away, forgiveness flooded my heart, and somewhere I was granted redemption for all my transgressions.

"I need this," she whispered. "It doesn't have to mean anything."

She pressed her breasts against me, positioning me so that I was leaning back on the arm of the sofa. Then she grabbed my ankles and pulled hard so that, with my help, she got me flat on my back.

She lifted the white T-shirt to straddle me. When she did so I caught a glimpse of her protruding pubic hair. I felt like a child seeing something that had been kept from him for what seemed like an eternity.

"Wh-what do you need?" I said, embarrassed by my stutter.

She moved down to my shins and reached up to catch the waist of my pants. With a quick tug she had both my pants and boxers down to my knees. Then she came up again.

Just before settling back down she said, "I need your warmth."

The feel of her hot sex sitting down on mine gave the hiss of her words a deeper meaning.

"Pull up your shirt," she said.

She began rocking gently back and forth and to the sides, doing things with my erection, which lay flat against my belly, that I would never have thought of on my own. I watched closely, looking for passion. But she was in control. The feeling was inside and she was keeping it there. She laid her hands upon my chest. I could see a finger against my erect nipple but I couldn't feel it.

"Was he your lover?" I asked. It was the last thing on my mind.

"Axel?"

"Sure."

"Sure," she repeated.

"What were you guys doing?"

"You mean how did we do it?"

"No. Those bonds. That letter."

"He loved me," she said. "He wanted to help me cross over from where everybody else was."

I understood every word, every inflection. She moved side to side and I felt her excitement down between my thighs even if it didn't show on her face.

"You love him?"

"If I tell you about him will you tell me something?"

I nodded and gulped.

"What do you want to know?" she asked.

"Do you love him?" I asked even though there was another question in my mind.

"It's more than that," she whispered with a sneer and an evil twist of her hips. "He reached out and saved my life. He took me in his house and then left me there with all those treasures. He introduced me to friends and family and never walked into a room where I couldn't go with him. And he never gave me a dime I didn't work for and he did what I told him to do."

The idea of a man obeying this woman brought a sound from my chest that I'd not heard before, not even from some infant that was all feelings and desire.

"He let me help him," she said. "He recognized that I was smart and educated and that I could understand him better than all those old white men and women that made him ashamed."

"Were you helping him with those bonds?" I asked, again a question I didn't care to ask.

"That was him. That was his devil."

She lifted off of me and cold concern rose in my face. She smiled and came back down.

"My turn," she said with a swivel.

"What?"

"What's making you so sad?" she asked.

In a flood of words I told her about Feather and about Bonnie, who was saving her while in the arms of an African prince in the Alps. It sounded like a bad movie but the words kept coming. It was almost as if I couldn't inhale before finishing the tale.

Her fingernail got caught on my nipple. A shock made me jump and press hard against her sex.

"Oh!" she said and then snagged the nipple again.

She'd found another way to pleasure us both. My breath was coming harder.

In between her rocking and snagging she said, "All men feel that women do them wrong. They feel like that all the time. But that's just silly. Here you got a woman givin' up everything to save your little girl and all you can think about is a passing fancy or even maybe another lover. What do you think they're doin' right now?"

I reached out and pinched one of her nipples and then the other.

She liked that but only showed it by inhaling deeply.

And to show me that it wasn't too overwhelming she began to speak again.

"It's like when Axel's older cousin Nina got jealous of me bein' in his bed. She loved him in another way; like Bonnie loves you. You shouldn't be jealous of her. You should be happy that she can give your little girl life."

Those were the words I had wanted to hear, needed to hear for days. I opened my mouth but she spoke first.

"No," she said, pinching my nipples hard and then pounding down, her sex against mine. "No. No more. Come to me."

I came all at once, before I was ready. She smiled but didn't slow the hammerlike rhythm against my erection. It hurt but I didn't throw her off or complain. And after a few seconds I had another orgasm. I guess that's what it was. It happened somewhere inside my body. All of a sudden there was a dam I didn't know about and it broke open and everyone in its path was drowned.

WHEN I AWOKE, the woman who might have been a murderer was lying along my side with her head nestled against my shoulder. I knew almost nothing about Philomena Cargill and yet she had touched me in a place I couldn't even have imagined on my own. Was she like this for all men? A fertility goddess come from Africa somewhere to bedevil mortal men with something they could never know without her? Her hand was on my limp sex. But as soon as I saw it I began to get hard again.

"We should get cleaned up," she said, awakening to my arousal.

"Yeah. Yeah."

There was a jury-rigged shower nozzle attached to the wall above the small bathtub in the restroom. We washed each other. Physically I was as excited as I had been on the couch but my mind was free.

"Where does Axel's cousin live?" I asked.

"Down in L.A. somewhere." In her mind she was still in Berkeley.

"And is she related to the family business somehow?"

"Nina's father was the man who started the company. He's Tourneau, Rega Tourneau."

"Was he part of the company before the war?"

"Oh yeah."

"Is he still alive?"

She began to lather my pubic hair, working deftly around the erection. "He's very old. Ninety I think. Nobody in the family likes him."

After the shower I was still straining with excitement. Cinnamon stood in front of me, smiling, and asked, "Are you going to leave now?"

I wanted to leave because I knew somehow that I'd lose something of my soul if I let her make love to me again.

"No," I said. "I'm not going anywhere."

42

I didn't leave Philomena's until early the next morning. It had been a long time since I'd spent a night like that. Georgette was wonderful and passionate but Cinnamon Cargill was the spice of sex with no impediments of love at all. Where Georgette kissed me and told me that she wanted to take me home forever, Cinnamon just sneered and used sex like a surgeon's knife. She never said one nice or kind thing, though physically she loved me like I was her only man.

When she'd leave the room to go to the toilet she seemed surprised, and not necessarily happy, to see me when she returned.

She told me all about old Rega Tourneau. He was the family patriarch, born in the last century. He had married Axel's father's aunt and so there was some family connection there — though not by blood.

"The old man had a sour temperament," Philomena said.

"When he was a boy he was caught in a boiler explosion that scarred his face and blinded his eye."

When he retired he became reclusive and removed.

He had a disagreement with Nina about the man she married. Rega didn't like him and so he disowned his daughter. As far as Philomena knew, Nina was still out of the will.

Nina Tourneau eventually separated from her husband and tried to become an artist down in Southern California somewhere. When that failed she became an art dealer.

Then we made love again.

Philomena would have married Axel if he'd asked her to. She would have had his children and hosted his acid parties with catered meals and champagne chasers.

"But you never said you loved him," I said.

"Love is an old-fashioned concept," she replied in university-ese. "The human race developed love to make families cohesive. It's just a tool you put back in the closet when you're done with it."

"And then you take it out again when someone else strikes your fancy?"

Then we made love again.

"Love is like a man's thing," she told me. "It gets all hot and bothered for a while there, but then after it's over it goes to sleep."

"Not me," I said. "Not tonight."

She smiled and the sun came up.

I forced myself to get dressed and ready to go.

"Do you have to leave?" she asked me.

"Do you love me?" I asked.

It is a question I had never asked a woman before that day. I had no idea that the words were in my chest, my heart. But that was the reply to her question. If she had said yes I would have taken a different path, I'm sure. Maybe I would have taken her with me or maybe I would have cut my losses and run. Maybe we would have flown together on the bearer bonds to Switzerland, where I would have taken a flat above Bonnie and Joguye.

"Sure I do," she said with a one-shoulder shrug. She might as well have winked.

I breathed a deep sigh of relief and went out the door.

I PARKED MY LOW-RIDER car across the street from an innocuous-looking place on Ozone, less than a block away from Santa Monica beach. It was a little after seven and there was some activity on the street. There were men in suits and old women with dogs on leashes, bicyclers showing off their calves in shorts, and bums shaking the sand from their clothes. Almost everyone was white but they didn't mind me sitting there. They didn't call for the police.

I drank my coffee, ate my jelly doughnut. I tried to remember the last good meal I'd had. The chili at Primo's, I thought. I felt clean. Cinnamon and I had taken four showers between our fevered bouts of not-love. My sex ached in my pants. I thought about her repudiation of love and my surprising deep need for it. I wondered if my life would ever settle back into the bliss I'd known with Bonnie and the hope for happiness I had discovered in Cinnamon's arms.

These thoughts pained me. I looked up and there was Jackson Blue walking out his front door, his useless spectacles on his face and a black briefcase dangling from his left hand.

I rolled down the window and called his last name.

He went down behind a parked car next to him. At one time seeing him jump like that would have made me grin. Many a time I had startled Jackson just because he would react like that. He dove out windows, skipped around corners — but that day I wasn't trying to scare my friend, I got no pleasure witnessing his frantic leap.

"Jackson, it's me . . . Easy."

Jackson's head popped up. He grimaced but before he could complain I got out of the car with my hands held up in apology.

"Sorry, man," I said. "I just saw you and shouted without thinkin'."

The little coward pulled himself up and walked toward me, looking around to make sure there was no trap.

"Hey, Ease. What's wrong?"

"I need help, Jackson."

"Look like you need three days in bed."

"That too."

"What can I do for ya?"

"I just need you to ride with me, Blue. Ride with me for the day if you can."

"Where you ridin'?"

"I got to find a white woman and then her daddy."

"What you need me for?" Jackson asked.

"Company. That's all. That and somebody to bounce ideas off of. I mean if you can get outta work."

"Oh yeah," Jackson said in that false bravado he always used to camouflage his coward's heart. "You know I'm at that place sometimes as late as the president. He come in my office and tell me to go home. All I gotta do is call an' tell 'em I need a rest day an' they say, *See ya*."

He clapped my shoulder, letting me know that he'd take the ride.

"But first we gotta go tell Jewelle," he said. "You know babygirl gotta know where daddy gonna be."

We walked back to his door and Jackson used three keys on the locks. The crow's nest entrance of his apartment looked down into a giant room. It was like staring down into a well made up to be some fairy-tale creature's home.

"Easy here, baby," Jackson announced.

She was standing at the window, looking out into a flower garden that they worked on in their spare time. She wore a pink housecoat with hair curlers in her hair like tiny, precariously perched oil drums.

Jackson and I were in our mid-forties, old men compared to Jewelle, who was still shy of thirty. Her brown skin and long face were attractive enough, but what made her a beauty was the power in her eyes. Jewelle was a real estate genius. She'd taken my old manager's property and turned it into nearly an empire. The riots had slowed her growth some but soon she'd be a millionaire and she and Jackson would live with the rich people up in Bel Air.

Jewelle smiled as we descended the ladderlike stairs to their home. The walls were twenty-five feet high and every inch was covered in bookcases crammed with Jackson's lifelong collection of books.

He had eight encyclopedias and dictionaries in everything from Greek to Mandarin. He was better read than any professor but even with all that knowledge at his disposal he'd rather lie than tell the truth.

"Hi, Easy," Jewelle said. She loved older men. And she loved me particularly because I always helped when I could. I might have been the only man (or woman for that matter) in her life who gave her more than he took.

"Hey, J.J. What's up?"

"Thinkin' about buying up property in a neighborhood in L.A. proper," she said. "Lotta Koreans movin' in there. The value's bound to rise."

"Me an' Easy gonna take a personal day," Jackson said.

"What kinda personal day?" Jewelle asked suspiciously.

"Nobody dangerous, nothing illegal," I said.

Jewelle loved Jackson because he was the only man she'd ever met who could outthink her. Anything she'd ask — he had the answer. It's said that some women are attracted to men's minds. She was the only one I ever knew personally.

"What about your job, baby?" she asked.

"Easy want some company, J.J.," Jackson told her. "When the last time you hear him say sumpin' like that to me?"

I could see that they'd talked about me quite a bit. I could almost make out the echoes of those conversations in that cavernous room.

Jewelle nodded and Jackson took off his tie. When he went to the phone to make a call Jewelle sidled up next to me.

"You in trouble, Easy?" she asked.

"So bad that you can't even imagine it, J.J."

"I don't want Jackson in there with you."

"It's not like that, honey," I told her. "Really . . . he just gonna ride with me. Maybe give me an idea or two."

Jackson came back to us then.

"I called the president at his house," the whiz kid said proudly. "He told me to take all the time I needed. Now all you got to do is feed me some breakfast and I'm ret-to-go."

43

Jackson made us go to a little diner that looked over the beach.

The problem was that the place he chose, the Sea Cove Inn, was where Bonnie and I used to go in the mornings sometimes. But I made it through. I had waffles and bacon. Jackson gobbled French toast and sausages, fried eggs and a whole quart of orange juice. He had both the body and the appetite of a boy.

The waitress, an older white woman, knew Jackson and they talked about dogs — she was the owner of some rare breed. While they gabbed I went to the pay phone and called EttaMae.

"Yes? Who is it?"

"Easy, Etta."

"Hold on."

She put the receiver down and a moment later Mouse picked it up.

"You in jail, Easy?" he asked inside of a big yawn.

"At the beach."

"How's Jackson?"

"He's somethin'."

"Your boy Cicero is what a head doctor girlfriend I once had called a psy-ko-path. I think that's what she called me too. Anyway he been killin' an' causin' pain up an' down the coast for years. They say he was a rich kid but his folks disowned him after his first murder. I know where he been livin' at down here but he ain't been there for days. I got a guy watchin' the place but I don't think he gonna show."

"Crazy, huh?"

"Everybody say it. Mothahfuckah cover his tracks with bone an' blood. You know I be doin' the country a favor to pop that boy there."

"Yeah," I said, thinking that deadly force was the only way to deal with Joe Cicero. A man like that was dangerous as long as he drew breath. Even if he was in prison he could get at you.

"What you want me to do, Easy?"

"Sit tight, Ray. If you get the word on Cicero give me a call."

"Where at?"

"I'll call Etta tonight at six and tomorrow morning at nine. Leave me something with her."

"You got it, brother."

He was about to hang up when I said, "Hey, Ray."

"What?"

"Do you ever get scared'a shit like this?" I knew the answer. I just didn't want to get off the phone yet.

"Naw, man. I mean this some serious shit right here. It'a be a lot easier takin' down that armored car. That's all mapped out. All you gotta do is follow the dots on a job like that. This here make ya think. Think fast. But you know I like that."

"Yeah," I said. "It sure does make you think."

"Okay then, Easy," Mouse said. "Call me when you wanna. I'ma be here waitin' for you or my spy."

"Thanks, Ray."

WE HAD JUST FINISHED rutting on the cold tiles next to the bathtub when Philomena told me about the gallery where Nina Tourneau worked. She enjoyed giving me information after a bout of hard sex. The force of making love seemed to give her strength. By the time we were finished I don't think she was that worried about dying.

The gallery was on Rodeo Drive in Beverly Hills. I put my pistols in the trunk and my PI license in my shirt pocket. Even dressed fine as we were Jackson and I were still driving a hot rod car in the morning, and even though he had a corporate look I was a little too sporty to be going to a respectable job.

I parked in front of the gallery, Merton's Fine Art.

There was the sound of faraway chimes when we entered. A white woman wearing a deep green suit came through a doorway at the far end of the long room. When she saw us a perplexity invaded her features. She said something into the room behind her and then marched forward with an insincere smile plastered on her lips.

"May I help you?" she asked, doubtful that she could.

"Are you Nina Tourneau?"

"Yes?"

"My name's Easy Rawlins, ma'am," I said, holding out my city-issued identification. "I'm representing a man named Lee from up in San Francisco. He's trying to locate a relative of yours."

Nothing I said, nor my ID, managed to erase the doubt from her face.

"And who would that be?" she asked.

Nina Tourneau was somewhere in her late fifties, though cosmetics and spas made her look about mid-forty. Her elegant face had most definitely been beautiful in her youth. But now the cobwebs of age were gathering beneath the skin.

"A Mr. Rega Tourneau," I said.

The name took its toll on the art dealer's reserve.

Jackson in the meanwhile had been looking at the pale oil paintings along the wall. The colors were more like pastels than oils really and the details were vague, as if the paintings were yet to be finished.

"These paintin's here, they like uh," Jackson said, snapping his fingers. "What you call it? Um . . . derivative; that's it. These paintin's derivative of Puvis de Chavannes."

"What did you say?" she asked him.

"Chavannes," he repeated. "The man Van Gogh loved so damn much. I never liked the paintin's myself. An' I sure don't see why some modern-day painter would want to do like him."

"You know art?" she asked, amazed.

At that moment the chimes sounded again. I didn't have to look to know that the police were coming in. When Nina whispered into the back room I was sure that it was to tell her secretary to call the police. After the riots people called the police if two black men stopped on a street corner to say hello — much less if they walked into a Beverly Hills gallery with paintings based on old European culture.

"Stay where you are," one of the cops said. "Keep your hands where I can see them."

"Oh yeah," Jackson said to Nina. "I read all about them things. You know it's El Greco, the Greek, that I love though. That suckah paint like he was suckled with Picasso but he older than the hills."

"Shut up," one of the two young cops said.

They both had guns out. One of them grabbed Jackson by his arm.

"I'm sorry, Officers," Nina Tourneau said then. "But there's been a mistake. I didn't recognize Mr. Rawlins and his associate when they came in. I told Carlyle to watch out. He must have thought I wanted him to call you. There's nothing wrong."

The cops didn't believe her at first. I don't blame them. She seemed nervous, upset. They put cuffs on both Jackson and me and one of them took Nina in the back room to assure her that she was safe. But she kept to her story and finally they set us free. They told us that we'd be under surveillance and then left to sit in their cruiser across the street.

"Why are you looking for my father?" Nina asked after they'd gone.

"I'm not," I said. "It's Robert Lee, detective extraordinaire from Frisco, lookin' for him. He gave me some money and I'm just puttin' in the time."

Miss Tourneau looked at us for a while and then shook her head.

"My father's an old man, Mr. Rawlins. He's in a rest home. If your client wishes to speak to me you can give him the number of this gallery and I will be happy to talk with him."

She stared me in the eye while saying this.

"He disowned you, didn't he?"

"I don't see where that's any of your business," she said.

I smiled and gave her a slight nod.

"Come on, Jackson," I said.

He shrugged like a child and turned toward the door.

"Excuse me, sir," Nina Tourneau said to Jackson. "Do you collect?"

You could see the question was a novel thought to my friend. His face lit up and he said, "Lemme have your card. Maybe I'll buy somethin' one day."

THE POLICE were still parked across the street when we came out.

"Why you didn't push her, Easy?" Jackson asked. "You could see that she was wantin' to know what you knew."

"She told me where he was already, Mr. Art Collector."

"When she do that?"

"While we were talkin'."

"An' where did she say to go?"

"The Westerly Nursing Home."

"And where is that?"

"Somewhere not too far from here I bet."

"Easy," Jackson said. "You know you a mothahfuckah, man. I mean you like magic an' shit."

Jackson might not have known that a compliment from him was probably the highest accolade that I was ever likely to receive.

I smiled and leaned over to wave at the policemen in their prowler.

Then we drove a block south and I stopped at a phone booth, where I looked up Westerly.

44

W hy you drivin' west, Easy?" Jackson asked me.

We were on Santa Monica Boulevard.

"Goin' back to Ozone to pick up your car, man."

"Why?"

"Because the cops all over Beverly Hills got the description of this here hot rod."

"Oh yeah. Right."

ON THE WAY to the nursing home Jackson stopped so that he could buy a potted white orchid.

"For Jewelle?" I asked him.

"For a old white man," Jackson said with a grin.

He was embarrassed that he didn't pick up on why we needed to switch cars and so he came up with the trick to get us in the nursing home.

We decided to send Jackson in with the flowers and to see how far he could get. The ideal notion would be for Jackson to tell the old man that we had pictures of him in Germany humping young women and girls. Failing that he might find a way to get us in on the sly. Every mansion we'd ever known had a back door and some poor soul held a key.

I wasn't sure that Rega Tourneau was mastermind of the problems I was trying to solve, but he was the centerpiece. And if he knew anything, I was going to do my best to find out what it was.

Westerly was a big estate a few long blocks above Sunset. There was a twelve-foot brick wall around the green grounds and an equally tall wrought iron gate for an entrance. We drove past it once and then I parked a few woodsy blocks away.

For a disguise Jackson buttoned the top button of his shirt, turned the lapels of his jacket up, and put on his glasses.

"Jackson, you really think this is gonna work? I mean here you wearin' a two-hundred-dollar suit. They gonna know somethin's up."

"They gonna see my skin before they see anything, Easy. Then the flowers, then the glasses. By the time they get to the suit they minds be made up."

After he left I lay down across the backseat.

There was an ache behind my eyes and my testicles felt swollen. Back when I was younger that pain would have been a point of pride. I would have worked it into street conversation. But I was too old to mask pain with bluster.

After a few moments I fell into a deep slumber.

Haffernon was standing there next to me. We were locked in a bitter argument. He told me that if he hadn't done business with the Nazis then someone else would have.

"That's how money works, fool," he said.

"But you're an American," I argued.

"How could you of all people say something like that?" he asked with real wonder. "Your grandparents were the property of a white man. You can't ever walk in my shoes. But still you believe in the ground I stand on?"

I felt a rage growing in my chest. I would have smashed his face if a gun muzzle hadn't pressed up against the base of his skull. Haffernon felt the pressure but before he could respond the gun fired. The top of his head erupted with blood and brain and bone.

The killer turned and ran. I couldn't tell if it was a man or woman, only that he (or she) was of slight stature. I ran after the assassin but somebody grabbed my arm.

"Let me go!" I shouted.

"Easy! Easy, wake up!"

Jackson was shaking my arm, waking me just before I caught the killer. I wanted to slap Jackson's grinning face. It took me a moment to realize that it was a dream and that I'd never find a killer that way.

But still . . .

"What you got, Jackson?"

"Rega Tourneau is dead."

"Dead?"

"Died in his sleep last night. Heart failure, they said. They thought that I was bringing the flowers for the funeral."

"Dead?"

"The lady at the front desk told me that he'd been doin' just fine. He'd had a lot of visitors lately. The doctors felt that maybe it was too much excitement."

"What visitors?"

"You got a couple'a hunnert dollars, Easy?"

"What?" Now awake, I was thinking about Rega Tourneau dying so conveniently. It had to be murder. And there I was again, scoping out the scene of the crime.

"Two hunnert dollars," Jackson said again.

"Why?"

"Terrance Tippitoe."

"Who?"

"He's one'a the attendants up in there. While I was waitin' to see the receptionist we talked. Afterwards I told him I thought I knew how he could make some scratch. He be off at three."

"Thanks, Mr. Blue. That's just what I needed."

"Let's go get lunch," he suggested.

"You just ate a little while ago."

"I know this real good place," he said.

I flopped back down and he started the car. I closed my eyes but sleep did not come.

"YEAH, EASY," Jackson was saying.

I was stabbing at a green salad while he chowed down on a T-bone steak at Mulligan's on Olympic. We had a booth in a corner. Jackson was drinking beer, proud of his work at the Westerly Nursing Home. But after the third beer his self-esteem turned sour.

"I used to be afraid," he said. "All the time, day and night. I used to couldn't go to sleep 'cause there was always some fear in my mind. Some man gonna find out how I cheated him or slept wit' his wife or girlfriend. Some mothahfuckah hear I got ten bucks an' he gonna stove my head in to get it."

"But now you got a good job and it's all fine."

"Job ain't shit, Easy. I mean, I like it. Shoot, I love it. But the job ain't what calms my mind. That's all Jewelle there."

He snorted and wiped his nose with the back of his hand.

"What's the matter, Jackson?"

"I know it cain't last, that's what."

"Why not? Jewelle love you more than she loved Mofass and she loved him more than anything before he died."

"'Cause I'm bound to fuck it up, man. Bound to. Some woman gonna crawl up in my bed, some fool gonna let me hold onta his money. I been a niggah too long, Easy. Too long."

I was worried about Feather, riding on a river of sorrow and rage named Bonnie Shay, scared to death of Joe Cicero, and faced with a puzzle that made no sense. Because of all that I appreciated Jackson's sorrowful honesty. For the first time ever I felt a real kinship with him. We'd known each other for well over twenty-five years but that was the first time I felt true friendship for him.

"No, Jackson," I said. "None'a that's gonna happen."

"Why not?"

"Because I won't let it happen. I won't let you fuck up. I won't let you mess with Jewelle. All you got to do is call me and tell me if you're feelin' weak. That's all you got to do."

"You do that for me?"

"Damn straight. Call me anytime day or night. I will be there for you, Jackson."

"What for? I mean . . . what I ever do for you?"

"We all need a brother," I said. "It's just my turn, that's all."

TERRANCE TIPPITOE was a small, dark-colored man who had small eyes that had witnessed fifty or more years of hard times. He had told Jackson to meet him at a bus stop on Sunset at three-oh-five. We were there waiting. Jackson made the introductions (my name was John Jefferson and his was George

Paine). I set out what I needed. For his participation I'd give him two hundred dollars.

Terrance was pulling down a dollar thirty-five an hour at that time and since I hadn't asked him to kill anyone he nodded and grinned and said, "Yes sir, Mr. Jefferson. I'm your man."

A time was made for Jackson to meet Terrance a few hours later.

Before Jackson and I separated back in Santa Monica, he agreed to lend me the two hundred.

The world was a different place that afternoon.

45

I went back to the hospital and got directions at the main desk to Bobby Lee's new room. Sitting in a chair beside Lee's door was an ugly white man with eyebrows, lips, and nose all at least three times too big for his doughy face. Even seated he was a big man. And despite his bulky woolen overcoat I could appreciate the strength of his limbs.

As I approached the door the Neanderthal sat up. His movements were graceful and fluid, as if he were some behemoth rising from a primordial swamp.

"Howdy," I said in the friendly manner that many Texas hicks used. I didn't want to fight this man at any time, for any reason.

He just looked at me.

"Easy Rawlins to see Robert E. Lee," I said.

"Right this way," the brute replied in a melodious baritone. He rose from the chair like Nemo's *Nautilus* rising from the depths.

Opening the door he gestured for me to go through. He tagged along behind — an elephant following his brother's tail.

Lee was sitting up in the bed wearing a nightshirt that wasn't hospital issue. It had white-on-white brocade along the buttons and a stylish collar. Seated next to him was Maya Adamant. She wore tight-fitting coral pants and a red silk blouse. Her hair was tied back and her visage was nothing if not triumphant.

They were holding hands.

"You two kiss and make up after the little tiff and trifling attempt at murder?"

I felt the presence of the bodyguard behind me. But what did I care? It was gospel I spoke.

"I told Robert everything," Maya said. "I have no secrets from him."

"And you believe her?" I asked Lee.

"Yes. I've realized a lot of things being so close to death. Lying here I've come to understand that my life has had no meaning for me. I mean, I've done a lot of important things for others. I've solved crimes and saved lives, but you know if someone is on a path to hell you can't save them."

His mouth was still under the sway of the drugs they'd given him but I perceived a clear mind underneath the weave of meandering thoughts.

"She sent Joe Cicero to our meeting," I said. "Then Joe emptied a clip into your chest. He almost killed you."

"She didn't know that he'd do that. Her only desire was to get the bonds. She's a woman without a man. She has to look out for herself."

"Wasn't it your job to get the bonds and give them to Haffernon?"

"He only wanted the letter."

Those five words proved to me that Lee's mind was running on all six cylinders. If I had become used to the idea of that letter, then I might not have noticed him slipping it in there.

"What letter?" I asked.

Lee studied my face.

"It doesn't matter now," he said. "Haffernon is dead. I've received notice."

It was my turn to stare.

"The only problem now is Joe Cicero," Lee said. "And Carl here is working on that problem."

"Cicero can't be in this alone," I said. "He has to be working for someone. And that someone can always find another Chickpea."

Lee smiled.

"I must apologize to you, Mr. Rawlins. When you first walked into my offices I believed that you were just a brash fool intent on pulling the wool over my eyes; that you only desired to make me do your bidding because I was a white man in a big house. But now I see the subtlety of your mind. You're a top-notch thinker, and more than that — you're a man."

I can't say that the accolades didn't tweak my vanity, but I knew that Lee was both devious and a fool, and that was a bad combination to be swayed by.

"Can I speak to you alone?" I asked the detective.

He considered a moment and then nodded.

"Carl, Maya," he said in dismissal.

"Boss . . ." Big Carl complained.

"It's okay. Mr. Rawlins isn't a bad man. Are you, Easy?"

"Depends on who you're askin'."

"Go on you two," Lee said. "I'll be fine."

Maya gave me a worried look as she went out. That was more of a compliment than all her boss's words.

After the door was shut I asked, "Are you stupid or do you just not care that that woman sent an assassin after you?"

"She didn't know what he intended."

"How can you be sure of that? I mean you act like you can read minds, but you and I both know that there ain't no way you can predict a woman like that."

"I can see that some woman has gotten under your skin," he said, leveling his eyes like cannon.

That threw me, made me realize that Bonnie was on my mind when I was talking about Maya. I could even see the similarities between the two women.

"This is not about my personal life, Mr. Lee. It's about Joe Cicero and your assistant sending him after you, after me. Now you and I both know that he'd have taken the same shots at me if I'd gone through that door first. And I don't have no bullet-proof vest."

"If what you told me is correct he needed you to gather information."

"Then he'd have grabbed me, tortured me."

"But that did not happen. You're alive and now Joe Cicero will be under the gun. I shot him you know."

"How bad?" I asked.

"It's hard to say. He jerked backward and fired again. I let off another shell but he was running by then."

"Can't say that he's dead. Can't be sure. And even if you could, and even if Carl gets him or the police or anybody else — that still doesn't account for who's doing all this."

"The case is over, Mr. Rawlins. Haffernon is dead."

"You see?" I said. "You see? That's where you're wrong. You think life is like one'a those Civil War enactments you got up in your house. People gettin' killed here, Bobby Lee. Killed. And they're dyin' 'cause'a what Haffernon hired you for. They're not gonna stop dyin' just because you call the game over."

I have to say that Lee seemed to be listening. There was no argument on his lips, no dismissal in his demeanor.

"Maybe you're right, Mr. Rawlins. But what do you want me to do?"

"Maybe you could work the Cicero-Maya connection. Maybe she could pretend that she still wants to work with him. Somehow we get on him and he leads us to his source."

"No."

"No? How can you just say no? We could at least ask her if it makes sense. Shit, man, this is serious business here."

"It's too dangerous."

"What's dangerous is tellin' a hit man where your boss is goin' and not lettin' your boss in on the change of plan. What's dangerous is walkin' out of a bar and havin' some man you never met open fire on your ass."

"I can't put Maya in danger."

"Why not?"

"Because we're to be married."

46

I left the hospital in a fog. How could he do that? Get engaged to a woman who not forty-eight hours before almost got him killed?

"She almost took your life," I'd said to him, floundering for sense.

"But she's always loved me and I never knew. A beautiful woman like that. And look at the way I was treating her."

"She could'a quit. She could'a demanded a raise. She could'a taken her damn phone off the hook. Why the fuck does she have to send a killer after you?"

"She was wrong. Haven't you ever been wrong, Mr. Rawlins?"

ON THE DRIVE BACK to Santa Monica I was angry. Here I was so hurt by Bonnie, who with one hand was trying to save my little girl's life and with the other caressing her new lover. Now

Lee forgives attempted murder and then rewards it with a promise of marriage.

I opened all the windows and smoked one cigarette after another. The radio blasted out pop songs that had sad words and up beats. I could have run my car into a brick wall right then. I wanted to.

"HERE WE GO, Easy," Jackson said. "Here's all the names in the register for the last week."

Terrance Tippitoe hadn't been subtle in his approach. He'd torn out the seven sheets of paper in the guest log and folded them in four.

I perused the documents for maybe twenty-five seconds, not more, and I knew who the mastermind was. I knew why and I knew how. But I still didn't see a way out unless I too became a murderer.

"What is it, Easy?" Jackson asked.

I shoved the log sheets into my pocket, thinking maybe if I could implicate the killer in Rega Tourneau's death then I could call in the cops. After all, I was on a first-name basis with Gerald Jordan, the deputy chief of police. I could slip him those sheets and the police could do the rest.

"Easy?" Jackson asked.

"Yeah?"

"What's wrong?"

That made me laugh. Jackson joined in. Jewelle came to sit behind him. She draped her arms around his neck.

"Nuthin's wrong, Blue. I just gotta get past a few roadblocks is all. Few roadblocks."

Jackson and Jewelle both knew to leave it at that.

* * *

I WASN'T THINKING too clearly at that time. So much had happened and so little of it I could control. I had to have a face-to-face with Cicero's employer. And in that meeting I had to make a decision. A week ago the only crime I'd considered was armed robbery, but now I'd graduated to premeditated murder.

Whatever the outcome it was getting late in the evening, and anyway I couldn't wear the same funky clothes one day more. I figured that Joe Cicero had better things to do than to stake out my house so I went home.

I drove around the block twice, looking for any signs of the contract killer. He didn't seem to be there. Maybe he was dead or at least out of action.

I took the bonds from the glove compartment of my hot rod and, with them under my arm, I strode toward my front yard.

Tacked to the door was a thick white envelope. I took it thinking that it had to have something to do with Axel or Cinnamon or maybe Joe Cicero.

I opened the door and walked into the living room. I flipped on the overhead light, threw the bonds on the couch, and opened the letter. It was from a lawyer representing Alicia and Nate Roman. They were suing me for causing them severe physical trauma and mental agony. They had received damage to their necks, hips, and spines, and she had severe lacerations to the head. There was only one broken bone but many more bruised ones. They had both seen the same doctor — an M.D. named Brown. The cost for their deep suffering was one hundred thousand dollars — each.

I walked toward the kitchen intent on getting a glass of water. At least I could do that without being shot at, spied on, or sued.

I saw his reflection in the glass door of the cabinet. He was coming fast but in that fragment of a second I realized first that the man was not Joe Cicero and second that, like Mouse, Cicero had sent a proxy to keep an eye out for his quarry. Then, when I was halfway turned around, he hit me with some kind of sap or blackjack and the world swirled down through a drain that had opened up at my feet.

I LOST CONSCIOUSNESS but there was a part of my mind that struggled to wake up. So in a dream I did wake up, in my own bed. Next to me was a dark-skinned black man. He opened his eyes at the same time I opened mine.

"Where's Bonnie?" I asked him.

"She's gone," he said with a finality that sucked the air right out of my chest.

THE MORNING SUN through the kitchen window woke me but it was nausea that drove me to my feet. I went to the bath-room and sat next to the commode, waiting to throw up — but I never did.

I showered and shaved, primped and dressed.

The bonds were gone of course. I figured that I was lucky that Cicero had sent a proxy. I was also lucky that the bonds were right there to be stolen. Otherwise Joe would have come and caused me pain until I gave them up. Then he would have killed me.

I was a lucky bastard.

After my ablutions I called a number that was lodged in my memory. I have a facility for remembering numbers, always did.

She answered on the sixth ring, breathless.

"Yes?"

"That invitation still open?"

"Easy?" Cynthia Aubec said. "I thought I'd never hear from you again."

"That might be construed as a threat, counselor."

"No. I thought you didn't like me."

"I like you all right," I said. "I like you even though you lied to me."

"Lied? Lied about what?"

"You acted like you weren't related to Axel but here I see that you signed into the Westerly Nursing Home to visit Rega Tourneau. Cynthia Tourneau-Aubec."

"Tourneau's my mother's maiden name. Aubec was my father," she said.

"Nina's your mother?"

"You seem to know everything about me."

"Did you know what Axel was trying to do?"

"He was wrong, Mr. Rawlins. These are our parents, our families. What's done is done."

"Is that why you killed him?"

"I don't know what you're talking about. Axel told me that he was going to Algeria. I don't have any reason to think that he's dead."

"You worked in the prosecutor's office when Joe Cicero was on trial, didn't you?"

She didn't answer.

"And you visited your grandfather only a few hours before he was found dead."

"He was very old. Very sick. His death was really a blessing."

"Maybe he wanted to confess before he died. About trips to the Third Reich and pornographic pictures of him with twelve-year-olds."

"Where are you?" she asked.

"In L.A. At my house."

"Come up here . . . to my house. We'll talk this out."

"What is it, Cindy? Were you in your grandfather's will? Were you afraid that the government would take away all of that wealth if the truth came out?"

"You don't understand. Between the drugs and his crazy friends Axel only wanted to destroy."

"What about Haffernon? Was he getting cold feet? Is that why you killed him? Maybe he thought that dealing with a twenty-year-old treason beef would be easier than if he was caught murdering Philomena."

"Come here to me, Easy. We can work this out. I like you."

"What's in it for me?" I asked. It was a simple question but I had complex feelings behind it.

"My mother was disowned," she said. "But the old man put me back in the will recently. I'm going to be very rich soon."

I hesitated for the appropriate amount of time, as if I were considering her request. Then I said, "When?"

"Tomorrow at noon."

"Nuthin' funny, right?"

"I just want to explain myself, to help you. That's all."

"Okay. Okay I'll come. But I don't want Joe Cicero to be there."

"Don't worry about him. He won't be bothering anyone."

"Okay then. Tomorrow at twelve."

I WAS ON A FLIGHT to San Francisco within the hour. I rented a car and made it to an address in Daly City that I'd never been to before. All of this took about four hours.

It was a small home with a pink door and a blue porch.

The door was ajar and so I walked in.

Cynthia Aubec lay on her back in the center of the hardwood floor. There was a bullet hole in her forehead. Standing over her was Joe Cicero. His right arm was bandaged and in a sling. In his left hand was a pistol outfitted with a large silencing muzzle. He must have been killing her as I was walking up the path to her door.

My pistol lay impotent in my pocket. Cicero smiled as he raised his gun to point at my forehead. I knew he was thinking about when I had the drop on him; that he wouldn't make the same mistake that I had.

"Well, well, well," he said. "Here I thought I'd have to chase you down, and then you come walking in like a Christmas goose."

With my eyes only I glanced to the sides. There was no sign of the man who had sapped me the night before.

Beyond the young woman's corpse was a small coffee table upon which sat two teacups. She'd served him tea before he shot her. The thought was grotesque but I knew I wouldn't have long to contemplate it.

"Lee is going to put the cops on you for the Bowers killing and for Haffernon," I said, hoping somehow to stave off my own death.

"I didn't kill them. She did," he said, waving his pistol at her.

"But you were at Bowers's house," I said. "You threatened him."

"You know about that, huh? She hired me to get the bonds from Bowers. When I told her what he'd said she took it in her own hands." He coughed and I glanced at the teacups. A tremor of hope thrummed in the center of my chest.

"Haffernon too?"

He nodded. There was something off about the movement of his head, as if he weren't in full control.

"Why?" I asked, playing for time.

"He was getting weak. Didn't want to do what they had to do

to keep their nasty little secret. That's why I had to kill her. I knew that" — he coughed again — "sooner or later she'd have to come after me. Nobody could know or the whole house of cards would fall. That's why I work for a living. A rich family will take your soul."

"Why not?" I asked, as bland as could be. "Why couldn't anybody know?"

"Money," he said with a knowing, crooked nod. "Sometimes it was just that she wanted her inheritance. Sometimes she was angry at the kid for taking all that wealth for granted when she and her mother had been living hand to mouth."

He straightened his shooting arm.

"And she knew you from your trial about the torture?"

"You do your homework, nigger," he said and then coughed. Blood spattered out onto his lips, but because he had no free hand he couldn't rub it off to see.

I leaped to the left and he fired. He was good. He was a right-hander and dying but he still hit me in the shoulder. I used the momentum to fall through a doorway to my left. Screaming from the pain, I made it to my feet. I was halfway down the hall when I heard him behind me. He fired again but I didn't feel anything.

I fell anyway.

As I looked back I saw him staggering forward, shooting once, and then he fell. He didn't move again.

I was on the floor next to a bathroom. I went in, trying not to touch any surface. I got a towel from the rack next to the tub and used it to staunch the bleeding from my shoulder.

When the blood was merely seeping I checked Cicero. He was dead. In his jacket pocket was an envelope containing twenty-five thousand dollars. In a folder on the coffee table I found the bonds and the letter.

There were many photographs on the shelves and window-sills. Some were of Cynthia and her mother, Nina Tourneau. One was Cynthia as a child on the lap of her beloved grandfather — pornographer, child molester, and Nazi traitor.

I took the bonds, leaving the letter for the cops to mull over. The teacups had the same strong smell that the cup had at Axel's house. Only one had been drunk from.

47

I drove my rental car for hours, but it seemed like several days, bleeding on the steering wheel and down my chest. I drove one-handed half the time, using the stiffening fingers of my right hand to press the towel against the shoulder wound.

It was a minor miracle that I made it to Christmas Black's Riverside home. I don't remember getting out of the car or ringing the bell. Maybe they found me there, passed out over the wheel.

I came to three days later. Easter Dawn was sitting in a big chair next to my bed, reading from a picture book. I don't know if she knew how to read or if she was just interpreting the pictures into stories. When I opened my eyes she jumped up and ran from the room.

"Daddy! Daddy! Mr. Rawlins is awake!"

Christmas came into the room wearing black jeans and a drab green T-shirt. His boots were definitely army issue.

"How you doin', soldier?" he asked.

"Ready for my discharge," I said in a voice so weak that even I didn't hear it.

Christmas held up my head and trickled water into my mouth. I wanted to get up and call Switzerland but I couldn't even lift a hand.

"You bled a lot," Christmas said. "Almost died. Lucky I got some friends in the hospital down in Oxnard. I got you medicine and a few pints of red."

"Call Mouse," I said as loudly as I could.

Then I passed out.

The next time I woke up, Mama Jo was sitting next to me. She had just taken some foul-smelling substance away from my nose.

"Uh!" I grunted. "What was that?"

"I can see you gonna be okay, Easy Rawlins," big, black, handsome Mama Jo said.

"I feel better. How long have I been here?"

"Six days."

"Six? Did anybody call Bonnie?"

"She called Etta. Feather's doin' good, the doctors said. They won't know nuthin' for eight weeks more though. Etta said that you and Raymond were doing some business down in Texas."

Mouse sauntered in with his glittering smile.

"Hey, Easy," he said. "Christmas got all yo' money an' bonds and shit in the draw next to yo' bed."

"Give the bonds to Jackson," I told him. "Let him cash 'em and we'll split 'em three ways."

Mouse smiled. He liked a good deal.

"I'll let you boys talk business," Jo said. She rose from the chair and I watched in awe, as always impressed by her size and bearing.

Mouse pulled up a chair and told me what he knew.

Joe Cicero made the TV news with his murder of Cynthia Aubec and her poisoning of him.

"They say anything about a letter they found?" I asked.

"No. No letter, just mutual murder, that's what they called it."

That night Saul Lynx arrived in a rented ambulance and drove me home.

Benita Flag and Jesus were there to nurse me.

Two weeks after it was all over I was still convalescing. Mouse came over and sat with me under the big tree in the backyard.

"You don't have to worry about them people no more, Ease," he said after we'd been gossiping for a while.

"What people?"

"The Romans."

For a moment I was confused, and then I remembered the accident and the lawsuit.

"Yeah," he said. "Benita showed me the papers an' I went ovah to talk to 'em. I told 'em about Feather and about you bein' so tore up. I gave 'em five thousand off the top'a what Jackson cleared and told 'em that you was a good detective and if they ever needed help that you would be there for 'em. After that they decided to drop that suit."

There weren't many people in Watts who wouldn't do what Ray asked. No one wanted to be on his bad side.

THEY FOUND AXEL Bowers in his ashram and tied Aubec to that crime too. The papers made it an incestuous sex scandal. Who knows, maybe it was. Dream Dog was even interviewed. He told the reporters about the sex and drug parties. In 1966 that was reason enough, in the public mind, for murder.

A few days later I received a card from Maya and Bobby Lee.

They were on their honeymoon in Monaco. Lee had connections with the royal family there. He said that I should call him if I ever needed employment — or advice. That was the closest Lee would ever come to an offer of friendship.

I sent the twenty-five thousand on to Switzerland. Feather called me once a week. Bonnie called two times but I always found an excuse to get off the line. I didn't tell them about my getting shot. There was no use in worrying Feather or making Bonnie feel bad either.

I lived off of the money Jackson got from the bonds and wondered who at Haffernon's firm bought off the letter. But I didn't worry too much about it. I was alive and Feather was on her way to recovery. Even if the moral spirit of my country was rotten to the core at least I had played a part in her salvation — my beautiful child.

IT WAS A MONTH after the shooting that I got a letter from New York. With it was a tiny clipping saying that an inquiry had opened concerning the American-owned Karnak Chemical Company and their dealings with Germany during the war. Information had come to light about the sale of munitions directly to Germany from Karnak. If the allegations turned out to be true a full investigation would be launched.

The letter read:

Dear Mr. Rawlins:

Thank you for whatever you did. I read
about our reptilian friend in the Bay Area. I
just wanted you to see that Axel had an ace
up his sleeve. He probably gathered the information in Egypt and Germany and sent it to
the government before he told anybody about

the Swiss bonds. I think he wanted me to have
them if anything happened to him. He couldn't
know how slow the government would work.

   It was nice meeting you. I have a low-level
job at an investment firm here in New York.
I'm sure that I will get promoted soon.

   If you're ever out here come by and see me.

                                        "love"
                            ·   Cinnamon

There was a dark red lipstick kiss at the bottom of the letter.

   I sent her the two books I had taken from her apartment and a
brief note thanking her for being so unusual.

FIVE WEEKS LATER Bonnie and Feather came home.

   Feather had been a little butterball before the illness. She was
just a wraith when she got on that plane to Switzerland. But now
she was at least four inches taller and dressed like a woman. She
was even taller than Jesus.

   After kissing me and hugging my neck she regained her com-
posure and said, "Bonjour, Papa. Comment ça va?"

   "Bien, ma fille," I replied, remembering the words I learned
while killing men across France.

WE ALL STAYED UP late into the night talking. Jesus was
even animated. He had learned some French from Bonnie over
time and so now he and Feather conversed in a foreign language.
Her recovery and return made him almost giddy with joy.

   Finally there was just Bonnie and me sitting next to each
other on the couch.

   "Easy?"

"Yeah, honey?"

"Can we talk about it now?"

There was fever in my blood and a tidal wave in my mind but I said, "Talk about what?"

"I only called Joguye because Feather was sick and I knew that he had connections," she began.

I was thinking about Robert E. Lee and Maya Adamant.

"When I saw him I remembered how we'd felt about each other, and . . . and we did spend a lot of time together in Montreux. I know you must have been hurt but I also spent the time making up my mind —"

I put up my hand to stop her. I must have done it with some emphasis, because she flinched.

"I'm gonna stop you right there, honey," I said. "I'm gonna stop you, because I don't wanna hear it."

"What do you mean?"

"It's not either me or him," I told the love of my life. "It's either me or not me. That's what I've come to in this time you were gone. When we talked at the airport you should'a said right then that it was always me, would always be. I don't care if you slept with him or not, not really. But the truth is he got a footprint in your heart. That kinda mark don't wash out."

"What are you saying, Easy?" She reached out for me. She touched me but I wasn't there.

"You can take your stuff whenever you want. I love you but I got to let you go."

JESUS AND BENITA moved her the next day. I didn't know where she went. The kids did. I think they saw her sometimes, but they never talked to me about it.